Praise for the S[
and New Pulp

"...One of the leading New Pulp writers of today... able to bridge nearly any genre... Van brings a special touch to anything he writes and creates."
--*Tommy Hancock, author of* Yesteryear

"(His Sentinels series) offers a fresh take on the superhero theme."
--*Kirkus Reviews*

"Nobody—not even Abnett and Lanning—is doing cosmic superheroes as well as Van Plexico is doing them. Period."
--*Barry Reese, award-winning author of* Rabbit Heart *and creator of the Rook*

"Amazingly talented."
--Sean Taylor, author of *Show Me a Hero*

"Van Plexico is responsible for me losing more sleep than any other author."
--*Larry Davis, Dragon*Con SF Literature Track*

"A gifted writer... Wow does (the) fun come across to the lucky readers."
--*Ron Fortier, award-winning author of* Boston Bombers *and the* Captain Hazzard *novels, on* Stellarax

"I ate dinner with one hand while holding [*Lucian*] with the other... I asked my husband to drive me to work so could finish the last pages on the way. Go get it and read it!"
--*Bonnie J. Sterling, Bonificia Reviews.*

"I was enthralled. I had a hard time putting (his books) down and after each ended I wanted to read more."
--*Mark Haleuga, Coordinator, Gotham Pulp Collectors Club*

Books by Van Allen Plexico

Sentinels:
The Grand Design
  1: When Strikes the Warlord
  2: A Distant Star
  3: Apocalypse Rising

  Alternate Visions (Anthology) *

The Rivals
  4: The Shiva Advent
  5: Worldmind
  6: Stellarax

Order Above All
  7: Metalgod

Other Fiction:
Hawk: Hand of the Machine
Lucian: Dark God's Homecoming
Gideon Cain: Demon Hunter *
Blackthorn: Thunder on Mars *

Nonfiction and Commentary
Assembled! Five Decades of Earth's Mightiest *
Assembled! 2 *
Super-Comics Trivia *
Season of Our Dreams
Assembled! 3 * *(forthcoming)*

*Editor

HAWK
HAND OF THE MACHINE

A *Shattered Galaxy* Novel

———

VAN ALLEN PLEXICO

WHITE ROCKET BOOKS

DAVID —
BLAST
EVIL !!

Thanks —

Van Allen
Plexico

This one's for Leesa

A stand-alone novel, this book also fits within the following extended universe storylines from White Rocket Books:

Portions of this book, in slightly altered form, previously appeared in *Pro Se Presents* in February and March of 2012.

HAWK: HAND OF THE MACHINE

Copyright 2012 by Van Allen Plexico

Cover art by Rowell Roque and Atlantis Studios

A White Rocket Book
www.whiterocketbooks.com

ISBN-13: 978-0-615-64131-7
ISBN-10: 0-6156413-1-8

First printing: June 2012

0 9 8 7 6 5 4 3 2 1

They are not legends, my brothers. They are very real.

Or, at least, they were.

Once, ages ago, before the coming of the Adversary and before the Shattering, the galaxy was filled to overflowing with life— with multitudes of sentient races occupying every nook and cranny, from the depths of the core to the farthest-flung spiral arms.

That was the time of the Hands.

They were a part of humanity, born of original Earth stock, yet ever they stood above it. They strode among the stars like giants. Like the gods themselves.

Valiant Hawk. Rugged Falcon. Brilliant Condor. Fierce Shrike. Cunning Raven. And so many others.

And above them all, the lord commander of the Hands, mighty Eagle. A born leader, a master strategist, and an imposing physical specimen. He could outthink them all, except perhaps Condor; he could outfight them all, except perhaps Falcon; and he could out-plot them all, except perhaps Raven.

They served the great Machine that watched over and protected the galaxy. In that way, they served us all.

We loved them for it. Yes, and we feared them, too.

They were great and powerful, awesome in their majesty. And when their wrath was aroused, they could strike down upon their foes with a terrible, unrelenting fury.

They were the protectors of the galaxy. They were the Hands of the Machine. And they could do no wrong.

Or so we believed.

Even after the Shattering, when the Adversary was defeated and what remained of the galaxy at last knew peace again, some few of the Hands still lived, patrolling the depths of space.

And then something happened, and most of them went away.

But with the great Adversary defeated, what cared we that the Hands were vanishing? Our worlds were now safe. We had no further need for such powerful, mercurial, capricious guardians.

Or so we believed.

And so now, centuries later, as hints creep in from every corner of the galaxy that something—something dark and disturbing— is returning, we cry out for help. But our protectors, our legends, our gods—the Hands of the Machine—do not answer. We can only conclude that they are no longer there to hear our entreaties. We declare that they are all extinct—or else never existed at all.

Or so we believe...

PART ONE

After the Shattering:
The Nineteenth Millennium

1: HAWK

Hawk awoke naked and screaming in the heart of a shattered galaxy.

He sat up. Instantly a wave of sensations flooded his mind, threatening to drown him—to sweep him away into gibbering insanity.

As he rocked back and forth, moaning, he brought his hands to his head. Something dangled from his arms, he saw: tubes, thin and fluid-filled, attached by needles to his flesh, his veins. Eyes focusing slowly, he grasped them and ripped them out.

He wasn't screaming any longer. In the few seconds since he'd awoken, he'd begun to sort through the layers of sensory overload and separate the various kinds of input he was receiving—light, sound, touch, taste, smell. The last two were strongest at the moment; a smell of smoke, thin but growing, in the air, and the taste of blood and metal in his mouth.

Warning, his instincts screamed at him silently. *Be prepared to move!*

The next sensation to penetrate his mind came via touch: the feeling of something cold beneath him. He realized he was sitting on the edge of a metal table of some kind. And that he was naked.

The world spun around him as he tried to look out at his surroundings. A sense of nausea crept up from the depths of his stomach, causing him to grip the cold table's edge tightly with both hands.

Where was he? For that matter, *who* was he?

As his consciousness slowly emerged from the long dark in which it had lain, submerged, for so long, he found far more questions than answers waiting for him.

On top of everything now, though, was one single overriding sensation—the skin-prickling feeling of danger. Danger all around; danger everywhere. Even the sounds in the room—

Sounds. Yes. His hearing came back, filling his head with deafening sounds. *What is that noise? Alarms,* he knew then. *Yes.* Followed by, *No more delays—move!*

He pulled himself off the table's edge and his bare feet smacked the floor. Unsteady at first, he wobbled, bracing himself by gripping the tabletop again. With his free hand, he rubbed at his sticky, itchy eyes.

His vision cleared then, and he immediately wished it hadn't.

The room was filled with the mind-jarring swirl of flashing and pulsing lights; lights of every color imaginable. They washed the room in their painful glare.

Shading his eyes and squinting against the visual assault, he could just make out his surroundings. He stood at the center of a small, round room, surrounded by consoles and computers and medical equipment that would have seemed quite disturbing, if he'd had his wits about him.

Flashing lights, wailing alarms. Clearly something was terribly wrong here—wherever *here* was. But what was it that was wrong? Was it *him?*

Possibly, he understood.

Time to move.

His hands moved involuntarily to his chest and he pulled at the wires and tubes attached to him there. Then he looked around for something to wear, but found nothing that would serve.

Shrugging, he padded cautiously out of the room, into a broad corridor that was also washed in red glare. At the far end, a sliding door stood half-ajar. He ran for it.

Halfway down the hall, a new sensation came fully to his mind. It had been there all along, of course, but he hadn't quite been able to process it. Now, its intensity ratcheting upward exponentially, it moved itself firmly to the forefront of his consciousness and made itself known beyond any doubt.

It was pain. Searing, blinding pain.

It sliced into his brain like a flaming brand and drove him to his knees. He clutched his head between his hands as he fell, wailing, his voice lost in the cacophony of alarms.

Within the pain, though, something was forming amid his jumbled thoughts; a tiny bit of rationality and order in the sea of agony and discord. As the pain at last receded, that which it had left behind emerged in its wake.

A memory?

Yes. A memory.

The pain had nearly vanished now and he found that he could focus. He turned his attention to this new thought that had risen into his awareness.

Part of the memory was a name, the other part a visual image.

The name rang clear and true in his head: *Hawk.* He allowed himself to taste it; to roll it around in his mouth along with the blood and the metal and say it softly aloud. *Yes.* It felt right. It was true. His name indeed was Hawk.

The image clarified into the outline of a vehicle—a spacecraft. He knew then with absolute certainty that a spacecraft was docked somewhere in the facility, waiting for him. *Where?*

He thought about that quickly, and it came to him that he possessed that knowledge, too—that he knew where to find it.

But why should he wish to? Was he supposed to go somewhere? Or—was this place simply too dangerous now? Had it been compromised by...by his enemies, whoever they might be?

The details, he decided, didn't matter at the moment. All he truly knew—knew without a doubt—was that he had to get out. For a number of reasons, none of them terribly clear to him at the moment, he knew had to get away from this place and get away *now*.

What he had until then taken for his own shaking, he now understood to be the floor itself vibrating violently. He ran.

As he sprinted through darkened, vacant corridors, Hawk allowed himself to wonder what kind of ship it would be, and how he would be able to fly it. For some reason, this thought didn't bother him. He felt certain he would *know* how, when the time came.

The other questions—the much larger questions—lurked just out of reach, awaiting his full attention. They were the same ones he'd first considered when he'd awoken: Who was he? *Where* was he? What was going on?

Some mostly-submerged memory told him he had no time to spend dwelling on such impractical points; at least, not yet. Get clear, get away from this—from wherever this was, and from whatever was happening—and then worry about the big picture.

The floor under his feet vibrated again, shaking more violently than before. The walls, most of them seemingly carved from stone, were actually beginning to crack. The bundles of thick wires and cables and tubes that were bracketed to them at chest-height bounced up and down with enough force to rip some of them free and leave them dangling and swaying. Sparks sprayed out intermittently from junction boxes as he passed them.

On he ran, not encountering any other living beings along the way. By this time he felt as if he'd run more than a mile through the darkened maze, and all with no conscious understanding of where he was going. He trusted his instincts the entire way.

Instincts, as it turned out, would not be enough.

Rounding a corner, he ran nearly headlong into two figures— big, hideous, nightmarish figures—that had been coming the other way. As he brought himself to an abrupt halt and the two creatures did likewise, his eyes flashed across them, instantly registering the details of their appearance.

They were insectoid, tall and slender, with jet-black chitinous exoskeletons. Their heads, long and narrow and triangular in shape, shone with a scattering of blood-red eyes across the middle portion that seemed to glow. As they moved on their two sets of back legs, their bodies appeared to flow like a liquid, rearing up to a height of more than eight feet. Each of them raised its two front appendages in menacing fashion. One "arm" was rounded off at the tip into a sort of cylinder with an open end, and Hawk instinctively understood this to be a weapon. The other "arm" ended with a curved segment that angled to a sharp point; obviously a vicious slashing and cutting weapon that needed no further interpretation.

These were the enemy. As deadly and dangerous an enemy as could be imagined. This too Hawk knew not consciously but viscerally, as a gazelle knows a lion.

But Hawk was no gazelle. He didn't run. Instead, he lashed out.

Moving with blinding speed and catlike agility, Hawk dropped into a crouch even as one of the figures was just beginning to raise its cylinder arm. Sweeping out with his feet, he took the legs out from under that one, then sprung upward and brought his fists into the midsection of the other.

A sharp pain bit into his left shoulder.

Leaping backwards, he saw that the first invader had managed to stab him with the tip of its dagger-like arm segment. Now it charged towards him, rising up to an even greater height, its deadly arm plunging forward.

Hawk ducked and lunged, the slashing appendage missing him by less than an inch as it plunged down. He grasped that rock-hard arm just above the bladed portion and twisted hard.

The creature emitted an awful cry and scuttled sideways, just as Hawk's foot came up in a powerful kick. The triangular head snapped back and the creature dropped, stunned.

Still holding the dagger-arm just above the bladed portion, he spun about and drove the incredibly sharp tip into the chest of the other invader as it sought to rise.

Two savage chops with the flat of his hands and Hawk had sent both of the insectoids to the floor, severely injured if not dying. He found he somehow knew exactly where to hit them.

Hawk stepped back from them, not feeling the pain from his shoulder and only absently wiping at the blood running down his side. His heartbeat remained steady; he hadn't so much as worked up a sweat.

Standing over the hideous creatures, he gazed down at them impassively, studying their long, sharp mandibles and glowing red eyes. He frowned. Somewhere deep within the mists that obscured his memories, a warning was sounding—had been sounding since he'd first seen them. Yes, he definitely knew these creatures, and he instinctively knew how to fight them.

And he hated them.

Why? Who were they?

A sudden fear sweeping through him, he brought his hands to his face. He moved them rapidly over the surface—inadvertently leaving streaks of blood across it—feeling the features, reassuring himself that he looked nothing like this grotesque creature. No—he was…human? That sounded right. *Human.*

Forcing his eyes away from the invaders and looking around, Hawk saw that he stood at an intersection of four wide corridors. The lights still pulsed and flashed in no discernible rhythm, creating a bizarre, funhouse atmosphere. He knew that he had to keep moving, but he found that for the first time he was unsure of which way to go.

Before he could decide, the clatter of approaching feet echoed toward him.

"There he is!"

Hawk looked up to see a trio of white-lab-coated medical/scientist types rushing towards him. They were humans like him, he noticed—even as he wondered why this would be an issue. Older, they were, and short in comparison to Hawk. Two were female. They halted in their tracks and gawked at him, startled by the streaks of blood across his face and down his chest. Then they looked down at his two insectoid victims.

Hawk remembered again that he was naked, but the three scientists seemed unconcerned about that fact. They looked back up at him.

"You did this?" the male scientist asked, his pale eyes shifting restlessly. He rubbed at his bald head and his thick mustache.

Hawk nodded. He was tense, his every sense heightened, his breathing low and smooth.

"Good. Your programming progressed that far, at least."

"I told you a Hawk was the best choice, regardless of the...*other* issues," one of the female scientists stated, her expression smug.

"It's not as if we had many other choices available in the genetic vault," the bald man snapped at her. "A Cardinal would scarcely have been of any real use now."

"He's been injured," the other female pointed out needlessly. Her dark features were pinched into a frown and her white hair was tied up in a bun.

"Escort us to the escape pods," the first female said, pointing with a fair-skinned if wrinkled hand, "and then we can tend to your wounds."

"And upload the rest of your data when we reach the other base," the dark-skinned female added.

None of this made any sense to Hawk. "What *are* those things?" he demanded, pointing at the insectoids he had fought.

"Skrazzi. Servants of the Adversary, of course," the male scientist replied, frowning. "They have returned—they are attacking our base." Meanwhile the two women exchanged worried glances, the meaning obvious: *He doesn't know.*

"We must get you to the other base," the man went on. "The attack disrupted your awakening process. There are probably numerous gaps in your—"

The floor shook violently, causing all three scientists to stumble against the nearest wall. A low rumbling sound echoed all around.

Hawk easily balanced himself on the balls of his feet and rode the quake out.

"They've blasted into the reactor system," the fair-skinned female growled, her green eyes darting back and forth.

"More of them are coming," the male scientist declared, studying the screen of a tiny device he clutched in one trembling hand. "We have to go. Now!"

"To the life pods," the dark-skinned female cried, pointing down one corridor.

"No," Hawk found himself replying sharply. Then, before any of the three scientists could act, Hawk shoved his way past them and dashed down a different corridor, his bare feet slapping the smooth stone floor.

"Wait!" cried one of them—the man. "You are not ready! You have not yet been prepared for—"

The voice faded away and vanished into the distance, amidst the din of alarms and explosions. Hawk was not interested in the little scientist people or in what they had to say. One look at them and he'd known they were enemies to him—enemies almost as insidious as the black-clad raiders he'd dispatched. Besides, he now knew exactly where he needed to go, and it was not with them or to their "escape pods," which promised no escape, only death in the void.

Why he needed to go there, he wasn't sure. But the thought had come to him in a flash of insight, and he knew it was right.

Passing another broad intersection and continuing on a short distance, he reached the end of the corridor at last. There he confronted a dull gray metal door. A set of what looked to be controls for it were set into the wall to the right. No sooner had he begun to study them, however, than the sound of agonized screams echoed towards him down the long corridors. Screams that very abruptly stopped.

The scientists, he thought. *I don't believe they made it to their precious pods.*

And now he could also hear the clattering of many hard feet on the smooth metal floor, coming from the cross-cutting corridor behind him.

He whirled and looked about. There was nowhere to go, nowhere to hide.

Quickly he returned his attention to the door mechanism. Rows of colorful buttons and lights. He frowned; no instant solution was leaping from his fog-enshrouded brain this time.

The sounds of feet clattering on the hard floor were growing closer—much closer.

He leaned back into the wall as far as he could, out of direct line of sight of the approaching enemy, making himself as flat as possible.

Two black insectoid invaders scuttled past, their weapon-arms gleaming in the strobing light.

He inhaled and exhaled slowly.

Two more hurried past and continued on.

He waited, and now sweat began to trail down the side of his face. This base—whatever it was—had indeed been overrun. He had to get out, and get out *now*.

Yet another pair of invaders entered the intersection. They slowed, their triangular black heads moving slowly as their glowing red eyes probed here and there.

Hawk held his breath. He knew somehow that while he was capable of fighting and beating these creatures, they were at least as capable of killing him. There was no doubting that he had been very fortunate in the previous encounter, sustaining only one real injury—an injury that had only now begun to seriously trouble him. His shoulder was throbbing; blood continued to run from the wound. What he could do about it he wasn't sure, but leaping into combat again was probably not the best way to address it.

One of the invaders had moved on but the other still stood in the intersection, not moving. Then slowly it turned, its red eyes flashing, to stare directly at him.

Hawk sprang out, using the wall to propel himself forcefully. He drove the creature hard into the opposite wall and struck down with an open-handed blow at the cylinder arm, understanding that it represented perhaps an even greater danger than the dagger-arm. Then he gripped the enemy's triangular head and twisted hard. The creature collapsed to the deck.

Hawk's victory celebration was short lived. Three of the others that had passed his hiding place by were now hurrying back, their cylinder-arms coming up to level at him.

He didn't wait for them to strike first. Leaping forward, blood splattering from his shoulder as he moved, he seized the first invader by the upper portion of the dagger-arm and pulled it toward him, then twisted it about. In the process, Hawk bent and cracked the arm at the elbow. A muffled cry rewarded his efforts.

One of the three invaders was rushing ahead, its cylinder-arm pointed at him. Hawk twisted his captive's body around and used it as a shield, uncertain as he did so of precisely what he was blocking.

Unable to see around the creature he was holding, he could only *hear* the tack-tack of the attacker's feet on the hard floor, accompanied by a low buzzing sound. This was followed immediately by a cloud of black particles filling the air; Hawk quickly realized this represented the carapace of his captive as it was being shredded, perhaps at the molecular level.

The answer came to him quickly. Disintegrators. The creatures' cylinder-arms were organic disintegrator guns. As crazy as it sounded, it was the only answer that made sense.

Ragged gasping sounds were coming from the invader he held. Black blood splattered across the floor, followed by the creature's limbs as they separated from the rest of it. Holding his breath to avoid inhaling the particles, he grasped the main bulk of the quickly-dissolving body in both hands and hurled it into its approaching comrade, sending both of them crashing to the deck.

The other two invaders had hung back, observing what was happening. Perhaps sensing that this human represented a greater danger than they had expected, they approached very slowly. Hawk could see them further down the corridor, even as the one he'd knocked down sought to extricate itself from what remained of the bleeding carcass of its comrade.

Hawk spared a second for a quick glance down at his own body—a body not at all familiar to him. He realized once again that he was still naked. Naked, and facing six—now five—deadly attackers.

As he looked down he spotted one of the severed arms of his "living shield"—the dagger-arm—where it lay near his right foot. He dove for it, snatched it up, rolled, and was flinging it even as he came up from the floor.

The bloody black bone-blade struck one of the attackers square in the center of the chest and drove it back, staggering and falling. Its partner spared it a brief, seemingly startled glance, then rushed forward with an inhuman cry, brandishing its own weapon-arms.

The attack was wild. Clearly, this one had been driven into a rage by what it had witnessed. It came at Hawk at a dead run, not even bothering with its ranged weapon, simply going with a straight-ahead bull rush.

Faster than the eye could see, Hawk side-stepped, twisted, reached out with powerful hands, and grasped the triangular head. Leveraging his weight and momentum, Hawk snapped the head cleanly away. The body continued on in a straight line until it impacted the wall, at which point it collapsed in a twitching heap, oozing dark ichor.

The blazing-red clusters of eyes dimmed as Hawk gazed down at the severed head. Disgusted, he tossed the thing away and wiped his hands on his bare sides, his victims' blood mingling with his own.

He spared no time in celebration. He knew that more of the invaders might well be on their way, and in fact might be waiting for him at the door he'd wanted to open. He sprung forward, panther-like, racing back in the direction he had come from—the direction of the door he'd felt compelled to open.

To his surprise, only the dead bodies of the invaders he'd killed greeted him.

He spun about, keen eyes searching. He moved to the intersection and carefully leaned out, checking in every direction.

Nothing.

Could that be all of them? Had they brought so few? Or had he so frightened the strange attackers that they had fled back from whence they'd come?

These scenarios struck him as unlikely.

A moment later, he had his answer. The sound of an entire battalion of invaders—invaders racing at a dead run down the cross-cutting corridor—came to him.

They knew about him. They knew exactly where he was. One of his victims must have managed to send a signal to its comrades.

His head was spinning now, his feet growing unsteady. He understood that his blood loss, combined with his exertions, had pushed him nearly to his physical limit.

He had no time to contemplate such things. He had to get out—*now*.

Returning his attention to the door lock mechanism, he frowned down at it, his fingers brushing lightly across its surface. It was a small box set into the wall just to the right of the gray door. It had no buttons or switches of any kind visible. How did it work?

His every instinct, and perhaps some portion of his lost memories, told him with great urgency that what he needed lay on the other side of that door.

But—how to open it?

The sounds were much louder now. He knew a veritable army was coming, and that there was no way he could defeat so many creatures—particularly in such a weakened state, and in such a confined space, and with no weapons of his own. No clothes, even!

He wanted to punch the door control box. He wanted to scream at it. Finally, in utter frustration, he shouted, "Open!"

Nothing happened.

He touched it with his right hand and shouted again, "Open!"

Nothing happened.

The creatures were nearly upon him.

Did the door know who he was? Did it only allow certain individuals to pass?

Keeping physical contact with the box, he shouted his name: "Hawk!"

The device knew him, though he did not know himself. From somewhere deep inside the mechanism, a click sounded, followed immediately by a deep, resounding clang that came from within the wall. As he stared at it, not quite believing what he was seeing, the door began to slide open.

Hawk wasted no more time. Within half a second he had leapt through the now-open portal and was rushing forward again.

He covered about fifteen yards of dark corridor in only a few quick strides. Long, narrow, bright lights flared to life around him in rings as he ran. From the sounds, he could tell the pursuing invaders had reached the door as well, and it was still open.

The buzz of the strange weapons came to his ears again. He felt slashes of pain along his right leg and down his left side.

He stifled a cry of pain. They were literally *disintegrating* him!

At the far end of the now-brightly lit corridor, a smaller hatch stood open.

Having no real idea what lay beyond, Hawk dived through it. He rolled on the hard surface and came up ready, hands out and prepared to strike.

"Registering external threat," came a voice from all around him. *"Securing main hatch."*

The round door snapped closed with a clang. Lights came on, bright at first but then dimming to a tolerable level.

Shielding his eyes, Hawk stumbled forward, his body wracked with intense pain. He looked up, searching for the source of the voice he'd heard. There was no one else there.

He slumped against a curved metal wall, nausea rushing over him. Looking down, he saw what looked like broad gouges in his flesh, and realized that blood was rapidly pooling on the dark gray floor, all around his feet. There was no real pain yet, but he knew it was coming and coming soon, if he was still conscious to feel it by then—or still alive.

"Orders?"

The voice again. It sounded male, but was silky smooth. Hawk gazed all around, frowning.

"Who—?"

"Detecting hostile parties outside main hatch. Shall we launch?"

He had been right—the pain was coming now, and coming hard.

"Who are you?" he called out, his vision swimming.

The voice grew less harsh; it was almost feminine when it came back with, *"You have sustained severe trauma, Hawk. Please enter the medical unit immediately."*

"Who are you?" he demanded again, his voice angry though weak. "I don't know what you're talking about!"

"Calculating probability of early disconnection from datadump system. Subject is missing vital knowledge. Executing emergency override. Launching now."

The room lurched, causing Hawk to stumble again, now away from the wall he'd leaned upon and toward a coffin-shaped box set into the wall—the hull?—just a few feet away. Its broad gray lid was up, open. He collided with it, held on as the room jerked again. He looked inside. For all of its morbid shape, the inside appeared quite comfortable, with thick white cushioned lining. Tubes and wires coiled in the gaps between the cushions, along with rows of lights, all currently dim.

"Please climb into the medical unit, Hawk."

He did want to lie down, he decided. Very much, he wanted to lie down. But—in a coffin?

The room—the ship?—rocked violently and he fell forward, into the box. The lid slammed down instantly, sealing him inside.

Gas filled the space. Needles jabbed him all around.

The universe went away for a time.

2: FALCON

Falcon did not look up as the great oaken door to his room creaked slowly open.

A sliver of white light shone through, penetrating the gloom and crossing the dank stonework. There it fell across his brown-robed and hooded form, seated on the floor in the far corner.

"He has been with us for over a week," came the voice of the sister assigned to the housekeeping of this level. "And he hasn't left this room for three days." Her voice was shaky, strained with concern as well as something more—perhaps a tinge of fear.

"Three days," a deep, rumbling, male voice replied. "Well. And you know without a doubt that he has not left the building in all that time?"

"He has not, my lord," the sister replied in a hushed tone. "I am certain of it."

The man laughed hollowly.

"I'm sure you are," he said.

He pushed his way roughly past the sister and moved fully into the room. The glare from the hallway framed him in a white halo, revealing a tall, gaunt man clad in the blood-red robes of the Inquisition. Jewels glinted on his fingers and on the golden insignia of office dangling from a chain about his neck. Atop his head rested a broad round hat that obscured his features in shadow, save for a long, beaklike nose. Crossing the room quickly in four long strides, he loomed over the huddled figure, staring down at him, his hard, weathered face betraying scorn and disgust.

Tentatively the sister crept up behind him, her voice cracking as she managed, "You—you don't actually believe that he could have had anything to do with the violence, do you, Inquisitor?"

The inquisitor did not deign to look back at her, or even to reply. All of his intense attention remained focused, laserlike, upon the seemingly pitiful figure at his feet.

"Your name," he boomed.

No reply.

The inquisitor's mouth twisted downward in displeasure.

"Do you know who I am?" he loudly demanded. "You will give me your name. Now!"

Still nothing.

The red-robed man glanced back at the sister. "Does he speak?"

"He does, Inquisitor," she replied. "I have heard him." Motioning with a trembling hand, she pointed down at the hooded figure. "Even now, he speaks."

"Speaks?"

Puzzled, the inquisitor knelt before the man, and became aware that indeed he was mumbling something in a low voice.

"I cannot make out his words."

He leaned closer toward the hooded figure.

This is what he heard:

"—answer me, you cursed Machine...Are you afraid? Why won't you answer—"

"The man is a heretic," the inquisitor declared, standing up suddenly. "He blasphemes against the God Machine!"

He brought back his booted foot to deliver a kick.

"No!" cried the sister, rushing forward. "He's...confused," she said, "perhaps even mad, but—"

"He speaks basest heresy," the Inquisitor boomed, "and he will answer to the Inquisition!"

The red-robed man swung his foot forward—but it never impacted the man on the floor. For a split second the Inquisitor wondered just what had happened, as the shock of his leg being forcibly stopped in mid-kick passed up his spine. He blinked and looked down.

A hand—a rough, thick, scarred hand—had emerged from the brown robe and had caught his lower leg in a viselike grip.

Rage rushed through his system. He glared down. "You— you *dare* to—"

The man on the floor looked up then, his other hand snatching back his hood.

The Inquisitor gasped.

"You!"

A sharp twist to the ankle and the Inquisitor was sent tumbling to the hard stone floor. His broad round hat fell off and landed beside him.

The sister scrambled back toward the doorway, seeking to get out of the way.

The Inquisitor rolled onto his back and sat up, brushing his lank black hair from his eyes—eyes that widened as he saw the other man already standing, looming over him.

"You," he gasped again, this time in a softer tone—one filled more with wonder than disbelief. "Impossible," he added, though he didn't sound entirely convinced.

The other man's robe fluttered open to reveal that he wore a uniform of some sort, mostly of a deep red but with dark blue trim, its texture visible and complex and somehow metallic. His sharp, piercing eyes—one human, one mechanical and softly glowing red—stared down from a heavy-set, rugged face beneath a bald head. And his face—a face as scarred and ragged as his hand—was partly covered by metal components and electronic circuitry.

"Yes," Falcon replied. "Me."

The sister gawked openly at Falcon, then looked at the Inquisitor. She'd never seen a member of the Holy Order so taken aback, so discomfited.

"Who—who are you?" she asked in a hushed tone, stumbling backward. Then, looking down at the Inquisitor, in a louder voice: "Who *is* he?"

The Inquisitor awkwardly struggled to his feet and stared at Falcon, seemingly uncertain of how to react or respond. He took a tentative step forward, his narrow eyes moving to take in the big, muscular figure that stood revealed.

"Though his cyborg features obscure it, his vestments are those of a sacred Hand."

The sister gasped. Then she gathered herself.

"But—but there *are* no more Hands!"

Her eyes moved from Falcon to the Inquisitor.

"That's right, isn't it? We have prayed for so many years, but the Machine has never sent us one. It no longer answers us at all."

Now her eyes stared upward, at the room's ceiling—though her eyes were focused beyond it, as if they could penetrate the surface and see all the way into the heavens beyond. "We had to conclude they're all gone—all dead!"

"So we have believed," the Inquisitor replied. "And so it may yet prove to be." He continued to study the larger man's red and blue uniform and mechanical enhancements while the subject of his scrutiny merely glowered back at him.

"He—he has been conversing with the Machine, then?" The sister's voice trembled noticeably now. "Or merely trying to?"

The Inquisitor ignored her, focusing entirely on the man who stood before him.

"I know this pattern from the ancient records," he stated. "You wear the uniform of a Falcon."

No reply.

"Many false Hands roam this galaxy now, wearing stolen or copied outfits, engaging in the most disgusting criminal activities. If you are *not* a Hand—and I see no way that you could be—the repercussions for you will be most severe."

No reply.

The Inquisitor's impatience grew.

"What evidence can you offer," he demanded, "that you *are* who your appearance would have us believe you are?"

"I do not answer to you," Falcon whispered.

"No, you answer to the God Machine, charlatan, and to his prophet, the great Cardinal—as do we all," the Inquisitor barked. "And I am one of his holy representatives on this world!" He took one step forward, reaching toward Falcon.

The gray-gloved hand moved like lightning, catching the Inquisitor's wrist in an iron grip.

Crying out, the Inquisitor dropped to one knee.

Falcon shoved him away.

"I came here seeking peace," Falcon said then, his voice rising. "A respite from the noise that rages in every corner of this galaxy, clouding my mind—preventing me from hearing the *voice*."

He glared down at the Inquisitor.

"But I should have known your kind would trouble me even here."

The Inquisitor was back up instantly, his eyes flashing.

"A voice? You seek to hear a voice?"

He looked back at the sister, as though seeking her moral support.

"And just whose voice would that be?"

"The voice of your precious Machine," Falcon growled.

"Heresy," the Inquisitor crowed, jabbing a slender figure at his quarry. "The God Machine no longer speaks to the faithful directly! It has not in over a thousand years. All know this to be true."

The sister earnestly nodded but said nothing.

Falcon took a menacing step forward, leaning in toward the holy man.

"The cursed Machine once spoke to me constantly. Incessantly! For much of my life—my too-long life—it scarcely afforded me any peace."

The Inquisitor stubbornly stood his ground but his eyes betrayed a sliver of doubt—doubt about his own beliefs. Then he gathered up his courage once more and shot back, "You are a liar and a charlatan. The God Machine is silent and all true Hands are long dead!"

"Believe what you will, priest," Falcon muttered, shoving past the Inquisitor and through the doorway as the sister scrambled out of the way. "I care not."

"The Holy Inquisition will have you, fraud! We will force the truth from you—and cleanse you of this blasphemy!"

Falcon whirled. He moved forward much more quickly than his bulk would have suggested, and jabbed a gloved finger at the Inquisitor.

"You are welcome to try, priest," he said.

And with that he exited the room.

The sister watched him go, then turned back to the Inquisitor, her eyes wide and imploring.

"What—what will you do?" she cried.

The holy man had a small communications device in his hand. He smiled at her, though she could clearly see the nervousness that lay behind it.

"I will call in the Inquisition, of course," he said. Moving to the window, he stared down as the big man passed through the front door and out into the street, the other sisters scrambling quickly to get out of his way.

"And they," he concluded, "will strike down upon this false Hand with a terrible and glorious fury."

3: HAWK

Consciousness returned slowly, emerging as from a deep fog. He felt as if he'd slept for a week, maybe more.

His eyes flittered open.

"Whuh—"

His speech was slurred, his mouth gummy. Maybe, he thought, he *had* been asleep for a week.

Darkness all around. Darkness—no, wait. Not entirely. Now he could see tiny lights, a few of them red, most of them green, winking on and off. How far away were they?

He reached out with his right hand and instantly his fingers brushed against the lights, and against the foamy cushions he now could see all around him.

He knew then: He lay within a coffin. A high-tech coffin, but a coffin nonetheless. He remembered falling into it, before.

Claustrophobia swept over him in waves then. He had to get out!

Both hands moved up, pressing against the lid, mere inches above his chest. Nothing. He pushed harder, but it would not budge.

Frustration growing, he shouted incoherently, banging his fists against the cushions.

A moment later, the last of the red lights changed to green. With a pop and hiss, the lid slowly swung up. Cool air rushed in.

Hawk blinked. He sat up. He looked around.

His eyes were still sensitive, despite the dim lighting that surrounded him. As they adjusted, he could see that he was still inside the little room he'd stumbled into earlier, when the bizarre alien creatures had been chasing him. Fortunately, the lone doorway into the room was still closed—and he was still alive—so clearly they had not been able to force their way in.

He eyed the door warily. Were they still lurking just outside, waiting to pounce on him? Dare he even try to open the door?

Where would he go if he did?

Placing his hands on the edge of the box, he pulled himself up, then swung his legs out and dropped carefully to the floor.

Looking back into the coffinlike structure, he saw that all of its lights had gone dark now, and the tubing had retracted back into its sides.

Just how long had he slept in there?

The next thing he became aware of was that he was still naked. Naked and increasingly cold—it was much cooler out in the room than it had been inside the box.

On the far side of the room he could see vivid blue and red colors standing out against the otherwise light gray walls. He moved closer and saw that it was a set of clothing of some sort, hanging from a peg.

He looked at the clothes, shrugged, reached out and grabbed them. What were the odds they would fit him? Probably not terribly good, but almost anything would beat another minute with *nothing* on.

Surprisingly, as he finished putting them on, he found they fit him perfectly. Almost as if they had been *made* for him.

He looked down at himself then and could see a snug-fitting, heavily textured, thick jumpsuit of dark metallic blue, with deep red trim across the shoulders and chest. The red continued down the tops of his long sleeves in almost a...*feather* pattern. The material felt thin and light at first blush but quickly revealed itself to be incredibly strong, tough, and resilient. Squinting his eyes and studying it as closely as possible, he found that it was composed of thousands or millions of tiny, self-contained components, like almost microscopic bubbles that were clinging tightly to one another and together forming a set of clothes.

Shaking his head in astonishment at the wondrous material, he pulled on the gray-silver boots along with a dark belt fitted out with numerous pouches, all fastened closed. He knew he'd have to inspect the contents of those pretty soon, to be exactly sure of what he was carrying around with him.

Still keeping one eye on the hatch, concerned that at any moment the horde of invaders might break through, he held up his hands and stared at them. What he saw was a pair of strong, broad hands, olive-skinned, with fine, dark hair.

He brought those hands down to his side and felt the shape of a holster there, under the right one. At first he assumed it was hanging from the right side of his belt, but a more careful check revealed that it actually was formed of, or extended from, the material of his uniform itself. Fascinating, he thought. And—a holster implied a gun. But where was it?

He looked all around the small room for any sign of it, at the same time attempting to make sense of where he was now. The more he thought about such things, though, the more his head throbbed in pain. The location of this little room brought with it too many other questions, one after the other. What was that strange place he been *before* coming into the little room? Who were the strange invaders he'd fought? For that matter, who was *he*?

The voice he'd heard earlier sounded again now, causing him to look up with widening eyes.

"What are you looking for, Hawk?"

His eyes narrowed and he backed against one wall.

"Who's there?"

A pause, and then, *"I see the medical treatments did nothing for your mental state. That is unfortunate."*

"Who are you?" he demanded. "Show yourself!"

Another brief pause, and then, *"I am all around you, Hawk. I am your ship."*

"What?" Hawk stared, his mouth opening and closing soundlessly. "A ship?"

"This ship. The ship you are currently aboard."

"Aboard?"

Hawk turned in a slow circle, regarding his surroundings with increasing understanding.

"I'm aboard a ship?"

"A spacecraft, yes. Your spacecraft."

Hawk blinked at this revelation.

"*My* spacecraft. A talking spacecraft."

A pause, then the voice stated, *"I am talking, as you put it, out of necessity. I would have no need to communicate audibly with you if your Aether receptors were functioning. I had hoped they would be back on line by now, given your time in the medical tank. Alas, you remain deaf to the Aether."*

None of that made the slightest bit of sense to Hawk. He was still stuck on the previous point: "I own a spacecraft."

"Indeed you do," the voice replied patiently. "As a Hand of the Machine, you could hardly perform your duties without one. Without me, *that is to say."*

Hawk took this in. He found that, almost instinctively, he understood what the voice was saying—what a spacecraft was, for example—though before hearing such a thing spoken aloud, he never would have thought of it.

"So—are we now moving through space?"

"Yes. I took the liberty of launching us from the base during the attack."

"Show me."

For a long moment, nothing happened. Then a heretofore hidden door slid silently open on the opposite side of the room from the entry hatch.

Hawk eyed the newly-opened portal.

"What is that?"

"Come in and see."

Setting his jaw, Hawk crossed the cabin in four quick steps and leaned through into the new room.

What he saw startled him.

Instantly he understood he was looking at the ship's cockpit. Just ahead of him was a single curved seat, broad and tall and layered with exotic fabrics and materials. Ahead of that, the control panel sparkled with lights and displays. And above that, filling the entire forward area, was a window that revealed the vast panoply of space.

The seat and the control panel both captured his attention for a moment, but what seized his mind and refused to let go was what he could see through that broad window.

He gasped and took a half-step back.

There before him was displayed a vision of apocalypse: ruins of planets and fields of rubble and the wreckage of massive starships—*fleets* of wrecked starships.

What he could see was devastation on a scale almost unimaginable.

What he could see was a shattered galaxy.

Closing his eyes tightly, he turned away from the window and leaned against the nearest bulkhead.

"What is this, ship? What am I seeing?"

"*Seeing?*" A pause. "*Ah, yes—your memories have been affected more severely than I first understood. Your unfortunate and premature disconnection from the machines has left you extremely disoriented.*"

Hawk ignored all of this. "What am I seeing?" he demanded again, more loudly and intensely.

"*You are seeing the results of a war of galactic scale and scope. A war so widespread and so devastating that little of this galaxy remains as it was before.*"

Hawk breathed in and out for a few seconds and then turned back to the window, staring out, his forehead creased in confusion and disbelief.

"So much destruction," he whispered. "So much…"

"*Yes.*"

"Who did this? Who caused it?"

"*Ah,*" the ship replied after what seemed like a moment's consideration. "*You arrive at the nub of the question now.*"

Hawk's confused expression morphed into a look of rage. He whirled about and struck the bulkhead with his right fist.

"Enough of your double-talk, ship! Tell me who did this!"

"*The Adversary caused this,*" the ship replied. "*The Adversary from beyond our galaxy. Though of course a number of the more hostile races native to this galaxy played their parts as well. A 'scorched-galaxy' strategy against the enemy resulted in just that—a scorched galaxy. A* shattered *galaxy.*"

Hawk considered this. He had so many questions, but he knew that an understanding of his opponents, as quickly as it could be acquired, took priority.

"This 'Adversary,'" he repeated. "That's an army? Or a single person? A person like me?"

"*Of the Adversary himself, I cannot say. But his army was indeed made up of living, sentient individuals,*" the ship answered, *"though they were, for the most part, nothing like you."*

"Are they still here?   Still in this galaxy?   Still in this vicinity?"

The ship paused for several seconds before answering; when it did, its voice was oddly hesitant.

"My understanding was that they had all been defeated... destroyed... long ago.   Or else driven from this galaxy—or what is left of it. But..."

"But what?"

"But clearly that is not the case."

"Why?"

"Because the enemy that attacked you at the base—the insectoid beings all of black.   Their race—the Skrazzi—was an ally of the Adversary; indeed, they served him with more complete devotion and fervor than nearly any other beings."

Hawk took this in.

"So either they never left," he stated slowly, "or else..."

"Or else they have returned," the ship finished for him. *"Yes."*

He gazed out at the shattered galaxy all around him once again. He shuddered.

"I think I begin to understand," he said. "At least, that much of it."

He climbed up into the pilot's seat, settling comfortably into the contoured cushions. A portion of the control panel extended automatically out so that it rested within easy reach. Lights flickered across its black glasslike surface.

"Ship," he said, eyes focused and intent now, "I believe you should tell me everything you know. Now. From the beginning."

His hand moved instinctively to his side, fingertips brushing against his empty holster.

"And you can start by telling me where to find my gun."

4: FALCON

Falcon sat at a small, circular table at the back of the cantina, his brown robes wrapped tightly around his body and his hood pulled low over his head, obscuring his face in shadow. The small crowd of customers at other tables carried on their own conversations or sat engulfed in their own solitude and utterly ignored him.

He'd made his way there more than an hour earlier, his robes helping him blend seamlessly in with the ranks of workers from the nearby monastery and convent. Though for obvious reasons few of those individuals seemed to frequent this particular establishment, he was apparently not so out of place as to attract excessive attention. So he sat at the back of the room and he drank and he brooded, all the while contemplating the hated voice that still echoed, so many centuries later, within his head.

Downing the contents of the glass in his right hand, he set it on the stained tabletop and looked at the bottle his thick, calloused fingers gripped in his left. He spent a few moments trying to decide if the bottle was half-full or half-empty, but decided that such philosophical questions were not high on his agenda at the moment, no matter how much they might tell him about his outlook on life.

His eyes—his normal right one and his mechanically augmented left one—scanned the room, taking in the sight of the other patrons. Workers, mostly, from the mines, along with a few shopkeepers and a smattering of other, less savory types. His eye detected no special weapons, no unexpected defenses or other telltale high-tech items that would mark a true enemy, a true threat.

Pouring another glass, he considered just how much longer he would be able to stay on this backwater mining world. It had promised safety and security and perhaps even a bit of sanity, lo those many weeks earlier when he had arrived. But, as usual, someone had to stick their nose into his business; take offense at his words, his actions. It never failed, and he honestly wondered why it even surprised him anymore.

He would have to leave soon. This he knew beyond question. He would find no peace here. This world was not at all what he had hoped it would be. The people here had apparently elevated the Machine to "God Machine" status, worshipping the cursed thing as a deity.

A deity. Some kind of benevolent sentience. He snorted. If only they knew—if only they understood the truth.

Groaning, he squeezed his eyes closed and raised his fists, grinding them into the sockets.

You don't fool me, Machine! I know you're still out there. Speak to me!

But of course the voice would not answer.

He almost laughed at the irony. There had been a time, long ago, when he had begged the voice to be silent—to leave him alone—and it would not. And, even before that, there had been a time when he had happily and faithfully served the Machine with no questions asked.

In the days just after the Shattering, the Machine had grown more controlling, more tyrannical, in its relationships with all of its surviving Hands. Eventually it had passed into what Falcon considered outright dictatorial behavior, seeking to directly control the actions and even the thoughts of its agents. For the most part, it succeeded.

After only a few years of that, Falcon had felt he was starting to lose his own grip on sanity, and suspected the Machine already had. He could not free himself from its thrall, but he secretly prayed to whatever deities there might be that it would at least fall silent—would grant him peace for just a short while. As much as he hoped and prayed, though, it never would leave him alone for very long. And every time it came back and spoke to him again, issuing terse and often contradictory directives, he felt a bit more of himself falling under its absolute sway.

And then, one day, its presence had vanished from the galaxy. Its voice fell utterly silent.

By then, he had lost contact with whatever few other Hands still survived—if any others did. And without the Machine to coordinate and relay their communications, he had no way of knowing or finding out.

So, in the years since, he had wandered from place to place, doing whatever good he could, keeping his head down, and generally railing at the Machine—his god that wasn't there—whenever he had a spare moment. Generally he demanded that it wake up, that it pay attention to him, that it *respond* to him. That it tell him what had happened to silence it.

It never did.

Angrily he knocked the glass aside, put the bottle to his lips and drank deep, finishing it. Then he banged it down on the tabletop, empty, and stared off into unfocused nothingness.

A disturbance at the door a few moments later brought him back to reality.

Here they come.

He was on his feet and moving even before the glint of light off weapons barrels shone through the opening doorway. He didn't rush to confront them—not at all. Instead he moved quickly toward the rear of the bar, aiming for the kitchen doorway and escape out the back.

His pursuers had anticipated this, of course. Men with guns were filing in through that door, too.

He stopped, standing stock-still, as soldiers came at him from both directions and formed a broad circle around him.

They were local Church troops, he could tell; probably the best the Inquisition could pull together on such short notice. They wore brown fatigues marked heavily with the flame-within-a-circle symbol of the Church and the Inquisition. They carried a variety of small arms.

Falcon waited, standing there at the center of the room. The other customers realized quickly what was happening—what was about to happen—and fled, many of them leaving their personal belongings behind in their haste to scramble past the soldiers and out the front doorway.

The troops had eyes only for Falcon. They ignored the departing throng and glowered as one at him, guns in hand. There had to be more than dozen of them; perhaps twenty in all.

"Surrender, heretic," one of the Church soldiers demanded then. "There are many of us, and you are unarmed. Come with us. Now."

Falcon's natural eye glinted in the pale light. He slowly and deliberately moved both of his arms away from his sides, hands open, and peered back at the man who had spoken.

"You've been misinformed," he told the soldier. "Who ever said I was unarmed?"

Two gunmetal gray pistols dropped from the sleeves of his brown robes into his waiting hands. He leveled each of the weapons at the same instant—one pointed forward, the other behind him—and opened fire. Even as he did so, he lurched forward, falling beneath the level of the table at which he'd sat.

In the first split-second, four Church soldiers were struck by slugs from his pistols and began to crumble to the floor. In the next, the remaining soldiers opened fire. Unfortunately for them, they had not been sufficiently trained in combat within such close quarters, with friendly forces directly in their line of fire. Each side managed to take out half of the other side before their commander, screaming maniacally over the weapons discharges and cries of pain, managed to get them all to hold their fire.

By that point, Falcon had slipped past the battalion in front of him and leapt through the open front door, out into the street.

He started to his feet again quickly, guns at the ready. The surviving soldiers inside the cantina were still in the process of extricating themselves from one another and had not yet exited in pursuit. But before he could fully stand, a blow struck him hard to the side of the head—the more human side—and he tumbled over with a grunt.

"He is here!" called the voice of the one who had struck. "Here!"

Falcon rolled over and gazed up.

The Inquisitor stood over him, robes flaring, a malevolent expression on his face. In his right hand he clutched a sort of golden scepter—clearly, the object he'd used to strike Falcon.

He was waving his other hand at the soldiers, who were now filing out of the cantina in pursuit.

"Heretic!   Fraud!   This will be your end!   My men will slaughter you!"

Falcon leapt to his feet in a move remarkably nimble for such a big, bulky figure.

"Let them try," he growled.   And with a shove he sent the slender man to the ground, then raced down the street.

Bullets and energy blasts zipped around and past Falcon like angry bees.   He ignored them as he directed one pistol back behind him and fired two quick shots.   The two nearest soldiers of the Inquisition dropped, dead.   Reholstering his gun, he came to the building he had been seeking and dashed through its open front door.

The Inquisitor was back on his feet and screaming at his soldiers to pursue.   They appeared to be increasingly reluctant to do so, however; more than a dozen of them lay dead now, and the survivors were having clear second thoughts about hurrying to confront this foe.   But after a barrage of threats and warnings, the remaining dozen or so troopers in their brown uniforms rushed through the doorway into the building Falcon had entered.

The Inquisitor stood there in the middle of the street, waiting.

He did not have to wait for long.

A mere moment after the last of the soldiers crowded through the door, the building exploded in a conflagration of fire and sound.   The Inquisitor was swept from his feet and hurled backward across the street, impacting the wall of the building behind him.   Flames gutted out in every direction as the building collapsed and disintegrated, destroying everything and everyone that had been inside it along with it.

For nearly a minute, the Inquisitor couldn't move, couldn't think.   He lay there, head spinning, staring up at the sky.   Then a voice rumbled down to him.   It was jumbled and incoherent to him, seeing as how his head was still ringing, but it gave him something to focus on.   Shaking his head to clear it, he sat up and looked for the source of the words.

Falcon stood over him.   His brown robe had been cast aside, revealing the red and blue uniform beneath it.   Bionic implants shone through in a number of places. Pistols hung in holsters at his side. The red light of an artificial eye flickered. In his hand he held a small device—the detonator for the bombs he had planted earlier.

"You...you *are*...a Hand," the Inquisitor gasped, taking in just what he was seeing. "Truly you are!"

Ignoring him, Falcon reached down with a rough, calloused hand. The Inquisitor flinched, but instead of assaulting him, Falcon grasped the golden scepter the Inquisitor had carried. He lifted it, studied it momentarily, and then almost casually he brought it down across his bent knee, snapping it in half.

"Relax," he intoned, his eyes moving from the stunned Church man to the blazing ruins across the street. "I've about had my fill of this planet. I'll be moving on now."

He tossed the two broken pieces of the scepter down onto the slender, scowling man.

"And leaving you in peace."

He gazed one last time at the fire roaring nearby—a fire that had consumed the remaining half of the Inquisitor's troops. Then he turned and walked slowly in the opposite direction.

"Which is more than can ever be said for me," he muttered softly to himself.

5: HAWK

Hawk sat back in the flight seat and inspected his newly-located pistol, while listening as his ship filled him in somewhat on his own life story.

He was already feeling more confident, more in control of his mind and his body. He still deferred to the ship for information and advice, but his natural tendency as a Hand was asserting itself—he was the master here, and the vessel merely his mechanical assistant. Now that he knew this, he felt he had his feet under himself at last.

And indeed he *was* a Hand, he understood now. A Hand of the Machine—the great artificial intelligence which had been built ages ago in some secret and long-forgotten location by the most advanced faction of the human race. In the years before the Adversary had attacked with his vast hordes, the Machine and its corps of Hands and other officers and specialists had commanded mighty fleets and armies that kept the peace across the galaxy, working in concert with some forces, against others, but always in the interests of law and order and justice.

Then came the Adversary, and everything had changed.

As the enemy's mighty forces had advanced from star system to star system, enslaving and destroying all before them, the Machine had kept up the fight, continuing the war even after all the vast star empires were swept from the skies by the black hordes of the Adversary.

The apocalyptic battle had finally come, the ship had explained. Wave after wave of enemy ships had struck the defenses of the great races. In numbers uncounted and uncountable they came, and the clash went on and on for months, for years—perhaps for centuries. And at the end the great enemy had been defeated, or at least driven utterly away. The hostile alien races in his thrall were mostly crushed, their holdings reduced to isolated little star empires. He himself had vanished. But at such a cost: the great star empires that had resisted him were forever smashed, broken, their starfleets annihilated, their planets and suns exploded and left as burned out cinders wandering blindly and erratically through the dark and icy void. And their galaxy itself was shattered; to its core, it was shattered. It was naught now but the corpse of a formerly thriving organism, slowly dying, its dead suns and broken worlds tumbling into darkness.

But within that corpse life still clung, still endured.

Some of the younger races, having failed because of their much less advanced technology to draw the full attention of the Adversary during the war, matured within that shattered galaxy and moved further out into space, creating their own fledgling spheres of influence. Others slowly recovered what they had lost, and began to assert their dominance again.

Humanity was chief among those, and its surviving colony worlds had grown into a number of squabbling and competing empires scattered across the remains of the galaxy, in the spots where life was still possible.

Clashes among the colonies were inevitable over time, as were wars with the other races that humans encountered. Chaos and catastrophe reappeared within the galaxy, and spread—now entirely the work of its own sentient beings, with no outside provocations necessary.

The Machine had gazed outward at the wreckage of so many civilizations, and had seen the violence and bloodshed that the native inhabitants of the galaxy were creating among themselves. And it found such a thing unacceptable.

It attempted at first to maintain what little order was possible in that environment, dispatching its few surviving Hands as lone agents and enforcers of the law. Without the vast armies they had once commanded, however, they were nowhere near as effective.

For all its might and all its intelligence, the Machine could not move, could not reach out and put things right. Once, before and even during the war, it had possessed many outside resources, but all of them had been destroyed by the time of the end of that conflict. As one after another of the remaining Hands perished in combat and conflicts across the disk of the Milky Way, the Machine could do nothing but watch.

Finally, the mighty intelligence itself had fallen silent, its few remaining agents left on their own.

"And you are such an agent—a Hand of the Machine," the ship had told him. *"You are a Hawk. Your job is to patrol the galaxy, enforcing the Machine's law and the Machine's peace— even if the Machine itself no longer answers our calls."*

"And there are other Hands who have survived?"

"...Yes, it is believed that some few remain, scattered here and there across the human worlds. No one knows just how many."

Hawk considered this, then nodded.

"Can we not travel to the Machine itself and discover what has caused its silence?"

"That is impossible," the ship replied.

"Why?"

"Because no one knows the location of the Machine. Its location has remained one of the great mysteries of the galaxy for nearly two thousand years."

Hawk absorbed this information.

"Where do we go for resupply, repair, and the like?" he asked after a moment.

"The Machine scattered bases for its Hands across the galaxy, for just such contingencies, as well as for the creation of new Hands," the ship said. *"The base where you were awoken— somewhat prematurely, due to the attack—has been lost to us, obviously. But I have found the nearest, and we approach it now."*

"Good."

Hawk studied his pistol closely for perhaps the sixth time since the ship had told him where to retrieve it from storage. It was apparently his back-up weapon, his primary gun now lost somewhere aboard the base he'd fled earlier. Even so, he found it endlessly fascinating—and wondered if he had been genetically programmed to feel that way about the tools of his trade.

He held the weapon up, allowing the cabin's light to play over its gleaming, blue-silver surface. For all its high-tech façade, it was a grim and obviously deadly piece of equipment. Two cylindrical barrels, one over the other, ran its length; one fired bursts of concentrated energy, the other metal slugs. Both a small battery pack and a clip of ammunition were plugged into the body just ahead of the trigger guard. He found he looked forward to getting to test-fire it soon.

For that matter, he was looking forward to getting to do just about *anything*. He found himself restless, anxious to stretch his legs a bit, in a space less confined than the interior of the ship. The time stuck inside the medical casket had only increased his claustrophobia and his desire for freedom. He hopped up and stalked around the cabin, nervous, though at least relieved to have a greater understanding of just who he was and why he existed. A certain amount of peace seemed to flow from that, though a degree of anxiety, as well—though for what reason he could not presently guess.

"Closing in on the base now," the ship intoned.

Hawk forced himself to sit down again and wait, his eyes locked on the flashing blue circle in the holo display. Then he shifted his attention to the window itself, and realized that he could now see the base growing larger with his naked eyes.

Not an asteroid as the previous one had been, this was an actual space station, manufactured from metal and crystal parts. It formed a great wheel, slowly spinning, with a dozen spokes all leading inward to a central hub. It was toward this hub that the ship traveled now, and Hawk could do nothing but watch and wait.

He saw them before the ship's sensors detected them—before it could identify the energy spikes that flared on the far side of the station. Strange, organic-looking vessels moved into view from where they had lurked behind the station. Their dark hulls, half-melted in appearance and streaked with red and orange, appeared to shimmer in the darkness. He knew without asking whom they belonged to.

"Ship—!"

Their forward momentum halted instantly as the ship reacted to what it was now detecting ahead.

"The Adversary! His servants have arrived here ahead of us!"

"It doesn't take a computer mind to grasp that," Hawk growled. "Get us out of here!"

The blue-silver, triangular ship spun about on its axis and accelerated, hyperdrive engine kicking in.

"They are firing upon us," the ship reported.

"I guessed that much. Can they hurt us?"

"Oh yes," the ship replied, *"without a doubt. Their weaponry is quite formidable. But,"* it continued, as the acceleration seemed to increase, even through the distorting effects of artificial gravity, *"they have to* hit *us to hurt us."*

The enemy vessels raced forward in the display, the distance between them and Hawk's ship narrowing.

"Can't you go faster?"

"Speed within normal space is irrelevant," the ship answered him in an emotionless voice. *"We will escape into the Above as soon as the engines can cycle up again. Only a few seconds."*

The ship shook violently as fire from the enemy vessels struck it. It shook again, harder.

"We may not have seconds, ship," Hawk shouted, angry at being unable to directly influence events around him. "Go faster!"

"Yes—I see your point," the ship said.

It lurched again, though whether from weapons impact or from sudden acceleration Hawk could not be sure. Then the tactical display blurred and the hyper-realm engulfed them.

"Can they not attack us here?" Hawk asked after a few seconds, his eyes sliding across the bizarre, shimmering waves that represented in the visible light spectrum the hyperspace travel effect.

"We are in what some have called the Above," the ship answered, "and relative distances here are meaningless. Even if the enemy ships entered just behind us, they might as well be on the far side of the galaxy while we are here."

Hawk took this in, finding that somehow he seemed to understand it better than he felt he should. Again that odd, nagging sense of being in control of only half his faculties— though half represented a sizeable gain on his condition a short while earlier.

"What about when we emerge into normal space again?" he asked.

The ship hesitated for a moment.

"The theoretical possibility does exist that they could emerge just behind us, yes," it said then. *"But that would require them to know exactly where we are going. And since even I do not know where we are going, nor have you given me orders to that effect..."*

"Right," Hawk replied. He sat there a moment, considering, and the ship said nothing. The hyper-realm of the Above continued to flow past the window. Then, "So...where *should* we be going?"

The ship was silent for several seconds before coming back with, *"That is the larger question we confront, is it not?"*

"What do you mean?"

"I mean that, under normal circumstances, and given that the Machine is now silent, you as a Hand would have the authority to determine our agenda and our mission."

"Ah," Hawk said, understanding. "But since I don't really have all of my memories available..."

"Precisely. Because you lack the knowledge and capacity to make such decisions for us, and without the Machine to guide us, we are what you might refer to as... loose ends."

Hawk considered this. The ship sounded almost...*afraid*...of having no one in authority to guide and direct it. He, on the contrary, felt somewhat relieved that a vast, mechanical mind was not issuing commands to him.

And yet the Machine had for all intents and purposes *created* him, and had given him this amazing, sentient vessel to carry him here and there across the galaxy... It made perfect sense that he should be obligated to obey its instructions, carry out its orders—was that not why he existed in the first place?—and perhaps even find out what had become of it. He would be extremely ungrateful to behave otherwise, he felt.

And besides—based on what the ship had told him about the current state of the galaxy, he was truly needed out there. A *Hand* was needed. And, like it or not, that's who and what he was.

"Alright," he declared after bringing this bit of reflection to its conclusion. "So, if we proceed from the assumption that the Machine needs us to help it, just about as much as we need it to help us...Then I believe our first order of business should be to locate it."

If the ship had possessed the ability to laugh, it probably would have.

"You propose to attempt to solve the greatest mystery in all the ages of the galaxy, as our first mission?" it asked, sounding as astonished as a ship's AI could sound.

45

Hawk ignored this.

"If the Machine were still intact and still able to communicate with its agents," he continued, "how would it do so?"

"You would feel a sort of sensation within your mind," the ship replied. *"A tickling...an itching that could only be remedied by quiet meditation. During that meditation, the Machine would speak to you, loudly and clearly, over what we call the Aether connection—a communications beam that can travel through subspace or through the Above, crossing vast distances nearly instantaneously."*

Hawk considered this.

"You said something earlier," he remembered. "That my Aether receptors weren't functioning—right?"

"That has been my suspicion, yes," the ship replied. *"I have been unable to communicate with you in that manner, despite repeated attempts. I believe those functions were damaged during your excessively violent and hasty awakening."*

"I would hear you in my head, then?" Hawk asked, tapping the side of his skull. "If my *receptors* worked properly?"

"Yes."

Hawk snorted. "It was bad enough when I first heard you speak out loud. That alone nearly made me think I'd gone mad." He looked up at the ceiling, in the direction of the main speaker. "So, even if the Machine did try to contact me, I wouldn't be able to hear it."

"I fear not."

"So—it might still be out there, trying to talk to me, and I'm just not able to hear it." He frowned, thinking. "But what about you? You haven't heard anything from the Machine in all the time since you were..." He sought the right word. "...Activated?"

"No. Nothing."

"But you would, though—if the Machine was still functioning, right?"

"I would hear it, yes," the ship stated, *"if it chose to communicate with me. My receptors are not damaged, nor is my transmitter."*

"And it hasn't."

"I am not a Hand," it said, *"merely a tool—a servant—of one. It might not consider me worthy of direct communication."*

Hawk thought about this but didn't say anything. He wouldn't have known what to say.

The ship didn't speak for several seconds, either, until, *"Though the historical records in my databases contain the information I have relayed to you, even so I had hoped the Machine's silence represented some temporary situation that had been remedied in the time since my programming. But now I fear it has truly and perhaps permanently gone silent."* The ship paused, then, *"I fear some terrible fate has befallen it."*

"That's what we need to find out," Hawk said. "And—if this Adversary you spoke of has indeed returned—we don't have much choice in the matter. We need allies—and I can't think of a better one." He looked up at the speaker. "Can you?"

The ship did not reply. Another long and oddly uncomfortable silence ensued.

After a while, Hawk grew frustrated with his mechanical associate's reticence to continue the conversation and stood, moving about the ship's central cabin. His muscles were still stiff from the medical treatments he'd undergone, and he engaged in a series of exercises, each of which seemed to come naturally to him as he moved. That part of his memory, at least, was intact.

As he considered his physical muscles, he realized that his subconscious was nagging at him about some other set of muscles—perhaps metaphorical, he decided after a moment's wondering. Those "muscles" were the ones he used to pilot the ship. It came to him then that he had no idea how to do such a thing.

"Ship," he called. "There has to be a way that I can actually *fly*…um…you. As opposed to just asking you to take me places. But I don't know what that way might be."

The ship did not reply for several seconds, and Hawk's ire began to rise again. Then, *"Yes,"* it said, its mechanical tone indicating reluctance, *"that is correct. Unfortunately,"* it continued, *"to do so you must mentally interface with my systems, and this is done via the Aether connection. Which you are unable to access."*

"Oh," Hawk sighed, disappointed. Then he brightened. "Maybe we should try it anyway. We can't be sure that just because one part doesn't work..."

The ship might have been considering this for as much as two seconds before it replied, *"Highly unlikely. The Aether receptors within your brain that are unable to access the network connection are the same ones that interface with my navigation systems and—"*

"Let's try it anyway," Hawk insisted. "What have we got to lose?"

The ship held out for another few back-and-forth exchanges before at last relenting.

"Very well," it said. *"We will attempt something very basic to begin with. Please take your position in the pilot's seat and concentrate on altering the course we are traveling."*

Hawk climbed into the pilot's seat and sat back, making himself as comfortable as possible. He closed his eyes and concentrated on the ship around him, and on the limitless space beyond.

He felt it then—the slightest twinge, as though sensing other limbs attached to his body; limbs that had been paralyzed for a seeming eternity but were now working again. He opened his eyes.

The ship was curving around, the stars streaming past gracefully in the forward view. As he watched, the ship's course settled back into a straight line again.

"Did I do that, or did you?" Hawk asked, now very wide-eyed.

"You did," the ship replied. *"Well. How...extraordinary."*

Hawk grinned. He was ecstatic—this represented perhaps his most positive accomplishment yet.

"Maybe the receptors in my head aren't dead," he speculated as he spun the ship about and increased its speed. "Maybe they're just... rusty or something. Atrophied. Needing a little more exercise."

"Perhaps," the ship replied.

"In any case," Hawk added, "it's a start."

At that moment a series of alarms resounded throughout the cabin.

Hawk almost leapt out of the seat in reaction, but quickly settled his emotions and frowned out at the starfield in front of his ship. Far in the distance, but growing perceptibly larger by the moment, loomed an artificial construct of vast size and complexity. Quickly it resolved into a conglomeration of very different shapes and colors, as though its builders had cobbled it together from whatever pieces were available; from the leftovers and castoffs of a hundred different worlds and space fleets. Squared-off boxes and rectangles connected almost awkwardly to smooth cylinders and spheres, mixed in among even more complex components. Clearly it was some sort of stationary base; Hawk could not imagine something of such awkward shape and size moving terribly easily through the void at any real speed.

"Is all that noise necessary?" he called out over the cacophony. He started to verbally order the ship to shut the alarms off, but then he reconsidered and attempted instead to concentrate on the alarms, ordering them to mute themselves.

Instantly the raucous sounds ceased.

"Apologies," the ship's voice said, *"and very well done."* It paused, then, *"We are approaching a major facility of the local political entity—the Hanrilite Empire. They have detected our presence. You will be expected."*

Hawk frowned at this. "Expected? Expected for what?"

"For dinner, I would imagine," the ship replied.

"Dinner?"

"As well as for a general inspection. That has been the usual protocol."

"Inspection? I'm to be inspected?"

"You are to do the inspecting, Hawk. You are, after all, a Hand of the Machine."

"They can tell this already? Without having met me, or even spoken with me?"

"They probably feel they should give you the benefit of the doubt, at least to start with."

Hawk grunted an acknowledgement.

"They are hailing you now," the ship added. *"Shall I put it on speaker?"*

"Sure," Hawk said distractedly, standing next to his seat and clasping one hand in the other behind his back. It was a stance he moved into smoothly and easily, without thinking, as if it were second nature to him.

A crackling sound filled the cockpit area for an instant, followed by a woman's voice, clear and crisp.

"Welcome, Hand," the voice said. "On behalf of the Captain, I offer greetings and the hospitality of our station to you." The words were spoken perfunctorily, as though she were reading them off a note card.

"You have my thanks for your kind welcome," Hawk replied automatically and with genuine warmth, the words falling into place effortlessly and seeming correct enough. As the ship didn't instantly contradict or cut him off, he continued. "May I ask the name of your captain?"

"Our station commander is Captain Katar Fomas," the woman answered. "He invites you to come aboard at your leisure, and dine with him."

All of this puzzled Hawk greatly. He scarcely knew himself—his abilities, his duties—at all, and yet others clearly respected him, or at least his office and position. Better, he thought, to allow that to continue, than to say anything that might damage his standing in their eyes before he'd even met them. As well, the ship seemed both demanding and somewhat reluctant to fill him in on everything he needed to know. Perhaps getting away from it for a while, and meeting other individuals, might help knock a few cobwebs loose.

"Thank you," he said aloud. "I would be honored."

"Excellent. Please proceed to landing bay delta. Navigational data is being transmitted to your ship's intelligence now."

"Very well."

"And if you would wait there, a welcoming party will arrive shortly."

After a couple of seconds, the ship chimed in, *"The data has been received and the communications link severed."*

Hawk sat back on the cushioned seat and rubbed his chin. "This could be interesting," he said, more to himself than to the ship. "I have no real idea what I'm going to say or do."

"You can keep our audio link open if you need to consult with me," the ship stated. *"I can provide you with an earpiece..."*

"That's okay," Hawk said quickly. "I'll contact you if I have any questions."

"As you wish."

Hawk's sleek, triangular ship slid easily into the massive station's docking bay. A few moments later, his sidearm in place in its holster, Hawk crossed the interior cabin.

"The official asked you to wait here for the welcoming party."

Hawk raised one eyebrow.

"And a Hand is expected to do as he is told? To meekly wait for them to be ready for me?"

The ship said nothing for a moment. Then, *"You are becoming more a Hand with every passing moment."*

The hatch slid silently open.

Hawk smiled grimly and stepped through.

The station may have been vast on the outside, but the interior spaces felt extremely cramped—not to mention dark, musty, and cold. There was a slight smell of decay in the air and the dim lighting only served to somehow heighten that impression. Hawk frowned as he looked about the reception area beyond the bay. A couple dozen humans and a scattering of alien life forms milled about in clumps here and there, some of them accompanied by floating palates of what must have been their luggage. Visitors, probably, to be down here in the landing facility—vacationers, business people, diplomats, and so forth. One or two of them cast glances at him before looking quickly away.

He became conscious of his rather unique clothing. A nearly skin-tight, bright blue and red metallic uniform scarcely blended in with all the dark business suits. Idly he wished he'd changed into something more nondescript—assuming there were any other clothes for him aboard the ship.

Instantly his uniform shimmered, the feeling like tiny insects crawling over his skin. Looking down, he saw that the vibrant red and blue had faded to dark gray. A slight smile crept across his lips. Then he realized that his pistol had disappeared entirely; even the holster was gone. A sense of panic struck him. He wondered—had it been taken from him somehow? Had it simply dissolved, teleported away, become invisible? He reached down and felt for it. Nothing. It wasn't just invisible, it was entirely gone. He grew increasingly concerned and started to contact the ship to ask about this, only to feel a blocky shape extruding from the side of his gray uniform. The holster was there again now. His fingers quickly reached down and confirmed that the pistol was still inside. He blinked; it had been extremely disconcerting to see the holster simply take shape as if from nothing. He relaxed about it, and the sidearm and holster vanished again, reabsorbed into his uniform.

So. His technology was even more advanced than he'd already guessed. Very well.

Since no welcoming party had been waiting to greet him—or whatever they had in mind—he started forward, then paused as he noticed an open entrance to a dimly lit room off to one side. He headed over for it and saw that it was just what he had suspected at first glance: a bar.

It might be useful, he thought, to gather a little informal information before the local authorities arrived to lead him off to whatever official functions he was expected to take part in.

He slipped through the doors, moved between a few lightly-occupied tables, and leaned against the broad, gleaming metal bar. An old guy straight out of central casting approached from the other side, wiping his hands on a tattered apron. He was heavyset, with a thick mustache and balding head. Tattoos covered his left arm. Barely glancing at Hawk, he asked what he'd have.

Hawk wasn't entirely sure how to respond.

"What's the local favorite?" he asked after a couple of seconds of thought.

The bartender narrowed his eyes, actually focusing them on Hawk for an instant, then nodded once and reached under the bar, producing a mostly-empty bottle and a narrow glass. He filled the glass halfway and slid it across.

Hawk lifted the glass, held it up, and gazed at it. He brought it to his lips.

"Hi."

He blinked and looked to his right. A young woman had silently slipped onto the barstool next to him. She had short, very light blonde hair and large, green eyes. Her shimmering red dress, such as it was, was tight enough to make his uniform seem baggy by comparison.

"Hi," he returned, nodding.

"What're you drinking?" she asked.

"I have no idea."

She started to laugh at this, then hesitated as she met his eyes. She looked from them down to his uniform; even though it was now dark gray, its shape remained the same, and the feather-motif areas along the sleeves still stood out as a darker gray. Then her eyes flashed back up to his face and her smile faded as she took in his appearance.

"Excuse me, officer," she said, sliding quickly off the stool. Before he could reply, she had zipped out the exit.

The bartender had witnessed this exchange; now he approached again, his expression much more earnest. He nodded to the drink Hawk was still holding. "That's on the house...*officer*," he said in a quiet voice. "And if you need to inspect the—"

"No, no," Hawk replied, frowning. "That's not necessary." It was slowly dawning on him that, even in his somewhat camouflaged state, he still stood out to the inhabitants of this station. They could tell that he was a...a *whatever* he was. An authority figure, at any rate. And they clearly respected that. Or feared it. Or some combination.

"But I am curious," he continued in a lower voice, while he had the bartender's attention. "Is there anything I should know—anything the local authorities might not want to volunteer to me?"

The bartender hesitated, perhaps simply unsure, perhaps weighing the advantages of divulging information against keeping quiet. After a few seconds, he moved in closer. "There are rumors," he said in almost a whisper. "Some say the Captain is—"

Whatever the man was about to say, Hawk would never know, for at that instant a small crowd passed through the entrance. They were clad in dark green military uniforms with black leather trim, and they moved in a clipped and precise motion. As they approached the bar, Hawk could see that there were six of them. They took up position with half on either side of him, standing at attention.

Hawk turned his back to the bar and waited, unsure of exactly what was happening.

Another figure, taller and clad in dark blue, walked through the entrance and strode directly up to Hawk, standing at the center of the formation. He nodded formally.

"Our apologies for the delay, sir," he said. "If you are refreshed now, the Captain respectfully requests your presence."

The little army led Hawk on a winding journey back across the landing bay reception area and through a large metal door set into the far bulkhead. From there, they passed along what seemed like miles of nondescript corridors. Along the way, the officer in blue offered the occasional additional apology for not having been waiting for Hawk when he arrived. Hawk waved these away as unnecessary. Meanwhile, he wondered exactly what was going on. He had the nagging sense, paradoxically, of being treated as both an honored guest and a prisoner—though why that should be, he couldn't guess. So he kept his thoughts to himself and his gun hand at the ready as he continued on with the others.

As they traveled through the poorly-illuminated corridors, Hawk began to realize that several very distinct types of inhabitants dwelled aboard the station. There were humans, such as the soldiers who were escorting him along. They seemed to occupy the upper reaches of the local social class system, based on the way they acted toward and spoke with the others. Then he would see the occasional alien beings of various species, some appearing insectoid in form, some mammalian, some completely unrecognizable, but nearly all of them utterly and completely different from human beings. In larger numbers than either of these, however, were the outright robots—totally mechanical constructs of gleaming alloy and crystal—tasked with various menial-labor jobs such as construction and repair. Hawk noted that the entire station looked to be in a perpetual cycle of construction and repair, and to desperately need even more of both.

Then there was one other type of being he occasionally glimpsed as he walked along with the soldiers through the heart of the station, and this type troubled him deeply. His discomfort with these creatures went beyond mere latent xenophobia over the strangeness of aliens to human eyes. At first Hawk was not sure what to think of them. They were humanoid in form, or at least many of them were. Parts of their bodies were clearly organic, but other parts gleamed metal or glass. A much greater proportion of most of their bodies looked to be mechanical than organic. They worked at their tasks—scrubbing, repairing, trundling along dragging cargo palates in their wakes—with the same single-minded focus as the pure robots, but there was simply no getting around the fact that they had mostly human faces. Blank, mindless human faces. Hawk stared at the first couple but then had to look away; he found them terribly disturbing.

After what seemed like at least half an hour of traveling, the group passed into a much nicer section of the station. The walls were all freshly-painted in a light gray and the floor was covered with a lush, blue-green carpet. At last they arrived at a massive pair of double doors that slid silently into the walls on either side as they drew near.

"Come in! Come in!"

The voice boomed out as Hawk stepped over the threshold and into a broad dining hall. The first thing he noticed was that it was easily the cleanest space he'd encountered on the station thus far. The smooth, spotless white walls curved upward to become an arching ceiling high above. Before him lay a massive table that extended nearly the entire length of the room.

It was covered in various dishes; the look and the smell nearly took his feet out from under him. At the far end of the hall, arms raised in welcome, stood what had to be the station's captain, a very dark-skinned man with a broad smile.

From a distance, Hawk could tell the man was tall and powerfully built, though starting to go a bit flabby around the edges, judging from how his uniform bulged in places. That uniform was a crisp dark blue with lots of gold trim and decorations. It sparkled as the man moved around the table's corner and approached with a jaunty gait.

"Captain Fomas," Hawk nodded as the man extended his hand. They shook.

"Welcome aboard my station," Fomas stated formally, giving a slight bow. Then he gestured toward a seat. "Please, please— join me, if you would. I was just sitting down for a light lunch."

Hawk glanced again at the dazzling spread of fancy dishes that had been prepared and laid out on the table. *A light lunch?* Returning the man's smile then, he nodded. "Thank you, Captain."

Moments later, an elderly servant had seated Hawk in a high-backed chair that looked to have been formed from white plastic, matching the others around the table—a table that featured golden candlesticks and silver utensils. None of it remotely matched, and it all made for an odd combination of chintz and extravagance.

The captain sat a short distance away, helping himself to a pile of sliced meat of some sort from a massive bowl. Hawk sat back, his senses heightened, watching the man while taking in everything else around him.

Another servant approached and placed a broad, deeply curved plate on the table before him. As the captain had scarcely paused in his eating and was currently working on another helping, Hawk helped himself to a modest selection of items from close by.

After several minutes of silence, Fomas began to speak in formal tones, in between bites.

"It is good, yes?"

Hawk nodded. "Very much so." He took another bite of a rich casserole.

"I do what I can to provide the comforts of home."

Hawk looked up at him. "Where is home?"

The captain froze, then smiled his broad smile again.

"Ah—there you have me, I'm afraid." He spread his arms in a wide gesture to take in everything around them. "I have no home—no real home—other than this station. And so I devote all of my efforts, all of my energies, to its welfare. To making it a *real* home, for me and for my crew." He continued to focus intently on Hawk as he shoveled another helping of one of the casseroles onto his plate. "Speaking of which—it was only a short time ago that the last Hand visited our humble facility."

This interested Hawk greatly.

"Another Hand? Which one?"

"Honestly I don't recall who he was supposed to be," Fomas replied somewhat cryptically. "I can have the records examined."

Hawk nodded, puzzled at this.

"In any case," the captain went on, "you can see how the timing of your arrival comes as something of a surprise."

"I suppose," Hawk replied. He had nothing else to say to that, so instead he took a bite of a succulent red fruit and nodded vaguely.

"Well, given the way these things usually go. Of course, we consider it a high honor that you have come here," the captain went on—and Hawk noted that he was not eating now, instead staring directly at him, "but—if it is not impertinent of me to ask—what brings you here now?"

"No specific reason," Hawk replied with a slight shrug. "Just a routine visit."

"I see. Yes," Fomas said, appearing somewhat relieved by the answer. He took another bite. "Well, fine. I'm sure you will find whatever it is you're looking for."

Hawk frowned slightly at this reply but didn't say anything. He was trying his best to absorb both what was being said and what was merely being implied, and having a difficult time at both tasks at the moment.

A young woman appeared, clad in servants' uniform, her curly black hair tied atop her head. She leaned in over Hawk's left shoulder to place a tall plastic cup before him and fill it with a golden liquid from a pitcher. Hawk nodded once to her, lifted the cup and sipped. Cold. Sweet and tangy. Not bad. He was afraid to ask what it was, for fear it was something he should be quite familiar with. Instead he turned his attention to his plate and took up a fork. Fomas did likewise.

"Yes," the captain said after a few seconds, "we are but a humble trading center. Little here of any interest here to a Hand. There are so many more places that you are needed. I'm sure your precious time and resources would be better spent elsewhere." He looked up and smiled. "Not that you are unwelcome, of course."

Hawk returned the flat, emotionless smile. "Thank you, Captain. That's appreciated. And I'm sure you're correct."

The conversation paused there for a time, as a somewhat uncomfortable silence descended. Both men continued to eat.

"Your station is fascinating," Hawk said, breaking the silence at last. He was growing full—the food, whatever it was, had turned out to be quite rich—and there was only so much of it he could eat. The beverage had seemed alcoholic at first, giving him a slight buzz, but then his head had suddenly and quite rapidly cleared. He'd begun to suspect that his uniform was administering some sort of agent to his bloodstream to neutralize the alcohol. Yet another amazing thing it could do.

The captain looked up from his plate and smiled. "It is quite a complex facility, yes."

"It appears to be made up of many different kinds of components."

"Quite true," Fomas agreed, even as he resumed eating. He reached for a still-sizzling leg of some sort of animal, dragged it onto his plate, and took a bite. "This station was cobbled together over many centuries," he said around the food, "as pieces became available. Some parts of it are very old indeed."

"I see." Hawk nodded. "And it looked from outside as if other parts are extremely new."

Fomas shrugged and continued to chew.

They ate for another minute in silence. Servants entered and carried away some of the dishes. Hawk was startled to see them setting down new ones in their place. Just how much did this man eat?

Forcing his attention away from the astonishing display of gluttony, he asked, "How did you acquire them?"

"I'm sorry?"

"The components that go into this station. How did you acquire them?"

Eyes widening, the captain shrugged. "By various means. Many were purchased by previous commanders. Some vessels arrive here in damaged condition and occasionally will trade portions of their structures to us for repairs or fuel. Other items were salvaged after battles. All quite legally, of course," the captain added, smiling that broad smile again.

Hawk continued to regard Fomas for a moment after the man had concluded his answer, giving no visible indication as to whether he believed him or not. Then he returned his attention to the dinner before him and continued to nibble at the food on his plate.

Slowly the captain's smile faded, eventually passing all the way into a slight frown.

Hawk was keeping the man in his peripheral vision, affecting an air of nonchalance but inside deeply concerned. Something seemed a bit off about this captain, and about his station. And that sense was only increasing the longer he sat there.

"If I might be permitted to ask *you* a question or two?" the other man asked suddenly.

Hawk looked up, somewhat surprised. "Certainly," he said.

"How long have you worn the uniform of a Hand?"

"Not terribly long. Why do you ask?"

"It is just that…" The captain hesitated, took a sip of his drink, and smiled half-heartedly. "If you will forgive my saying so, you do not seem very much like the other *Hands* I have met during my tenure here."

The way that Fomas had said the word Hands—the way he had stressed it, almost to the point of sarcasm—struck Hawk as particularly odd. He might as well have wiggled his fingers in the air to make quotation marks as he said it, as if indicating that whatever Hands he had met were not actual Hands.

Hawk gazed back at him levelly. "Are you questioning my legitimacy as a Hand?"

Fomas laughed sharply. "Oh, heavens no," he said with a grin and a wink. "I'm certain you're just as much a Hand as all the other *Hands* that show up at stations like mine, extracting their usual share of the profits in return for...*protection*." He sipped at his drink again. "I have been a captain long enough to know how the game is played. And do not doubt that I respect the power you doubtlessly command. However you may have come about it." He put his fork down and sat back in his seat. "But I must be honest with you, sir. You come to me unexpectedly, with no advance notice, and in this particular guise..." His expression darkened. "Usually I am given some sort of warning before one of you descends upon us here." He cleared his throat. "It should be quite clear to you that you have made me—and my staff—extremely uncomfortable. And so I must ask myself, 'What does this man want? Does he want the usual payoff...or something else? Something more?'"

Hawk took all of this in with considerable surprise, and considered it for a moment.

"Let me be sure I follow you," he said, leaning forward. "You're saying that other Hands who have visited your station have attempted to *extort money* from you?"

Fomas stared back at him blankly.

"Is that what you are saying?" Hawk pressed.

Fomas's eyes narrowed, and then he unleashed a powerful burst of laughter.

"Please, sir," he, "do me the honor of at least somewhat respecting my intelligence. We are both grown men. We both know how this works." He placed his hands flat on the table and leaned slightly forward in Hawk's direction. "I cannot imagine what you think you will gain by playing coy." He gestured again at Hawk's uniform. "Or by these scare tactics.

A *Hawk*, of all things!" He shook his head, then leaned back again. "I have placed all my cards on the table for you. Beyond that, I am at a loss."

Now it was Hawk's turn to lean forward.

"Captain, I have no idea what these other Hands—*false* Hands, I assume, based on what you are saying—have done to you and your station in the past. But I assure you, I am *not* here to extort money. My sole purpose at the moment is to warn the sentient beings of our galaxy that the great Adversary has returned."

Fomas gazed back at Hawk with a look of perplexity.

"You are telling me you are *not* here for a payoff?" he asked, his voice filled with incredulity. "Then why *are* you here?" He frowned, his tone growing defensive. "To take over my station, perhaps?"

Hawk watched as the captain subtly moved one hand down under the table, pressing something; most likely a hidden alarm button.

"You're not hearing me, Captain. I am here for the reason I stated, as a Hand of the Machine," Hawk answered in a calm, flat tone. He had not moved a muscle in the past few seconds; his breathing had slowed and his senses had heightened. His entire body was now poised to act as a weapon, should he be attacked.

"You actually believe you are a true Hand?" the captain barked then. "This is not some elaborate ruse with you—you're serious? And your only concern is about some mythological enemy? You expect me to believe such a thing?" He started to laugh. "What do you take me for?"

Hawk turned his head ever so slightly to one side, allowing himself to see the door behind him in his peripheral vision. Something within his eyes adjusted slightly and in response bright red shapes stood out along the wall, moving from either side. He understood then that he was seeing into the infrared, making out the heat signature forms of soldiers in the corridor outside, on the other side of the wall, closing in on the dining room entrance.

"If you are truly being extorted by impostor Hands," Hawk said then, his voice sharp, "I believe my business lies with *them*—tracking them down and eliminating them—rather than with you and your station."

Fomas blinked at this.

The doors behind Hawk slid open. He didn't bother to turn around.

The sound of boots on the tile floor. A voice sounded from just behind him in clipped, military tones. The officer in blue, most likely. "Captain?"

Fomas raised one hand. "My mistake, Sergeant," he said. "All is well, I believe. But—" He looked at Hawk, smiled faintly, and continued, "—stay close, please. Just in case you are needed after all."

"Sir."

The sergeant retreated from the room and the doors slid closed behind him.

Fomas stared at Hawk now as if seeing him for the first time.

"I believe you were just saying something about wanting to eliminate the men who extort my station," he said.

"If there are people pretending to be Hands and engaging in those sorts of activities, then certainly I will do everything in my power to eliminate them."

"I like the sound of that," Fomas said with a smile. "I like it very much." He paused, then, "You are claiming that you are an actual, genuine Hand," he asked, his tone growing formal, "here on behalf of the great Machine that defends our shattered galaxy. Is this so?"

"It is so."

The captain laughed now, but for once it was a bemused laugh, touching on wonder, rather than sharp and dismissive.

"Only two possibilities, then," he said. "You're either a madman—in which case, you'll get yourself killed sooner rather than later, on your own, without any help from me or my men…"

Hawk gazed back at him, half-smiling. "Yes? Or?"

"Or else, gods help me, you truly are a Hand. Actually a *Hawk*, no less! In which case, you have far, far bigger issues to deal with than my lowly operation here."

Hawk took one last drink from his cup and set it down, then pushed his chair back and stood. "I believe the dinner is concluded," he said.

"And *I* believe we understand one another," Fomas stated, also rising. "Rogue Hands make a far more enticing target for your efforts—whether you're a divine being or a divine fool—than my modest little station and anything I may be doing here. Yes?"

"That is fair to say, yes," Hawk replied. "For now." He moved toward the doors. "But once I've disposed of the impostors and I return—should I ever do so—I trust there won't be anything going on here that a Hand of the Machine would disapprove of."

Fomas swallowed. As dark as he was, he'd actually grown somewhat pale. "Heavens help me, I'm beginning to believe you are who you say you are."

"I am," Hawk stated flatly. "Thank you for your hospitality. The food was quite good."

He turned on his heel and strode through the open doors, moving calmly past the army of soldiers waiting in the corridor. They all watched him pass them by, their eyes wide.

He moved quickly, his mind instantly recalling the path he had taken to reach the dining hall and working in reverse. Some of the soldiers hurried after him, trailing like a ship's wake behind him.

Emerging at last onto the reception deck, he almost walked into the middle of a disturbance. Screams and sudden motion broke through his extreme concentration and caused him to halt in mid-step. Looking around quickly, he took in what was happening: A man was holding a woman around the neck and pointing a pistol of some kind at her head. He was backing away from a small group of station guards, none of whom seemed to quite know what to do. The man was shouting something in a language not immediately understandable to Hawk.

Hawk moved to the side of one of the guards and quietly asked, "What is the situation here?"

The guard gave Hawk a quick double-take, then must have decided there was no reason to withhold the information. "That man is a criminal," he said. "He was traveling on forged documents. We detected his true identity—he's wanted for multiple counts of murder and other charges across four systems. He's taken a hostage now, though, so—"

The guard trailed off as Hawk moved away from him and stepped out into the open space surrounding the hostage-taker. The man was tall—at least a foot taller than the woman he was holding in front of him—but was hunched down behind her. His hair was sandy brown and sweat trickled from his face.

"Let her go," Hawk called to him in a clear, firm voice. "Surrender now."

The man's bloodshot eyes focused on Hawk. "Back off! Back off or I'll blow her away!"

Hawk raised both his hands, fingers spread wide, as if indicating he wasn't armed.

"This is your only warning," he called back. "If you harm that woman, you will not live to regret it."

"Her life means nothing to me!"

"Her life isn't the one you ought to be concerned about."

"Back off! Back off or I will kill her!"

Hawk's holster extended out from his uniform's leg. Faster than the blink of an eye, he drew the gun and fired it in one smooth motion, then returned it to the holster with hardly a pause in between. The holster retracted and vanished.

The hostage-taker staggered back, his eyes rolling up in his head. A small dark spot shone on his forehead. He collapsed to the deck, even as the woman wrestled herself free of his grasp.

The guards rushed forward. Two of them caught the woman before she could fall, while the others surrounded the criminal. Hawk turned and began to move toward his ship, where it sat on the landing deck a short distance away.

A couple of soldiers who had trailed him moved to intercept.

"How—how did you do that?" one asked, face a mask of amazement.

"I am a Hand of the Machine."

"What? That's crazy!"

Hawk ignored him and continued toward his ship.

The other soldier was the sergeant. He moved in front of Hawk and raised a hand. Hawk halted, staring at him with a frown.

"Did you—did you kill him?" the sergeant asked, seemingly unaware of the shocked expression he wore as well.

"He deserved it, but no—he's only stunned. He'll be well enough in a couple of hours." He started to move past the two soldiers, then paused. "You should make certain he's locked up somewhere securely by then."

The sergeant worked his jaw silently. In the end he only nodded.

With that, Hawk resumed walking towards his ship.

The guards and the trailing soldiers watched him go with unabashed astonishment.

Once he'd boarded, the sergeant clicked open his communications link and signaled Captain Fomas.

"Sir—did you see that?"

"I was watching over the surveillance channel, yes."

The sergeant ran a hand over his forehead. It was damp.

"Sir—I think that man actually *was* a Hand. Actually a *Hawk!*"

There was a pause, and then Fomas's voice came back, a slight tremor running through it. "I am increasingly inclined to agree with you, Sergeant," he said. "And that thought frightens me to death."

Hawk sat back in the cockpit of his ship and attempted again to mentally interface with the controls. Things clicked for him even easier this time than they had before. Smoothly the ship lifted from the deck and spun about, then shot out into space.

As the black depths embraced him once more, he leaned back against the cushioned head rest and stared up at the ceiling.

"How did I do that?" he asked aloud. "How did I make that shot—without even thinking about it?"

"Your reflexes are built in," the ship replied. *"They are as much a part of you as your face, your hair, your status as a Hand. They are who you are."*

Hawk pondered this for a moment.

"I must admit I was concerned you would get yourself into trouble," the ship said then, changing the subject. *"But here you are, alive and well. My fears were obviously misplaced."*

"Not necessarily," Hawk replied. "I nearly did." He laughed. "The station's captain seemed to have encountered a number of *false* Hands over the years. Apparently masquerading as a Hand has become quite the ticket to the good life."

"Given the number of hidden bases the Machine created across the galaxy for his army of enforcers—that would be individuals like you, of course—it is not surprising to think that some of them would be discovered by unscrupulous types, raided, and their contents stolen and used for nefarious purposes."

Hawk nodded.

"The whole conversation did raise an interesting—and very disturbing—question, though," he said. "If the Machine *is* dead, or deactivated, or insane, or whatever, and I am truly *alone...* then how am I any different from any of these impostor Hands who are using stolen uniforms and technology to pretend to be Hands and engage in extortion?" He lowered his gaze to the black depths that filled the forward view. "Absent the Machine overseeing us all and sending us on missions of critical importance around the galaxy, what makes me—a genuine Hand—any different from the impostors?"

"I find the question insulting," the ship replied immediately. *"But I know that you mean it in earnest, so I will attempt to answer it."* A pause, then, *"Two major factors stand out: One, you are not using your abilities and technology to extort money, but for the benefit of others. That makes you different, obviously. You are a true Hand. Your duties and responsibilities are to safeguard the welfare of all. And two, we do not know that the Machine is in any of those conditions you named. It simply may have chosen to keep silent for now, for reasons we cannot guess. We owe it to the galaxy to discover the truth—and, in the*

meantime, to do our job. If the Machine yet exists, then you are one of its chosen agents, and you are therefore most assuredly different from any shameful impostor."

Hawk considered this. He stroked his chin absently as he watched the star field outside move as his ship curved around and took up a new heading.

"So, having been awake such a short time, I find myself already burdened with two missions. I must warn of the Adversary's return, and I must discover what has truly become of the Machine." He stroked his chin thoughtfully. "And I have no idea how to do either of those things." He gazed up at the cockpit ceiling. "What do I do?"

The ship said nothing for a moment, and Hawk crossed his arms in frustration. Then its mechanical voice echoed out: *"I am able to facilitate your efforts in many ways, Hawk,"* it said, *"assisting you with transportation and medical care and logistics and resources, and even the occasionally useful bit of information. But,"* it cautioned, *"I am not capable of actually drawing up your strategic plans. That task falls to you and to you alone."*

Hawk took that in and thought about it.

"No, not necessarily," he said.

"But, as I said, I cannot—"

"I understand *your* limitations," Hawk interrupted. "You're an artificial intellect—though that same restriction didn't seem to prevent the Machine itself from ordering us around in days gone by—and cannot help me decide upon my best courses of action."

"The Machine is far greater than I am," the ship snapped back. *"Such restrictions do not apply to it."*

"Okay." Hawk leaned forward, peering at the visual display, seeing wrecked planets and shattered stars littering the night sky. "But—my point is that another human—another *Hand*, perhaps—wouldn't be limited in the way that you are."

"Another Hand?" The ship paused for a moment, then, *"Hawk,"* it replied, *"based on everything I have processed since your awakening and my activation, you may need to prepare*

67

yourself for the possibility that you are one of the few Hands remaining in this entire, vast galaxy. Perhaps the only one."

Hawk breathed in and out, nodding. He gestured back toward the station they were streaking away from.

"The captain of that facility seemed to think there are no more Hands. He didn't even really believe I was one."

"That may be so," the ship replied, *"though it would represent a terrible tragedy for intelligent life forms everywhere."* A pause, then, as the ship seemed to be considering its next words carefully. *"We know one thing is true, however. Even if there are no others, you are most assuredly a Hand. I suspect, given the current state of this galaxy, that you will have ample opportunities to demonstrate that fact very soon."*

Hawk snorted humorlessly.

"You may be right. And I might be up to the task. Maybe. But still," he said, exhaling slowly and gazing at the darkness that lay ahead, "it would be awfully nice to have some help."

6: RAVEN

Raven's eyes flickered open.

Deep, dark, nearly black eyes, they moved in quick little jumps, from left to right, up to down. Behind those eyes, however, Raven's mind was only just awakening, just beginning to try to make sense of the scene before her.

Where am I?

She had scarcely more than two full seconds to study her environment before the assault began.

This is what she saw:

She was in a dank, dimly-lit chamber. A broad, round, open space in the center of the floor and the corresponding wide gap in the ceiling revealed that the entire complex was constructed of multiple levels. She was standing against a metal slab of some sort which projected out very close to the edge of the hole in the floor of her level. Wires and tubes lay coiled all around, ultimately connecting to wall sockets on either side of her. No other living being was visible anywhere. Through the gap in the ceiling, the room appeared to go up and up into the dark distance; as her eyes flickered downward, a similar sense came to her from that direction.

Those impressions were formed quickly; she had no additional time to study her surroundings. For at that moment she was assaulted from within and without.

First came the mental invasion: Information flooded into her mind with the force of a torrent, taking her legs out from under her and sprawling her on the cold metal floor.

Get up, boomed a voice that echoed through her head. *Quickly. There is danger here.*

Raven wasted no time in questioning the voice—who it was, where it had come from, or why it was speaking to her. She reacted instantly, springing up onto her feet with catlike agility and taking four quick steps forward. As she ran, the wire that had been connected to the back of her head popped loose. She ignored this, though a part of her consciousness noted that the wave of information assaulting her mind ceased.

A second attack came hard on the heels of the first. This one was physical, signaled by metal ringing sounds echoing up from where she had just been standing. *Ricochets from gunfire,* she knew at once. Someone was shooting at her.

Moving instinctively, she ducked and rolled, sprang upwards, soared out over the abyssal drop-off, and grasped a projecting metal bar with both hands. Continuing her momentum forward, she swung upward, somersaulted, and with all the skills of a great gymnast, landed gracefully on the metal latticework flooring, one level higher and on the opposite side of the chamber.

Surely, she thought, that would throw off the attacker—at least, long enough for her to assess her tactical situation.

And she knew with complete certainty that she was quite adept at assessing tactical situations. The torrent of information that had flooded into her brain in the split second before she'd moved into action was slowly resolving itself into accessible knowledge, and that knowledge included the fact that she was a *Raven*, an internal affairs operative for the Machine. A quick glance down at her uniform—tight red material with blue trim and a low, green collar—confirmed this. As such, she more than possessed the power and skills to protect herself—and to bring all hell to her enemy, wherever that person might be lurking.

Her supreme confidence served her well, driving her forward with a single-minded determination. She clung to the shadows—the darkest depths of the already dark chamber—and moved quietly, stealthily.

For several moments only a deathly silence reigned; naught but the drip-drip of water from some hidden source far above as it fell down through the openings to land far below, and the soft tinkling of chains that dangled from a piece of heavy machinery set into the wall above and to her left.

Then the enemy struck. A barrage of gunfire from some sort of automatic slug-thrower gun raked the wall just over her head as she crouched in darkness. She sprung out, body extending and then tucking in tight as she landed near the edge of the hole in the floor. Another spray of bullets sent sparks flying past her head and vibrated the floor. She gripped the metal latticework beneath her with both hands and swung out, her back to the void as she pivoted and dropped down.

The blinding flash of laser or energy-beam weaponry dazzled her vision but she held on until her momentum had carried her in a tight arc back over the floor of the section beneath her. Letting go then, she performed a mid-air spin with her arms tight to her body before landing in a crouch.

Silence all around. Silence—but she could feel it now. The enemy was near. Approaching, approaching...

Pitching forward, she caught herself on the floor with her left hand, spun around and lashed out with her right foot, bringing tremendous force to bear.

Her foot struck something—struck it hard—but whatever it was, it did not yield to the force of her blow. Raven staggered back from the force of impact, dropping onto her seat, then sprang upward just before a massive fist from the shadows smashed down onto the spot she had just occupied.

Bullets sprayed out at her again from the darkness, and only her astonishing gymnastic ability prevented her from becoming perforated. She leapt and spun and dived and twisted and somehow managed to stay a half-step ahead of the fearsome attack.

And even as she moved, her eyes snuck occasional quick glances in the direction of her foe. Though he'd never once emerged fully from the shadows, she had gotten the impression that he was big—very big—and covered in some sort of armor. Clearly he was armed with a variety of weapons systems. And he was extremely dangerous.

But so am I, she thought. And, *Enough of this.*

Even as she sprang from a ledge and soared across the open gap in the floor, her hand reached to her hip, searching for the pistol she knew should be there.

It was not.

Frowning, she hit the opposite deck and rolled to a stop, her hands feeling for any other weapons.

Where are they? Where—?

Her fingers closed around the hilt of a bladed weapon of some kind. The memories injected into her brain instantly cried out, *"Katana!"*

Her powerfully-muscled legs launched her across the space between her and her enemy even as she drew the sword from its sheath on her back and swung it out in a broad arc.

The blade met something—something big and broad and tough—and slashed it.

An unearthly cry resounded from the darkness.

Bullets sprayed out again, but Raven was no longer where she had landed. Dancing to her right, she crouched and slashed out again.

Another cry, another spray of bullets. Again the target had already moved.

Another slash, followed by a downward stroke.

Now bellowing in rage, the big adversary stumbled forward—into the light. Raven could see him clearly. She leapt upward and caught an exposed piece of pipe, so that now she was hanging out over his head, looking downward.

Standing more than eight feet tall, the muscular behemoth wore rugged black armor trimmed in silver. A faceless helmet jerked from side to side as he searched for her. Guns bracketed onto his forearms cycled and spun, preparing to open fire the instant the target was reacquired.

"Who are you?" Raven whispered to herself as she studied the strange figure.

The helmet jerked upward and he stared straight at her. His arms redirected themselves at her, guns powering up.

Raven dropped onto his back, her sword clutched tightly in her right hand. A sword, her injected memories told her then, that had been constructed of a complex alloy and that could cut through almost anything.

The gunfire sprayed out, bullets missing her by mere millimeters.

One quick motion with her sword.

She leapt away even as the bullets kept firing. But now, she knew, they were firing through pure reflex alone.

For the attacker's head had been cleanly separated from his body. It dropped to the deck with a sickening thud.

The big, headless armored body kept firing its weapons for another few seconds—and, ironically, during that time, the bullets came closer to hitting Raven than they had at any point previously—before the ammo ran out and the body slumped lifelessly to the floor, guns still cycling and clicking impotently.

Raven stood over it, breathing heavily, her sword held tightly in her right hand. As she breathed, as she came to be certain her foe had been defeated, she allowed her grip to loosen and the tip of the long blade tilted downward.

She formed the words in her mind, then: *Machine. Are you there? Can you hear me?*

Silence for two seconds. Three seconds. Then, an almost monotone voice echoed within her head. *Excellent*, it said. *Well-handled. You have the makings of a superb Raven.* The voice paused for a moment, then continued. *And, at this time, a superb Raven is precisely what is needed.*

You are the Machine? she asked the voice.

Alas, no, came the inner reply. *I am but an echo of the Machine's consciousness stored within your ship's intelligence. I am here to assist you.* A pause, then, *My first act of assistance was to order the base's automated systems to move your body, even as you were awakening, out of the recovery room and into a maintenance and utility shaft. My hope was that the invading forces would not find you until you were fully awake and could defend yourself. It was very close, but the stratagem succeeded.*

I see, Raven replied. *Thank you.* She frowned then. *And why can I not communicate with the Machine itself?*

The Machine remains silent, the voice stated, *as it has been for these many centuries. It speaks to no one.*

Raven took this in, puzzled.

Silent? What are you saying? What is wrong with it? And then, *Centuries? My implanted memories recall the Machine speaking to me and to the other operatives often.* She blinked her eyes rapidly, startled. *How old are my memories? Just how long has it been since the last Raven traveled the spaceways of this galaxy?*

It has been a very long time, Raven.

She was frowning now. *Why is that?*

A pause, then, *Your line was ended and the records were sealed. There has been no new Raven since the days of the Shattering.*

The Shattering. Instantly she knew what it was, understood its significance. Her implanted memories reached far enough toward the present for that much, at least, to be included.

She felt no great emotion when thinking of the Shattering. Her predecessor had witnessed it—or the beginnings of it, anyway—and had grieved over the fate of the untold trillions and trillions of victims, all dead at the hands of the Adversary. That, she understood, was over and done—and had been done for a very long time, to use the words the voice had used. The Shattering was ancient history.

No, the emotion that welled up within her now was of a much more personal nature. She felt her heart pounding within her chest as she asked, *My line was ended? For what reason? On whose authority?*

I have given you all the information I possess, it replied. *Do your own implanted memories tell you nothing?*

Raven bit back an angry retort, closed her eyes, and attempted to calm herself. She thought back—back into the depths of memories that had been downloaded into her; downloaded from the computers in which they had been stored after being extracted from her predecessor.

I—I cannot make sense of my old memories, she said after several seconds of effort. *They are jumbled. And they end very suddenly—as if my predecessor suffered some sort of unexpected and traumatic event.*

The voice said nothing in response.

Raven considered what she had just learned for a few more seconds. The implanted consciousness obviously could not or would not tell her anything more. The downloaded memories from her predecessor were all but useless, at least so far— though she hoped that meditation and extreme concentration might eventually restore some of them. If she wished to discover what had happened to cause no Ravens to be awakened for centuries, she would have to investigate that for herself.

Her mind came back to the present. *Why was I awakened, then?* she asked the inner voice.

You are needed.

Why me? Why after so long?

A pause, then, *The situation is dire. Very few Hands still exist. Many of the old bases and installations have been destroyed. Hands that have not been awakened for many years are now being brought to life.*

I see.

Raven slid her sword back into its scabbard and then looked around, now even more wary of additional enemies.

What do you want of me?

Many things, the voice said. *False Hands roam this galaxy, pretending to act in the Machine's name when in fact they merely serve themselves. They must be dealt with. Harshly.*

Raven nodded. *Of course. Dealing with genuine Hands that had turned renegade was always one of my prime functions. False Hands should prove a far lesser challenge.*

Additionally, the voice went on, *entire armies of humans and aliens have recently begun to cooperate with one another, attacking whole worlds in synchronized actions, and even eliminating a number of Hand creation and storage installations and destroying the ancient genetic matrices. You have just encountered part of one such group.*

This was quite disturbing to her. Entire varieties of Hands— eliminated forever? Their genetic lines destroyed? She shivered at the thought. How many remained? Were there any Falcons out there anymore? Condors? Shrikes? She started to add "Hawks" but then thought better of that particular one.

And what of Eagle himself?

Who are these enemies? she asked. *What do they want?*

Unknown. The pattern, however, is disturbingly familiar.

Raven accessed what she could of her stored memories. Fragments of images and sounds flashed through her thoughts, never quite enough to latch onto and fully understand. It all made her head throb painfully.

Not the Adversary, she thought back at the voice in her mind when she had recovered somewhat. *Surely that's impossible. My implanted memories tell me the ancient enemy was defeated—destroyed—though at catastrophic cost to the entire galaxy.*

Unknown, the voice repeated. *But these new events do perfectly match his and his forces' past behavior, and that fact alone is sufficient to take the greatest precautions. Discovering answers to those questions would also constitute a portion of your duties.*

Very well.

Beyond all of that, however, your primary duty is to discover why the Machine no longer speaks. Has it been damaged? Has its body been compromised by some enemy force? Has it merely forsaken us all?

Raven nodded to herself. This was something she very much wondered as well. And, she told herself, if she could get the Machine talking again, she would present it with a very pointed series of questions.

She wiped her hands together.

"Alright. Where do you need me to go?" she asked out loud.

To your ship, to begin with, the voice boomed back. *To me.*

"Where are you?"

The image of a map appeared before her, projected into her mind. The path she should take flashed in red.

Nodding, she moved into action. Her long legs carried her swiftly along the metal decks and catwalks and up four ladders and two flights of stairs. During the entire time, her breathing scarcely altered its pattern.

Reaching the top of the chamber, she glanced around and spotted a metal door with a wheel at its center. She approached it carefully, her gloved fingers moving out to touch it.

"What's on the other side?" she asked, automatically looking up as if she were addressing some deity.

Only this ship. I detect no danger.

She started to turn the wheel.

The voice cried out in her head then, almost enough to shatter her brain.

No! No! Danger! They were hidden—cloaked—but now—

Too late. The heavy door was swinging open.

Raven instinctively drew her blade as she gazed out at the sight that greeted her.

Ahead of her stood a veritable army of faceless armored warriors, all clad in black and silver.

They rushed towards her.

1: HAWK

Hawk's ship streaked through the hyperspace realm of the Above even as he himself dropped into the comfortable pilot's seat. A holographic image formed in front of the forward window, displaying what the ship had explained to be a tactical overview of the general sector of the galaxy they were very rapidly passing through—or over, or around. The physics of it all didn't quite make sense to Hawk, but he had other things of greater concern to him at the moment.

Hawk studied the three-dimensional display intently. He found that while some of the higher scientific concepts yet eluded him, he was beginning to gain a greater sense of his own role, his own place in this galaxy, after long conversations with the ship and his own deep introspection. He found he wasn't entirely uncomfortable with it.

Learning came quickly to Hawk. The ship only had to show or tell him something once for him to grasp it in its entirety. Occasionally, the merest mention of a subject had caused Hawk to make an intuitive leap and grasp the full concept. The ship hypothesized that this was because *some* of the information had managed to be downloaded into his brain, even if it was not immediately available for retrieval. Discussing it with the ship seemed to bring it back to his consciousness with increasing clarity.

"No enemies in the area?" he asked the ship, though he was fairly confident he was interpreting the display correctly.

"That is correct."

"Then," Hawk said, "this would appear to be a good opportunity for you to fill me in on more of my history."

Silence for several seconds.

"Ship? Have you no reply?"

"I am not at all certain that would be the best course for you to take," the mechanical voice stated.

"Why not?"

Nothing.

"I'd like to know something of the other Hands," Hawk pressed. "Did we never cooperate with one another?"

"Certainly there was a time when all the Hands—or most of them, at least—worked together to great effectiveness," the ship allowed.

"Do you have records of this? Can you show me?"

Silence.

"I order you to show me!"

"…Very well. I will transmit this memory record to your mind. Stand by."

Hawk sat back and closed his eyes. And here is what he saw…

PART TWO

**Before the Shattering:
The Seventeenth Millennium**

—

Rheinstadt

1: EAGLE

The gargantuan flagship *Talon* ripped a hole in the fabric of space-time and deposited itself instantaneously into orbit above the planet Rheinstadt. The warships into whose midst it appeared, their proximity alarms suddenly blaring, scrambled to clear out of the way and allow it a wide berth.

On the command bridge, like some misplaced god, stood the massive, muscular form of Eagle, supreme commander of the Machine's Hands. His arms were crossed against his chest and his piercing blue eyes gazed out from beneath a close-cropped covering of pale-blond hair. He wore a skin-tight uniform of metallic blue so dark it was nearly black, with fine red and gold trim along the sleeves and legs. A pair of matching gloves hung from his belt, along with a massive golden sword.

From the tactical display filling one end of the bridge, Eagle's eyes flicked over to the man standing to his right. Almost as tall, not quite as muscular but heavier and somehow seemingly even more imposing, this Hand wore red as his predominant color. His nose was blunt and his head was shaved clean.

"Smooth transition, perfect locationing," Falcon noted with a slight smile. "The Captain hasn't lost his touch."

Eagle ignored the remark. He had no time for compliments for the ship's personnel. He expected perfection from each of them, usually got it, and accepted it as the norm. Instead he moved to stand behind the main tactical officer and leaned forward, looming over him, studying the holo displays. "Report," he barked.

The tactical officer had been bombarded with data over his Aether connection from the moment the *Talon* had emerged from the Above and into normal space. He sorted through it rapidly, seeking the pertinent information. "Seventeen ships in orbit," he reported, not daring to so much as glance back at his commander. "All of military configuration."

Eagle nodded. He turned his attention briefly to the array of starships now filling both the tactical display and the sweeping, transparent wall that constituted the forward portion of the bridge. The great blue-white orb of the upper half of a planet occupied the lower half of the view. "And all of them Indonian, yes?"

The officer accessed the Aether again, just to be certain, even though the tactical readouts that floated above their heads had circled each of the ships in green with identification codes listed alongside.

"Indonian Empire," he confirmed. "Every one of them."

"I could've told you that," Falcon commented wryly, "since nobody's shooting at us."

"Most of their landers are already down," the officer continued. "Drop-ships and shuttles. I'm reading their transponder codes on the ground near the center of the major continent." He paused, parsing through more data as quickly as it came to him. "There's at least one major action underway on the surface," he added then, "in the area surrounding the capital city." He frowned at one particular data string, then nodded in understanding. "Someone has a force field up," he explained. "Very powerful. Covering the entire city."

"Very well." Eagle stood back, taking in the entirety of the veritable sea of information that currently filled the forward section of the bridge, from holographic visuals to 2-D displays to lines of text and numbers that flowed, snakelike, through the air between the various sections and stations. "And what of the enemy?" the big man demanded at last. "What do we know?"

"What do we *need* to know?" Falcon asked, before the officer could respond. "It's the Rao. Again." He snorted. "We know how to deal with them."

Eagle shot him a look of barely-contained patience.

"We take nothing for granted, as you well know," he stated firmly. Turning back to the tactical officer, he asked, "Who erected the force field over the city? Is it Indonian or Rao?"

The officer manipulated controls and images flowed across the holographic display, pulled in from various transmission sources in low orbit and on the ground. Everyone on the bridge paused to stare at them and study them.

"It would appear," came a new voice from off to one side, "that the Rao have already captured the city and set the field up themselves, to hold what they gained."

Hawk stepped through the double sliding doors and onto the main deck of the bridge. His vivid blue and red uniform flashed as he moved into the bright lighting of the rear section. Falcon glanced back at him with a slight frown while Eagle ignored him entirely.

As the display images zoomed in, Hawk's impressions were confirmed. The alien Rao in their modular metallic armor had overrun the capital city and activated a gigantic force field over the entirety of it. Sometime afterward, military forces of the Indonian Empire—the human government to whom this planet at least nominally belonged—had arrived from space and laid siege to it. Thus far, they had been unable to pierce the bubble. Meanwhile, from the look of it, Rao forces outside the field were engaged in extremely violent and bloody actions against the Indonians.

Eagle took it all in very quickly, his finely-tuned tactical mind working through possibilities. Then he nodded once. "Very well. Signal the drop-ships. Firewing and Iron Raptor units first."

The tactical officer acknowledged the order and touched a series of lighted squares on the panel before him, even as he transmitted a series of codes via the Aether connection. In response, all along the exterior of the vast, cylindrical *Talon*, assault pods began disengaging and rocketing away, quickly forming up into a mass wave as they cleared the immediate vicinity of the big ship. Moments later, their small rear engines firing, they tumbled down toward the surface of Rheinstadt.

"First two units are away," the tactical officer announced, turning to regard his commander.

"So what are we waiting for?" asked Hawk, starting toward the doorway.

Falcon laughed, shaking his head at the younger Hand.

Eagle turned to face him now, finally. He regarded the younger Hand circumspectly. "You seriously wish to go down with the assault teams?" he asked.

"You don't?" Hawk shot back. He frowned at his commander. "Have we grown that lazy?"

"He makes a good point," Falcon stated. "I think I'll join him."

Falcon started forward. Hawk turned toward the door. Eagle raised a hand.

"Wait."

Both men halted instantly. They knew Eagle afforded them a remarkable degree of familiarity with him, but his authority remained absolute, within the bounds of the Machine's orders that ran before all their business.

"I haven't given either of you permission to go anywhere," the big commander noted, his voice very low but filled with power.

His expression now dour, Falcon stood with his hands clasped behind his back, waiting. He'd known his commander just long enough to be completely uncertain as to how the big man might react.

Hawk merely grinned back at the blond giant. "You don't want us getting soft, do you?" he asked, a twinkle in his eye.

Eagle glared at the smaller man for a long moment, then inhaled deeply and exhaled slowly. "No," he said. "No, I do not." He moved forward himself now, striding past the other two Hands and towards the doorway. "Though I'm not entirely certain that killing a few Rao qualifies even as a meaningful training exercise."

Hawk and Falcon followed along in their godlike commander's wake as he exited the bridge. Moments later, the three of them had boarded a heavily-armored shuttle and were blasting down towards the planet's surface. Even as they departed the *Talon*, the first wave of assault pods were impacting the surface of Rheinstadt and the assault troops of the Firewing and Iron Raptor units were emerging, weapons blazing. The startled and surprised Rao defenders who were positioned outside the force field dome, caught utterly flat-footed, struggled to recover and mount a defense.

By the time the three Hands took the field, scarcely a one of them was left alive.

2: FALCON

Falcon, the brutish demolitions expert of the three Hands present, completed his work and signaled to the others. Fifty meters away, standing atop a jagged outcropping of rock, Eagle gave the go-sign. Falcon nodded back and then sent a mental signal via the Aether to activate all the detonators simultaneously.

The resulting series of explosions shook the very foundations of the planet Rheinstadt.

Minutes earlier, remote-guided borers digging their way through miles of bedrock had deposited the last of the explosive devices deep under the capital city, locating them in prime positions to knock out the generators powering the Rao force field. It had been a simple enough operation, as Falcon had expected it would be. The Rao could be extremely tough and resourceful when dealing with standard military forces, but they simply couldn't match the tactical abilities, the technology, or the sheer ruthlessness of the Hands of the Machine and their legions.

The great, green-glowing Rao force hemisphere, some twenty miles in diameter, that entirely covered the planetary capital shifted abruptly from green to red, then slowly faded to muddy amber, then disappeared entirely. With it gone, the massive fortress complex that dominated the city's skyline stood revealed for the first time. Members of the Firewings and Iron Raptors gazed up at the dark edifice in wonder.

As debris continued to rain down all around, Eagle leapt from the outcropping and landed solidly on his tree-trunk legs. Reaching to his hip, he drew forth his sword, a broad-bladed weapon seemingly wrought of solid gold but much stronger, and raised it high. "The Rao shield is down," he shouted, his voice booming out and easily reaching every member of the assault army with little or no need for amplification over the Aether. He pointed with the sword toward the massive fortress that towered before them. "Your enemy awaits!" He charged forward then, the others rushing along behind him. "For the Machine," he cried. *"For the galaxy!"*

Falcon stashed the detonator components away in a belt pouch and, hoisting his massive firearm, hustled after the others. Ahead, he could see Hawk pause to engage a lifter-pack that he'd strapped to his back. Its long and narrow wings unfolded and stretched out to either side, quickly lofting him into the air. He zoomed over the heads of his legion and quickly caught up with Eagle at the vanguard of the assault, his ever-present pistol in hand.

The battle for Rheinstadt was joined in full.

And it went about as expected.

Wave after wave of armored Rao warriors rushed out of concealment behind the outermost buildings that lay in the shadows of the great and ancient fortress complex. Firewings and Iron Raptors, following standard assault plans designed by Eagle and by absent Condor, sliced their way through them, quad-rifles and force swords blazing an arc of destruction. The Firewings, resplendent in their vivid red and orange micro-thin armored uniforms, drew the preponderance of the enemy's attention—and they tended to like it that way. The Iron Raptors, meanwhile, in their grim gray and black body armor, stomped along on the flanks, heavy arm-cannons blazing death at their foes.

At the rear, the recently-arrived armies of the Indonian Empire, whose government claimed the planet, could only look on in astonishment and awe. They had hoped to receive help from the Machine and its renowned Hands and their legions, whose reputations had grown in only a few decades to mythological proportions. They had trusted that such assistance would be sufficient to tilt the balance of the conflict in their favor. Seeing the Hands of the Machine in action, though—seeing them with their own eyes, blasting their way through forces that had easily overcome the planet's defenses and then had held off their relief mission—that was something altogether different.

Falcon watched them gather themselves and charge along on the heels of the Machine's legions. He grinned. In some of their recent interventions, the local forces hadn't even bothered—or found the guts—to join in. Many had simply sat back and watched. That sort of thing never really bothered Falcon. Truth be told, the indigenous troops often got in the way more than anything else. But he understood that, afterward, they would need to feel as if they had contributed something useful to the campaign, if only to make them easier to deal with during the mopping-up phase. So he deliberately held back and allowed two companies of Indonian infantrymen to flood around and past him before he himself started to trudge forward, his massive autocannon charged and firing, Rao defenders cut down and left in piles in his wake.

3: HAWK

As the Indonian ground forces finally managed to drive the Rao from their defensive positions outside the city and back into the shadows of the skyscrapers, Hawk found himself battling side-by-side with one of the higher-ranking officers of the Indonian Empire. Glancing over at the man even as he deflected a sizzling energy blast and returned fire, Hawk called out, "So, why was it you Indonians needed our help here? Couldn't you have just blasted that force field yourselves, from orbit?"

The officer returned Hawk's glance and frowned in consternation. "We could have, yes," he replied testily after a moment. "But we preferred not to demolish our own capital city and kill all of its inhabitants—a likely outcome of that approach. Perhaps you find that a quaint notion."

"Not at all," Hawk said, swinging a fist wide to knock down an amber-armored attacker. "You will notice that we didn't go that route, either."

"Exactly," the man said. "A more surgical strategy was needed—one that we were unable to provide. Thus the call was made to the Machine."

"And here we are," Hawk finished. "The surgeons of the galaxy. That's us." He laughed. "I'm sure Falcon will be delighted by that description."

"Indeed I am," came a booming voice from behind them. Falcon's massive form stomped up alongside. "Though *amused* is probably a better term." He directed the huge multi-cannon cradled in his right arm toward a concentration of Rao troops hiding behind some rubble and opened fire. Orange spears of energy lashed out, blasting the chunks of concrete into much, much smaller chunks of concrete—and the Rao into much, much smaller chunks of Rao.

Hawk watched his friend devastate the foe, the grin on his face fierce and somewhat proud. Then, sparing a glance back at the Indonian officer, he suppressed a chuckle as he beheld the man's astonished expression.

"You wanted the best," Hawk called to him as his lifter-pack carried him aloft again. "You got the best."

The soldier was still staring up in awe as he dwindled away in the distance. Hawk accelerated and began to fire down at the Rao in their defensive positions from his fifty-meter vantage point, instinctively dodging their return fire as he soared along in the direction of the city center.

After a few minutes of battling his way through the Rao defensive lines by air, Hawk circled around a still-mostly-intact concrete building—and then it was his turn to stare in astonishment at what he beheld.

At the center of a maelstrom of amber-armored Rao warriors stood Eagle, his golden sword in his right hand and a multi-cannon cradled by his left arm. As Hawk looked on in awe, Eagle slashed and blasted his way through wave after wave of the enemy. The pile of bodies grew rapidly all around him, soon nearly eclipsing him from the view of anyone who lacked Hawk's altitude.

"Do you need some help?" Hawk called down to his commander.

"I trust you do not *mean* to insult me," the juggernaut of a man shouted back up, even as he casually decapitated two Rao soldiers with one mighty swing and blasted another point-blank in the helmeted face.

Cringing at his error and knowing he should say nothing more, Hawk simply saluted and zipped on ahead.

He hadn't advanced far into the city proper when he saw a strange sight: Rao and Indonian soldiers alike were hurrying away from a half-demolished building. They weren't even fighting each other; it was as if they had somehow forgotten they were enemies here. As if something far more important— or far more deadly—had taken the field.

Or was about to.

Hawk swooped down and landed smoothly on the rugged pavement, the wings of his lift-pack folding themselves away instantly. The Rheinstadt sun had dropped below the level of the buildings ahead, so that long shadows now trailed out in his direction from the skyscrapers and ruins closer to the center of the capital. Just ahead, in the space cleared moments earlier by both armies, an almost cavelike opening gaped in the side of the nearest building, darkness filling it as if it were a doorway into the void.

Hawk had been ignoring the standard-level chatter coming across his Aether connection, originating mostly with the always-talkative Firewing legion. Now, however, the alert status on the messages began to shade from yellow toward red. Keeping his eyes trained on the dark opening ahead of him, he mentally dialed up the Aether link and paid attention. What greeted him was a series of warning messages from both Firewings and the Indonian troops in the immediate vicinity. They were all pulling back, though none could say exactly why. They only knew—knew at a very deep, intuitive level—that something bad was happening.

Something bad was *coming*.

A flickering of light within the dark cave mouth brought Hawk's attention back to his local surroundings. Frowning, he squinted in that direction. Standing about twenty meters away from the entrance, he was the only living thing within a hundred meters, as far as he could tell, aside from a handful of Rao warriors only a short distance away—each of whom was ignoring him, focused entirely upon the dark opening instead.

The flickering light in the dark passage vanished for a moment, returned, then strengthened. As it grew it oscillated across the spectrum of visible light—and beyond, as Hawk's ocular implants revealed.

A wave of palpable fear washed out and impacted Hawk. It felt as real, as solid, as an ocean wave feels to someone standing on the beach. The surviving Rao warriors gave way, scrambling aside as the light grew to near-blinding levels and then divided, now emanating from two separate and distinct sources.

Hawk resisted the fear assault far better than had any of the others nearby, but even so he couldn't help stumbling backwards, the shattered pavement crumbling beneath his feet.

At that moment two bizarre figures moved out into view. Tall they were, yes, but extremely slender. Lightning-quick were their movements. They wore a kind of armor that looked as if it had been formed from colored glass. Waves of light of every color swirled in and around them, like some strange sort of eldritch energies trapped and contained within the substance of the armor itself. They carried long, straight, transparent swords that appeared to have been carved from pure crystal, and light danced in and around those weapons as well.

The two strange beings stood atop the broken ruins of the building's entranceway and gazed down at Hawk with unmistakable malevolence.

"Dyonari," Hawk muttered, mostly to himself. "Huh." And then, louder, "What are you doing here?"

The nearer of the two aliens, its head tilting slightly to one side, emitted a sound like dry leaves being crushed. At the same moment, a new wave of sensation washed over Hawk. He could tell it was some sort of psychic energy reaching for his mind, but this time it wasn't composed of pure fear. Even so, he started to resist—or at least to attempt to—but then realized it merely carried a "voice," speaking to him in a way that he could understand the words.

"Pawn of the Machine," the mental voice of the Dyonari before him said. "Why do you and your kind involve yourselves in this matter?"

"I might ask you the same question," Hawk said aloud, trusting that the translating effect worked both ways. "We assumed this was merely a Rao territorial raid. Your worlds are far from here."

"We now act for a cause beyond ourselves," the strange being said by way of answering. "Our efforts contribute to a higher purpose than mere expansion of our empire."

"Oh, really?" Hawk frowned, even as he brandished his pistol and dropped into a defensive stance. "And what purpose might that be?"

The two Dyonari lowered their shimmering swords and then each raised an empty hand, palm outward. They did this at a speed that was, for them, quite slow compared with their other movements.

"Our selfishness of old has given way to something greater," the psychic voice said. "All of our efforts are now directed toward the higher purpose we have found. We now serve at the command of—"

A dark blur passed between Hawk and the two eerie aliens and he tumbled backwards, instinctively leaping out of the way. He rolled to his feet, pistol at the ready, only to behold a sight he hadn't at all expected.

His commander, the great warrior Eagle, had leapt into battle, engaging the two Dyonari in combat. His massive sword slashed again and again, sunlight flashing from it and lending it the aspect of a golden lightning bolt hurtling down upon his foes.

The Dyonari moved now with a speed that put their previous swiftness to shame. Working in tandem as though each comprised only half of the same body, their movements perfectly coordinated, they unleashed their full array of skills and all their psychic fury upon Eagle, driving him back from the cave mouth.

Hawk scrambled across pavement shattered by Falcon's earlier explosives, leaping over chunks of debris along the way. He nearly tripped twice, mainly because he refused to take his eyes off the cataclysmic clash happening only a short distance away.

Eagle gave way at first, falling back a step at a time. Soon, though, he gathered himself up and held his ground, his sword deflecting the attacks of his enemies, the heavy pistol in his left hand blasting away; it had replaced the multi-cannon at some point since Hawk had seen him last.

For several long seconds that felt to Hawk like hours or days, Eagle battled toe-to-toe with the two Dyonari Swordmasters— and Hawk knew them to be so, now, beyond any doubt. The ancient and powerful empire of the alien Dyonari produced many fine warriors, but none quite like their rare and deadly Swordmasters, who blended expertise at edged weapons with well-honed psychic talents and martial arts skills. The Swordmasters could wear down your mind before they carved up your body, and they rarely lost a fight.

Now Hawk looked on as his commander faced two of them at once.

"Well now," came a deep voice from behind him. Hawk recognized it at once and didn't bother to turn. "This was worth the whole trip to Rheinstadt, all by itself," Falcon observed, his voice remarkably casual.

"Should we intervene?" Hawk asked, the effects of the fear-blast still not entirely dissipated from his psyche. "Shouldn't we help?"

"Are you serious?" Falcon asked, snorting a laugh. "If we tried that, he'd kill us himself."

Hawk could only nod slightly at that comment, knowing it was probably true.

And so, instead, the two Hands watched as their commander continued to battle the two aliens alone.

The combat had stretched on for over ten minutes now, though Hawk was almost certain his chronometer had stopped and a day or more had passed. During most of that time, neither side had gained an advantage, the three of them locked in a stalemate as Eagle deflected all incoming attacks but could never quite land a solid strike of his own upon either enemy.

Then, at around the fifteen minute mark, Eagle scored a hit. A blast from his gun caught a spot in one Swordmaster's glasslike armor, along the calf, where it had previously been weakened by a glancing blow from Eagle's sword. The armor gave way, shattering to reveal the slender, bluish leg within. Pale blood flowed out and the Dyonari dropped to one knee. It raised its sword to ward off the blow it knew was coming, but it was too late. Eagle's golden blade flashed down and the Dyonari's head separated cleanly from its shoulders.

Before the body could hit the ground, Eagle pivoted around in a half-circle. The other Swordmaster, taken momentarily aback by the sudden and violent end of its partner's life, hesitated for only a tiny instant. That was more than enough.

Eagle's sword jabbed out, his powerful muscles driving in irresistibly upward, spearing it through the torso of the second Dyonari.

The alien choked and stumbled backwards, transfixed by the golden blade.

Eagle drew his weapon out with a sharp tug and then swung it around in a broad arc, like a baseball player swinging for the stands.

The second Dyonari's severed head tumbled down and joined that of the first on the ground.

4. HAWK

Eagle had allowed himself to take a seat on the remains of a concrete pillar, though he wasn't happy to be spotted by the Firewings and Iron Raptors in such a sorry state. But his exertions—more than a quarter-hour of battling against two Dyonari Swordmasters—had taken a good bit out of him, giving him no choice but to rest for a time. It hadn't hurt when Hawk had noted that, far from thinking less of the commander after this battle, the troops would only grow his legend all the more for what he had accomplished.

Now he simply observed tiredly as Falcon barked out orders and organized the legions into ranks, preparing them to board the recovery shuttles that were even now descending from the *Talon*.

As the first of the troop transports descended on pillars of flame over the ruins of the city, Hawk approached his commander and saluted.

"What troubles you?" Eagle asked, even as he gazed up at the darkening sky. "And I know that something does. You've never been any good at hiding your emotions."

Hawk hesitated a moment, then, "It's the Dyonari, commander."

"Oh? Have they somehow reconstituted themselves? Must I strike them down again?"

A chuckling sound behind him told Hawk that, once again, Falcon had approached without his notice.

"They are still down for the count," the demolitions expert reported with a grin. "Decapitation tends to cause that, I find." He moved between the other two men and directed his attention from his commander to Hawk. "Perhaps you would like for them somehow to be *more* dead?"

Hawk ignored this. He kept his attention focused on Eagle.

"What do you suppose they were doing here?"

"I don't know, Marcus," Eagle answered, using Hawk's familiar name. "It looked to me as if they were helping the Rao."

"And that doesn't strike you as more than a little bit odd?" He spread his hands wide. "When have the Dyonari ever helped *anyone* but themselves?"

Eagle shrugged. He turned to the bald man to his left. "What do you say about this, Titus?"

Falcon shook his head.

"I can't venture a guess," he answered. "I don't pretend to understand aliens or their motivations." He chuckled. "Or their languages, for that matter."

"That's just it, though," Hawk interjected quickly. "I *could* understand them."

Eagle frowned at him. Falcon gave him a quizzical look. "What?" he asked sharply.

"The Dyonari are telepathic," Hawk said. "We already knew that, with regard to their Swordmasters in particular—and one of them was telling me something."

"Telling you what?" Eagle demanded, sitting forward.

"It didn't make a lot of sense," Hawk said, thinking back. "Something about how they were cooperating with the Rao because they now serve a 'higher power,' or words to that effect."

Eagle stared back at him for a long moment, blue eyes locked unwaveringly onto him and seeming to slice into his very soul. Hawk returned the gaze, puzzled by its utter intensity but not backing down from it. Then the tension broke, with Eagle looking away, sitting back and relaxing again.

"It could mean anything," the big commander stated flatly. "But I will ask Cardinal to look into it."

Falcon groaned audibly.

"You have something to say, Titus?" Eagle asked, eyeing Falcon narrowly.

The demolitions man returned Eagle's steady gaze. "Must you get Regulus involved, Agrippa? Doesn't that red-robed buffoon have enough to do already, sniffing around everyone's private business and accusing half of us of apostasy with regard to the great and holy Machine?" He snorted. "Next thing you know, the man will have his own Inquisition set up, putting all of us on trial for some imagined violation or other."

Eagle looked about to say something sharp, but then apparently decided against it. Instead, he allowed himself to reveal a half-smile at the others, and said, "I will ask him to be restrained. And discrete."

"That'll be the day," Falcon scoffed—but he smiled as he said it.

Hawk smiled too, meanwhile watching as the second troop transport set down smoothly a few hundred meters away; Iron Raptors were already marching up the boarding ramp of the first. "I'll need to speak with Cardinal, then," he noted. "I was able to record the Dyonari's words, and I'm sure he'll want to hear them firsthand."

Eagle sat up again, tense.

"You did what?" he demanded.

Hawk's frown grew deeper. He glanced from Eagle to Falcon; the demolitions man's eyes were wide; he merely shrugged slightly.

"You will erase it," Eagle ordered. "Permanently."

"I—but—" Hawk blinked.

Eagle glared at him. Hawk would have sworn at that moment that his commander—his friend—was about to charge at him.

"Of course I will erase it, if that is your order," Hawk went on. "But—why would you wish that I—?"

"They're telepathic, just as you stated a moment ago," Eagle snapped. "There's simply no telling what psychic time bombs they left hidden within your recording, like viruses in a computer routine." He exhaled slowly and deeply, his blond brows furrowed as he all-but-glared at Hawk. "Erase it, Marcus—erase it utterly and immediately."

"I—yes, of course." He closed his eyes for a few seconds, then nodded. "It's gone. Completely."

Eagle met his eyes again, held them for a second, then nodded. "Thank you."

His tone softened a bit. He flashed a half-smile at Falcon and then at Hawk.

"You could have potentially exposed us to any number of malicious telepathic threats, with a recording made in that environment," he continued to explain. "The risk was simply too great."

"I understand," Hawk said aloud, even as he thought to himself, *Honestly, I'm not sure I understand anything anymore.*

Falcon started to add to the conversation, but then cut himself off before he could speak. He was gazing upwards at something—and his expression was not the same as it had been when the ships coming down to join them were only transports. Curious, Hawk turned around and angled his head back to see what was happening.

A single, small, triangular ship was descending rapidly. It swooped down over their position, curved around gracefully, and set itself down in an open field very nearby.

"Uh oh," Falcon muttered.

"Is that who I think it is?" Hawk added.

"Indeed it is," Eagle confirmed. Now he did stand, determined not to be seen lounging around by this latest arrival.

The hatch on the side of the tiny ship slid up and a single figure emerged. As the pilot strode across the field and approached, Hawk could tell that it was a female, not terribly tall by anyone's standards, but slender and lithe. She wore a uniform that matched in its design elements those of the other Hands present; predominantly red, her boots were blue and her gloves a golden brown. A green seam circled her collar. Her hair was long and dark and her eyes slightly almond in shape. She halted a short distance away and stood there, staring back at them in silence.

"Raven," Eagle said by way of greeting, inclining his head slightly. Falcon and Hawk welcomed her as well.

She gave each of the three Hands a quick looking over, her expression all the while one of scarcely-contained disapproval.

"We weren't expecting you," Eagle said. "I didn't request—"

"The Machine does as the Machine will do, Eagle," she interrupted sharply. "You know that better than any of us."

"You're here on the Machine's orders, then."

Raven didn't bother to answer that. She gave the three of them one more quick looking over, then began to walk forward again, past their position, toward the city.

"And what did our master send our lovely Internal Affairs agent here to do?" Eagle asked as she passed him.

Raven paused in mid-step but didn't turn back. Her hand did briefly touch on the hilt of the sword sheathed behind her. After a moment she said, "I'm simply here to make certain everything is being done by the book."

Eagle nodded slowly at this, casting glances at the other two Hands; they offered barely-disguised looks of impatience and disapproval.

"Well then," Eagle called back to her, "I'm sure you won't be disappointed. Everything went as smoothly as could be."

"We'll see," Raven said. Then she started toward the city again.

Behind her, the other three Hands merely watched her walk away in silence.

PART THREE

**After the Shattering:
The Nineteenth Millennium**

1: HAWK

Hawk opened his eyes as the memory-recording ended.

"That…was instructive. Thank you, ship."

There was no reply.

"Ship?"

Still nothing.

Hawk continued to frown. He drummed his fingers on the side console. Perhaps five or six minutes passed.

"Ship?" Hawk called out, frustration getting the better of him. "Respond. Now."

A yellow light on the control panel in front of him began to flash.

"Now what?" Hawk demanded.

"I am detecting a signal," the ship answered, breaking its long silence.

"Why haven't you answered me?" Hawk demanded.

"The signal," the ship continued, ignoring his question, *"is being transmitted by….a Hand."*

Hawk's eyes widened, his annoyance with the ship already melting away as this new turn of events registered.

"A Hand? Another one?"

"I believe so, yes." The ship's smooth mechanical voice sounded almost relieved. *"It is a distress call, requesting assistance."*

"Alright then," Hawk said, "bring us out of hyperspace and set a course for it."

But even as he was speaking the order, the streaking visual effects of the Above as seen through the front viewport vanished, replaced by the mottled blackness of normal space.

"Already done."

Hawk grunted wordlessly. He didn't much care for what had just happened. The ship was doing things without being told. That had been acceptable when he had been completely disoriented and injured, and didn't even know who or what he was... But now—now that he was at least somewhat in control of his mind and body, now the ship had to obey him completely... right?

The disturbing thought came back to him: *Maybe not.*

With the ship now fully emerged back into real space, Hawk could see a planet looming ahead, nearly filling the forward viewport.

"Taking us down."

Hawk nodded. He decided not to press the issue, at least for now. So far, the ship was doing what he would have ordered it to do anyway. But, still...

"Do you know yet who specifically is signaling us?" he asked.

A pause as the ship inspected the signal, then, *"I believe so. And it is unexpected. They almost never request assistance—or need it."*

Hawk waited, annoyance growing within him. Finally, as if only incidentally remembering that it had been asked, the ship saw fit to answer him directly.

"The signal," it said, *"is apparently being sent by... a Falcon."*

2: FALCON

Falcon sat within a clearing atop a low hill, some miles outside of the town to which he had recently brought such devastation.

Only a few years earlier, he might have laughed at the notion that he had come to this world seeking only peace and solitude, and now he was leaving it after having destroyed so many of its citizens and property. Yes, once he might have laughed at that fact—but not now. Now the bitter experiences of playing out that role time and again had taken their toll, and only weariness and a grim fatalism remained.

A thin column of smoke off to the south marked the town's location. Clearly the fires were nearly out now. Perhaps they had not spread too far, caused too much damage.

His eyes, human and augmetic, flickered from the horizon down to the small silver device in his left hand. A tiny red light flashed on its surface.

Still nothing in range. But soon, surely. Soon...

He'd begun signaling for pickup even before he'd planted the explosives in the town. He doubted another officer of the Machine would happen within range and offer transport—it had been years now since that had happened, and he had *never* encountered another like himself, another Hand—but the old robotic supply vessels tended to cruise through inhabited systems with surprising frequency, and they provided reliable, if not necessarily comfortable, transportation between systems.

A sound in the distance escaped his notice at first, but gradually he came to realize that something was approaching. *Several* somethings, in fact.

Standing and looking out in the direction of the sound, he activated the telescopic components of his augmetic eye and studied what he could now see.

Hovercraft of some sort. At least four of them. Big, heavy, armed and armored.

So. This planet's "Inquisition" was nothing if not persistent. They were also likely taking this matter personally now, seeing as how he had been forced to kill so many of their soldiers in the town.

Fine, he thought. *Let them come.*

He gazed down at the little device in his left hand, still flashing red.

Maybe they will provide me some entertainment until someone comes to pick me up.

The minutes passed and the enemy drew closer. Falcon stood there, waiting for them, a bulky rifle now cradled in his right arm. Then the roaring grew louder. It was coming from two directions, and his telescopic mechanical eye revealed to him another flotilla of hover-tanks approaching from a few degrees further south. They were converging very rapidly on his position.

Eight or nine of them, at least.

The portion of his face that was still human frowned. The situation was growing a bit more precarious.

I am a Falcon, he thought. *Not a Condor, or even a Hawk. Everything about me was designed for combat engineering; for demolition work. Not for individual combat against a veritable army of foes...*

A third roar came from behind him. This time, he didn't even bother to look.

Surrounded. Alone, on a bare hilltop.

It doesn't take a Condor to know that these logistics are very poor.

His half-human face twisting into a scowl, he looked around quickly, locating the closest available cover. Then, rifle swinging in his right hand, he strode rapidly for the tree line.

In his left hand, nearly forgotten now, the red light on the little silver device stopped flashing, and a green light took its place.

3: RAVEN

Raven stood at the center of a broad swirl of the dead.

She leaned forward, her left hand resting on the pommel of her sword, using it like a cane or walking stick to hold herself up.

Her chest heaved as she struggled to breathe—to get enough air into her lungs to help her recover from the massive expenditure of energy she'd just endured.

Blood covered nearly every inch of her. How much of it was her own, she had no idea as of yet. She could feel no pain—none whatsoever—other than the bone-tired weariness resulting from her exertions. Her red and blue uniform had injected various chemicals into her body to keep her going well beyond her natural limits, and to keep her from passing out due to her injuries, whatever they might be.

She opened her eyes and looked down, seeing nothing but blood. Her sword as well dripped gore onto the sopping-wet field.

Slowly she raised her head and straightened her body, removing her weight from the sword and lifting it to her side. She shook the weapon once, twice, and the blood slid from its almost frictionless surface to splatter on the ground.

As the effects of the chemicals coursing through her veins—both natural and artificial—started to wear off, a terrible weariness came over her. She ignored it and looked around at her handiwork.

In a circular pattern that spiraled outward from where she stood, the dead lay where they had died—where she had slain them.

Dozens—hundreds—of alien warriors in black and gray uniforms and armored components were piled one on top of the other, each missing a head or arms or legs, or some combination thereof. Chaos, carnage, and destruction: she had visited those things upon her enemies, though the strain of it had very nearly killed her—as had the weapons of her foes, of course.

But now they all lay dead. All save her, there at the center of a maelstrom of destruction.

She gazed out at all that carnage, all that death, and she allowed herself a tiny smile, just at the corners of her narrow mouth.

You have done well, Raven, came the voice in her head—the voice of her ship's onboard intelligence coupled, it had claimed, with a sliver of the Machine's old consciousness.

"Thank you," she said aloud, her voice flat and emotionless.

Now—come aboard. For your mission has only just begun, and a great task lies before you.

Her breathing now level, she started forward, picking her way through the corpses. At one point she realized she still carried what seemed like gallons of their blood on her clothes; the fact that the quantity had not greatly increased in the past few moments indicated to her that it was almost entirely theirs, and not hers. Touching a tab on her belt, she caused her uniform to shimmer momentarily; the gore that covered her instantly slid to the ground, leaving her uniform spotlessly clean.

Now I just have to get it out of my hair, she noted, already planning a very hot shower once she was aboard her ship and it was underway.

Several minutes later, she was indeed aboard her vessel and enjoying the spray of water across her body. Every muscle still ached, including some that she could scarcely remember even using. But the pain was lessening, thanks to the shower and to medications provided by the ship. Victory, too, felt good. Very good.

Emerging from the small shower cabinet, she shook water from her long, brown hair and pulled her uniform back on, knowing that it would absorb all the excess moisture from her skin and slough it off. Then she dropped wearily into her pilot's seat and looked out the forward viewport.

A blue-white planet filled the window.

"We're still here?" she asked aloud.

"You must supervise the destruction of the enemy forces," said a smooth yet clearly mechanical voice from all around her—the ship, choosing to speak audibly rather than over the Aether link.

Raven frowned.

"Destruction? I thought I already destroyed them."

"You destroyed the scout force that had located and was assaulting the base," replied the voice. *"The main elements of the Adversary's forces are only now landing on this world, and in full force. They are moving to occupy several key strategic locations."*

Raven took this in, studying the holographic tactical display that appeared in front of her in the cockpit. Several red circles flashed here and there, data spooling out beside each of them, giving troop dispositions and numbers. The numbers were very, very large.

"I take it they weren't just after me, then," she stated.

"No. Though certainly you were one of their objectives, and would have been a fine prize for them. Your elimination would have constituted a major victory for them—whoever they are."

"That's good to know, I suppose," she said with a half-smile. "Makes me feel so important and needed."

"I understand that this is part of your human need to be flippant and sarcastic," the voice told her, *"and I indulge you in it. But do not doubt your value to the Machine, to the cause, and to this galaxy."*

"We don't even know if the Machine still exists," she pointed out.

"We must trust that it does," the voice replied. Unfazed, it continued, *"If this force is not some new manifestation of the Adversary's legions, it at least appears to represent every bit the threat the old enemy did. Though much of this galaxy lies now in shattered ruins, life yet endures—but for how much longer, if this threat is not stopped?"*

Raven sobered and nodded. The fragmentary information that had been injected into her mind prior to her awakening filled in most of the spaces; she "remembered" the great war that had shattered the galaxy, and the armies of the Adversary being defeated and driven away, back into the blackness between the galaxies.

"I understand," she said.

But, she wondered to herself, did she truly understand? If this enemy was the old Adversary, why had it returned? Why now? And if, as the voice had intimated, very few other Hands remained alive, what could one woman—albeit one woman very skilled at slaughtering the enemy—do against a foe as vast and implacable as that?

Particularly if the Machine itself was silent? And just what did that silence portend?

The ship/Machine intelligence was not privy to her inner musings. It continued on, *"Measures are being taken now to remove the enemy's influence on this world. It will not be allowed to gain a foothold here—not so long as one of our automated weapons vessels lies in space nearby."*

Raven stood and walked into the main cabin, stretching her still-sore muscles. Remembering her missing pistol, she brushed her fingertips across a blank gray wall panel, causing it to open. A blue-silver weapon extended silently out from its storage recess and she took it, sliding it into the holster that extended automatically out from the hip of her uniform.

When she returned to the cockpit, bright lights were flaring all across the planet's surface.

"This enemy, whether it represents some new threat or the return of our old foe, must be made to understand that this is the greeting it will receive no matter where in this galaxy it goes, no matter what it attempts to do."

Raven watched as Armageddon played out beneath her. She realized with a start that she was of two minds about what she was witnessing. A part of her reveled in the thrill of victory. Another part of her, however—a part deep inside, entirely hidden from view—objected somehow. What of the planet's natives? Did the planet even *have* natives? She had not bothered to ask, or to find out. Why? Was she so completely task-oriented that such a thought had never occurred to her, until now?

What did such a thing say about her? About her very humanity?

"Remote instruments tell only so much," the voice said then. *"I prefer a human interpretation."* It paused, then, *"Your*

biological readings reveal suddenly elevated blood pressure, Raven. I take this to be a result of witnessing our great victory today."

"Of—of course," she answered, sweat forming along her upper lip.

The voice continued with scarcely a pause. *"You are satisfied, then, that the enemy has been destroyed on this world?"*

"Yes," she answered, her throat suddenly very dry. "Everything has."

"Very well. The mission awaits. Get some rest. We will hyper-jump shortly. Your briefing will begin when we reemerge at our destination."

Raven heard this only peripherally. Her eyes remained locked on the nuclear explosions continuing to blossom across the planet's surface—explosions that were still flaring to horrid life when her ship spun about and vanished into the Above.

4: HAWK

The heat of a very fast entry into the planet's atmosphere already dispersed by the ultra-high-tech material of its hull, Hawk's ship swooped down from the sky and shot toward a broad, forested area dotted with grassy hills. As it drew closer, Hawk could see with his naked eyes a series of explosions alternating with bright gunfire on the ground.

"Whoever this Falcon is, and whatever he's doing, he definitely looks like he could use some help," Hawk observed.

The ship did not reply. Instead it executed a broad curving sweep over the area of the battle, scanning as it went.

"Falcon is there," it said at last, causing the holographic display to come to life in front of Hawk. A flashing blue light appeared at its center, within the trees just beyond a bare hilltop.

"His predicament does appear dire—he is surrounded by numerous attackers."

"Who's attacking him?" Hawk wondered aloud.

"That is unclear as of yet."

Before either Hawk or the ship could take any further action, a string of explosions flared below.

"Zoom in," Hawk ordered. "Let me see what's happening."

The holographic display switched from a tactical map to a close-up of the action. Hawk could now see that the attackers' forces included some sort of hovering tank contraptions, each complete with an array of weapons projecting out from a central turret. This Falcon had originally faced as many as a dozen of them, but in the last few seconds, at least three of them had exploded.

"He is using the classic approach of a Falcon to dealing with this threat," the ship observed with what almost sounded like admiration in its semi-mechanical voice.

"And what would that be?" asked Hawk.

"The approach of a demolitions expert. He is luring them into pre-set traps, and blowing them up."

Hawk considered this and realized that there was something to what the ship was saying. He knew he never would have thought of that strategy. His instincts told him he would have sought a way to perhaps commandeer one of the vehicles and use it against the others, or else flee the area and regroup elsewhere, an arsenal of anti-tank weapons in hand.

Another of the tanks exploded. The enemy continued to advance on Falcon's location.

"Who is attacking him?" Hawk wondered out loud. "Whoever they are, he must have done something to really tick them off."

Another exploded. Unfortunately for Falcon, that left more than half of the original force still intact and advancing.

The ship had not said anything for several seconds now, and Hawk had just started to wonder what it was up to when he saw on the display that they had pivoted about and were now streaking down at the enemy's line, weapons firing into the row of tanks and soldiers.

As they swooped over the front ranks of attackers, Hawk could see in the close up view the insignia the soldiers wore on their uniforms: a flame within a circle.

The ship became aware of this at the same moment, and instantly stopped firing.

"What are you doing?" he demanded. "Their line was about to break! They would have had to fall back!"

"I am not permitted to harm them," the ship replied.

"They don't appear to have any problem with harming this Falcon," he growled back. "Or us, for that matter." On the screen, he could see several of the soldiers firing up into the air, attempting to hit Hawk's ship. "Who are they, that you're not able to shoot them?"

"They are devoted the Machine," the ship replied. *"Their insignia reveal this."*

Hawk frowned.

"Devoted? You mean, like they worship it? Like a god?"

"Precisely." The ship paused, even as it swooped around above the battlefield again. *"The Machine always found such devoted followers to be very useful, from time to time. Thus we are not permitted to harm them."*

Hawk was incredulous.

"Even when they're shooting at our guy down there? At another Hand?"

"Yes. We will have to rescue him without harming his foes. And we must persuade him to stop attacking them, as well."

"You're able to look at what's happening down there and say that *he's* attacking *them*?" Hawk found such a concept laughable—though, to be honest, in the last few seconds the momentum definitely seemed to have shifted from the Machine-worshipping army to the lone Falcon.

As they dropped closer to Falcon's position, Hawk got a glimpse of him at last. He was a big guy—big and bulky and rugged. His uniform was similar to Hawk's, but mostly dark red instead of mostly blue. What looked like mechanical components covered part of his face and body, and he carried a weapon in his right hand that was both large and dangerous-looking. He fired off a shot here and there, while with his left hand he drew forth some sort of grenade from a pocket and hurled it at his opponents. Yet another explosion rocked the countryside.

"That guy is definitely tough," Hawk observed.

The ground rushed up and the ship settled onto a grassy hilltop. The outer hatch slid open.

"Retrieve him!" came the ship's voice, loudly.

"I thought I gave the orders here," Hawk growled back. Receiving no reply, he gritted his teeth and, biting back further arguments, dashed out the doorway onto the thick grass.

The man called Falcon was about thirty yards away, his eyes flashing from the direction of the enemy to Hawk and back. When he saw Hawk standing there in his blue and red uniform, he started and did a double-take. Then, raising his big gun, he fired again at his pursuers.

Hawk realized immediately that there was something odd about Falcon's eyes—he could tell this even from so far away. The next time the man looked his way, he realized what it was: One of Falcon's eyes was human, but the other was mechanical—a shining jewel, almost—set within a silver metal, skull-like half-face.

"Come on!" Hawk shouted, waving a brown-gloved hand. "Quick!"

The man in red fired off two more shots before racing through the thick grass towards the ship.

"Well, well," the big man growled as he stood before his rescuer, openly staring at him. "A Hawk. To say I wasn't expecting *you*...That would be something of an understatement."

He moved his right hand then, and Hawk expected that he might be reaching out to shake hands. Instead, he saw that the big man was gripping his bulky weapon more tightly, and moving it up into position so that its massive, gaping barrel aimed directly at Hawk.

"No," he continued, "I wasn't expecting you by a long shot."

5: FALCON

"And yet here I am," the dark-haired man in blue was saying, his dark, piercing eyes clearly noticing how Falcon had shifted the gun. "Here to help you," he added, now very plainly indicating the weapon, nodding toward it. "So, no need to shoot me or anything."

Falcon was taken aback. "A Hawk," he repeated, not quite sure he could believe it.

The other man nodded.

Falcon frowned. A Hawk, seriously? The guy couldn't possibly be real.

His cyborg eye performed a very quick scan of Hawk's facial features, cross-referencing them with memories from a very long time ago.

Everything checks out, he realized upon comparing the data. *To the tiniest detail, it checks out. Whoever this guy is, he's definitely not a cheap thug masquerading as a Hand to extort cash, or anything like that. And even if he was—why choose to imitate one of the most hated individuals in history? The very architect of the Great Betrayal and the Shattering? No— something very different, very unexpected is going on here.*

The guy still hadn't made any hostile moves. He acted totally sincere. Falcon wondered at this. All the while, ancient memories flooded back. The man looked so much like his old friend, it was extremely disconcerting.

Could he actually be from the same genetic stock? Is that possible?

No, Falcon told himself. *It has to be a ruse—a trick of some kind. It has to be. It can't actually be Marcus.*

Falcon gripped his weapon more tightly. He had killed false Hands before. None of them had ever looked like a Hawk, though. For that matter, none of them had ever looked *this* much like *any* other Hand. If this was a fake, though, why would anyone intentionally choose this particular guise?

It made no sense at all.

Another explosion echoed from the distance, and Falcon glanced back. Another hovertank had encountered one of his traps. He chuckled a little at that thought. What a bunch of idiots these Inquisition guys were turning out to be. *That's what they get for worshipping that knucklehead Cardinal as some kind of messiah,* he thought. *If only every enemy were so stupid.* Then he looked back at Hawk again, and reminded himself that not every enemy was stupid—and that some of them were quite formidable.

Still, the guy wasn't making any hostile moves. And he wasn't, after all, pretending to be a Raven—which, arguably, would be worse.

He had to do something. Shoot the guy? Refuse his help and run him off? Or just play along and see what was really going on?

He made his decision.

"So." The cyborg warrior's human eye bored in on Hawk. "You picked up my signal, and you're here to help."

Hawk nodded.

"Alright. Not the reception committee I was expecting, to say the least. But I won't turn it down, given the situation."

As if to punctuate Falcon's words, an energy blast from one of the remaining hovertanks crackled through the air very near to Hawk's head.

"Let's go, then," Hawk replied, apparently oblivious to Falcon's misgivings, or at least unconcerned about them. He gestured with one hand at the ship's hatch.

The big cyborg continued to eye him warily, then looked past him at the triangular ship that rested on the grass beyond.

"Yeah," he breathed. "Okay. Let's do it."

They crossed the short distance to the ship quickly, weapons fire striking all around. Falcon trundled through into the central cabin, Hawk just behind him. The hatch snapped instantly closed and the ship was aloft and zooming away before the encircling army had any real idea what had just happened.

As they ascended quickly into orbit, Falcon moved to the center of the main cabin and looked around. The human portion of his face twisted slightly in an expression somewhere between condescension and contempt. Dull, bare gray walls. Boring as anything. How could anyone live in an environment like this for any amount of time at all?

Falcon shook his head at the mere thought.

Hawk moved past him to the cockpit, watching the tactical display as they moved into higher orbit. Then he turned back, meeting the level gaze of the other.

Neither man spoke for several seconds. They stood there, taking the measure of one another.

The silence lingered a few seconds more before being shattered by the mechanical voice of the ship. It said, *"Welcome aboard, Falcon."*

Falcon ignored this. He had no interest in the ship's artificial intelligence—a glorified cruise control. He continued to study Hawk.

"Is something wrong?" the man in blue asked at last.

"Whatever could you mean?"

"I mean... I have been led to believe that we're on the same side... And I rescued you—or we did, the ship and myself—and yet you're staring at me as if I were as much of an enemy as those people we just left behind."

Falcon parsed through this unexpected statement, attempting to make sense of it.

"What do you mean," he asked, "when you say you have been 'led to believe' that we're on the same side?"

Hawk stared back, frowning.

"You're a Falcon, right? I'm a Hawk. We're Hands. Hands of the Machine."

Falcon squinted at him with his good eye. He pursed his lips.

"Well, but..." the big man said. "Do you know who I am?" He hesitated, then, "Or who *you* are?"

Hawk shrugged.

"You're a Falcon. I'm a Hawk. Are we not on the same side?"

Falcon did something then that threw Hawk for a loop. He laughed. He laughed quite long and quite hard.

The ship's voice cut into their awkward conversation. *"This is very fortuitous for all concerned, Falcon,"* it said. *"Your assistance will be most useful, and most appreciated."*

Falcon's eyes never left Hawk. "How so?" he called up to the ceiling.

"As you may have surmised by now, this particular Hawk was somewhat damaged during his recent awakening. He is only beginning to understand who he is, and why he exists."

"His awakening?" Falcon repeated, surprised. "As in, his actual legitimate awakening as an honest-to-goodness genetic copy of a Hand of the Machine? Not some con man who somehow acquired the ship and the uniform and…"

Falcon trailed off, stunned by what he was hearing and thinking. The Machine—or someone else—actually activated and awakened a genuine Hawk, for the first time in a thousand years.

He shook his head, his eyes narrowing as he continued to study Hawk.

Why in the name of sanity, he wondered silently, *would anyone do that?*

Hawk was just standing there, gazing back at him evenly and patiently.

"That is…interesting, indeed," Falcon stated after several seconds of deep thought.

"And what is more," the ship continued, its voice sounding almost embarrassed now, *"there was a trauma suffered at the moment of awakening. Consequently, he has no memory of his kind's past."*

These words registered instantly with Falcon. Involuntarily he moved back a step and actually gasped.

Hawk wasn't sure how to react to this. He stood there, waiting.

"You…you have no memories of your previous life, or lives, as a Hawk?" Falcon asked, his human eye widening.

Hawk shook his head.

Falcon was still staring at him, but now the big man's rugged face had morphed from cold and hard to expressing a sense of wonder.

"Then...then you know nothing of the Great Betrayal?"

"The what?" Hawk shook his head again. "All I know," he replied, "is what my ship has told me, in the short time since my awakening."

Falcon registered this. "Ship," he said, thinking things through methodically, "why are you speaking to us aloud and not via the Aether?"

"Hawk's Aether receptors are not functioning properly," the ship replied. *"He cannot fully access the network."*

"Huh. That's actually to the good," Falcon muttered. Then, louder, "You will not recite any more ancient history to him. Nothing about his previous life."

"What?" Hawk asked, puzzled.

The ship sounded almost indignant. *"That is not—"*

"Hand override code omega blue," Falcon snapped. He added a string of numbers.

"Acknowledged," the ship answered in a dull and flattened voice when he was finished.

"What did you just do?" Hawk asked, growing somewhat angry.

"Don't trouble yourself about it right now," Falcon replied with a half-smile, waving the question away. "You have lots of other things to be more concerned about."

The big cyborg turned his attention from Hawk to the ship's forward console again, as if that was where the artificial intelligence sat.

"You're attempting to contact the Machine, aren't you, ship?" he asked it.

"I have attempted to do so regularly since my activation," the voice replied, *"but I have been unable to make contact."* The ship paused. *"If by some chance the Machine is still functional, I hope to reestablish contact soon—and then we can all report in and receive updated instructions at last."*

Upon hearing this, Falcon's reaction was instantaneous. Before Hawk could move a muscle, the big man shoved past him into the cockpit area.

"What—?" Hawk began.

Falcon bent over the forward console and his gloved hands moved rapidly from one panel to the next as he studied the displays and controls. Then he nodded and reached out, grasping the small handles on one particular panel tightly. With a savage yank, he pulled the panel out of its housing in the cockpit console and held it before his face, staring at its revealed crystalline components.

"What are you doing?" demanded the ship, its voice as filled with emotion as Hawk had yet heard it. *"Stop that immediately! Replace that component! It is a vital portion of my interstellar communications array!"*

"Exactly," Falcon whispered, as he traced the connections of the various tiny components on the circuit boards. Then, before Hawk could stop him, he raised the entire panel over his head and brought it sharply down onto the deck, shattering it.

"NOOOO!" screamed the ship.

Hawk had his pistol out and was leveling it at Falcon's chest.

Falcon looked up from the ruins of the communications array to the weapon trained at him, and then to Hawk's face. He met the man's gaze with a grim calmness and laughed again.

"You're welcome," he said.

6: RAVEN

Raven was floating in a serene, dreamless state when she suddenly became aware of a droning, buzzing sound that was intruding into her consciousness. Slowly, slowly she responded, climbing upward toward the light—and then with a start she came awake.

She was lying back in the cushioned seat of her ship's cockpit. Sweat trailed down from her forehead into her hair.

Her reflexes kicked in. She sat up. Her green eyes flashed about.

A blue light on the console in front of her was flashing, and the noise that had brought her back to reality, she understood then, was warning her about the hyperdrive. It was shutting down—and the alarm meant that it was shutting down prematurely. Either some component within the engine was failing…or it was being affected by an outside force.

She leaned forward, reaching out and tapping commands onto the forward console. Data streamed across the holographic display that hovered a few inches in front of her. She struggled to sift through it, making sense of what she was being shown.

She exhaled slowly, annoyed by the confusing set of readings she was receiving. All of the diagnostic programs indicated that the hyperdrive engine was functioning perfectly. And yet, here she was, back in normal space. It was bizarre—as if something was suppressing the engines' effects and dragging the ship out of the Above.

Before declaring the situation to be entirely influenced by outside forces, however—which raised a whole new set of potential problems—she decided to inspect the engine herself. She pulled herself out of the seat and started for the rear of the vessel.

As she moved, she winced at the soreness still evident in her muscles, and regretted that her sleep had been interrupted; the accelerated healing her suit and her ship could provide during such times was too valuable to squander.

She had been trying to piece together her old, implanted memories before she had fallen asleep, to little avail. Deep meditation had brought her to what felt like the precipice of revelation, but each time she felt she could at least sense the outlines of her previous self's memories, something pulled her back. It was infuriating—and the more emotional she became over it, the harder it was to maintain the meditative state. Finally she had given up and simply dozed off.

"Ship," she called out as she pulled off her gloves and ran her bare fingertips over the smooth gray access panels. "Still no contact with the Machine, or with any other Hands?"

"Negative. Subspace communications are not functioning."

She clicked the first panel open, then frowned.

"The channels are jammed? Or the equipment itself is not functioning?"

"Unknown. All systems report active, but I am entirely unable to access subspace."

Again, puzzling but at least consistent. The hyperdrive worked by opening a portal into a higher level of reality—the Above, as it was called—where great reserves of energies could be harnessed to propel a ship far beyond the speed of light. Conversely, the communications system worked by directing a signal through a *lower* level, the Below, where time moved at a much faster rate. Thus a signal traveling great distances in the Below could re-emerge at a point far across the galaxy with hardly any time having elapsed in our reality. Ships could travel through the Below as well; until the development of engines that would work in the Above, that had been for many centuries the primary means of interstellar transportation. But it was extremely unpleasant for the passengers and crew, who had to freeze themselves and endure a centuries-long voyage through that dimension, waiting to re-emerge in normal space only a short time after they had departed.

The upshot was that both hyperspace travel and subspace communication required the ship to be able to open a portal into the Above or the Below. At the moment, it seemed her ship—for all the indications otherwise—was simply not able to do so.

"Scan this sector and fix our current position," she called out as she worked. "Locate any Machine or Hand bases nearby."

A few minutes later she had removed several access panels and pulled most of the drive components from their housings. While not a certified hyperdrive engineer by any means, she'd been injected with enough knowledge of the systems to at least diagnose the most obvious and likely problems. She squinted down at the crystalline boards, studying the circuits and connections. As she'd expected, nothing seemed amiss.

"No bases in the immediate vicinity," the ship's voice informed her then.

Having replaced the gray panels over the access ports, she returned to the cockpit and perched on the forward edge of the seat. She touched a series of controls to dismiss the holographic display and then stared out through the viewport at the velvet blackness surrounding her, thinking. She was drifting motionless in space. Readouts indicated the sublight engines were in perfect shape—but of course they said the same about the hyperdrive and the communications system.

"Give me control," she ordered the ship.

The Aether connection meshed her mind with the ship's systems. Visualizing a joystick control extended upward from the control panel, she gripped it. Now she could execute tight maneuvers on her own. She activated the engines and the ship leapt forward, then responded with precision to her tiniest movements. She swooped and spun and barrel-rolled, dancing the small, triangular ship through the void with an almost preternatural deftness.

"No problems there," she said to herself as she settled the ship into a smooth, slow glide. Yet still the blue light flashed, indicating no hyperspace capability.

She leaned back in the cushioned seat, closing her eyes and fighting to suppress the growing level of frustration that was building up in the pit of her stomach.

"Ship. Full diagnostic. Discover what is wrong with the blasted hyperdrive."

A long pause, and then the smooth voice replied, *"The hyperdrive is functional and undamaged."*

"Then why, for pity's sake, are we just sitting here, dead in space?"

"Unknown. All evidence indicates that the hyperspace/ subspace effect is being suppressed in this immediate vicinity by an outside force or agent."

"How in the name of the Machine is that even *possible*?"

"Unknown."

She cursed.

Seconds ticked by.

"Are there any inhabited planets within immediate range?"

"Negative."

She cursed again, louder.

What to do? Several scenarios presented themselves, but none seemed particularly desirable—especially with no Hand base nearby. One option was that she could aim the ship in the direction of the nearest base and then seal herself in the medical coffin, letting it freeze her until she arrived, or until a friendly ship encountered her. It could take decades—centuries—at least. And meanwhile, she would be completely cut off from whatever was happening with these new attackers. And perhaps vulnerable to them, too.

It was all simply intolerable. She'd been awoken into this body just in time to encounter some new menace and battle a phalanx of them, and now she was trapped like a fly in amber and could do nothing—couldn't travel, couldn't even communicate with anyone else in the galaxy. *Intolerable!*

In fact, if the Machine still existed, it might even write her off entirely and awaken a new Raven. What would such a thing mean for her, once she finally made it back to civilization? Would she be cast out as a redundancy—a superfluous duplicate? Would she be destroyed?

She was lying still in the pilot's seat, ruminating over all of this, when the alarm wailed again.

She sat up, her heart thumping. "Now what?"

"A hyper-portal is opening directly in front of us."

She gazed out through the viewport and her face twisted with confusion. There, just ahead, floated a shimmering blue circle. The ship was headed directly for it.

"But—I thought we'd determined that wasn't possible here."

"Correct," the ship replied. "I am still unable to create a portal myself."

"Then what—*who*—?"

The blue circle leapt toward her ship with a startling suddenness.

"Evasive!" she cried.

Before either she or her ship could react, the blue circle engulfed them.

Reality went away for a time.

1: HAWK

The big cyborg tossed the ruined crystalline circuit board to the deck. His human eye moved from it up to Hawk's face. He stood there, waiting, almost challenging Hawk to take some sort of action in response.

But Hawk was too stunned and confused to so much as move. That was understandable. Of all that he'd learned since his awakening in the besieged base, two things stood out as most important: that he was a member of a group of agents—Hands— who worked together against the enemies of Man, and that a Hand's ship was his most valuable support system and source of information.

And yet what he had just witnessed flew all in the face of those two facts. Falcon had intentionally damaged Hawk's ship—and then told him, "You're welcome!" Hawk was dumbfounded and couldn't manage to speak for several moments.

The ship, however, found its voice, and its outrage, much more quickly.

"What is the meaning of this, Falcon?" it demanded loudly. *"You have damaged my subspace communications array!"*

Falcon snorted.

"You are apparently as ignorant as your brain-damaged charge, here," the big man called out to the ship's intelligence. Then he turned to confront the very confused man in blue. "I'm going to go ahead and assume—at least for now—that you truly are a Hawk," he said. "That being the case, it had to have been a colossal error for you to be brought back into existence at all." He laughed sharply. "But here you are," he continued, "and as such—as a *Hawk*—you have absolutely no business trying to communicate with the Machine, whether it's still out there or not." He looked around menacingly. "Nor does your ship."

Hawk's face reflected deep confusion. "Why exactly not?"

Falcon looked as if he were about to answer, then hesitated. "Believe me," he said, his brown human eye meeting Hawk's almost black ones, "you're much better off this way." He stepped back and shook his bald, partly metallic head. "You do *not* want the Machine to know where you are right now. Or, honestly, any of the other Hands."

"Believe you? Why *should* I believe you?" Hawk moved around to block Falcon as the bulkier man sought to pass in the confined space of the main cabin. "From what I understand, we all—all three of us, counting the ship—were more or less created by the Machine, and we all work for it."

Falcon stared down at the gray deck at his feet for a moment. Then he looked up at Hawk, and both his human and mechanical eyes seemed to be burning with fiery intensity.

"That's the problem," he growled at Hawk. "Or part of it, anyway."

"I don't understand."

"And I can't say everything I'd like," Falcon snapped back, looking up at the ceiling, then all around the cabin. "At least, not for the moment."

Hawk frowned at this but did not reply. It was obvious that something—the ship itself?—was constraining Falcon's ability to explain himself. He considered this for a few seconds, while Falcon succeeded in moving past him and leaning into the cockpit area.

"Ship," Hawk said loudly before Falcon could cause any further mischief. "Are you able to shut off your monitoring of our conversation for a brief time?"

The ship said nothing at first, though whether this was because it did not in fact know the answer immediately, or because it was reluctant to admit it, Hawk couldn't tell.

"I can," it said at last, in an almost petulant tone. *"But why should I?"*

"I have matters to discuss with my brother Hand," he replied, even as Falcon eyed him strangely. "Matters I'd prefer kept between the two of us, at least for now."

"Between the two of you? But—I am not certain that I should allow—"

"Allow?" Hawk repeated incredulously. "You serve the Machine, do you not? And after the Machine, you serve me. That is what I have learned, and remembered, thus far."

"...*Yes, that is true,*" the ship said, its voice now definitely petulant.

Hawk touched an unassigned control square on the forward console. "Then transfer that function to this control. I will turn off your hearing now, and turn it back on shortly."

"...*Very well.*"

Hawk pressed the square.

"Ship. Can you hear me?"

Silence.

"Ship! I order you to answer me if you can hear me."

Silence.

Hawk nodded and glanced up at Falcon, who looked on dubiously.

"Nice. But—you trust this ship?" Falcon asked.

"Less than I did two minutes ago," Hawk answered. "But—why did you rip the comm system out?"

"As I said, you do *not* need to be trying to communicate with the Machine right now—if ever. And your ship definitely needs to be kept quiet." He hesitated, then snorted softly. "Not that the Machine is listening anymore, of course. Just a precaution. You never know when it might decide to wake up and start paying attention to us all again."

Hawk was attempting to take all of this in.

"I said I didn't trust my ship," he told the big man across from him, "but of course I don't trust *you*, either."

Falcon snorted his distinctive laugh.

"I should hope not. You don't even know me yet." He rubbed his rough chin. "And if I had been nearly any other Hand, you'd probably be dead by now."

Hawk just stared at him.

"And what, precisely, am I supposed to take from that statement?" he asked at last.

"Nothing but fact. If the Machine knew you existed right now—if any of your brother or sister Hands knew another Hawk had been awoken and even now traveled the highways and

125

byways of this galaxy, they would surely have no compunctions whatsoever about terminating you."

Hawk peered back at his new guest, eyes narrow.

"And will you tell me *why* that should be?"

"No."

"No?"

"Not just yet. It's a somewhat…sensitive topic." Falcon looked around the cabin somewhat nervously. "I need to get a feel for things first. For how things stand."

Hawk appeared to be considering this. Then he nodded. He dropped back into one of the cabin seats, arms crossed in front of him, and regarded the big man, at last having the opportunity to take the measure of him.

"Alright. For now. So—can you at least tell me why you'd want to help me? Why you prevented my ship from trying to contact the Machine?"

"It's simple, really," the cyborg answered, slowly lowering his heavy bulk into the seat across the cabin. "Because the ship is a slave to the Machine. It follows a compulsion to attempt to contact our mechanical master. As do we."

"We?"

"Of course," Falcon replied instantly. Then his eyes narrowed and he studied Hawk. "You feel it, don't you? In the Aether? That constant, nagging sense that you have to talk to the thing—you have to try your best to find a way to establish a communications link to it?"

Hawk shook his head. "I really don't know what you're talking about." He stared back at Falcon. "You experience this, then?"

"Constantly. Incessantly. And it grows worse the more time that passes since the last time I was able to speak with it."

Hawk nodded slowly. "And how long ago was that?"

"A thousand years."

Hawk nearly laughed, then realized the big man was serious.

"A thousand years? It hasn't replied to you in that long?"

Falcon shook his head. "Obviously, something has gone wrong somewhere."

"Apparently so."

Falcon scratched at the human portion of the top of his head distractedly.

"So you can imagine that it's more or less driving me insane," he added. "I don't really *want* to talk to the Machine. Not anymore. But between the implanted compulsion and my own natural curiosity—wondering just what has happened to it, to silence it this way—I can't help but keep trying to open a connection. Unsuccessfully."

Hawk absorbed what Falcon was saying, seated there in the cabin of his ship. The big cyborg seemed honest enough, and really had no reason to lie, as far as Hawk could tell. Even so, something was still bothering him.

"So," Hawk asked after a few seconds, "why do you suppose *I* don't feel this compulsion to try to communicate with the Machine?"

Falcon shrugged. "Your ship said you have a problem with your connection to the Aether—the hyperspace network we use to communicate with one another, control our vessels, and so on. In your particular case, that may have turned out to be quite a blessing." He leaned in closer. "Tell me about your awakening."

Somewhat reluctantly, Hawk recounted the story—his earliest memories.

"You're free of the compulsion, it sounds like to me," Falcon concluded after Hawk had quickly outlined the story, "because you got disconnected too early. While they were still programming you with everything a Hawk needs to know. Something must've gone haywire and messed up the part of your brain that receives the signal—and the compulsion to connect that comes along with it." Falcon rubbed his stubbly chin. "If that's the case, your awakening couldn't have been very pleasant, if my guessing is close to accurate."

Hawk involuntarily flashed back to his first moments of life—finding himself lying naked and screaming on a metal table.

"Not pleasant, no."

"And now I know why they'd awaken a new Hawk," Falcon added.

"Why?"

"They—the inhabitants of your base—were under attack by apparently overwhelming forces. They must've thought they were all about to die anyway. 'Might as well awaken a Hawk and see if he can save us,' they probably thought."

Hawk remembered the scientists begging him for help. He shoved the memories away.

"What about you?" he asked the cyborg. "If every other Hand would try to kill me, because we're all slaves to the Machine and have to follow its orders, why are you sitting here, having this pleasant little conversation instead?"

"Oh, a couple of reasons."

"Yes?"

"For one, we were always friends."

"Is that so?"

Falcon shrugged. "For my part, sure."

Hawk considered this and nodded.

"Okay," he said, "but beyond just our great old friendship— what else is keeping you from trying to toss me through the hatch? Did the Machine not leave sort of standing orders to that effect before it went away?"

"Oh, it definitely did," Falcon replied. "Terminate on sight orders, sure. But—unlike other Hands—I have a choice about obeying it or not."

Hawk perked up. "And how is that?"

Falcon grinned and, reaching up with his right hand, tapped the largest patch of silver metal visible on his face. It looked to Hawk as if nearly half the man's skull was metal.

"Did you think every Falcon looks like this?"

"I have no idea."

"They don't."

Hawk's brows furrowed.

"Then what—?"

"I was on a mission—this was just after the Machine went silent, when those of us that were left were still trying to make a go of being Hands, even without the Machine to coordinate for us." He sighed and shook his head in remembered frustration. "That didn't work out too well." He snorted. "So anyway, I was checking out an old mining site I'd heard had been overrun by outlaws. They spotted me. Half the nearby town must have come out to fight me. There was a battle. Go figure." He shook his head wearily. "And an explosion. I got trapped—buried under a ton of rocks. Half a mountain came down on me, it seemed like."

"You seem to make a habit of taking on entire cities, all by yourself," Hawk observed.

"Figuring out how to take down a city was always something I was good at," Falcon replied, rubbing thoughtfully at his chin. "It's the 'by myself' part that hasn't worked out so well."

Hawk couldn't help but smile crookedly at this.

"So how did you escape?" he asked after a second.

"The townspeople dug me out. And they fixed me up—or, at least, they fixed me up the best way they knew how. The best they could, given their somewhat limited level of technology." He raised one partly mechanical arm and pointed at the shiny half of his head. "They used salvaged industrial parts."

Hawk took this in, eyes widening.

Falcon shrugged.

"It kept me alive, so I guess I should be grateful. I'm nearly half metal and plastic now, though. But the good thing—or the bad thing, depending on how you look at it, and on who's doing the looking—is that I no longer felt the compulsion to *obey* the Machine. Talk with it, yeah," he added, "but not do exactly what it says." He rubbed at his temples. "Even so, the compulsion to try to talk to the thing is awful, especially since it never answers. Some days I suspect it's driving me insane. Other days I'm pretty *sure* that's true."

Hawk nodded, but now he was looking away, off to the side, considering other implications.

"The thing I still don't understand," he told the big cyborg at last, "is why you seem *glad* to be free of the Machine's commands. Are we not its Hands? Should we not be *happy* to serve that which created us? And, from what I have gathered, does it not send us out on missions that are of grave and vital importance to the safety and security of the galaxy?"

Falcon stared back at him, head tilted slightly to one side. He inhaled and exhaled slowly, then looked down at the deck and laughed softly.

"I'm sorry," he said after a few seconds. "It's just that I never imagined I'd be having this conversation—not with a Hawk!"

Hawk looked on, studying the man, waiting.

"In fact, at this point, the only interaction I thought I'd ever be having with a fellow Hand was dodging a Raven's sword and blaster, if the Machine came back online and decided to wake one up to send after me."

"A Raven?" Hawk spoke the name slowly, considering the ramifications of it. "So there *are* other Hands besides our types."

"Oh, there are a few. Not sure why the Machine went with the whole 'bird' motif, but it's been that way for what seems like forever, so..." He shrugged. "Raven's not around anymore—her line was terminated, just like yours."

"Why is that?"

He shook his head.

"Not sure, really. The line was put on ice, back during the big war." He grinned unexpectedly then. "But she was something to see, before that." He snorted. "She even made *me* nervous."

"What was her purpose?"

Falcon exhaled slowly, thinking back. "Raven was a pretty decent spy and infiltrator. Clandestine operations—that kind of thing. But she was also the police of the police, so to speak. Sort of an 'internal affairs' agent. Meaning, if one of us got out of line, the Machine would dispatch Raven after us, to straighten us out. And by 'straighten us out,' well, you can imagine..."

Hawk was surprised at the look of respect Falcon displayed while speaking of this person.

"Then she was tough enough, powerful enough," he asked, "to take down a Hawk or Falcon?"

"In her own way, yeah," Falcon said. "She was good at surprise and sneaky stuff. A Raven's not gonna just run up and launch a frontal assault at you or anything. But let her get the drop on you, and she'll cut your head off before you know what's happened."

Hawk absorbed this and filed it away, nodding. Then, "Ravens are always women, then?"

"Poor Hawk, you really are a blank slate, aren't you?" Falcon chortled. "Oh yeah. Raven was a 'she,' for sure. The Machine used a separate genetic template for each of us. A really *old* set of templates, I think," he added. "So all Falcons would look like me—or like I *used* to look, at least—and all Hawks like you. There are a few others, too, or at least there were." He pursed his lips, thinking. "Oh—and there's only one of each Hand in service at a given time. Or that's the way the rules used to work, anyway, though nowadays, who knows?" He shrugged again. "So don't think to be running into any more Hawks anywhere in the galaxy. Not legitimate ones, anyway. Or any more Falcons—unless the Machine decided at some point to write me off as a loss and move on. Which, come to think of it, could have happened a long time ago." He laughed. "Which is why I was so surprised to see you coming to *rescue* me and not '*retire*' me."

Hawk rubbed his smooth chin, considering all that he'd been told. He stood.

"All right," he said. "Thanks for the history lesson." He walked to the cockpit and eyed the square that would bring his ship back into the conversation. "Though you still haven't told me why the Machine is a thing to be shunned—why you consider it a good thing that you and I don't have to obey it."

"Well, the whole idea of 'freedom' aside," he snorted, "I think that, somewhere along the way, the Machine became insane." He met Hawk's startled expression with one of amusement. "How's that for a reason not to obey it?"

"Insane?" Hawk stared back, puzzled. "But—it's…a machine! A computer mind, right? Is that even possible?" He scratched at his chin distractedly. "How could that be possible?"

Falcon shook his head.

"How should I know? But it's true." He rubbed his massive, scarred hands together. "There's no question it once did good things—*great* things, like defending the galaxy from the Adversary—but those days are long gone. Toward the end, the orders it issued made no sense at all. Then it finally just fell silent." He sighed. "The last few Hands I talked with, way back then when it was happening, thought someone had finally located the Machine and damaged it or destroyed it. Maybe that's true." He snorted. "I just think it finally broke down— lost its mind, so to speak. And when all you *are* is a giant mechanical brain, that's a mighty big loss. So it figure it just sort of fell dormant."

Hawk's mouth was slightly open. He shook his head back and forth slowly, as if not quite able to conceive such a thing. Everything his ship had told him thus far—and everything that was coming back to him from his interrupted programming— argued that the Machine was perfect, that it was infallible. And yet... And yet everything Falcon had said so far had seemed entirely believable, once he'd considered it. He gazed down at his hands, then back up at the big man.

"And you know this—you *believe* this—because—?"

Falcon gave him a wry look and tapped his metal skull again.

"Because, in the days before it fell completely silent, I had to listen to its lunatic ravings almost every moment of every day. Some days I thought it was making me almost as crazy as it was." He laughed coldly. "And then, one day, it just stopped talking at all."

With that, Falcon fell silent. Hawk sat back, his fingers steepled in front of his chin, calmly regarding him, going over everything the big man had told him. He found this information far more disturbing on an emotional level than he ever would have expected. Clearly the Machine had implanted deep conditioning within its Hands—perhaps down at the genetic level, even—that caused them to *want* to obey the Machine, and to be concerned for its welfare.

Hawk found himself extremely ambivalent about the entire concept. So he changed the subject.

"Your type of Hand is a demolitions expert, then?" he asked after almost a full minute had passed.

"Among other specialties, yeah," Falcon said.

Hawk gestured toward the pieces of circuitry littering the floor. "You demonstrated that very effectively on my ship."

The big man stared back at him for a few seconds and then grinned.

"I like you," he said. "You're a lot like Marcus. But of course you would be."

"Marcus?"

"Your template. The first Hawk." He hesitated. "My friend."

Hawk stroked his chin. "Your friend. Really."

Falcon shrugged.

"When I saw a Hawk swooping down to save me," the cyborg rumbled after a moment, "I figured you were living on borrowed time. But now I think maybe I was wrong." He smiled. "Maybe you have a future after all."

Hawk couldn't help smiling in return. "I'm happy to hear that."

The silence that hung between them lasted for all of three seconds before an alarm wailed.

Hawk leapt to his feet and an instant later was seated in the cockpit area, bringing up the holographic tactical display. Falcon leaned in the doorway beside him.

"Two ships," Hawk reported, his partially-implanted memories once again serving him without his even realizing it. "Big ones."

Falcon nodded. "Switch to visual. Zoom in."

Hawk gave the order and the three-dimensional image before them shifted to the panoply of space, with the two tactical markers now replaced by the images of two rust-colored vessels rapidly approaching. Big and boxy and covered in what had to be weaponry, they looked extremely dangerous. Hawk said as much.

"There's something else," Falcon noted. He jabbed a thick finger at the side of one of the ships, just visible given their angle of approach. "Guess who it is."

Hawk studied the marking the cyborg was indicating. It was a stylized flame surrounded by a smooth circle. He blinked, feeling he should recognize it.

"You just saw this, down on the planet where you picked me up," Falcon growled. "Access your visual records."

Hawk frowned. "Yeah—I'm not really sure how to do that."

133

Falcon shook his head. "You're pretty messed up, alright." He pointed at the emblem on the ships again. "Flame within a circle. The seal of the Inquisition."

Hawk's eyes widened.

"Those guys? They have ships? Ships like *these*?"

"Apparently so. And I must have really ticked them off, because they've brought in some major reinforcements. And now they've found me. Which is no big deal, probably," he added with a shrug. "Their compatriots down on the surface wouldn't listen to me, but surely they will. I am, after all, telling the truth—I am a Hand."

Hawk nodded, his eyes locked on the rapidly closing warships.

"No," Falcon continued, "their finding *me* is no big deal. Finding *you*, however—well, that's going to be a major problem."

Hawk looked at him.

"I think you need to tell me why."

"Probably, yeah…"

The ship shuddered violently.

"…But at the moment, you need to concentrate on getting us out of here."

"Ship!" Hawk called. "Answer me!"

Nothing.

"You ordered it not to listen to you," Falcon pointed out. "Remember?"

"Oh…"

Hawk thought for a second, then leaned forward and touched a control. Instantly the voice of the ship rang out: *"Attack! We are under attack! Tractor beams locking onto us!"*

"Get us out of here," Hawk shouted back. "Jump! Go anywhere!"

"Too late," the ship answered. *"Engines are being overridden. Tractor beams are locked onto us. We are trapped."*

Hawk's face was a mask of frown lines. He looked to Falcon as if some magical answer would be forthcoming.

One of the Inquisition ships moved alongside them and opened a docking bay; Hawk's ship was slowly drawn inside.

Falcon dropped back into his seat, seeming almost relaxed, and examined his weapon. He looked back up at Hawk.

"This should be entertaining, anyway," he said.

B: FALCON

Falcon clicked off the safety on his massive firearm and rose to his feet like a wrathful god. He crossed the cabin in four big strides and took up position one side of the hatch, waiting, gun at the ready.

Hawk moved to the other side and crouched down, pistol aimed ahead. "What sort of strategy do you suggest?" he asked.

"Try to reason with them first," Falcon said. "After all, they're supposed to be on the same general side as us." He snorted. "And when that fails, kill them all."

Hawk took this in, considered it, and nodded. "Got it."

Falcon spared him a quick glance and a quicker smile. "Good."

For several seconds, nothing happened. Then the hull clanged around them, the sound like that of a bell ringing—if Hawk's ship were the bell. Hawk looked up, frowning, then resettled himself and aimed ahead.

"They'll override the ship's systems and force the hatch to open," Falcon stated. "It won't take long. Be ready."

Before Hawk could reply, the lights flickered off and back on. A whining sound came from just outside the ship. Then the hatch snapped open.

Hawk recoiled as energy blasts erupted through the opening. Falcon was already firing back into the darkness, his huge weapon on full auto as it spat blazing death back the other direction.

"I take it the 'try to reason with them' part has already passed," Hawk shouted at him.

Falcon ignored him and lurched out of cover, trudging forward. His massive autocannon sliced through the attacking ranks of crimson-clad Inquisition soldiers, carving out an avenue for his advance. Shrugging, Hawk followed along, his own pistol blasting.

They had made it nearly five meters inside the Inquisition ship before Falcon heard his new ally shouting a question: "What exactly are we trying to do here?"

"I told you—we kill them all."

"But… we just want to get away, right?"

Falcon didn't answer for a second as he gunned down four more attackers. Then, "Okay—we kill enough to persuade them to let us go… or enough that they aren't able to hold us anymore. How's that?"

Before Hawk could offer any sort of response, Falcon waved sharply at him and halted in mid-step. The soldiers ahead of them were pulling back suddenly, and that did not generally bode well. Then he spotted the wall panels sliding open just ahead and recognized the tiny speakers that were being uncovered. At Hawk's query he yelled back, "Sonics! Activate your countermeasures!"

Falcon had no idea if Hawk even knew what he was talking about, let alone if he was able to access that part of his uniform's capabilities. Fortunately, it seemed he was; when the sonics blared out, neither of them collapsed to the floor in agony.

When it hit, there was one singular instant of sound—a sound so loud, so piercing, that it felt as if it were drilling straight through his head—and then nothing. Utter silence. Falcon always found it weird when his super-high-tech uniform cancelled out the sound around him; when he really was hearing literally *nothing*—his uniform was emitting a sort of white noise that blanketed the hypersonic attack, along with every other sound in the ship's corridor. Falcon felt as if he stood within a bubble of soundlessness; as if his ears had ceased functioning entirely.

Doubting that Hawk could understand their military hand-signal language—at least, not this quickly, without ever having used it before—he simply motioned forward, leading his new acquaintance on the attack again.

Out of the corner of his eye, Falcon watched as Hawk shot two more Inquisition soldiers and stepped over their red-robed bodies. The kid wasn't bad. He was definitely a Hand. *A Hawk, yeah.* As bizarre as that sounded to him, after all the centuries that had passed, it had to be true. He started to motion to Hawk again, the rudiments of a new plan finally forming in his mind— *Hey, I'm not Condor the strategic genius! I just blow stuff up!*— when a small, round object bounced down the corridor at them. As it arrived, another one came bounding along behind it.

Falcon whirled, motioning frantically at Hawk. "Shock bomb! *Get down*—"

The first object exploded.

The concussive force drove both Hands down into the deck.

Falcon raised his head a couple of inches, trying to see what had become of Hawk. His head was spinning and he actually thought he saw stars spinning around his head—or maybe they were little birds. Hawk was down, not moving.

The second object exploded.

Time sort of blinked on and off for Falcon. The deck beneath his prone body shifted back and forth, as if he lay upon the deck of a sailing ship.

Black boots appeared in his very limited field of vision. The sonics had shut off, and so had his auditory countermeasure, so he could hear again.

"Well now," said a man's voice from somewhere high above. "If these two men are impostors, I'd hate to face a *real* Hand."

"This one's down for the count," said a voice from a couple of meters away.

The one that stood over Falcon gave a surprised laugh. He bent down closer.

"This bugger's still awake, believe it or not—though I'm sure his brains're scrambled pretty good right now."

Falcon attempted within his mind to unleash a string of threats and profanities, even as he tried to swing a punch at the man. In the real world, all that he accomplished was to emit a sort of groan and wiggle ever so slightly.

The Inquisition trooper laughed again and brought a rifle butt down hard on the human part of Falcon's head.

Darkness descended.

9: RAVEN

Raven's ship emerged from the hyperspace realm of the Above back into normal reality quite suddenly and unexpectedly, accompanied by a flash of vivid blue light.

She sat up, reaching for the virtual joystick controls, ready for anything.

Anything, that is, except the sight that greeted her.

Looming ahead of her was a star—a sun—in the distance. No planets, though—as the tactical holographic display confirmed. Nothing, in fact; no asteroids, no moons, nothing.

Nothing... except...

"Ship—what is *that*?"

To the right and slightly below her, relative to the ship's orientation, a broad gray...*wall*...curved past, shrinking and disappearing into the darkness in each direction. If it was another ship, it was an unbelievably huge one. In fact, as Raven's eyes attempted to adjust to the perspective, she came to realize that what she was seeing was much farther away than she had first believed.

Since it represented the only body anywhere near her ship, she focused her attention on it.

"Object configuration unknown," the ship announced. *"Scanning."*

While she waited for the ship to try to make sense of what lay before it, she watched the preliminary sensor data forming a sort of wireframe image within the holographic display. What she saw nearly took her breath away, and confirmed that her initial impressions of a "wall" had been very nearly accurate: it *was* a wall—a perfectly circular wall—that extended all the way around the star.

She blinked, frowned, and studied it more closely.

Yes, a wall all the way around a sun. It was as if the path of a planet's orbit had somehow been tightened into a circle instead of the usual ellipse, and then converted into solid material. *Into solid material.*

The implications were obvious to her as she considered them. Obvious—and staggering.

"A ring around the sun," she whispered.

"Yes," the ship replied. *"The object does entirely encircle the star."*

Raven thought about it for another few seconds.

"Too many questions," she said then. "Where did it come from? Is it new, or left over from the war? Who built it? Who could possibly have the power and the technology to create such a thing? Why would they—what's it for? And, most importantly—did it, or someone on it, bring us here?"

Another alarm wailed. This time, Raven scarcely reacted.

"Sublight engines offline, now, as well," the ship announced. *"And we have been seized in a tractor beam. We are being drawn forward—toward the ring."*

By now, Raven was done with being surprised, with being puzzled. And staying on edge for the entire time it would take her ship to be drawn to the Ring seemed entirely wasteful to her. So instead she relaxed back into the pilot's seat, laying her head on the cushions.

"Fine," she growled. "I guess that answers at least one of my questions—they wanted me here. Maybe we'll get some more answers when we get to that...*thing.*" She closed her eyes and began her slow-breathing exercises.

"Just wake me when someone shows up who wants to talk—or to fight," she added, before settling into a dreamless sleep.

10: HAWK

"You will be given a fair and equitable trial for your horrific crimes," the Grand Inquisitor told Hawk and Falcon. "Following that, you will be executed, of course."

With those words, the hatchet-faced man in the blood-red robes whirled about and strode majestically from the cabin, two armed acolytes following along behind him. In his hand he carried genetic samples from the two men that he had just collected.

Hawk watched them go, not knowing exactly what to say. He had awoken some time earlier only to find himself—and Falcon—bound to the wall by some sort of invisible force. That wall, it had turned out, was an interior bulkhead of a starcruiser. Quite likely the same starcruiser that had forcibly docked with Hawk's ship and captured them some time earlier.

Hawk was able to turn his head slightly to the side, despite the almost magnet-like force that pressed against him, and could see Falcon trapped in similar fashion a couple of meters away. The big man was wide awake and glaring back at him.

"So," Hawk said.

Falcon continued to glare.

Hawk waited.

Falcon exhaled slowly, then turned his head away and looked down.

"What?" Hawk asked. "You're angry with me? Why?"

Falcon still said nothing.

"Because we got captured?" Hawk scoffed. "Remember—they were chasing you before I even met you."

Still no response from the big cyborg.

"If I hadn't picked you up on that planet," Hawk pointed out a few seconds later, "these guys would've had you even sooner."

"But they wouldn't have been wanting to *execute* me," Falcon barked back. "Or, at least," he added after a second's reflection, "probably not."

Hawk frowned at this.

"You're saying you're in *more* trouble with this 'Inquisition' crowd because you're with me?"

"Oh, definitely," Falcon answered, still looking down at his booted feet. "Much more."

Hawk felt his emotions welling up. He wanted to shake his head but the force binding him to the bulkhead barely afforded him the freedom even to breathe.

"Alright," he said at last. "I think it's time for some answers. What exactly is it these guys don't like about me? What did I— or rather, an earlier version of me—do that was so horrible?"

Falcon looked up at him finally. His mechanical eye was impassive as ever, but Hawk would've sworn the human one looked to be filled with tears.

"You betrayed us."

Hawk was utterly taken aback by this. He opened his mouth but found he couldn't speak for several seconds. When at last he found his voice again, he managed, "You mean—I betrayed you, personally? Or the Hands?"

Falcon shook his head slowly, his mouth curving downwards.

"I mean you betrayed the entire galaxy."

Two hours later, the Grand Inquisitor returned, accompanied by many soldiers, and took Hawk and Falcon down from the wall. Under heavy guard they were led to a broad and high-ceilinged cabin that would serve as the courtroom. Hawk moved slowly, sluggishly. He felt as if the weight of the galaxy had descended upon his shoulders. In some ways, it had. Falcon had told him the bare bones of the story; the reason why Hawk was so hated by those in the galaxy who still remembered what he—or rather, the original version of him—had done.

"We face the most repulsive of crimes here," the Inquisitor stated as Hawk and Falcon were led inside and the proceedings began. The tall, slender man in red stood at the center of the circular room, the two defendants standing opposite a row of similarly-robed and hooded figures that were introduced as the tribunal panel.

The jury, Hawk guessed. *And a very impartial-looking lot, too.*

His defiance was hollow, however. Hawk couldn't find the energy to argue, to resist. After what Falcon had told him, he felt nothing but deep depression.

"The facts are these: Our agents on Maltheus discovered this demonstrably false Hand—" he gestured toward Falcon, "—doubtlessly using a uniform and weapons he found or stole to defraud the people of the galaxy. Upon discovery, this false Hand killed or wounded many of our brother Inquisitors on that world." He leaned in closer, his narrow face and long nose mere inches from Falcon's rough visage. "Those crimes alone are, of course, serious enough to warrant the death penalty. But then, *then...*"

Hawk watched as the Grand Inquisitor moved away from Falcon and approached him, regarding him as though he were a particularly troublesome insect that had somehow gotten inside their ship.

"*...then* we find him in the company of this man... Another false hand, obviously, *but*—" The Inquisitor stopped moving and stood just in front of Hawk, gesturing at him. "—but one who has chosen to present himself not as a Falcon or a Condor or even a simple legion soldier, but as...a *Hawk*."

Whispers washed across the chamber from the jury then; the words "traitor" and "betrayal" could be picked out in particular.

From what Falcon had told him earlier, Hawk understood why their reaction was as it was. He merely closed his eyes and listened, waiting.

The Inquisitor turned from the two and strode across the room to face the jury.

"While the thought that this cyborg might actually be a Falcon, having survived for so long without the Machine to guide him, is rather far-fetched, to say the least," the Inquisitor went on, "the idea that a *Hawk* has been recreated and reintroduced to the galaxy—particularly at a time when the God Machine no longer speaks with his children or interacts with us in any way—well, this is patently absurd." The Inquisitor motioned toward Hawk where he stood pinned to the wall. "This model of Hand was discontinued immediately after the Great Betrayal, many centuries ago. There was only one Hawk—and he was killed the moment his treachery was revealed."

The Inquisitor turned his back on the jury and stalked back over to the defendants. He jabbed a long, slender finger in Hawk's direction.

"Therefore, this man is unquestionably a fraud—a false Hand." He glared at Hawk with undisguised disgust. "And, what is worse, he has chosen to masquerade as the worst Hand of all—the great traitor to our galaxy—a Hawk!"

Hushed sounds of anger and revulsion echoed from the jury.

"Both the verdict and the sentence are more than obvious," the Inquisitor concluded. "Guilty, both of them—and death, swift and sure."

The Grand Inquisitor strode regally to one side as the jury members muttered to one another. After a moment, the figure serving as judge spoke up. His hood was pulled back and it was obvious he was a good bit older than the others gathered in the room; he had very short, white hair and deep creases across much of his face.

"Have neither of you anything to say for yourselves?" he asked, his voice still firm and strong.

Falcon cleared his throat carefully—a particularly disconcerting sound, coming from him. Then he said, "You want to be very sure I'm unable to escape from this restraint." He smiled in a kindly fashion to the judge, jury, and Inquisitor. "Because if I do—if I succeed in getting loose—then by the Machine itself, as I am a Hand, I swear I'm going to kill every one of you simpletons and idiots."

This actually took the Inquisitor and most of the others present aback. For a long moment no one spoke at all. Then the startled expression on the Inquisitor's face gave way to one of furious anger.

"Threaten us all you like, charlatan," he snapped. "Soon you'll be dead, just like anyone who dares to mock the God Machine."

Falcon shrugged and looked away, silent. He'd said what he wanted to say, and found no need to continue conversing.

143

Next to him, Hawk swept his eyes across the jury, seeing the looks of anger and contempt that filled every face. He shook his head, bewildered. "I don't fully understand what I—what the *original* Hawk—is believed to have done," he said. "I would very much appreciate hearing at least that much, before I'm executed."

The Grand Inquisitor laughed at this. "He pleads ignorance! He would doubtlessly have us believe he merely found this uniform, stole it, and has used it for various nefarious purposes without ever knowing anything about the original Hawk— without anyone who saw him ever telling him anything!" The Inquisitor laughed. "As if that somehow would make impersonating a Hand of the Machine a pardonable offense."

Hawk ignored this. He could see nothing to be gained by arguing that he actually was a Hand—that he actually was a Hawk. It sounded like, if anything, that would only make these Inquisitors execute him all the faster.

"I would simply appreciate being informed of the crime I'm being accused of," he stated.

The Inquisitor's face was nearly as red as his robes at the moment. He opened his mouth to ridicule Hawk once again, but the judge interrupted him. "I will allow it," the older man said.

The Inquisitor turned to look at the judge, his face betraying his surprise.

"You will play the recording?" he asked. "You would do that—for these two criminals, who are soon to be dead?"

The judge gazed back at him levelly. "If this man truly does not understand the severity of his act of pretending to be a Hawk, we have a duty to show him. Before he dies." The judge hesitated. "And it might do the rest of us some good to once again be exposed to the moral lessons it imparts."

The Inquisitor considered this for a moment and then bowed slightly to the judge. "Very well."

The lights dimmed and a holographic field shimmered into existence in the center of the chamber, even as the Grand Inquisitor hurried to get out of the way. Images began to appear, floating in midair.

"This is a recording from Hawk's own consciousness—from the time before the Shattering," the judge announced. "Legend holds that it was delivered to the Machine by the mighty Eagle himself, before…" His voice trailed off.

The Inquisitor stepped forward again, glaring at the two prisoners, even as the image of a planet's surface filled the holo display, rapidly growing closer—as though it had been filmed by a parachutist, or from an aircraft coming in for a landing. The vista beneath the viewpoint of the recording was of a great city, vast and ancient-looking. A tremendous domed structure grew quickly in the center of the image, with outlying buildings surrounding it.

"See, then, the Great Betrayal of our galaxy by the Hand of the Machine called Hawk," the Inquisitor said. "And let this, impostors, be the last thing you ever see."

PART FOUR

Before the Shattering:
The Seventeenth Millennium

—

Scandana

1: HAWK

As gentle as a feather and as invisible as the wind, Hawk descended onto the roof of the planetary palace. The broad red sun dropped below the horizon just as his feet touched down.

"I'm moving into position now," he signaled to the others over a secure Aether channel as the reactionless thrusters in his backpack switched off. The merest thought directed the pack to shut down and detach from his back; it fell to the hard roof with a clatter and lay there as he sprinted for cover. The cloaking field that had at least partially concealed him from electronic surveillance switched off. The outer layer of his normally blue and red uniform had darkened to nearly black.

"Good luck, Marcus," came the voice of the commander over the Aether connection. "I'm holding everything else back, in the hopes that you can do this surgically and with a minimum of collateral damage."

"Understood, Eagle," Hawk replied. "I'll do my best."

"Eagle here didn't like my suggestion of simply detonating Merlion's entire wing of the palace from space," came a deep, resonant voice over the connection. "I think it would be safer for everyone, but…"

"Not for the innocent people—probably hundreds—who live in the palace, Falcon," Eagle pointed out. "And walking openly up to the front door would just be asking for Merlion to do something crazy. Not to mention, what we really want is to ask the man a few...*friendly* questions. No—this is the best way. Hawk will take him down with a minimum of violence and loss of life and property."

"That I will," Hawk agreed. He had reached a place of concealment behind an ornamental sculpture and gazed out at the long expanse of tan-colored stone that comprised the roof surface. A short distance from him stood a doorway leading down into the palace. His eyes switched through a variety of vision modes as he searched for signs of surveillance equipment, defenses, and so on. After a few moments he felt that he had successfully identified all of them and he ordered his uniform to adjust and adapt in order to block their probing sensors. Even so, something was bound to take note of him before too long; the palace defenses were simply too sophisticated. The best thing he could do, he knew, was to rely on speed—to move, and move quickly, toward his objective.

His objective was Lord Darwyn Merlion, chief advisor to Ludon Kail, the planetary governor of Scandana. By the purest chance, an encrypted transmission from Merlion had been intercepted by the Machine and decoded. Its contents were shocking: Merlion was providing ultra-sensitive technical and defense data to some outside entity. For whom the data was meant, no one could say—nor could they say if the governor himself was involved. But it was obvious beyond any doubt that Merlion at least had come into the service of a foreign power.

Because Merlion had control of both the planetary military and defense network and the quite formidable defenses of the royal palace, and in order to cause as little damage and disruption as necessary to the people and the infrastructure of Scandana, the Machine had ordered Eagle to launch a small, surgical raid on the palace—one that would result in Merlion being captured alive for interrogation.

Eagle had agreed and, given the wounds he had suffered in their recent operation on the planet Cassimo, had ordered Hawk to carry out the operation in his stead. Hawk was delighted by the assignment; it sounded to him both challenging and fun.

"You have a very strange notion of 'fun,'" Falcon had replied when Hawk had confided his enthusiasm for the mission. In return, Hawk had just shrugged.

Now he raced across the stone rooftop, only steps away from the doorway that let into the palace.

That was when the murderous crossfire nearly cut him in half.

Thousands of miles above Scandana, the flagship *Talon* orbited in full stealth mode.

"He's down," Falcon reported a few moments earlier. "On the roof. So far, so good."

Eagle said nothing. Gazing at the holo display floating before him, he might as well have been a statue—a dark-blue-clad statue of a particularly wrathful deity of some ancient warrior-race.

For several seconds neither spoke, and the only sound was the soft murmur of the other dozen or so crew members moving about as nondescriptly as possible. Seasoned professionals all, they did their jobs in near-silence and otherwise stayed out of the way of the mighty Hands they served.

Then Falcon cleared his throat and emitted the faintest, "Hmm." Frowning, he leaned closer to the display screen in front of him.

"What is it?" Eagle asked, his voice soft, his expression unchanged.

"Starting to detect some kind of electronic interference around the palace," the man in red reported.

"Jamming? By the governor's people?"

"Maybe. Can't tell yet."

Eagle nodded slowly. "Keep an eye on it."

"Right." Falcon touched a series of controls and send a string of mental commands through the Aether into the system, flagging key indicators. Then he sat back in a heavy, reinforced swivel-chair and slowly turned to face his commander. "So," he said, pursing his lips, "this is all good, then, isn't it?"

Eagle turned his head slightly and regarded Falcon, waiting.

"This kind of mission, I mean," he continued. "Being proactive. Going after potential problems—or potential traitors—before they can cause even bigger problems."

Still Eagle remained silent, merely looking at him.

Falcon shrugged. "Guess I'm just glad to see the Machine being a little more aggressive in enforcement and intervention." He watched Eagle for the space of a few more seconds before turning back to the displays.

"You don't feel we are violating the rights of Governor Kail," Eagle rumbled then, unexpectedly, "by staging this covert insertion into his palace?"

"No." A pause, during which time it was obvious Falcon had more to say on the subject. Then, "Maybe." He snorted, glancing back over at his commander, and settled on, "I don't know." He allowed a slight smile to cross his lips. "And don't much care, really. Just want to root out the bad guys." Now he did smile. "And happy to see the great Machine that gives us our orders feels the same way."

Eagle took this in and appeared to consider it for the briefest of moments. Then he turned back to the holo projection, his eyes narrowing to the point that the blue was almost entirely obscured.

"Perhaps," he said.

The word hung there between them for all of two seconds before the entire conversation became forgotten: Hawk was signaling them.

"I've run into a little bit of trouble," he said, his voice distorted with static. "Nothing I can't handle, though. Stand by."

Falcon regarded Eagle, a slight degree of concern evident on his features.

Eagle remained stone-faced.

Together they waited.

Hawk had dropped and rolled the moment the energy-weapon fire had lashed out at him, scoring still-smoking streaks along the hard rooftop surface. Coming up quickly, he snapped his head around, surveying the entire field before him in only an instant. Then he rolled again, scrambling behind a piece of equipment that might have been some sort of air conditioner unit.

He'd seen nothing. His attackers had not been visible.

Now that, he knew, could mean any number of things, some of them worse than others. Were the people who were shooting at him simply very-well concealed... or were they actually invisible?

He needed to know the answer to that question, immediately.

"Okay, guys," he called. "Let's all take a breath here. I'm a Hawk—a Hand of the Machine. Duly authorized under all interstellar treaties and agreements to be here and—"

Another barrage of blasts came his way, this time nearly taking off his left ear. He drew back, out of this new line of fire, cursing under his breath because he *still* hadn't seen whoever was shooting at him.

"Okay, fine—I get the sense that you people aren't too big on the niceties of interstellar law. That's fine. Just allow me to return to my ship, up there in orbit, and we can send down the lawyers to—"

More blasts, drawing even closer to him. Hawk growled deep in his chest and drew his pistol. After a quick and mostly cursory check of the barrel that fired bolts of pure energy, he switched to the underneath one—the barrel that fired projectiles. He wasn't generally as fond of that part of the weapon, but he had to admit that, on occasion, it had its uses.

Switching out the ordnance that was loaded into it for something that he believed might prove a bit more useful at the moment, he snapped the weapon closed again and, taking a deep breath, leapt out of concealment.

The shots just missed over his head as he rolled.

He came up, instantly assuming a shooter's low stance, and fired. From the projectile barrel, he fired—over and over.

A woosh. Another woosh. Another and another.

A smack. Another smack.

Two human shapes stood partly revealed now, directly in front of him, covered across their torsos in bright yellow paint. They both were looking down in surprise—if not outright astonishment—that they had both been hit and yet neither had been hurt.

"The paint's not what gets you," Hawk informed them—just before he leveled his pistol again and fired two very quick and deadly energy blasts directly into each of them.

Falcon looked up from his musings as the speaker linked to the Aether connection crackled to life.

"Okay, I'm inside," came the nearly-garbled transmission from Hawk on the top of the palace. "The locks on the door were a joke. Entering the main level now." He paused. "Aside from the two guards on the roof, so far, I haven't seen anyone."

Falcon frowned at this. He shot a quick look at Eagle, whose face indicated incomprehension as well.

"Say again, Hawk," Falcon transmitted. "You say you haven't *seen* anyone? Anyone *who?*"

"Anyone," Hawk replied simply. "Anyone at all."

Hawk raced across the broad antechamber just outside the governor's main receiving hall. Marble columns towered overhead, beneath a high, ornately carved, arching ceiling all of cream and gold. Centuries of history looked down upon him as he traversed the chamber. Vulnerable as he was, exposed like this, he just hoped that was *all* that was looking down on him at the moment.

The two huge, golden doors sealing off the main hall were unguarded. Hawk found this to be the most troubling development yet. Guards should be manning that post at all hours of the day and night.

He walked up to the doors, then paused and looked around again. A cry sounded from the distance, somewhere behind him, causing him to whirl about.

A woman was racing his way down one of the long side-corridors. She wore the white jumpsuit uniform of a member of the palace staff—probably a maid or kitchen worker. As she stumbled up to Hawk, he reached out and grasped her by the arms. He saw then that they were bloody, as from dozens or hundreds of cuts that covered them. Her eyes, when they flashed his way, were bloodshot and wild.

"What's the matter?" he demanded. "What's happened to you? What's going on here?"

She gaped at him as if he were the devil himself, recoiled backwards and tried to pull away.

"It's okay," he almost shouted at her as she fought him. "I'm a Hand. A Hand of the Machine. See?" Mentally he triggered the transformation of his uniform from its stealth black-and-gray to its standard metallic blue-and-red.

The only effect was that she shrieked again, even louder, and tore herself free. Spinning about, she dashed away in the direction of the main entrance.

Hawk watched her go. He could think of no good reason to try to restrain her, to tackle her—and clearly that's what it would have taken to stop her mad flight.

The woman had been hysterical, verging on insane. That much had been quite clear. And something here—some unknown force acting in this palace—had caused that, he knew.

Turning back in the direction he had been moving, he reached up and pushed at the partially-open double-doors. Cunningly balanced, they swung easily open. The huge hall lay before him. He walked inside.

The room was shaped like the nave of an old Earth cathedral, and at least as huge—at least fifty yards wide and twice that long. Brightly-colored banners and tapestries covered the walls. The arched ceiling soared far overhead.

Hawk strode down the center aisle, his boots making an unexpected crackling sound on the cream-colored marble tile. Puzzled, he gazed at the floor, wondering what he was stepping on. Then, frowning, he pulled the glove from his right hand and bent down. His fingertips brushed the cold surface.

Ice. The tile was covered over by a thin layer of ice.

He realized then that the temperature in the hall had dropped noticeably even in the short time since he had entered. His uniform was easily compensating, warming him, but the trend was continuing—the air was becoming frosty as he breathed.

Standing, he gazed toward the far end of the room, and there he could make out various multicolored shapes lying on the floor all around the raised dais that held the planetary governor's seat. His eye implants adjusted quickly, zooming in, and revealed to him that the shapes were actually people—men and women—lying motionless on the cold floor.

Were they all dead? Could that be? And—*why?*

He sprinted the remaining distance and then stared about in horror.

"Eagle. Falcon," he sent mentally over his Aether link, even as his eyes swept the horrific scene before him. "Do you read?"

No response.

"Hawk to the *Talon*," he repeated, more insistently. "Eagle. Falcon. Please reply."

Nothing.

He ordered the micro-relays in his uniform to switch momentarily to standard radio wave and route the signal to the tiny audio implant in his left ear, but was punished for this action by a blast of static that would have nearly deafened him if his own internal processor interface hadn't instantly kicked in with a firewall block.

Switching back over to the Aether, he routed extra power to the signal. The only result was that he could mentally "hear" a low hissing and popping; a sort of thought-wave static. He cursed. Either both his Aether connection and his radio link were malfunctioning, which was almost unheard-of, or everyone aboard the flagship was napping all at once.

Of course, a third possibility existed as well. Someone could be deliberately jamming him.

But how could such a thing be possible? Radio waves were one thing, but the Aether link used by the Hands of the Machine operated by briefly routing a hyperwave signal into the Above, both expediting its speed and boosting its strength. Who could be able to jam something like *that?*

And yet no one aboard the *Talon* was answering.

He shoved that problem to one side of his mind and returned his attention to the scene around him. The sight of it still caused him to stagger backward a step and nearly fall.

The bodies that filled this entire end of the governor's hall—dozens of bodies, male and female, slumped over their seats limply or lying sprawled on the tile—were most assuredly dead. Every one of them. That much was obvious.

Hawk made no effort to assist any of them. Clearly there was no point. For there was something else about them—something far more disturbing than the simple fact that they were dead.

"By the stars," he whispered.

Their heads were missing. Every single person in the room had been decapitated.

He stared all around.

"How could this have happened?"

He shook his head slowly in astonishment. He felt as if he needed to sit down, but his instinct for duty was too strong. He stood there a moment longer, looking all about, taking it all in, trying to process what he was seeing. Then he was in motion again, walking around, through, and past the bodies.

There was no blood. It was as if something had cauterized the cuts instantly. Somehow, for Hawk, this made the grim tableau even more disturbing and horrific.

He reached the dais, all the headless bodies behind him now, and hurried up the low steps. The governor's chair, as much a throne as anything, stood before him. Thankfully, it was empty.

Broad and grim and black as though wrought from pig iron, the chair recalled the grimmest of monarchical seats on old Earth. Its back towered some twenty feet high and its interior surface was covered with lush and vibrant red cushions. Hawk ignored it entirely, for something else had caught his attention now: a slight crackling in the air; a very localized disturbance in the electromagnetic spectrum. He had no idea what to make of that, but then he noticed that his Aether connection buzzed just slightly louder as he moved into the area of the disturbance. Following it as if it were a homing beacon, he walked around the throne and behind it to where the dais met the rear of the room. The wall it touched was of smooth gray stone, with no doorways visible. Hawk knew how these facilities were generally designed, though. He switched his visual implants to scanning mode and quickly located the hidden seams that indicated a doorway. Reaching out, he ran a hand along the line. When his fingers touched the right spot, the door soundlessly slid aside and revealed a dark opening in the wall. The light of the hall served only to illuminate the first few steps of a stairway winding down into a sudden and overwhelming blackness. The buzzing and crackling in his ears and his implanted senses grew louder.

"Falcon? Eagle? In case I'm getting through to you somehow—I'm going into a hidden chamber beneath the governor's receiving hall."

Still nothing in response. Frowning, Hawk glanced back one last time at the headless bodies littering the room. Then he stepped forward into the darkness.

A few minutes earlier, aboard the *Talon*, Eagle had stalked over to the nearest communications officer and barked, "Why are we no longer receiving his signal?"

"Some kind of interference, sir," the blonde woman answered, not cowed by the sheer brutal force of Eagle's frustration made manifest.

"Interference—of the *Aether* connection?" Eagle scoffed. "How can that be?"

"Is such a thing even possible?" Falcon asked, looking up at his primarch from one of the forward tactical stations he was currently occupying. "I've never heard of it happening."

"Nor have I."

Falcon strode to the communications station and leaned in close to the officer there.

"You will continue trying to contact Hawk, and will alert us the moment the connection is restored."

"Of course, sir," the woman replied.

"In fact, patch the Aether frequency into the bridge audio. Let's actually *hear* what we're receiving."

She did so. Immediately a soft hum filled the bridge. It matched what they had been able to detect over their mental Aether interface with the ship.

"That's all we're receiving, sir," she told Falcon.

"Continue working at it," he said. "And in the mean time," he added, "you will invent such technology as necessary to penetrate this blasted interference."

She looked up at him, eyes wide, only to encounter a half smile and a twinkle in the bald warrior's eye. Suppressing her own smile in return, she nodded. "I will do that, sir, yes." Then she returned her attention to her console, redoubling her efforts.

Eagle clasped his hands behind his back and moved to the center of the bridge. His massive chin angled slightly upward, he gazed out at the blackness that filled the viewport, then down at the brown-white landscape far below. The *Talon* was in geosynchronous orbit so that they would remain stationary relative to the capital city and the governor's palace complex; even so, it was scarcely visible from so far away.

"I don't like this," he rumbled at last.

"Nor I," Falcon agreed. "It has to be for a reason. Someone is covering something up."

Eagle pursed his lips at this, but offered no comment either way.

Long seconds passed. The communications officer worked at her station. Only low static continued to flow from the bridge speakers.

"It was a mistake to send only one man." Eagle half-turned and his piercing gaze fell upon Falcon.

The other man said nothing, instead blankly returning the look.

"I believe we should redress that mistake," the commander added.

Falcon moved to stand next to him in front of the viewport. The mottled planet surface appeared to unfold beneath their feet, leaving them towering over it like gods.

"Who should go, then?" Falcon asked.

Approximately two minutes later, a small, cloaked shuttle dropped out of the *Talon's* landing bay and accelerated toward the planet at high speed.

Round and round and down in the dark went Hawk, his pistol in hand, his eye implants on night-vision mode still struggling to cope with the utter darkness in which he found himself. The stairway spiraled deeper and deeper into the bowels of the palace—perhaps, Hawk began to suspect, below that now and into the planet's surface itself.

At last a bit of light appeared below him and he began to reduce the night-vision effect. Moments later the stairs ended and he emerged into a long and broad chamber that seemed to have been carved out of sheer rock. The smooth, dark walls, streaked with veins of white and red, curved upwards and became the ceiling, some fifty feet above his head. Two rows of flickering lights were suspended from above, filling the entire room in a pale yellow glow.

The buzzing and crackling across the Aether had grown quite noticeable now.

Hawk moved into the chamber and took in what little there was to see.

About halfway across the room stood a bank of equipment: control panels and computer units arranged in a horseshoe shape, with massive cables leading along the wall in the opposite direction from Hawk.

Puzzled, he approached and studied the equipment but couldn't determine the use of any of it.

As he circled around it and reached the far side, the buzzing in his senses grew louder still. He continued on to the opposite end of the chamber and passed through an open doorway that led into a similar but smaller room. Entering, he gasped.

This room was circular rather than oblong, with a high, domed ceiling far above. The blank walls shimmered with red and purple light that washed over them in waves. The source of that light was what took Hawk so aback.

Floating in the center of the room was a sphere some twenty meters in diameter, seemingly composed entirely of reddish light, its surface mottled and rippling. It hovered in the air, its lower curving surface just above Hawk's outstretched hand.

Staring up at it, looking through the surface at what was inside, Hawk gasped.

The sphere of light was filled with heads.

"No," he muttered, gazing up in horror at the grim tableau. "Why—why would—?" He moved slowly around the sphere, taking it in from every angle. "What could this possibly be for?"

The heads floated upright, drifting slowly about one another in no discernible pattern. Male and female, of various ethnicities, they stared out through blank eyes. Blank, Hawk realized then—but not dead.

"By the Machine..."

The heads were still alive. The eyes were open and staring, the mouths working soundlessly. Blazing, eldritch energies coruscated around each of them.

Tearing his eyes away from the macabre vision, Hawk quickly examined the rest of the room. On the far side of the sphere, covering part of the floor, he found an array of what looked like antennas. The shimmering energy from the sphere—from the heads inside the sphere, apparently—flowed visibly down into the antennas. From there it followed cables that led through holes cut into the wall. No other openings or doorways were visible.

Hawk frowned. There had to be more here. What was this all for? Who was responsible?

A sudden, sharp cry from behind him caused Hawk to whirl about. A man was standing there, about twenty meters away, clad in a khaki-and-green uniform that Hawk recognized from pre-mission briefings as the official livery of the soldiers of the planetary governor's royal house.

"Who are you?" the man demanded—and then, an instant later, he clearly must have recognized the blue and red color scheme of a Hawk, or at least a Hand of the Machine, because his eyes widened and he called behind him for help.

"Just a minute—" Hawk began, trying to end a bad situation before it could even begin. He allowed his pistol's aim to move off to the side, bringing his left hand up in an open gesture. "I'm here on official business. There's no need to—"

It was too late. Even as several more identically-clad troopers rushed in through the doorway Hawk himself had used moments earlier, the first man drew his gun to fire.

Hawk leapt to one side, executing a remarkably athletic maneuver that involved a flying handstand with his free hand even as the other aimed the pistol and fired. By the time he was back upright on his feet, the guard's three blasts had all missed while the man himself lay dead, a victim of Hawk's one shot, which had struck him above the left eyebrow.

Six more troopers had rushed into the room in the time since the first man's cry. Now they all opened fire at once, from a variety of weapons including everything from slug-throwers to particle-beam guns to plasma-blasters. Hawk back-flipped out of the way of the first barrage, the onslaught ripping through the equipment behind him. His pistol was up and firing then, crisp and precise shots clipping two more of his foes in their torsos and bringing them swiftly down. From the burn marks visible on their uniforms, Hawk could tell they were wearing thin but strong body armor underneath—but it was no match for the primary weapon of a Hawk. His gun could penetrate virtually any substance instantaneously and even the personal guardsmen of a planetary governor lacked the resources to create an adequate defense against it.

The other four troopers were scarcely giving up. They continued firing, and only his remarkable agility was sparing his life thus far. Managing to stay one step ahead of the bullets and blasts, Hawk worked his way closer and closer to his opponents, then somersaulted over them and fired again, taking down two more.

The last two glanced nervously at one another and then rushed him. Hawk found that he was proud of them for not fleeing in terror, given that he had defeated and possibly killed five of their compatriots in only the short time the fight had raged. That did not, however, prevent him from blasting the one on the right at point blank range in the head, then delivering a stinging punch across the face to the other as the man moved in tight and sought to grapple.

Hawk's second punch drove the last soldier back another step; the man looked up at Hawk afterward with a mixture of shock and anger masking his face. He roared wordlessly and charged again, blasting away with his heavy energy rifle as he moved. Hawk shot him square in the chest and he dropped.

There was no time to celebrate his victory. The next attack seemed to come out of nowhere, and it consisted of just one single word, spoken not out loud but booming through his brain:

"PAIN!"

Hawk cried out in agony and fell to his knees.

"PAIN!"

Hawk screamed. His head was throbbing. He dropped his pistol and clutched the sides of his skull with both hands. It did no good whatsoever.

*"PAIN! LONLINESS! TORMENT! **PAIN!!**"*

The waves of sheer agony battered into Hawk and sought to drive him down flat into the cold stone floor. Secondary blasts of excruciating torment, almost like echoes reflecting and deflecting back down upon him again as they bounced off the walls and ceiling, hammered away during the microscopic gaps between the larger doses.

The onslaught went on and on, for what had to have been hours or even days. Hawk's personality retreated and hid in the depths of his brain, leaving only a pure animal persona to gasp desperately for air and clutch with clawlike hands at the emptiness around him.

Pain, pain, and pain. Pain without surcease, without ending.

Finally, after what felt like ten years or more of crouching down, merely trying to hang on, like a rafter thrown overboard and clutching at a rock in the rapids for dear life, Hawk managed to re-engage a tiny portion of his brain just long enough to ask himself, "Where is this coming from?"

He couldn't say. He had no idea. But he knew that discovering an answer to that question was the first step to ending the attack.

After what seemed like five more years of being crushed down into the floor by a ten-ton column of unrelenting agony, Hawk managed to raise his eyes and then his head just a tad; just enough to see the room around him, and to see his enemies.

They were there. One was directly in front of him, the others arrayed all the way around him in a circle.

The heads. The disembodied heads from the big tank. The weapons fire must have shattered the tank and freed them, he guessed, and now they were loose and on the attack.

They were floating a meter or so above the ground; crimson energies coruscated across their faces and through their hair as they bobbed and spun slowly along. Their expressions were all twisted with rage, their mouths open, their eyes blazing.

Telepathy, he understood then. They were all psychics of some sort. Their telepathic power was holding them aloft, and they also were using it to beat him down into the floor—to deliver massive doses of pure, unadulterated *pain* to his mind.

Understanding this somehow reduced its effects ever so slightly. Just enough, at least, that he could *think*—that he could deduce these things. The pain was still mind-numbingly intense, but some small part of his brain was able to pull away from it, wall itself off, and bark out sharp orders to his body.

UP, he commanded himself. *MOVE!*

He lifted his head higher and saw his pistol lying where he had dropped it. He understood then that in no way did he retain the ability at the moment to actually pick it up and fire it. Instead, he surged upward and blindly ahead, arms waving before him, until he bumped into the floating head just in front of him. His fingers closed in its hair, securing a firm grasp. At the same moment, his actions caused the barrage against him to weaken, as the telepath he attacked and all the others reacted with surprise at his actions. Taking advantage of this brief opportunity, he whirled about and slung the head directly at one of its compatriots on the far side of the circle.

The two heads crunched together in midair and both caromed away like billiard balls.

"NO!" cried the others, aghast. *"NO!"*

Their resolve was faltering, their numbers reduced, and their potency much weaker. Hawk snapped up his pistol and aimed it, then hesitated.

The expressions on the faces had morphed from anger to confusion and even sorrow. The waves of pain lashing out at him ceased abruptly.

Puzzled, he looked back at the big sphere that had floated in the center of the room. It had fallen and rested now against one of the control consoles, itself riddled with holes from the firefight with the guards. The sphere was cracked and the crimson light that had filled it earlier was now dimmed almost to the point of invisibility.

Hawk was uncertain of what to make of it all, but somehow he suspected the heads had been used as a kind of psychic battery, their telepathic energies drained into the sphere and then channeled elsewhere via the banks of electronic equipment that filled much of the room.

But—a battery for what?

The nearest head darted into his field of vision then, bobbing like a loose helium balloon. Its expression was no longer angry or sad but merely a sort of dull blankness.

KILL US, the thing's voice called in his mind. KILL US.

"What? No," Hawk replied out loud. "Surely there's something that—"

"NO," the voices all boomed at once. "NOTHING BUT PAIN HERE. BODIES GONE. ONLY SLAVES—FOREVER."

Hawk's expression soured as he considered what he had found on this world so far.

"Who did this?" he demanded.

"KILL US," the voices called.

Several more times he attempted to discover the identity of the person responsible, but the heads were beyond reason, beyond rationality. All they knew was pain—pain and anger. And the desire for release.

"PLEASE," the silent voices all called within his mind, in unison. "NOW."

Disgusted and filled with anger at the unknown perpetrator of this atrocity, Hawk raised his pistol.

"I will find who did this, and they will pay," he promised.

Then he fired, one shot after another. A few seconds later, it was done.

He stood there for almost a full minute, then checked his chronometer. Only something like ten minutes had passed since he had first entered the room. Shaking his head in wonder and in horror, he wiped at the sweat on his brow and considered what to do next.

That was when the hidden doorway opened.

"By the holy name," a voice called out, coming from off to Hawk's right. "What has happened here? What—"

He spun about, pistol at the ready, and saw the heretofore hidden doorway yawning open. A figure emerged through it.

They both gawked at one another. In the split second that neither was moving, Hawk saw that the other man wore a loose-fitting robe of black. His face was obscured in the shadows of a hood.

"What—?" Hawk began.

The other man whirled about and fled back through the doorway.

Hawk gave chase.

A metal door slid down between them, filling the opening.

Hawk leapt and struck the door with a flying kick. It did not yield.

Spinning about, he landed smoothly and aimed his pistol. He fired dead-center.

Nothing. The blast deflected harmlessly away.

Heart beating faster now that he felt he was on the verge of getting some answers to the insanity that had gripped the palace, he reached for a pouch at his belt. Opening it, he drew forth a small cylinder. Quickly he traced an oval on the face of the door, near the edges, all the way around. The line where he had drawn the oval flared brightly and sparks flew out.

Hawk lashed out with a powerful kick and the center of the door popped out, disappearing into the room beyond.

Hawk ducked through the hole he had created and found himself in another room, though this one was so dark, he

166

couldn't at first tell precisely how big it was, or even its shape. The only light came from two banks of madly-flickering candles some distance ahead of him. A short distance away, he could make out the vague form of a rectangle some four or five meters tall, wires and cables trailing from it.

A robed and hooded figure rushed towards him, screaming. Hawk's night vision revealed a long, wicked-looking dagger held high in the man's right hand, swinging forward. Hawk brought his pistol up and shot the man down. The figure crumpled at his feet, dagger tumbling away.

"Stop! Stop!!" came a desperate shout from somewhere in the darkness.

Hawk whirled, gun up and ready.

"Who's there?" he called, rapidly readjusting his ocular implants. "I am a Hand of the Machine, here on official business. Show yourself!"

Another figure in blood-red robes moved slowly into the light. His hands were open and raised.

"Don't shoot," the man said, continuing towards Hawk.

"Stop. Stop right there."

"Yes—yes, of course."

Hawk watched for a moment as the figure halted, hands still up.

"Who are you?"

"I—I'm Governor Kail," the shaky voice replied.

Hawk hadn't expected that answer. "You're the governor?"

"If I may—?" The man reached up slowly and pulled the hood back, exposing his face and head.

Hawk looked at him, meanwhile accessing the data file he had stored within his mind earlier. He compared the images. It did indeed appear to be the planetary governor who stood before him.

"Governor Kail," Hawk said, frowning deeply, "just what in the name of sanity is going on here? Were—were you responsible for the...the *heads* back there? For *any* of this?"

The governor stared back at him for several seconds, then abruptly he laughed.

Hawk frowned at this. He started to demand to know what was happening, but the governor cut him off.

"You may drop the pretense, Hawk," he said. "We both know why you are here. And let me add that you have done a marvelous job." He smiled broadly. "I doubt that anyone even suspects that *you* are the traitor in the ranks of the Hands."

PART FIVE

**After the Shattering:
The Nineteenth Millennium**

1: HAWK

The holographic display faded and the courtroom's lights came up again. The Inquisitor strode back out into the center of the circular space, a smug and self-satisfied look on his narrow face.

"What—that's it?" Hawk demanded, incredulous, from where he was pinned by some sort of gravitic force to the smooth wall. "That's all you have? From *that* you determined that I was guilty?"

"Not just from that," the Inquisitor replied sharply. "From the testimony of Eagle as well. And none would dare gainsay him." The man paused for a moment, then turned to the jury once again. "You will notice this man said the words, 'that *I* was guilty.' Still he maintains this pretense that *he* actually is a Hawk."

"And what betrayal exactly is this evidence supposed to convict me of? Can you at least clarify that a bit?"

"This man's gall is infuriating," the Inquisitor almost shouted. "As if every child in the galaxy doesn't know the answer to that."

"Humor me," Hawk said.

The judge interjected then: "For the sake of formalities, I will add that information to the official record." He cleared his throat. "It was found that Hawk assisted the other great traitor, Merlion, in handing over secret defense and military data to the one known as the Adversary. That being then assaulted this galaxy with his vast army and fleet of starships, made up of the forces of many different alien races, nearly all of them unknown to this galaxy at the time. The defeat of the Adversary required the sacrifice of millions of lives, the utter elimination of several of the most powerful races in our galaxy, and the shattering of thousands of star systems." The judge paused, then concluded, "For this, Hawk is considered one of the worst criminals and villains in history."

"And you seek to emulate him," the Inquisitor declared, facing Hawk and jabbing an accusatory finger at him. "The prosecution rests."

"This is a joke," Hawk exclaimed, fiery emotions rising within him. "Even if my... *predecessor*... in this role did somehow commit an act of betrayal—and the evidence of that seems pretty thin to me—that doesn't mean that *I* have—or that I would!"

"Silence!" The Inquisitor glared at Hawk, then turned back to the jury. "The evidence is clear," he stated formally. "There can be only one sentence for both of them."

"Hold on," Falcon growled, speaking at last. "When do we get to present the defense's side of the argument?"

"There is no defense's side of the argument," the judge stated flatly. "The jury will render its verdict now."

Hawk sighed. He glanced over at Falcon. The big man's good eye widened a tad. He was looking down on the proceedings from the vantage point of five feet off the ground, where he was held immobile by gravitic waves, the same as Hawk.

"Interesting justice system you people have," Falcon grumbled. Then, "Wait—you took genetic samples from us before. Any results back from those?"

The judge looked to the Inquisitor.

The Inquisitor gave a slight shrug. "That was a formality, for the most part."

"But you do have the original genetic records of the Hands stored somewhere, for comparison?" Falcon pressed.

"We do. But even so—"

The judge nodded once. "Let's continue to play this by the book," he intoned. "Show us the results of the genetic matching."

An apparently lower-ranking Inquisitor in a dark green robe emerged from the shadows and handed a small crystal to the Grand Inquisitor. He in turn inserted it into a niche in the wall. The holographic display activated again, showing two swirling patterns of lines and dots of many colors and shapes.

"These are the baseline genetic codes—the original codes for Falcon and Hawk, from before the Shattering. We have preserved them through the centuries along with our holiest artifacts."

He gestured and another pair of patterns appeared, off to one side.

"These are the codes of the two impostors we have captured here. As you can see when we move the two sets together, they will not match at all."

He gestured again and the two sets moved together.

They matched perfectly.

The room was dead-silent for perhaps three seconds. Then all hell broke loose.

Most of the Inquisitors were pointing at Hawk and shouting, but everyone was speaking at once, so no one could be heard. From what Hawk could make it out, they were basically reacting as if the devil himself had been brought aboard.

"Excuse me, people," Falcon boomed—and his shout got their attention. They all stopped again and stared up at him. "Thank you. Now, as you may have noticed, it wasn't just Hawk that was a match. So was I." He grimaced. "As I've been telling you numbskulls from the beginning." He forced a smile back on his rugged countenance. "So—since nobody's ever accused *me* of being anything other than a loyal and hard-working Hand of the Machine—will you please get me down from here?"

The Inquisitor looked to the judge, who looked back at him, then at the jury. No one seemed to have an objection at this point. An assistant deactivated the gravitic field and Falcon popped free of the wall, dropping the short distance to land with a heavy clang on the metal floor.

"Excellent," Falcon said, straightening up. "Now then." He turned to look up at Hawk for a moment, where he was still pinned to the wall. Then he turned back to the crowd of robed and hooded figures filling much of the rest of the circular chamber. He smiled an even broader smile at them.

"Remember how I told you that you should all hope I couldn't get down from your wall there? Because, if I got free, I would kill every last one of you?"

He blinked his red-glowing mechanical eye twice. A tiny whirring sound came from within the metal part of his skull.

"Well—I'm free."

A gunmetal-gray pistol dropped from a hidden compartment in his mechanical arm and slid smoothly into his hand. He raised it casually.

The Inquisitor and the jurors all gawked at him.

As Hawk looked on in astonishment, he opened fire.

2: FALCON

"Those Inquisition guys sure did make some funny noises when we blasted them and trashed their ship, didn't they?"

Hawk simply stared back at the big man who was lounging on the far side of the central cabin. They were back aboard Hawk's ship, having thoroughly demolished the vessel that had held them captive.

"What?" Falcon said at last, the silence from his counterpart growing long and uncomfortable. "You didn't like how I handled that?"

Hawk frowned. He looked around the cabin briefly before settling his gaze back upon the big cyborg.

"You certainly handled it in a...*definitive* fashion," he said at last.

"I sure did," Falcon replied with a grin. Then, seeing that Hawk wasn't smiling, he exhaled slowly and crossed his arms. "I suppose you were perfectly fine with having those goons execute you, then?" he pressed. "Because, if you didn't notice, they were pretty much going to *kill* you. And they were going to *let me go*, there at the end." He snorted, rubbing at his human eye with one rough hand. "Let me go—hah—they were going to do my bidding! They would've practically *worshipped* me, as the first genuine Hand they've probably encountered in centuries." He returned Hawk's level gaze then. "Well, the first genuine one they didn't want to put to death, anyway."

Hawk didn't reply. He merely sat back in the curved seat—a seat that had been engineered, centuries earlier, to perfectly fit his body—and brooded. Neither man spoke for some time, while the ship's intelligence kept them on course.

"Wait a minute," Falcon said, after what felt like half an hour had passed in silence. "You're not upset about me gunning down a bunch of murderous fanatics. You're thinking that maybe they were right."

Hawk's eyes flared as they locked on Falcon. "What?"

"You're wondering if that first Hawk really was guilty of what they accused him of," the big man replied, sitting up a bit as he spoke. "And if that means *you* deserve to be punished for it."

Hawk started to retort, then bit his tongue and kept quiet.

"Yeah—that's it, alright," Falcon said, nodding to himself. "I'm not always the quickest on the uptake in these kinds of matters, but I usually figure it out right in the end." He rubbed his chin. "You're beating yourself up over something you didn't even do—over something you're not entirely convinced your predecessor did, for that matter."

Hawk stood and moved across the cabin to where it connected to the cockpit. He started to go through, then hesitated and stood there for a moment.

"I'm somewhat responsible, though—right?" he asked, staring out the forward viewport at the stars streaming by. "I mean—he was me, and I'm him—isn't that so?"

"Of course not," Falcon said. "You are your own individual. Now, if your awakening process had gone as it was supposed to, then there might have been an argument to make that you are just a continuation of him. But it didn't. You don't have any of the first Hawk's memories. So you have no connection to anything he might have done. Not at all—not on a personal level." He shrugged. "So if the first Hawk made some bad choices, it doesn't mean you will. You are your own man."

Hawk appeared to be considering this. For Falcon's part, he considered that alone a major victory. All he had ever really understood in life—in his very long life—was how to tear things apart; how to find their tiniest points of weakness and rip them to pieces. The idea of actually trying to help someone—trying to build them back up, and put them back together—that was pretty much unknown territory for him. If what he was saying was having a real and positive effect on Hawk, then maybe he himself was capable of more than just destruction. And that made him feel very good, for the first time in a very long time.

Whether Hawk would respond positively or negatively to Falcon's persuasive monologue, however, would never be known. For at that moment, the ship's voice cried out, its mechanical voice almost frantic: *"Enemy approaching!"*

Falcon's face expressed astonishment and outrage. "What—is it those Inquisition idiots again? Did they track us?"

Hawk moved quickly into the cockpit area and climbed into the main seat. "What enemy?" he demanded.

Falcon leaned in through the door and together they gazed out through the forward viewport at what lay just ahead of them. The ship's intelligence brought up a holographic close-up in front of them.

The shimmering, dark hull; the bright streaks along the surface; the long, narrow, seemingly organic shape... There was no mistaking what they were seeing.

"The Adversary!" cried Hawk.

"Hyperdrive!" Falcon shouted to the ship. "Jump now!"

"Jump engine not available," the ship replied, strain evident even in its modulated tones. *"A field projected by the enemy is suppressing the drive. We have no access to the Above or to subspace."*

"How did they find us?" Hawk wondered aloud.

"Save the technical questions for later," Falcon barked. "Their suppression field might have a limited range, so—"

"Yeah," Hawk said, nodding. He gripped the flight controls and accelerated away from the enemy as rapidly as the sublight engines would allow.

"Ship, jump the instant we're free of the field!"

"I had already assumed those to be your standing orders," the ship answered him.

Huge, intense, blazing bursts of plasma shot past the forward viewport.

"I don't think your ship can take more than one hit from those before we're good and vaporized," Falcon told his fellow Hand.

"No kidding."

Hawk continued to jink the ship back and forth, even as he kept pushing the engines to the max, striving to increase the distance between them and the Adversary.

"Any lessening of the suppression effect?" he called out.

"Negative. Effect is constant at all distances thus far."

Hawk cursed.

Falcon considered the options that presented themselves, then leaned slightly over Hawk's shoulder, saying, "Turn us around. Go straight at them."

Hawk glanced backward, regarding his new companion with an expression that conveyed both a sense of disbelief and the notion that he might have to drop Falcon off at the nearest lunatic asylum, should they survive beyond the next few seconds.

"We're not going to do any good out here," the cyborg Hand pointed out. "If they're going to vaporize us, what difference does it make which way we're going at the time? And if they're going to drag us on board their ship, better that we do it on our terms, right?"

Hawk blinked, processing what the man was saying. Then, with a slight shrug, he curved them about and aimed directly towards the Adversary ship.

Predictably, Hawk's ship wailed in dismay.

"Quiet down or I'll have to mute you," Hawk told the artificial intelligence, and with an almost sullen and fatalistic resignation, it piped down.

"If they want us as prisoners—which might be the case, if they still remember this ship's design, and if they realize who we probably are—then they won't obliterate us."

"That's a lot of 'ifs,'" Hawk said.

Falcon merely shrugged.

Hawk's piloting skills clearly had been implanted successfully in his mind before his premature awakening. He managed to dodge the few blasts that came their way. In truth, however, it was clear to both men in the cockpit that the Adversary apparently wanted to capture them alive; otherwise, a broad barrage of fire would have taken them out quickly.

Falcon left the piloting to Hawk for a few seconds and moved to the main cabin, where he chose one particular panel along the gray wall. He touched it and waited a moment but nothing happened.

"Ship!" he called testily. "Open this thing now!"

"You are not authorized to—"

"NOW!" he roared.

The panel slid open.

Falcon reached in, gave the entirety of the thus-revealed armory a cursory glance, then reached in and began removing weapons with both hands. Some items fit precisely into niches in his cyborg arms and legs and torso; others he strapped on or stored in his belt pouches. Then he returned to the cockpit.

The enemy ship, which the tactical display revealed to be nearly a quarter-mile long, filled the forward viewport. Falcon whispered the remainder of his strategy into Hawk's ear and the dark-haired man didn't flinch; he merely nodded in agreement, having for the most part already guessed what Falcon was about. He was now hunched over the controls, his muscles taut, eyes focused with absolute intensity upon the tactical display as it fed him velocities, angles, and heading information. He aimed them precisely on a collision course with the bizarre vessel, twisting and curving the entire way.

When mere meters lay between their silver hull and the bizarre streaked surface of the enemy, Hawk spun them about and fired the thrusters at full power. The ship vibrated savagely, and then with a clang it stopped moving altogether.

Hawk sat back, exhaling slowly, prying his fingers stiffly free of the flight control sticks one by one.

"No time to relax," Falcon stated, already moving into the main cabin. "Come on."

Hawk joined him in the larger space, wondering exactly how they were going to proceed.

"Ship," Falcon said then, "do I need to lay this out for you, step by step, or—?"

"No," the ship answered. *"I understand. I do not like it, but I understand."*

Hawk, realizing that he was therefore the only one present who did not understand, waited to see what was about to happen. He did not have to wait long. A square segment of the floor just in front of him lit up a bright orange, then white. Then, mere seconds later, it faded back to its customary dull gray. Then it slid aside, retracting into the hull.

Falcon grinned. Hawk moved up alongside him and peered down.

A hole had been cut through the strange hull material of the enemy ship, and now a gray tube extended two feet down through it.

He looked back up at Falcon, somewhat puzzled.

"After you," the cyborg said with a half-grin.

Hawk's eyes widened.

"This was your plan? Going *inside* there?"

Falcon said nothing, but his humorless smile widened microscopically.

"Okay," Hawk said then. "But—why?"

Falcon patted the array of munitions now attached to his massive body. The grin widened all the way out.

"If we can't blow 'em up from outside," he said, "we'll blow 'em up from inside."

Then, before Hawk could object further, the big cyborg stepped over the edge and dropped into the enemy ship.

Cursing vividly, Hawk leapt after him.

3: HAWK

Hawk's ship disengaged from the hull of the enemy vessel and tumbled away like a piece of discarded flotsam for several seconds. Then its thrusters activated and it cruised smoothly into open space, even as blossoms of flame erupted from various spots along the other ship's hull.

Hawk took over and manipulated the controls with a mastery born of RNA injections his body had been given prior to his awakening. He spun them about so that the black ship filled the forward viewport.

"Nice work," he told Falcon, as they watched the big vessel spouting fireballs from a dozen places. It canted about, the nose moving downward and the tail end swinging slowly forward. "Their stabilizers are gone, at least. Looks like navigational controls, too."

"Let's not get ahead of ourselves," the cyborg cautioned. "We don't know what it takes to completely kill one of those things. In fact—"

Before Falcon could complete his sentence, the warning he was attempting to give came true. The fires died down, the ship moved back so that its nose pointed directly at them, and blasts of energy weapons fire sprayed out.

"Evasive," shouted Falcon, even as Hawk danced his little ship up and down, side to side. The blasts missed connecting with them by the scantest of distances, and Hawk could have sworn he actually felt the intense heat, even through the void of space, as the deadly plasma bolts zipped past.

"Do we have hyperdrive back?" the big man demanded.

"Negative," the ship responded. *"It returned for a moment, some seconds ago, but—"*

"Why didn't you tell us?" Hawk shouted, continuing to dance the ship amidst the barrage of fire.

"Before I could, it was suppressed again," the ship stated. *"They have a device that—"*

"I was sure I blew that part up," Falcon muttered. "I was sure that was it."

"Doesn't matter now," Hawk shot back, his eyes locked on the tactical display and his hands gripping the flight controls. "I'm open to any new ideas!"

Falcon growled deep in his throat but didn't say anything. The ship, for once, remained quiet.

A bolt of energy passed by so close that the viewport flared with blinding brilliance and the two occupants instinctively shielded their eyes with their hands. Hawk cursed, knowing it was only a matter of seconds—if that long—before the gunners on the enemy vessel got lucky and connected.

And then something unexpected happened: A bolt of energy flashed past them going the other way.

They didn't realize this at first, of course. The blasts moved too quickly for that. What they did perceive relatively quickly was that the enemy was no longer firing directly at them—though it was still firing.

Hawk frowned and, glancing back at an equally perplexed Falcon, demanded, "Ship! What just happened?"

"We are being approached by an unknown vessel of considerable size," it squawked. "The enemy ship is now firing on it—and being fired upon, in return."

The tiniest bit of relief crept over both men in the cockpit area, though it was as always tempered with caution.

"Who is it?"

"Unknown. Detecting massive power reserves—and many weapons directed at us, as well as at the enemy!"

A barrage of fire shot just past them then, coming from the new arrival and directed at their foe. Every shot struck home, and the enemy ship listed to the side again.

Falcon appeared to be doing mental calculations. He announced then, "It's just about time for my 'insurance' bomb to—"

The enemy ship flared brightly, then separated into two sections along a jagged line.

Falcon nodded, his mouth now pulled into a tight smile.

"Yep," he chuckled.

Another spray of plasma rounds from the cylindrical ship tore through both halves of the black vessel. The enemy was not firing back now, and whatever signs of life it had exhibited previously were now absent.

Hawk didn't waste time watching it die. He spun them around until they could see the new ship through the viewport. Though it was cylindrical, its thicker sections at the far end created overall an almost conical impression. Lights from tiny windows along its sides twinkled in the darkness, and red and green running lights strobed here and there, in a somewhat irregular pattern.

"That's not a Raven's ship, by any chance?" Hawk asked, not taking his eyes off the thing.

Falcon laughed humorlessly.

"Not even close."

"I figured as much," Hawk said. "Doesn't exactly say 'stealth' to me."

Falcon gazed out at the big cylinder, its hull mottled with discoloration.

"I don't have a clue what in the Above or Below that thing is. Looks pretty old. A leftover from the Shattering, I think. Some kind of pirate, maybe?"

Whatever it was, it was closing on them fast. Hawk dropped into the pilot's seat and the holographic tactical screen appeared before him.

"Just because these guys helped blow up our enemy," Falcon noted, "doesn't mean they want to be friends with us."

Hawk nodded. "I was thinking the same thing." He raised his voice. "Bring whatever weapons we have on line, ship," he called.

"I will," the mechanical voice replied, *"but I do not believe it will do much good. That vessel is heavily shielded. And its reactors are generating massive amounts of energy."*

Before Hawk could issue further orders, the ship interjected, *"I am receiving a signal."*

Hawk was puzzled. He looked up at Falcon. "I thought you ripped that system out?"

"Only the parts pertaining to the Machine," he growled. "Let's hear what they have to say. It should be good for a laugh, before they blast us to kingdom come."

The voice that crackled over the comm connection was haughty and imperious, with an odd accent that neither Hawk nor Falcon could place. "You are illegally traveling in a vessel belonging to a Hand of the Machine," it declared. "You will surrender your ship to me immediately."

Hawk and Falcon exchanged surprised looks.

"He has overridden my systems," the ship noted with alarm. *"Your visuals are now being transmitted to that ship."*

After a couple of seconds, the voice returned, now a tiny bit less haughty.

"Well, well," it said. "Can this be?"

"We are receiving a visual in return," the ship noted.

The tactical hologram disappeared. In its place now hovered the image of a face: lean, lined, with piercing blue eyes and a long, narrow nose and strong chin. Blond hair was combed or pulled back tightly from the face. In all, the image was of a man in perhaps his late forties or early fifties with something of a regal bearing, standing with his hands on his hips.

"Surely this is some sort of joke?" The dour blond man appeared to be studying his own display for a moment, first with an incredulous look, and then with pleasant surprise. "And yet, my sensors confirm what I'm seeing. A Falcon. Though," he added, "this Falcon appears somewhat worse for the wear." He paused, staring at them over the connection. "And...could that truly be a Hawk that I see?" He crossed his arms over his broad chest. "My, my. There has to be an utterly fascinating story behind *that*."

"You know us," Hawk replied, "but we don't know you."

"Oh, I know who he is," Falcon growled before the blond man on the hologram could say anything. "Or who he's supposed to be, anyway. Didn't expect to ever meet one again, though."

Hawk looked up from the seat at his cyborg companion expectantly.

"Hawk, meet the Machine's great and mighty logistics and tactical agent." He glared at the hologram, his human eye narrowed to a dark slit. "Meet Cassius—the Hand known as *Condor*."

4: FALCON

Hawk's ship passed through into the docking bay and settled gently to the deck. A large mass of figures emerged from doors located at the back of the chamber and hustled quickly into place around the ship—troops, obviously.

Falcon watched them on the holo display as they formed into tight, straight rows. They wore brown uniforms with red trim and carried a variety of very deadly-looking weapons, from energy rifles to blaster pistols to everything in between.

"You can see what I mean already, huh?"

Hawk was getting up from the pilot's seat, but looked back at the display. "How so?"

"He's Mr. Logistics and Tactics. They're lined up all parade-style, looking pretty and making a lovely show of it—but also in carefully-planned positions such that they can blow us away from any direction as soon as we walk outside."

Hawk took this in.

"Okay…so…but we're still going outside, right?"

"Of course."

They exchanged grim smiles and moved through the main cabin toward the hatch.

Falcon moved aside to allow Hawk the honor of stepping out first, since this was his ship. The fact that this also exposed Hawk first to any possible sneak attack was not lost on either of them.

Falcon smiled inside as the hatch opened and Hawk simply strode right out, chin up, without hesitating or looking around first. He couldn't help it—he found that he *liked* this Hawk. Maybe it was as simple as the fact that there hadn't been a genuine Hawk for him to interact with in all the centuries since the Shattering, but there seemed more to it, somehow.

Now you're getting all soft and mushy, he admonished himself. *There's a lot more to be concerned with right now than having found a potentially useful and trustworthy associate.*

Falcon followed Hawk out into the bright lights of the docking bay. His mechanical eye quickly adjusted, leaving his human one to squint at the glare.

From out of the ranks emerged a tall, gaunt figure in brown. Blond hair brushed back, aquiline nose, haughty air as he gazed at his new guests—whoever the man was, he certainly knew how to evoke the attitude of a Condor.

"Gentlemen," he said formally. "Welcome aboard my ship."

"Thanks for the assistance back there," Hawk replied, extending a hand. Meanwhile, Falcon looked around, soaking up the details.

Another second passed and then Condor smiled tightly and reached out, taking Hawk's hand and shaking it. "It was my pleasure."

The three stood there for several seconds, no one speaking. Falcon looked off to the side, his lone human eye blinking rapidly as his partly electronic brain reached out, out... Nothing.

He turned back to Condor. "No Aether reception, then?" he asked. "Neither you nor your ship?"

Condor looked only the slightest bit chagrinned.

"I'm afraid...I've suffered some difficulties along those lines," he answered, offering a flat smile. "And nowhere to go to effect repairs." He nodded to indicate Falcon's cyborg prosthetics. "Obviously you've encountered similar difficulties."

"I'm not able to connect to the Aether, either," Hawk volunteered.

Falcon flashed his new comrade a quick look of disapproval. He didn't like revealing anything he didn't have to—not even to an alleged ally.

"I see," Condor stated, glancing at Hawk. "So—the three of us are reduced to verbal communications, then, it would appear."

"I suppose we can make do," Falcon commented. He paused, sizing the blond man up. Then, "What I'd be interested to learn is how you found us. This is a mighty big galaxy for you to just happen to come along when you did."

Condor offered Falcon a somewhat surprised expression.

"You mean you don't know?"

"Don't know what?" Falcon asked, casting a slightly nervous glance Hawk's way.

Condor laughed, somewhat arrogantly at first but softening quickly to a friendly chuckle as he saw Falcon's expression hardening.

"We could scarcely miss you," the blond man replied. "Your ship has been screaming incessantly on every private Hand frequency for, oh…" He shrugged. "Hours, at least."

Falcon and Hawk both reacted with surprise at this news, but the big cyborg's expression soured very quickly. He glowered at Hawk, then at the ship where it rested on the docking bay floor.

"Screaming, eh?" he growled.

"Incessantly," Condor replied with a nod. "Calling out for any available Hands to come to its rescue—claiming that it was being menaced by a rogue Falcon."

The other two Hands absorbed this information in silence. Then Falcon sighed and shook his head, staring down at the metal floor.

"A rogue Falcon, it said?"

"That's right." Condor paused, then, "One who had already damaged its systems and might do so again. It was very emphatic about that part."

Falcon stared back at Condor, and now he couldn't help but begin to smile and snort a laugh. The blond man returned his gaze somewhat noncommittally.

"Hawk," Falcon rumbled, turning halfway toward the third man, "you need to have a serious talk with your ship's intelligence." He considered for a second, then added, "or else maybe I could. With a hammer."

Before Condor could rejoin the conversation, an underling approached with a bow and said something quietly to him.

"Your ship is requesting that my people repair its subspace communications array," Condor informed them after the trooper had been dismissed. "In fact, 'requesting is far too mild a term. It is practically *demanding* it, to any of my cybernetic units that will listen. It seems the ship is upset that it can no longer attempt to contact the Machine. As if the Machine were still listening," he added.

"Yeah, well, about that," Falcon began.

Condor dismissed it with a wave.

"I will have my technicians look it over," he said, "but not immediately. Other requirements must take priority."

Falcon exchanged significant glances with Condor at that.

"Assuming you are agreeable, Hawk," Condor added. "It is, of course, your ship."

"Of course. No hurry."

"I suspected that would be the case," Condor said with what might have been a wink.

Falcon grinned. Though nothing had been said openly—at least, not yet—Falcon was getting the strong sense from this particular Condor that he was by no means a fanatical devotee of the Machine and that he, too, enjoyed his freedom from the great computer mind's thrall. If that was the case, things might at last be looking up.

"So," Falcon went on at last, breaking the brief silence and turning to directly face the man in brown. "What have *you* been doing for the last thousand years or so?"

Condor smiled a warm but almost smug smile back at him.

"Not quite a thousand, actually," he answered. He hesitated for a few seconds. "I'm a more recent edition." His bright blue eyes met Falcon's mismatched pair. "I don't believe you and I have ever actually met."

"No," Falcon replied with a chuckle. "You're definitely not the Cassius I knew before." Nonetheless he offered the man his hand and they shook. His smile faded quickly afterward and his eyes remained locked onto those of the other man. "But, seriously—what *have* you been doing, since they woke you up?"

"Same old things," Con said. "Fighting the good fight. Going after the bad guys. Keeping an eye out for larger trouble." He gestured around them. "Doing the best I can with what's available, in these latter days we find ourselves in."

Falcon was nodding as the other man spoke, but within his own mind, he was puzzled. *Something's not right,* he realized. *No ship like this was ever part of the fleet of the Hands—and, even if Condor captured it somewhere along the way, only recently, it hasn't been maintained in any fashion the way a Hand's ship should or would have been.*

Condor gazed at Hawk for a second or two, as if unsure of what to make of him.

Falcon had expected this and stood ready to move into action if necessary—though one could have never told it, looking at his easy, casual stance.

"You don't have any problems with Hawk, here?" Falcon asked, cocking his human eye at the blond man.

Condor shrugged slightly.

"Not as such, no," he replied, his eyes shifting from Hawk to Falcon and back. "A lot of time has passed. Centuries." He glanced back at Falcon, meanwhile motioning with his head toward Hawk. "And he's not the same one, at any rate—right? He couldn't be."

"No," Falcon agreed. "He couldn't be."

Hawk followed the conversation but kept his silence.

"Fine with me to have him here, then," Condor said. "Hawk or no, I can use all the high-powered help I can get."

Falcon wasn't sure how to react to that. In a way, knowing the original Condor the way he had, a thousand years earlier, he would have expected the man to object strenuously to the presence of a figure as reviled as Hawk. But it certainly benefitted them all now for this version of Condor to be acquiescent about his presence. Consequently, he was hesitant to be overly suspicious or to say anything more. Falcon therefore just filed it all away and waited to see what happened next. In the meantime, he kept both his human and cyborg eyes on Condor.

"Are you experiencing some sort of trouble, then?" Hawk was asking.

The blond man smiled again and shrugged somewhat nonchalantly. "Nothing we haven't been able to handle, thus far," he replied. "But assistance is most assuredly welcome, and will certainly make things easier."

Before either of the other two men could inquire as to what exactly these "things" were, Condor nodded to the two of them and gestured toward the doorway at the rear of the bay. "If you would accompany me to the command level, we can continue this conversation in a more comfortable setting." He looked them over. "And we can discuss just *who* that was that you were fighting when I arrived…" He spared Hawk a pointed glance then. "…As well as a great many other things."

Hawk started forward. Falcon continued to look around, taking reams of mental notes.

"How did you two come to be together?" Condor was asking. "Is your ship nearby, Falcon?"

"It was destroyed," Falcon replied tersely. "A while back. Hawk was giving me a ride."

"Ah." Condor glanced at Falcon, and looked to be about to inquire about the man's cyborg implants and reconstruction, but then seemed to think better of it, at least for now. "Well. How fortunate that a brother Hand was in the neighborhood, eh?"

Falcon nodded once.

Condor smiled at them and then gestured with his left hand.

"This way, gentlemen."

He led the two other Hands past the ranks of soldiers and through the doorway.

It was now Hawk's turn to look around, as they traveled down a series of corridors.

"So this is the ship of a Condor?" Hawk asked.

The blond man glanced back at him, his expression showing more than a touch of puzzlement. Then he smiled, as though coming to the conclusion that Hawk had been joking.

"We salvaged this vessel from a battle zone that probably dated back to the Shattering," Condor replied. "It has its uses. Particularly with our larger ships from the old days now lost to us."

Falcon gave Hawk a slight jab in the ribs and a quick look that very clearly said, *"Don't ask any more questions that give away what you don't know!"*

They continued a short distance further until they reached a sort of elevator. The doors opened and they all walked inside. The doors closed and Falcon could feel a hint of movement.

No one said a word. Falcon figured Hawk was overflowing with questions, but another sharp look kept the dark-haired Hand's trap shut.

The doors whisked open. Condor led them out onto the command level—a broad, open area with high ceilings and wide, clear viewports lining the opposite wall for what must have been nearly a hundred meters. Various brown-and-red-uniformed individuals stood or sat here and there, at various consoles and workstations, presumably operating the ship. A few of them looked up as the doors opened, took in the new arrivals with no small degree of surprise, and quickly returned to their tasks.

Condor walked out onto a circular open area at the center of the vast chamber. He raised his arms out from his sides, presenting the command level to his guests.

"You have come along just in time, gentlemen," he told them. "We are preparing to initiate a new operation and your assistance may prove invaluable."

Hawk walked along behind him onto the circle, looking about. Falcon could tell the dark-haired man was awed by what he was seeing—but then, Hawk had only been awake a short time. He hadn't seen the things Falcon had seen in his much longer life, and hadn't received most of the memory downloads from his original self. Falcon hung back, near the doors, still studying his surroundings in minute detail.

Yeah, he told himself. *I was right. Even if they just salvaged this tub a day ago, it shouldn't look like this. Not with a high-ranking Hand and his personal army in charge.*

His gaze moved from the walls and equipment to the technicians operating the ship. His mechanical eye zoomed in on Condor tightly, studying his uniform, his movements, even his face.

No, no, no, he thought. *This whole thing is wrong.*

Still, he thought an instant later, *that doesn't mean it can't all be useful...!*

Falcon joined the other two on the central dais and stood just behind them, listening. Condor was saying something about the auspicious portents of their meeting at this juncture—or some such nonsense. Falcon tuned it out. Hawk seemed instinctually good enough at going through the motions of formalities and rituals to cover for both of them. Meanwhile, Falcon intended to get to the bottom of what was really happening.

But then something Condor said caught his ear.

"The artifact we have discovered at the far fringes of the galaxy is entirely uninhabited. But it offers almost limitless possibilities."

"What artifact is this?" Falcon asked, leaning in.

Condor eyed the man with a touch of disdain.

"As I was telling our brother here, it is a structure. A vast structure. I have come to believe that it was built by one of the last great civilizations of our galaxy, before or during the Shattering."

Hawk looked like he was about to ask a question—and probably a very stupid question for a Hawk to be asking, if said Hawk were in complete command of his memories and faculties. But before Falcon could say or do anything to stop him, Hawk closed his mouth and continued to listen.

Maybe the kid is learning...!

"It is utterly uninhabited now," Condor continued. "The alien race that built it is entirely gone—in all likelihood wiped out by a biological weapon of the Adversary, during the Shattering… or else by some sort of plague—perhaps an entirely natural one."

"And just what is it?" Falcon pressed.

"You will see soon enough," Condor stated. And by way of reply to their questioning looks, "As a Condor, I am invoking my rank and recruiting you both into my operation. Deputizing you, as it were, for the duration of this mission."

Hawk looked puzzled and glanced at Falcon, who gave him a half-shrug and a nod, as if to say, *Yes, a Condor can do that.*

Hearing no objections or other comments in response to his declaration, Condor continued. "I believe the artifact was intended as a refuge for the race who built it—a place for them to hide from the Adversary, or from some other massive threat, while having all the living space they could ever need."

"It's that big?" Hawk asked.

"Oh yes," Condor said. Then he continued, "Or else it may have been designed as a sort of ultimate weapon against that enemy. Or perhaps it was to serve as both." He smiled. "In any event, it is to be mine now. Ours, that is," he quickly corrected. Then he frowned and looked at the other two. "And the Machine's, of course—if we ever hear from it again." His frown deepened. "I don't suppose either of you has heard anything from the Machine…?"

Falcon shook his head once.

"No," Hawk answered, leaving it at that, afraid to say anything more.

Condor's frown softened and vanished. His tight smile returned.

"No—of course you haven't. Neither have I. Not in many years." He laughed softly then, even as he turned about to gaze out the viewports at the panoply of space that surrounded them. "You must forgive my exuberance," he added. "I have been operating on my own, more or less, for some time now, what with the Machine silent. All of my efforts have gone into preparing this operation. I've come to think of it as my own. I mean no disrespect towards our master."

"We understand perfectly," Falcon said, not meeting the blond man's eyes.

Condor gave him an inscrutable look.

"Yes, of course," he said.

Falcon added this odd conversation to his list of things that puzzled him about Condor. None of this sat well with him. It was true that it had been many, many years—centuries, in fact—since he had last encountered a Condor. It was also true that those years had done much to change Falcon from the gung-ho demolitions expert and loyal Hand of the Machine he had once been, happily serving alongside Eagle and the original Hawk aboard the *Talon*, to...to *whatever* he had become now. Even so, this Condor rankled somehow. Things were not quite as they seemed here—of that, more than anything else, Falcon was now certain.

"So you say the artifact you've found is a kind of ultimate weapon?" Hawk was asking. "What are its capabilities, then?"

Condor's smile widened. His blue eyes flashed.

"You will see," he said. "Soon enough."

He led the two off the command deck and back toward the lift, giving them directions to the guest quarters and asking that, after some rest, they rejoin him for dinner—at which time he would lay out his plans in full.

"For untold millennia this artifact has floated at the edge of the galaxy," Condor said as the other two Hands stepped into the lift. "It has waited for someone to find it—someone who knew how best to harness its great power and its vast potential." He gestured broadly again. "That day has come. Soon *I* will represent the major force in this galaxy."

"*We* will, you mean," Hawk said. "We Hands of the Machine."

The doors closed before Condor could offer a reply—if any at all had been forthcoming.

5: RAVEN

I'm dead, Raven thought, and knew it to be true. *I'm dead, but they're bringing me back to life.*

"She's awakening now, sir," the hollow voice said, barely penetrating and echoing within Raven's half-dozing brain. "She's almost back. This new body appears to be in perfect condition. We are about to download the various skill sets that—"

"I don't care," another voice snapped. "Deactivate her."

"What? Put her back to sleep?"

"Yes."

"But—that's highly irregular, sir. I don't believe we have *ever* terminated the waking procedure of a reconstituted Hand right at the point of wakefulness."

"I didn't ask you what was regular. I ordered you to shut her down. Now."

"I—but—" A pause, then, "Yes, sir. Whatever you say."

She was alive again. Her eyes were just starting to flicker open. Then the cold descended over her. Sleep welled up, embracing her, dragging her down...

No, she tried to say, tried to shout, but her voice was even more sluggish than her thoughts. *No. I don't want to die again. I don't—*

She awoke with a scream.

Leaping off the flight seat, she landed on the cabin floor in a ready crouch, prepared to use her bare hands to kill anyone near her.

There *was* no one near her. She was entirely alone.

She blinked. Her eyes were crusty and raw. Gradually reality reasserted itself.

She was inside her ship. Her own ship. And she was awake. Alive and awake.

Memories returned. Some of them, anyway.

She was aboard her own ship, and the incident she had just remembered had happened many, many years ago. More than a thousand years ago.

Had it been only a dream?

No. No, she was certain of that. It had definitely happened.

She had died, presumably in the line of duty, and a new body had been awakened for her—standard procedure for all of the Hands of the Machine. But then, someone had ordered the technicians to stop the process and to shut her down—to put her back to sleep, indefinitely.

Who had done that? And why?

She stood there in the ship's central cabin for several long moments, her arms wrapped tightly around herself as if to drive a residual chill away. Then she swallowed hard, forcibly put such matters aside, and called out to her ship.

"Status report."

The ship laid out the situation for her in succinct terms: It seemed that the tractor beam that had grappled onto them when they had emerged from hyperspace had pulled them across the gulf of space until the ship lay just alongside the dull gray ring. From a distance, the ring had appeared to be rotating about the sun very slowly; up close, that was shown to be an optical illusion, or rather an artifact of the thing's tremendous, gargantuan size. It was actually spinning at blinding speed.

"Just how fast is it moving?"

"Sensors show the ring to be rotating about its sun at a speed of seven hundred and seventy miles per second," the ship reported.

Raven whistled aloud.

"How does it not fly apart?"

"We must assume the ring is made of an exceptionally strong substance."

"No kidding." She continued to stare out at it. "Why rotate the thing that fast?"

"Such a speed would impart angular momentum sufficient to generate artificial gravity quite similar to human standard."

Raven considered this.

"They're spinning it for gravity. Centrifugal force. Okay. So there could be someone living on it. Walking around on the inner surface."

"Unable to scan through to the inner surface of the ring. The outer shell is composed of an unknown substance, with a density sufficient to block all sensors."

"Okay…"

She pointed at a tiny band of blue, very narrow but long, that glowed far out across the distance. It was invisible near the sun, due to the glare, but farther out the two blue lines could faintly be made out. They appeared to be moving downward as the ship was drawn closer toward the ring.

"That's the inner side, on the other side of the sun from us, right?"

"Precisely."

"There's nothing blocking it from us. So—what do you detect there?"

"Insufficient data," the ship answered crisply, almost defensively. *"The distance is too great, and there is too much interference from solar radiation between here and there. And, unfortunately, now—"*

Even as the ship said the words, Raven watched the thin strands of blue continuing downward relative to her view, until they disappeared entirely behind the blank gray wall that now filled her viewport.

"—now we have drawn level with the ring's plane, blocking the rest of the structure from view and from sensors."

Raven sighed and continued to stare out the viewport at the great gray bulk as it silently whizzed past. All of this inaction was wearing on her; she felt a strong desire to attack…*something*. Idly she wondered if her sword could cut through the super-dense gray matter that comprised the ring. She found herself entertaining the fanciful notion that she could open the hatch of her ship, lean out, and give it a try.

After a short time, she frowned and spoke up again.

"Is the ring slowing?" It certainly seemed to be, as she watched one segment after another of the gray wall move past in an unending procession.

"Actually, the tractor beam has increased our speed relative to the ring's rotation."

"Matching velocities," Raven concluded. "Taking us up to the same speed as the ring. They're bringing us in for a landing, I think."

The ship said nothing in response to this, so Raven busied herself with checking over her weapons and suit functions. Then satisfied that she was as ready as she could be, she sat on the deck near the hatch, lotus-fashion, with her katana laid across her legs, and she waited.

She did not have to wait long.

The ship resounded with a deep *clang*ing sound as it was forcibly docked to the underside of the mighty ring.

Raven inhaled deeply and exhaled slowly. The fingers of her right hand gripped the leather handle of her sword while she drew her pistol from its holster with her left.

"Uniformed men are approaching the hatch," the ship reported.

"Show me."

A holographic display appeared in the center of the cabin. On it, Raven could see a dozen men in dark green uniforms with silver helmets marching in two columns toward the hatch.

"Only twelve?" Raven scoffed, contempt filling her voice. "Who do they think they've captured?"

She waited to see what manner of weapons they would use to try to open the hatch. What she saw instead puzzled her.

The men waited unmoving just outside the hatch, standing at attention, six on either side, facing inward.

"What are they doing?" she wondered aloud, knowing her ship had no more idea than she did. Indeed, it did not attempt to answer.

After nearly a minute of waiting, she saw another figure stride boldly up to her ship, passing between the ranks.

"A woman," she noted, puzzled.

Indeed it was a woman who now stood just on the other side of the hatch from her. A tall, slender woman clad in a form-fitting green uniform of a design very similar to Raven's own, with blue gloves and boots. She wore her long, blonde hair pulled back severely from her face and tied in back. A pistol like Raven's hung from her belt on either side, both resting against her hips.

"No, no," Raven whispered. "It can't be. They're all dead."

The ship recognized the woman's look, as well, and filled in the details.

"You are correct. This woman is dressed as a Shrike—but that unit was—"

"I know," Raven snapped, cutting the ship off.

The woman had high, regal cheekbones and piercing dark eyes that moved from the assembled soldiers to the ship. She gazed directly up at where the holographic imaging was originating from; the effect was that she appeared to be staring directly at Raven.

She spoke: "Attention occupant of this vessel. I know that you can see and hear me. I will ask but once: Are you a loyal Hand of the Machine?"

Raven's eyes widened.

"We've been captured by our own people?" she whispered. "This makes no sense at all."

"If you are," the woman outside continued, her voice strong and commanding, "then open your hatch and present yourself. You will find you are among friends—friends who have a need of your particular abilities. In the name of the Machine."

Raven waited, holding her breathing steady. Her fingers tightened on her sword's hilt.

"If you are not—if you have somehow stolen this vessel—then surrender now, or your punishment will be severe. Most severe indeed. Also in the name of the Machine," she added.

Raven considered the situation carefully. There was what appeared to be happening: another, higher-ranking Hand, coming to her rescue. And then there was what Raven somehow felt was more likely: a trick.

But if she didn't open the door, they'd surely blast their way through, she was certain. And a damaged ship was not something she wanted, assuming she was able to get away.

"Ship," she called out. "Evaluation."

Instantly, the ship replied, *"As the ship of a Raven, my programming shades toward the suspicious by nature—I am designed to look beyond surface appearances, even as you do. That is your role as a covert operations and internal affairs agent of the Machine's forces. From that perspective, I agree that there appears to be more at work here than this alleged Shrike is letting on."*

"So—?"

"Given our current logistical situation, I agree that you have no choice but to open the hatch and hear this person out."

Raven took this in and nodded.

"You have ten seconds to open the hatch," the woman in green called out.

Raven stood and holstered her pistol. Reluctantly she slid her katana back into its sheath on her back. Then she gestured at the door. It slid open. She stepped out, directly in front of the woman in green.

"A Raven," the woman said, her eyes widening slightly as she realized who she was seeing. "Well, well." Then a slight smile played about her dark red lips. "I am glad to have you aboard," she added quickly.

Raven nodded once. She saw that she was several inches shorter than this alleged Shrike, but she met her eyes firmly. "Thank you," she said. "Not that I had much choice in the matter."

The woman nodded.

"Yes. I'm afraid our automatic systems scan adjacent quadrants constantly for Machine-created ships. As you can imagine, they are always being piloted by unauthorized individuals. Criminals who have stolen them from our remaining bases. We re-acquire the ships and equipment and...*punish*... the guilty."

"I see," Raven replied. "That's a practice I heartily approve of." Her eyes flicked from the blond woman to the soldiers all around. "What is this place?"

"We will discuss that shortly," Shrike said. She started to move in the direction of the ranks of soldiers and Raven walked alongside her.

"I have to ask you," the blonde woman said after a moment, "where did *you* acquire this uniform and the ship? You look very authentic, very impressive."

Raven frowned at her. "Excuse me?"

Shrike halted and gazed down at the dark-haired woman. "Let's not cling to the pretense," she said. "We both know that there hasn't been a Raven in a thousand years. That model was discontinued with extreme prejudice, during the Shattering."

Raven tensed.

"I have no idea what you're talking about," she growled, her hand brushing the grip of her pistol. "Or who you really are."

The blonde woman turned to her, frowning.

"My primary function is to police the other Hands," Raven continued. "I can spot a phony a light-year away. So the question is not who *I* am, but who *you* think you're kidding."

Shrike glared at her, started to say something sharp and then apparently changed her mind. She whirled about, gesturing toward the rows of soldiers, about to issue some sort of order—

Raven had already leapt into the air, her gleaming sword drawn and swinging around in a broad, killing arc.

Shrike saw this out of the corner of her eye and just managed to lunge out of the way; the blade sliced neatly through the neck of the soldier who had stepped up behind her. His head tumbled to the ground just ahead of the rest of him.

Raven landed on the other side of the dead soldier and her pistol was already drawn, gripped in her left hand and firing.

Two more soldiers went down. Shrike danced away again, managing to keep at least one soldier between herself and Raven at every moment.

Raven somersaulted and struck with her sword, relieving two soldiers of their arms; they stumbled back, gurgling, blood spraying.

One soldier had his sidearm out and started to fire. Shrike struck out with the flat of her hand, catching her man at the elbow. He cried out in pain and dropped the gun.

"Alive," she shouted to the surviving troopers. "I told you all—alive!"

A heavily armored figure trotted up then, charging straight at Raven. Darts flew from guns built into his arms. Raven executed a ballet-like sequence of moves that resulted in every projectile missing her.

The armored man shrugged off two blasts from her pistol, then extended his left arm. Raven lopped it off above the elbow.

To his credit, he did not cry out; he charged again, three more soldiers coming up fast behind him.

At that same moment, Shrike leapt from the floor up at an angle so that her feet touched the side of Raven's ship. She sprang away from it, her momentum carrying her through the air such that she would pass just over Raven's head, a pistol-like weapon appearing in her hand as she did so. She pulled the trigger but, instead of beams or projectiles emerging, a cloud of gas sprayed out.

Raven swung her sword upward even as Shrike twisted in midair, the result being that she only sliced off a portion of Shrike's pale blonde ponytail as she passed.

That same instant, the bulky armored man struck again with his remaining arm.

Raven sliced it off and took the heads of two more of the soldiers before the jets of gas from Shrike's weapon at last caught her and sent her into oblivion.

6: HAWK

Hawk sat in a thick but worn cushioned chair and stared at his companion in puzzlement.

Falcon had been standing there, just inside the doorway to Hawk's compartment, for several minutes now, not moving a muscle. For his part, Hawk was reluctant to say anything—he wasn't sure how much he could trust this Condor, and he wasn't entirely sure how much Falcon trusted the guy, either—though it was clear that Falcon didn't really trust anyone very much.

Come to think of it, Hawk realized that he didn't know where his own true loyalties lay now. At first, upon hearing from his ship about the purpose of the Machine and about his own role as a servant of that entity and a sort of policeman for the galaxy, Hawk had felt he could resume that job with no objections. But then he'd met Falcon, and the big cyborg had planted enough questions in Hawk's mind with regard to more recent history that now Hawk was thoroughly confused.

So, for now, he was playing it all by ear, doing what he felt was right from moment to moment and striving to gain a fuller grasp on where his loyalties and obligations *should* lie.

Under the system of rank among the Hands, from what little he'd been able to gather so far, he understood that Condor outranked both Falcon and Hawk. That meant he should divulge everything he knew to Condor, and follow that man's instructions rather than relying on Falcon's somewhat questionable judgment, as he'd been doing since they'd first encountered one another.

But various things Condor had said, coupled with veiled commentary by Falcon since their arrival here, had Hawk questioning Condor's legitimacy—or at least his true agenda. It had, after all, been at least a thousand years since the Shattering; enough time for anyone to change who they were and what they believed in—and what they were willing to fight for.

And so, all in all, discretion seemed the better part of valor, at least for now.

With his ultimate boss, the Machine, no longer speaking to any of the Hands and apparently dormant for centuries, he felt justified in this approach. If the Machine came back online and demanded answers, he could simply explain that he had done the best he could, given his own lack of memories and the strange and uncertain loyalties of the Hands he had encountered since his awakening.

Would the Machine believe him? Would that argument succeed, or would it get him killed and his model, the Hawks, eliminated again? Why had a Hawk been awakened in the first place, if the model was so bad—responsible for the worst betrayal in human history?

So many questions yet remained, and they gave Hawk a terrible headache.

And because of that, he saw no need to be in any hurry for his ship to regain contact with the Machine. In hindsight, Falcon had probably done the right thing by ripping the circuitry out.

He looked over at Falcon again. The man still stood there, not moving. It was growing annoying, and Hawk started to say something. But then he realized that he was wrong—the man was not entirely still. There were movements—tiny, almost imperceptible movements—here and there. An eyelid flickering. A finger just barely twitching. A nostril flaring slightly. Almost as if it were all deliberate—as if it was some sort of code, or—

...ever going to catch on, ever going to remember, you twit? How long do I have to stand here and do this, before you...

Hawk almost, *almost*, reacted with a verbal exclamation as he suddenly discovered that he could understand what Falcon was "saying."

...figure it out? You are not only useless, but potentially a huge liability, apt to get us both killed, either by fanatical followers of the Machine or by this alleged Condor or...

It all clicked. The portion of his mental "programming" that included physical motion codes snapped back into place all at once, and he found that he could easily understand what Falcon was trying to communicate to him.

...by someone else. By the Above and the Below, you are so useless—

Is that so? Useless? Would you rather still be facing the Inquisition on that planet where I found you?

Ah! At last. Well—that only took three forevers.

My apologies.

Yeah. Anyway, here we are now. Okay. Several observations. You don't trust Condor. You're not even certain he is a Condor. And you know he's not remotely loyal to the Machine, whether he is who he says he is or not.

...Right. How did you know that?

I'm not as stupid and useless as you think.

Point to the Hawk. Next. I—

You want to see what this big weapon artifact thing is, before we make any moves.

Another point. You surprise me, Hawk.

Thank you.

Falcon considered for a moment, his tiny gestures ceasing. Then they started back up again, and Hawk could read, *Clearly we aren't going to do the bidding of this guy, just because of our old ranks with respect to the Machine. I don't think of myself as working for it anymore, and I don't think you do, either.*

Another issue for another time. But—no, I don't see any reason why we should obey this man's orders, whoever he is, and whether the Machine is still around or not, or whether its old military hierarchy still applies to us or not.

Falcon allowed himself a slight smile at that news.

Good.

But, Hawk added, *from what I'm remembering now, Condors are pretty powerful. If this guy truly is a Condor, or simply has access to all of a real Condor's weapons and powers, I'm not sure we can stop him or resist him. Plus—you saw when we arrived—he has an army at his disposal, and a great big ship, and—you get my point, right?*

Unfortunately, yeah. Falcon snorted softly. *But it's two against one, so he's screwed.*

Hawk suppressed a laugh.

Okay, then, he sent by the code. *You and I remain allies, at least for now. And neither of us cares for this Condor, so— Machine's hierarchy to blazes—if we don't like what he's up to, we take him down. Permanently.*

I believe there's hope for you yet, Brother Hawk, Falcon replied. Then he nodded once, turned on his heel, and exited the room.

Hawk lay back on the bed and stared at the ceiling, knowing that he needed to get as much sleep as he could whenever such an opportunity presented itself—though he seriously suspected sleep would not be quick in coming now. There was just too much going on in his head—and a great deal of it seemed beyond his control. Even so, he knew he needed to rest. Things had been interesting enough for him since he'd been brought into this life, and he had a sense now that they were about to get infinitely more interesting.

Who'd have ever thought, he mused, *that fighting eight-foot-tall insects with disintegrators for arms would represent the easy part of my first day?*

Then he closed his eyes, and sleep did finally claim him.

And as soon as it did, another blocked memory broke free and floated to the surface. It came fully-formed to Hawk's mind all at once, and he *remembered*—remembered that it had happened roughly two weeks prior to his solo mission to the governor's palace on Scandana. Two weeks before the events that caused him to be labeled a traitor.

He remembered very clearly. The planet was Cassimo; the objective, the imposing granite Fortress of St. Julian.

And here is what he saw...

PART SIX

Before the Shattering:
The Seventeenth Millennium

—

Cassimo

1: HAWK

Hawk stepped out of the still-steaming assault pod and gazed up at the towering granite edifice at whose foot he had landed. Shaking his head at the sheer size of his forces' objective, he turned back and motioned for the soldiers behind him to climb out.

As the Iron Raptors division, resplendent in their gray and black armor, moved around him and took up their carefully-planned assault positions, the assault pods of the Sky Lords began to land. So far, so good, he thought.

"Falcon," he called over the Aether connection. "Where are you, buddy?"

"Coming in for a landing now," replied the gruff voice of the demolitions expert.

An uncomfortably short distance away, a pod crashed to the ground and its hatch popped open. The first figure to climb out was Falcon, his massive sidearm at the ready.

Hawk watched him, expecting him to immediately begin sizing up the challenge that had been presented to him by the St. Julian Fortress. He did not do this. Instead, he turned in a slow circle, taking in the entire scope of the world he had just set foot upon, seemingly appreciating the planet he was about to wreak severe havoc upon. As Hawk watched him, he realized he himself had failed to do this.

Have I become so accustomed to military campaigns on one planet after another that I no longer even spare a moment to look at the place? To see what color the sky is? What the air smells like? What the plants look like?

Hawk put these thoughts aside, promising himself he'd think more along those lines later, and jogged over to Falcon's pod.

"What've we got?" the big man asked. "I'm assuming you've already scoped things out a bit," he added, offering his friend a flat smile as armored troopers climbed out from the pod behind him.

"A little," Hawk replied. "It's a granite fortress, five hundred meters tall. Built right up out of the natural rock of this plain." He gestured around, taking the opportunity to actually pay a little attention to what it all looked like, as well as to the tactical situation. "They've got a force field surrounding the whole thing. Not just a dome where you can blast the generators from underneath, like on Rheinstadt."

Falcon nodded, and Hawk could see that he was already starting to focus more on the objective at hand, his shrewd engineer's mind doubtlessly considering ways to remove that force field from their path—as well as whatever enemy soldiers might be within it—without overly harming the fortress.

They had come here, to the distant world of Cassimo, on the very fringes of human-occupied space, in response to a frantic call from the planet's colonial office—a call that was cut off midway through.

It seemed the planet had been overrun by alien forces unknown in composition and in origin. Those aliens had somehow gotten through the defensive fields of the two main cities and occupied them without doing any visible harm, and then—even more surprisingly—had penetrated the defenses of the ancient stone fortress of St. Julian that towered above them now. Humans hadn't built St. Julian; it had been there for a very long time when the first colonial ships had arrived a few centuries earlier. They had simply elaborated upon it, transforming it from a sort of plain-looking granite hive protruding from the otherwise flat local landscape to a gothic structure of power and personality, its battlements towering over the plains. In the process, they'd also vastly increased its defensive capabilities with the most modern of technology.

It would be a tough nut to crack.

Why the legions of the Machine were there to attempt to crack it at all was a convoluted story that had more to do with the invaders—whoever they were—than with the planet itself.

Cassimo hadn't been part of any human empire long enough to have established much of a population or even to have elected or otherwise chosen a planetary governor, but it was nonetheless considered valuable in future terms by the Machine. It was also seen as something of a test of humanity's will: if Cassimo were allowed to fall to invaders without a fight, the chances that humans would defend any of the dozens of other frontier worlds along the fringe became less likely, and thus all of them would become potential targets to any nearby alien powers wishing to expand in their neighborhoods.

Failure on Cassimo, in other words, could open humanity up to a whole new wave of warfare along the edge of its expanding sphere of influence.

And so here we are, Hawk thought. *About to fight for a planet that's not really worth fighting for, against enemies unknown to us, who even now sit securely inside one of the most defensible positions in the galaxy.*

Hooray for us.

"Looks like we're going to have to do this the hard way," Falcon was saying, a 'scope held up to his two hazel eyes. Carefully he studied the texture and form of the energy field that stood between them and the fortress. Then he looked beyond to what could be seen of the granite edifice itself. "I don't see any other way."

"I was afraid you'd say that," Hawk said.

Falcon lowered the device and looked at his friend and colleague.

"I'll get the breachers set up. You ready the troops."

Hawk nodded.

"Will do."

A short time later, Falcon called over the Aether connection to report that the field-breachers were in position.

Hawk, having strapped on a lift-pack, popped the wings out and shot into the sky, taking a quick visual measure of the state of deployment of his forces. He was pleased with what he saw. To his right, rank upon rank of Iron Raptors awaited the signal to advance. To his left, the Sky Lords had finished donning their own lifters and were quickly deploying into their prearranged positions.

"All set," Hawk reported to Falcon. "Ready when you are."

Falcon's only response was to activate all three field-breachers at once.

The overcast midday of Cassimo erupted with bright blue light as the machines he had set right up against the defensive field came to life, each of them spewing out energies at a frequency and wavelength perfectly tuned to counter the field.

In each of the three spots where the breachers now operated, holes some thirty meters across opened in the enemy force field.

"Go!" shouted Hawk. "Advance!"

The Iron Raptors rushed forward as quickly as their armored bodies could allow, their first ranks moving through one of the points of entry and into enemy territory. The Sky Lords lofted into the air and zoomed through the hole nearest to them, spreading out quickly on the other side.

Bright, blinding energy weapon discharge erupted immediately, signaling that the attackers were meeting stiff resistance already.

Hawk decided to remain in his current position a little longer, so that he could see the full scope of the engagement and determine if adjustments needed to be made.

Several minutes passed and most of their forces had passed through the breaches in the field. Advancement slowed across the short expanse of plain that lay beneath the outer walls of the fortress as enemy resistance increased. Hawk was considering his options and about to contact Falcon for a report when a deep, rumbling voice came to him from below.

"I would say you have things well in hand."

Hawk started and looked down.

"I assume you're about to join the festivities yourself," the voice added.

Hawk grinned and lowered himself gently down onto the plain alongside the newcomer.

"That's where I was headed, yes," he said. "Come to join us and get your hands dirty?"

"As a matter of fact, yes," replied Eagle.

The blond-haired commander of the Machine's forces grinned back at his comrade and raised a massive quad-barrel blaster strapped to his left arm.

"And I brought party favors, too."

Hawk laughed. "Those are always welcome." He gestured toward the nearest entry hole. "After you, sir."

Eagle's grin was now almost predatory. "Thank you, good Hawk."

He took two steps forward and then froze.

Hawk, striding across the smooth and damp soil surface, realized quickly that his commander was not with him. Turning back, he saw the big man in dark blue standing still, his gaze directed upward and distant. Puzzled, Hawk started to ask if something was wrong. Then he realized the man was having a conversation—and an urgent one, no doubt—via the Aether connection.

"You coming?" Falcon called over Hawk's own connection. "The water's fine."

"One moment," Hawk replied. He was growing a bit concerned. For one thing, the conversation was going on far longer than most of Eagle's usual communications, which tended to consist of him issuing orders in direct and succinct fashion. For another, the commander's expression had darkened considerably—and Hawk didn't like to think about things that could trouble the mighty Eagle.

"Hawk? Everything okay?"

"Apologies, Falcon," Hawk transmitted. "The big guy is here. Give me another minute."

"Ah," Falcon said over the link. "Understood."

Eagle motioned then, directly at Hawk. *Go, go,* he was mouthing as he waved toward the breach. Then he gestured toward himself and silently indicated that he was tied up with something annoying but important.

Hawk nodded back and lofted into the air again, then zoomed toward the hole in the force field. He didn't envy Eagle's position as commander sometimes; having to tend to what the big man usually called "administrative details" surely took a lot of the enjoyment out of their work as Hands.

Through the breach he flew and soon had caught up with his troops as they advanced slowly against the fortress. Red and green energy blasts—not to mention old-fashioned metal slugs and artillery shells—filled the air, making navigation dangerous, so he dropped down a bit.

"Over here," Falcon called a few seconds later, indicating a location along the base of the outer walls where the firefight looked to be particularly intense. "We're in."

Hawk and the troops at his command quickly redeployed in support of Falcon's attack. They approached the smoking, jagged hole the demolitions expert had blasted in the sheer rock face of the wall. Falcon waved Hawk down.

"What've you got?" Hawk asked, peering into the smoke and not able to make out a great deal. "Who's in there?" None of the Hands had been happy with the extreme lack of intelligence provided by the locals. The message they had managed to send during the initial invasion had been truncated; either it had been cut off in mid-transmission or disrupted en route. Even now, they didn't know exactly which alien foe they were facing. "The Rao again, right?"

Falcon gave him a funny look.

"We have seen the Rao," the big man agreed, "and that's who's shooting at us now, yeah—but I don't think they're not alone in there."

Hawk frowned at this.

"The Dyonari are with them again? Like on Rheinstadt?"

Instead of replying at first, Falcon brought the 'scope up to his eyes and tried to see through the hole and the smoke.

"Yeah, I think so," he muttered noncommittally.

Hawk turned to face him full-on, now. He could tell something was disturbing the man—and anything that disturbed Falcon was probably going to disturb him, as well.

"What? Somebody else is in there, too?"

Falcon snorted, shaking his bald head.

"I think so, yeah."

"Who?"

"Not sure," Falcon said. "Just…a funny feeling."

Hawk's frown deepened. This was not like Falcon at all.

"Then what do you—"

"Alright, gentlemen," came a booming voice from behind them. "That's more than enough speculating."

"There he is," Falcon grunted, turning and offering his commander a jaunty salute. "At last."

"Glad you could join us, Agrippa," Hawk added with a smile.

"Administrative," came the quick, unhappy reply. "You know how it is."

The big blond man in dark blue strode rapidly across the churned soil, soldiers scrambling to get out of his way as he came. The big quad-blaster was still strapped to his left arm, and he looked anxious to employ it.

"Not sure who we're up against, eh?" he asked as he reached them.

Falcon shrugged.

"Some Rao, maybe a few Dyonari—maybe in their 'advisory' role again, like we've seen recently in other spots."

"But that may not be all," Hawk pointed out. "Right?"

Falcon gave his friend a quick and ugly look, as if silently upbraiding him for raising that point in front of their boss. Then he turned back to Eagle.

"Not really sure," he said with a quick shrug. "Just…a sort of strange feeling, is all."

Eagle regarded his old friend with surprise.

"Feelings?" he asked, almost laughing. "From you?"

Falcon snorted.

"That's why I'd just as soon ignore them and press on," the bald man replied. "Seeing as how I'm not really good with them to begin with."

All three men laughed.

"Fine, then," Eagle said after a moment, sobering. "Time to charge on in there and find out who we're facing the easy way."

"Or the hard way," Falcon muttered. Then, louder, "Right—let's go. Iron Raptors!" he called to the remaining soldiers in gray waiting behind them. "Advance!"

The three Hands and their support troops charged headlong into the breach.

Forty minutes and three levels up into St. Julian later, an out-of-breath Hawk had managed to fight his way back over to an equally exhausted Falcon. They held one end of a broad, open courtyard tiled with orange cobblestones. The orange stones were nearly invisible, however; a seeming ocean of dead Rao soldiers in matte green body armor littered the floor all around.

"Seven of the Firewings are down," Hawk informed his comrade, "but they say they've secured the next section ahead. If we can eliminate the rest of the resistance here—"

"I'm working on it," Falcon replied, almost angrily. "I'd like to get to the top before Eagle catches up with us again." He motioned at the nearest Iron Raptor to his left. "Get them moving, Sergeant," he barked. "The Rao are tough, but nowhere near tough enough to stop one of our advances."

The sergeant nodded and saluted, but then hesitated.

"What is it?" Falcon growled.

"I—I don't think it's the Rao up there, sir," he reported nervously. "At least, they're not fighting like Rao."

"Who are they fighting like, Sergeant?" Hawk asked, before Falcon could.

The man never got to answer.

From just ahead and to the left, a section of wall along the courtyard's edge exploded outward, sending shards of rock and concrete flying. Immediately through the resulting hole charged a veritable army.

And it wasn't the Rao.

"Are you kidding?" Falcon shouted. "What are *they* doing here?"

A wave of black surged across the open courtyard.

"Skrazzi!" Hawk shouted. "Fall back! Get into cover!"

The Iron Raptors who had advanced into the courtyard were caught flat-footed by the attack. Those near the rear did manage to turn and effect what might charitably be called a strategic realignment into cover. Those at the front had no choice but to face the nightmare horde of alien attackers and fight for their lives.

The Skrazzi, eight feet of insectoid death incarnate with their scythe-blade left arms and organic disintegrator cannon right arms, slashed their way through the Iron Raptor division with hardly a pause.

Hawk opened fire with his pistol, scarcely a pause between shots as he instinctively aimed for the most vulnerable points in the big bugs' chitinous armor covering. Beside him, Falcon too laid into the black creatures, mowing down the front of the advancing wave.

As the last of the Iron Raptors leapt over the barricades and into cover, another big shape bounded out, moving in the opposite direction—headed directly into the tide of alien warriors.

"ATTACK!"

It was Eagle, of course. His eyes were fiery; the quad-blaster on his left arm blazed away while his massive golden sword sang a song of death as it sliced into the enemy's ranks.

The Skrazzi, shocked at this unexpected turn of events, faltered in their charge.

Seeing this, the Iron Raptors rallied and surged forward, opening fire with everything they had.

Hawk and Falcon leapt from cover and attacked as well, meanwhile calling up the reserve forces from behind them. It seemed that the Battle of St. Julian was fully joined now, and might well be decided in this single engagement.

An hour later, the Iron Raptors had reached the summit of the fortress and the last of the alien defenders had been rooted out of cover.

Hawk had halted about fifty meters up the final, curving, cobblestoned pathway that led to a sort of steepled temple at the apex of the complex. He was hunched over, breathing heavily, his pistol nearly depleted. Falcon stood nearby, directing his men to check the last few possible hiding places in the ancient brown stonework around them. Eagle had continued onward and upward, to the top, driving the last of the resistance forces before him.

Then the call they had always dreaded came to them.

"Eagle is down," one of the Raptors called over the Aether connection. "Repeat—Eagle is down!"

Hawk and Falcon instantly forgot everything else and charged up the narrow street toward the temple.

When they reached the summit, they found several Raptors, their helmets removed, standing over the fallen commander. A medic knelt beside him, administering something with an injector.

"What happened to him?" Hawk demanded, shoving through the ring of Raptors.

Falcon moved in quickly beside him and knelt, relieved at once to see the blond man was alive and awake.

"Ran into someone—something—unexpected, boys," Eagle managed to say.

They looked down from his face to his muscled torso and saw the wound then, to his lower chest. It wasn't pretty.

"I'll be alright," the blond man added weakly. "You should see the other guys."

"What did this?" Hawk asked, astonished that anything could ever harm their seemingly invincible commander.

A Raptor trooper caught Hawk's attention and motioned to the side. Two alien creatures lay there. Hawk and Falcon both stood and frowned at what they saw.

One was a Dyonari, resplendent in blue glass-like armor but also apparently dead. A long, golden spear that still shimmered with unearthly energies lay just beyond the strange being's fingertips.

"I knew it," Falcon breathed. "The Dyonari again." He cursed.

To the Dyonari's right, in a black heap, was a second alien—one that both Hawk and Falcon had first taken to be a Skrazzi. But, as they moved closer and inspected more carefully, they realized it was nothing like a Skrazzi. This other creature was swathed in black robes of some strange, roughly textured material—but, beneath the cloth, the creature was a strange and eerie conglomeration of pale organic and silvery-gray mechanical parts. In place of its head, a distorted metal skull-face leered at them.

"What is that thing, sir?" the nearest Iron Raptor asked Hawk.

"By the great Machine," Hawk could only gasp.

"You have to be kidding," Falcon added.

Hawk realized with a start that the ground all around them was covered in a thin and melting layer of ice.

"It's the stinking Phaedrons," Falcon was saying, practically spitting the word. "What's one of *them* doing here?"

"They're psychics," Hawk added, his mouth twisting in distaste. He gazed over at Falcon. "There's the source of your 'bad feelings,' I think. Psychic residue from this guy."

Falcon nodded slowly.

"I'll bet you're right. He was probably blanketing the whole fortress with a wave of fear, to cause us to hesitate—to fight scared."

They both moved back over to Eagle, who was being moved onto a floating stretcher unit.

"I'll be back in form in no time, gentlemen," the commander told them with as much of a smile as he could generate. "In the meantime, you need to wrap things up here and get our forces back up into orbit, quickly."

"What's happening?" Hawk asked. "Where do we have to be?"

"That's what all the chatter was, at the start of the battle. I received a message from the Machine. We're ordered to the planet Scandana at once." He grunted as the stretcher unit lifted him up into the air and hovered there while the medic adjusted various controls on a side panel. "It seems that Lord Merlion may be a traitor—a serious traitor. We've been ordered to capture him—or eliminate him altogether. And anyone else there who gets in our way."

Hawk's eyes widened. That wasn't the typical order the Machine sent them. Far from it.

"Whatever the guy's doing must be pretty serious," Falcon said then, obviously thinking thoughts similar to Hawk's.

Eagle shrugged—an action that caused him to wince in pain.

"Not sure," he said. "We'll discuss it further back aboard the *Talon*."

Hawk and Falcon nodded and the medic led the floating stretcher bearing Eagle away down the winding roadway. A shuttle was already swooping down to pick them up.

"I'll tidy up here," Falcon told Hawk as they watched Eagle's stretcher disappear around the curve. "You get the pick-up site organized."

"Will do," Hawk said. Then, as Falcon strode purposefully away and began to bark new orders to the men, Hawk paused. He thought he'd heard a sound from behind him. He turned and saw to some surprise that the Dyonari warrior was not entirely dead—it was raising its long, narrow head and looking at him.

"Human," came a croaking sound that was all that remained of its voice.

Hawk approached carefully. He knelt down beside the alien.

"What?"

"Your time…is nearly done," it breathed.

"Yeah, yeah—I've heard that from every other alien in the galaxy. Don't really need to hear it from you."

"Not an opinion," the creature stated firmly in its weak voice. "A fact. A new power has come to this galaxy. Its victory is at hand."

"A new power," Hawk repeated. "Right. And who might that be?"

The Dyonari inhaled and exhaled slowly; its breathing was extremely ragged and blue-green fluid ran from the corners of its mouth.

"One… who can *unify*… unify *all* of us," it said. "Unify…all life…in this galaxy."

"And who might that be?" Hawk asked, finding none of this remotely believable.

"One...who is...from... *outside*."

"Outside?" Hawk frowned down at the dying alien. "Outside of what? The galaxy?"

"The universe," the Dyonari replied.

Hawk could only frown at that.

"The walls...of this reality... have grown thin in places," the Dyonari continued, its voice very faint now. "He has come through... from *beyond*."

"And just who is 'he?'"

"He is the master," the Dyonari said, its voice almost inaudible now. "And he will be your adversary. He brings a new order to this galaxy. An order that is *beautiful*..." The voice faded out there at the end. Then it surged back, stronger, as much a coughing fit as a set of words—though Hawk could make out what it was saying clearly enough.

"...and *terrible*."

The alien's head slumped to the side.

Hawk stood. He had no idea what to make of this.

He looked around and saw Falcon gazing back at him, puzzled.

"Was that guy still alive?" the bald man called to him.

"For a few seconds, yeah," Hawk answered.

"What did he say? Anything interesting?"

Hawk hesitated.

"Maybe. We can talk about it later."

Falcon looked at him strangely.

"Okay, then," he said. "That's fine."

Falcon turned back to the men.

"Hey," Hawk called back to him.

"Yeah?" Falcon answered, looking back again. "What?"

Hawk frowned. He looked around at the dead enemy bodies all around—at Skrazzi and Rao and even a Dyonari and a Phaedron. All here together.

He thought about the word the dying Dyonari had used. He whispered it.

"Unified."

"What?" Falcon repeated.

"Nothing," Hawk called back, waving him off. "Later."

Falcon snorted and went back to work.

Deeply troubled now, Hawk slowly made his way back down the slope. As he went, he saw the shuttles from the *Talon* swooping down to pick them up. He increased his pace.

No time to worry about aliens and their strange and inexplicable activities now, he told himself. There's too much to be done.

Even so, a very disturbing series of thoughts now wormed their way through his mind, and he wouldn't sleep well again from that moment until their arrival in orbit around Scandana.

Awake.

Hawk sat up in the uncomfortable bed that had been prepared for him by Condor's troops and looked around, remembering where he was. And who he was.

Not the man whose memories I just recalled, he told himself. *That was a different person. A different Hawk. Not me.*

The door chimed again, and he realized that was what had woken him up.

"Sir?" came a voice over a hidden speaker. "Your presence is requested for dinner."

Hawk climbed out of bed and rubbed at his eyes, then crossed the room and signaled for the door to open. The gray panel slid aside to reveal half a dozen soldiers in uniforms the same shade of brown as Condor's uniform.

Hawk took in the sight of the armed men and frowned.

"I don't suppose," he asked them, "I have time for a quick shower, maybe?"

PART SEVEN

After the Shattering:
The Nineteenth Millennium

1: FALCON

The buzzing sound wormed its way into Falcon's head and pulled him out of a most enjoyable dream. He had driven the bad guys out of the village and saved the people from a hideous alien invasion force, and the maidens of the town were about to reward him with their ample—

Oh, come on!

He sat up, eyes open, the buzzing sound echoing within his little room.

"Alright, alright—I'm awake," he shouted, and the buzzing ceased.

Climbing to his feet, he shuffled into the washroom and remained there an inordinately long time, enjoying the shower and other amenities he'd had to do without for some time now.

At last a knocking at the outer door reached him and he switched off the water. Stepping out into the room, he pulled his red and blue uniform on—it instantly sloughed the water away from his skin, filtered it, and absorbed it into hidden reservoirs for possible later use. Then he motioned and the door slid open.

Outside stood Hawk—cleaned and pressed, too, it appeared— accompanied by a half-dozen of Condor's brown-suited soldiers.

Falcon raised one eyebrow at this sight. "Yeah?"

"Time for dinner," the other Hand told him. "Condor beckons us."

Falcon shrugged. "Lead on, then."

They made their way along endless corridors of dull gray, occasionally streaked with discoloration. Odd smells wafted through the air. In some areas, the lights flickered or didn't work at all. Their boots encountered grainy deposits here and there, punctuated by sticky spots.

"This vessel isn't in the best of shape, to put it mildly," Hawk said to the nearest soldier. "How long have you occupied it?"

The man looked at him as they all walked and appeared to consider answering, but then turned his head back to the front as if he hadn't heard the question.

"We are Hands of the Machine!" growled Falcon in a slightly loud and very gruff voice. "You will answer him!"

The soldier looked back at them again, and this time his face revealed severe conflict and consternation. Before Falcon could say anything further, however, the man replied in a shaky voice, "Nearly three years, Lord Hawk."

The two Hands exchanged knowing glances: This supposed Condor had allowed his ship to remain in such a state for *that* long? A proper Condor, Falcon knew, would have had the entire place scrubbed down so that even the rust spots shone within a week.

And even beyond that, the soldiers themselves scarcely appeared to Falcon as proper servants of a Hand—certainly not a high-ranking Hand like Condor. Their uniforms were nice and fancy, sure; but one had but to look only a tiny way below the surface to realize they were nothing more than dressed-up mercenaries and pirates.

But he looks *like a Condor, right?* Hawk managed to convey via the subtle movement code. *You said we're each made from the same template, over and over—so does this Condor physically look like the others—like he came from that template, that genetic sample?*

For the most part, Falcon replied. *But there are little things. Things I didn't notice at first, but which stand out now.*

At last they reached a broad, tall set of double-doors and, passing through, emerged into another long, high-ceilinged room. A long table filled the center and, at the far end, Condor stood from an ornate chair as they approached.

"My new friends," he greeted them as they were shown around the table to their places, on Condor's either hand. "Fate has brought us together at this critical juncture, and I embrace you, my brothers, with open arms." He raised a glass of something—wine, Falcon wondered? And then servants approached with full glasses for the two Hands.

"A toast," Condor went on, "to our successful alliance!"

Hawk and Falcon glanced at one another, took the glasses, and all three of them drank.

"By 'critical juncture,'" Hawk said then, "I take it you mean the return of the Adversary."

Condor looked at him, a touch of confusion momentarily flickering across his features. He blinked and pursed his thin, bloodless lips.

"The Adversary. Yes, of course," the blond man said after a moment. "Yes, in part. That is certainly something that we must look into." He smiled then. "But it is not the only situation that demands our attention."

Falcon contained a laugh. The guy clearly had no idea that the Adversary had returned—not until Hawk mentioned it. He started to communicate that to Hawk, then thought better of it and remained still, holding his half-empty glass and waiting.

Condor gestured at them. "Please, have a seat, gentlemen. We will eat, and then I will lay out for you my vision of the galaxy that is to come."

This ought to be good, Falcon thought, settling into an ornately-carved wooden chair. He glanced over and saw that Hawk looked as if he was about to say something else, but then stopped himself. *He's learning quickly,* Falcon thought. *Especially when to keep his mouth shut. Maybe the kid's not a complete impediment.*

Several courses were served, and Falcon was certain that he could identify only a small percentage of what he ate—but he didn't let that stop him. He hadn't eaten very well in a long time;

wandering across mostly Medieval-tech worlds was not a lifestyle that lent itself to fine dining.

As the last few of the plates were carried away, Condor favored them with another smile—a particularly reptilian smile, to Falcon's thinking—and laid his hands flat on the table surface.

"And now," he said, "I'm sure you would both like to know more about what I have in mind."

"You mean other than absolute loyalty and obedience to the Machine?" Hawk asked—and as he did so, Falcon glanced over at him, only to see a sort of mischief dancing in the man's eyes.

Okay, Falcon thought. *He knows what he's doing now. That was deliberate.*

Condor frowned at Hawk.

Hawk returned the look with an expression of utter innocence.

Condor's face darkened. A chill seemed to fill the room.

"Why this pretense?" the blond man asked finally, breaking the tension. "You are both aware by now that the Machine exerts no hold over me."

Falcon snorted. "I'm beginning to wonder if there's anyone left in the galaxy that cares about it, or even remembers it," he muttered. "Aside from some very misguided inquisitors."

"The answer to that might well be, 'No,'" Condor snapped. "As you two surely know very well, whatever peace exists today in this shattered galaxy is not enforced by some ancient computer mind. It's enforced by people like you and me—free agents—those with the power to make a difference, and the willingness to *use* that power."

"I've been from one side of the galaxy to the other in the last thousand years, and I haven't found much peace anywhere," Falcon commented.

"Precisely," Condor stated.

"Wait. Free agents?" Hawk asked, leaning forward. "You see us as free agents?"

Condor smiled thinly. "Let us be candid with one another," he said, sitting back, his blue eyes flickering from one of them to the other. He spread his hands wide. "Loyalty to the Machine was a fine thing, during the days it was reciprocated. But now—now it's silent, perhaps dead and gone, and new forces must emerge to replace it. To fill the power vacuum." He smiled.

"You're saying you feel no loyalty to the Machine any longer?" Hawk asked.

"As if you two do," Condor replied.

Hawk and Falcon both frowned, then glanced at one another.

"Oh, come now, gentlemen," Condor said with a sly smile. "I understand what you are doing here—feeling me out, testing my reactions, my loyalties—making it seem as if you two are loyal soldiers and *I* might be some sort of rebel. But you have no secrets from me." His gaze shifted from one of them to the other. "You cannot imagine that I did not have surveillance cameras in your quarters, or that I do not understand the secret movement code you have been employing."

Hawk looked to Falcon again, concerned.

Falcon shrugged.

"I suspected you'd see us," the cyborg casually stated, "and figure out what we were saying."

"You did?" Hawk asked, still somewhat wide-eyed.

"Sure. But I knew by then that Condor was a free agent, and wouldn't be turning us in, any more than we would him. None of us feels any particular loyalty to the Machine—if it even exists anymore."

Condor's smile widened.

"Ah, wonderful. So we are, all three of us, free agents. And that gives me hope—hope that the three of us may yet salvage this relationship, and indeed make it into a profitable one for us all." He spread his hands. "Being free, we are free to work together—to work for interests other than those laid down so very long ago by the Machine."

"Which interests would those be?" Hawk asked, still trying to get a handle on the situation.

"He means our own interests, of course," answered Falcon.

"Precisely," said Condor.

Hawk took this in, his dark eyes moving from Condor to Falcon.

Condor watched him closely for a few moments as silence reigned. Then he turned toward Falcon.

"I have to confess," he said, "I wonder about your friend—about this Hawk."

"Why is that?" asked the cyborg.

"He seems to lack a certain...*enthusiasm*."

Hawk stared back at Condor, still saying nothing.

"Hawk is fine," Falcon said. "Not a problem at all. Don't concern yourself."

Condor turned back to stare at Hawk while continuing. "Are we certain his loyalties no longer lie with any other organization—or entity?"

Falcon scoffed. "Hawk can't even *remember* the Machine, much less be compelled by any leftover programming from it."

Condor nodded, then looked back sharply at Falcon.

"What about you?"

Falcon waved a dismissive hand.

"Oh, I remember it very well." He rubbed at his chin. "But like I said a minute ago, I've crossed the galaxy and back, and never once in all that time did I hear a peep from our old lord and master, the Machine."

Condor continued to stare at him for a few moments, then nodded. "Very well. The two of you only confirm what I have long suspected: that the Machine's power and influence are virtually nil. Even if it still exists, it cannot control its main servants, the Hands, any longer. Thus we are free to do for ourselves, as we please."

He raised his right hand, palm upward.

"And free to modify ourselves—to find new realms and reserves of power."

Suddenly rays of colorful light emerged from his hand as if shining directly up through the skin itself. The light grew in intensity, filling the room, becoming blinding, and shifting through all the colors of the spectrum before fading to nothingness.

Condor lowered his hand. He looked at the other two as if expecting them to fall over in amazement.

Falcon stifled a yawn, though he definitely took note of what he had just seen, and filed the information away for future reference.

Hawk continued to look on in silence.

Exhaling slowly, Condor appeared to accept that his demonstration had had little effect on the others. He sat back, regarding them through narrowed eyes.

"That all sounds well and good," Hawk said, speaking up at last. "But there's one big problem."

"What do you mean?" Condor asked.

"The Adversary has returned."

Condor's eyes widened slightly. "You were serious about that?"

"Very much so," Hawk answered.

Condor considered this for a few moments.

"I cannot see how that is a concern of ours," he said at length. "Even if it is true—even if the great Adversary has returned with his hordes of warriors—we three cannot begin to hold back such an assault."

"Not just the three of us," Hawk agreed. "But with the Machine on our side—"

"The Machine?" Condor all-but-shouted. "I thought we just agreed it's asleep—or dead. Or whatever giant computer brains do when they wear out."

"Then maybe we will have to wake it up, or fix it."

"Whoa—wait a minute," Condor said, his hand slicing through the air in front of him. "What exactly are you saying here?"

"I'm saying that we will *need* the Machine," Hawk replied, "and we will need it back at its full strength, functioning properly, coordinating attacks and defenses and creating new soldiers and ships and weapons."

Condor was still staring at him blankly, as if not remotely comprehending what he was talking about.

"I told you," Hawk continued, urgency creeping into his voice. "The Adversary has returned. You just saw one of their ships— fought it—saw how tough they are to kill. We have to prepare. Every resource must be marshaled."

Falcon eyed his comrade with curiosity. He'd heard Hawk's tale about the black, insect-like creatures he'd fought upon awakening, but somehow it hadn't seemed entirely real. This

Condor, on the other hand—he was quite real, and quite dangerous. And Falcon could reach right out and touch him if he wanted to. This, to Falcon's way of thinking, made Condor the more immediate threat—and thus that was where he was directing most of his concern and his attention.

Condor's puzzled look slowly transformed into a smile. He regarded Hawk with what looked to be barely-veiled contempt and condescension. "This is a big galaxy, my friend," he said. "You say that the single warship we encountered earlier had some connection to the old Enemy. While this is good intelligence to have—if it proves true—and I appreciate you giving it to me..." He shrugged. "I find it difficult to believe that this foe represents such a clear and present threat to—"

An alarm had begun to blare throughout the ship. Condor frowned and turned to one of his aides, demanding to know what the trouble was.

"A squadron of spacecraft approaching fast," the brown-uniformed woman replied, after listening to a voice over her earpiece.

"Who are they?"

"Unknown as of yet. But they are taking an attack vector in approach."

Condor at first appeared concerned, but then he looked back at Hawk and Falcon and his old, arrogant smile flashed across his face.

"Gentlemen! Perhaps now you will have the opportunity to witness the effectiveness of my flagship's weapons and defenses firsthand."

He stood, followed by the other two, and issued quick orders to the nearest crewman to take the food away and save it for later. Then he led the two Hands out of the dining hall and back along a series of twists and turns until they emerged onto the ship's bridge.

The holographic display hovered in midair just ahead of them as they walked out onto the circular command platform. Condor cast only a quick glance at it before turning to the nearest officer.

"Situation?" he demanded.

"Pretty obvious," Falcon observed, staring at the tactical hologram. "Four ships approaching fast."

"Their weapons are active, according to our sensors," the officer told Condor.

"Who are they?" asked Hawk.

"Dead is who they're about to be," Condor snapped.

"Configuration unknown," the officer stated, "but they're very similar to the ship we destroyed that was attacking these Hands."

Now they were close enough for a long-range visual image: conical in shape, they streaked through space; their splotchy black hulls, streaked in red, were jagged along the surface as if covered in horn or bone, with an ugly, organic look that somehow sent chills up the spine.

"You want to tell me those aren't the same guys we just fought?" Falcon demanded of their host.

Condor appeared troubled but said nothing.

"Hawk was right," Falcon continued. "The ancient enemy is back. I know those ships from my implanted memories of the Shattering. They belong to one of the major races that served the Adversary."

Condor still didn't move or say anything, and the other two Hands glanced at one another, growing concerned. Finally, the blond man turned back to them, his easy bravado reasserting itself. "Perfect," he said. "Then I will be making Hawk quite happy by destroying them."

The two Hands stood aside as Condor assumed the central position on the raised dais and barked out orders to his crew. In response, the big ship's weapons opened fire. From their positions, Hawk and Falcon could see blazing blasts of red and green energy streaking away into the void.

A few seconds later, and confirming what they had all seen with their own eyes through the ports and via the holo display, an officer informed them, "No hits, sir. All four ships are unharmed."

"How can that be?" Condor demanded, scowling.

"Shielding, deflection, stealth tech—who knows?" Falcon said. "The point is, you're going to have to do better if you're going to take them out. Otherwise…"

Condor shook his head in annoyance and turned back to the display. Even as he did so, the first two ships shot past, their own weapons striking Condor's ship's hull with resounding force. The artificial gravity clicked off for an instant and everyone floated an inch or so above the deck before it switched back on and yanked them back down; two technicians tumbled awkwardly across the floor.

"Divert power to our defenses," Condor demanded. "Now!"

The second of the two pairs of attackers streaked by, weapons blazing. Again the gravity flickered—this time for several seconds.

"Defensive screens are holding," one technician shouted over the din of explosions and the jumble of status reports echoing from the internal communications system. "But just barely. And we're losing gravity."

"I think we already figured that out," Falcon observed, hooking one foot around a slender column to brace himself in case it happened again.

"They're coming around for another pass," the tactical officer reported loudly.

"Fire everything we have as they approach," Condor ordered. "Blasters, missiles, mines—everything!"

All along the scorched and pitted hull of Condor's ship, weapons pods popped out from their housings. Blast-cannons extended. Racks of rockets slid out.

The attacking ships drew closer, preparing to fire.

Condor's ship unleashed everything from its mighty arsenal.

The light from the viewports washed across the Hands and the crew, nearly blinding them all despite the massive filters in place. The holo display crackled and disappeared for a few seconds.

When the brightness faded and something approaching normal vision returned, they all looked out and saw two of the ships shooting past, very close. Both were clearly dead now—burnt-out cinders retaining the massive velocity they'd had before.

They whizzed past Condor's big cylinder of a ship, moving purely on momentum, and disappeared into the blackness.

"What about the other two?" Condor demanded of his tactical officer and techs.

Before anyone could answer, two more black cones tumbled by, also clearly dead.

Condor hesitated for a moment, then turned and regarded his two visitors. His arrogant grin was much diminished, but he still preserved a bit of his bravado.

"There—you see?" He waved toward the viewports with one hand. "Gone!"

"What's left of the ship's weapons?" Falcon asked the officer who stood nearby, ignoring Condor.

The officer cast a nervous glance at his commander, who frowned but nodded.

"Blast-cannons at one-third power. Missiles and mines completely depleted."

Falcon and Condor eyed one another.

"Our first priority," Hawk stated as he stepped somewhat between the other two, "must be to repair and replenish this vessel's weapons. Because I very much doubt that was all—"

Before he could complete his sentence, Hawk was interrupted by the tactical officer.

"Another contact, sir," he called to Condor, who seemed in reaction to deflate a little.

"How many?" the blond man asked, almost wearily.

"…Just one, for now."

Condor brightened. "Same kind of ship?"

"Affirmative. But not in an attack vector."

Condor frowned. Somehow that was even more disturbing. "What's it doing?"

"Signal coming in," the communications officer reported. "Universal translation code."

All three of them looked to the comm station expectantly.

"They're requesting a truce," the woman at that station reported. "A parley."

Condor looked at Hawk and Falcon, puzzled.

"Is that—that doesn't seem right," he said.

"No," Falcon replied.

"Wait," Condor said then. "Of course." He laughed. "This must be their flight leader. He probably held back from the attack and now, with his squadron gone, he's scared. Maybe his ship was damaged in the fight. He can't get back home. Wants to discuss terms of surrender."

"What is the pilot saying?" Hawk asked the comm tech.

"…Nothing."

Condor grinned.

"Then allow him aboard."

"That's a mistake," Falcon growled.

"I tend to agree," Hawk said. "We don't know—"

"We know all we need to know," Condor said. "The guy wants to come aboard, and we need to know more about them." He laughed again. "And perhaps we can take his ship apart while he's here—learn a few things about how they evaded our first strike, and so on."

Condor would not be dissuaded, and so the little ship passed into the same docking bay where Hawk's ship rested. After it had settled to the deck and the atmosphere had been pumped in, a circular hatch formed on the side.

Hawk nodded as he watched on the display. "Same as the creatures I fought," he said, seeing the alien that emerged. Tall, black, hideous, and insect-like—there was no mistaking them.

"I would not allow it any further inside the ship," Falcon advised, the human portion of his face creased with concern.

Condor gestured to one of his nearby techs. "Have you scanned that ship? The pilot? Any weapons?"

"Nothing, sir," the tech replied.

"Nothing you can *detect*," Hawk stated. "But I've fought them—one on one." He jabbed a finger at the creature on the display. "They have biologically-engineered weapons. For instance," and he pointed at the creature's cylindrical-shaped left arm, "that thing is a disintegrator cannon."

Condor reacted with a start. He grabbed the intercom microphone and clicked the link open.

"No weapons beyond that point," he called down to the creature. "You'll have to stop right there and disarm. We will—"

What happened next astonished and somewhat sickened all of them. The insect creature stopped and stood unmoving on its rear two legs for several moments. Then it reached up with its long, deadly, curved-blade right arm and brought it down with a savage blow against its left, severing the limb just above the elbow.

The disintegrator-weapon arm dropped to the deck in a growing pool of ichor.

"That," Condor observed when he could speak again, "was... something."

"That's one word for it, I suppose," Falcon growled. "Definitely took the word 'disarm' literally."

"Its weapon is its arm," Hawk pointed out again. "That was the only way for it to 'disarm.'"

"It must truly want to parley with us if it was willing to do that," Condor said, staring at the creature on the display.

Falcon half-shrugged. "It was stupid. Or..." His voice trailed off as he seemed to be considering something.

"You're not going to let it out of the docking bay now, are you?" Hawk asked, keeping his eyes on the creature.

Condor considered that.

"It does still have the cutting arm," he noted, before drawing his twin pistols from their holsters. "But I have these. And I know you two gentlemen are surely more than prepared for—"

"It's moving again," Hawk pointed out.

The creature was nearing the doors leading out of the hangar deck.

"Stop," Condor called over the intercom.

It did not stop. It reached out gestured with its cutting arm and the doors opened.

"How did it do that?" Condor said aloud, mystified.

"Biological tech," Falcon explained. "It can't easily be identified by mechanical scanners, because until it's used, it looks like some sort of normal organ or physical process."

The creature was shuffling along one of the corridors now. Condor ordered his men to fall back while he considered what to do.

"It really has me curious now," he told the others. "I want to dissect it—and its ship."

But before the conversation could continue further, the creature apparently arrived at the location it was aiming for. It stopped in the corridor and leaned over, and dark fluids spilled out from the stump of its left arm. They formed a steadily growing puddle on the deck.

"Oh, that's disgusting," Condor said, watching.

"We have to evacuate," Falcon growled.

"What?"

Hawk nodded. "Yeah, I think he's right. I have a bad feeling."

Condor scoffed and stepped quickly down from the command dais. He strode across the bridge and through the doors, the other two Hands on his trail.

"Not a good idea," Hawk called after him as they went. Falcon said nothing, but his unhappiness was palpable.

They hurried along the winding corridors of the ship until, rounding a turn, they could see the alien creature perhaps twenty yards away. The pool of fluid surrounding it was quite large now. They halted.

"What are you doing?" Condor called out. "You wanted a parley, and I granted it."

The creature looked up at them, its clusters of red eyes blazing clear hate.

"We need to evacuate," Falcon said again, quietly but forcefully. "Now."

Condor ignored him, still staring at the creature. "Have you nothing to say to us, after all this?"

It emitted a hissing sound, then slumped lower to the deck. The fluids mostly formed a circular pool beneath it now, but traces were trickling away. One long trail ran almost to the Hands where they stood. Falcon stooped and sniffed at it. He nodded.

"You—your kind—infest our universe," the creature managed to vocalize in somewhat recognizable words. *"You... must be... cleansed."*

"Condor," Falcon all-but-shouted, grabbing the tall man by one arm and yanking him around furiously, "these chemicals are combining to form an explosive. They're going to blow!"

To his credit, Condor only stared dumbly at Falcon for a split second before the light came on in his eyes.

"When?" he demanded.

"Any second!"

Condor raised both hands, arms stretched out to each side. Lights flared all around, at first clear and bright, then swirling into many colors. The swirl of colors moved away from Condor and passed down the corridor until reaching the alien. There they halted, surrounding the insect creature.

"How are you doing that?" Hawk asked, watching in fascination. "What *is* that?"

"I'm manipulating quantum threads," Condor replied. "Perhaps I'll explain it in detail later. If we live," he added.

The swirling sphere of light changed quickly to an almost solid sphere, green in color, opaque.

"Will that be enough to hold it?" Hawk asked, bracing himself.

"You'll be one of the first to know," Falcon replied.

Condor leaned forward, arms extended, concentrating on solidifying the sphere.

With a muffled but very loud sound, the chemicals detonated.

The sphere changed instantly from green to red to deep purple. But it held—barely.

The shock threw the Hands to the floor, causing Condor to lose control of the sphere. He managed to prevent it from disintegrating first on the side facing them, but this effectively converted it into a shaped charge that blasted through the deck with horrendous force.

The ship shuddered. More explosions followed rapidly, even as the Hands sought to rise.

"Major damage to all systems," a technician reported over Condor's comm link. And then, before anyone could respond, the tactical officer's voice cut in. "More ships approaching! Same type, but…"

"What?" Condor demanded, on his feet again, ears ringing.

"There are dozens of them, sir!"

Hawk faced Condor, eyes intense. "We have to abandon ship now."

Condor looked away, but he was nodding.

"Hawk's ship is in the hangar," Falcon pointed out. "It will hold perhaps a dozen, at least for a short time."

"No," Condor said. "I don't trust it to keep me—us—alive against a whole fleet of those things."

Hawk looked at him in puzzlement.

"Well, unless you have another magic trick you can pull out…"

"Actually, I do," Condor told them. Some of his self-assurance crept back into his demeanor. "You wanted to learn more about my new weapon? I believe the time has come to show you." He motioned back down the corridor. "This way."

"A weapon?" Hawk called after him, following along behind Falcon. "We need more than a weapon! We need a way out of here!"

"Exactly," Condor replied.

They emerged into a broad, high-ceilinged room, one side of which was nearly filled with a very unusual collection of machinery. None of the pieces, ranging in size from smaller than Hawk's pistol to almost as large as Hawk's ship, seemed to match one another. It was as if they had been gathered from all over the galaxy, from dozens of different civilizations. Neither Hawk nor Falcon had a chance to study any of it very closely, however, because Condor had apparently already activated one of the larger modules by remote and now a bright swirl of light was forming in the center of the room.

Hawk hesitated a moment, reached down and drew out a small communications device. He opened a link to his ship.

"Get out of here now," he ordered it. "Get to safety if you can. I will track you down if and when I am able."

The ship started to argue but Hawk stifled it. "I'll be okay. It seems I'm leaving via an alternate route," he reassured it.

The swirl of light brightened and almost solidified. Now it formed a disk perhaps a dozen feet high and across.

The ship shook violently. Various members of the crew, at Condor's command, had abandoned their posts and were lining up outside the door.

"This way, gentlemen," Condor stated grandly, gesturing toward the swirling disk of light. "Greater wonders await you."

"I'll settle for just staying alive a bit longer," Falcon replied.

Hawk reached out and stopped Condor. "Before we go through, and just in case this… whatever it is… doesn't work— tell us the truth. You're not actually a Condor, are you? You were never a Hand."

The blond man glared at him angrily for a split-second, but then he softened and actually laughed softly.

"You're correct," he told Hawk. "I was never a Hand." He gestured around them. "I did all of this myself, with no help from any all-powerful computer mind to support me. But," he added, "Ask yourselves this question: Without the Machine behind *you* now, are you two any different?"

Then, with a smile and a wink, he stepped through and vanished.

The ship shook again, roughly. They could all tell it was about to come apart.

Eyeing the brown-clad crewmembers, Falcon leaned in close.

"The man makes a valid point—you know?"

Hawk's face was lined deeply. He shook his head. "I don't know if it means we should trust him more—or less." He looked up and met Falcon's eyes. "Not to mention what it says about us, and why we're here now."

Falcon snorted and, grasping Hawk by the shoulders, spun him around to face the shimmering disk. "That's an easy one, my friend," he chuckled. "We're *not* here now!"

Falcon propelled Hawk through the portal, then followed him into the circle of light.

The last member of Condor's crew made it through just before the ship exploded.

2: RAVEN

They were taking no chances with her.

Raven had awoken from the knockout gas attack to find herself bound almost mummy-like, covered neck-to-toe in broad, flat bands that held her completely immobile. She lay on her side on the floor, staring across the room she now occupied and taking in every detail, even as she probed the ropes as best she could for any weaknesses.

From her odd vantage she could tell very little; only that she was in a very large room with white plastic-looking walls and high ceilings. The translucent, glowing panels that comprised the ceiling over her were something on the order of thirty meters up. Banks of unfamiliar equipment ran along the sides of the room all around. It was all sort of eerie in appearance; half-melted and with shimmering lights beneath the surface. A quick rummaging through the stored memories of her previous lives confirmed it—the equipment looked like nothing she had ever encountered before.

Some time earlier, a cluster of troopers had entered the room, green-clad Shrike leading the way. She had conducted a brief conversation with someone via holo display, but the angle had been wrong for Raven to see who she was speaking with. Whoever it was, they held enough authority to cause Shrike to speak to them in respectful tones, if somewhat unhappy ones.

"...my decision that it was the safe thing to do. Clearly it was a Hand's ship and therefore represented a threat. And since she would have found us anyway—"

A man's voice coming through a speaker had interrupted her.

"You could have simply blasted her ship when you first identified it."

"I thought another Hand might prove valuable, if it could be turned."

"A Raven? You seriously thought to sway a Raven to our side?"

The slender blonde woman had emitted a miniscule sigh of frustration.

"I did not know she was a Raven until she came out of the ship."

A pause, then, "Very well. We will speak more of this soon. We will be coming through after dinner."

The monitor had gone black and Shrike had all but stomped out, her retinue of guards hurrying to keep up.

And that was how things had stood for the last hour or more, while Raven lay seemingly forgotten.

Finally Shrike reappeared in the doorway. She walked over and stared down at Raven, several of her soldiers behind her.

"I'm sorry for your rather uncomfortable condition," the woman in green said. "But of course everyone knows, or should know, how dangerous a Raven can be. So we have to be very careful."

"Who are you people?" Raven asked. "Why are you pretending to be a Hand?"

"Pretending?" She frowned, looking away for a moment, and seemed to deflate a little. Then, "I don't think of it that way," she said, more to herself than to Raven. "I suppose it depends on how one defines a Hand." Regaining some of her forcefulness, she strode confidently, almost majestically around Raven's incapacitated form. "I have all the abilities, all the talents of a Shrike. In effect, I *am* a Hand."

Raven scoffed.

"Just not a Hand of your *Machine*," Shrike continued. "I am free to do as I wish."

"Free? That's not how it sounded a little while ago," Raven pointed out. "It sounded like you have a boss every bit as dictatorial—every bit as in control of you—as the Machine would be."

Shrike frowned at that. "I have *chosen* the path I follow now," she said. "Unlike *you*."

"I serve the greater good of all life in the galaxy," Raven shot back. "Whom do *you* serve?"

Shrike's frown deepened.

"I've done my best to keep you alive thus far," she barked. "You should show me some gratitude."

"Release me and you may experience my gratitude in full."

Shrike emitted a sound full of frustration and anger. She backed away, hands on her hips, glaring at Raven.

For her part, Raven cursed inwardly at her own mistake. The woman had nearly gotten close enough... and then Raven had pushed her too far. A foolish mistake, unbecoming of her role.

After a couple of seconds, Raven spoke again, this time softening her tone somewhat.

"If what you are doing is in any way beneficial to the greater good, then perhaps we need not be antagonists," she said. "Leaving aside your status as a Hand—which is, in any case, not for me to judge."

The woman who claimed to be a Shrike looked back down at her. The lines on her face eased a bit.

"What are you saying?"

"I am saying there *could* be room for cooperation between us, if you would but share with me your plans so that I might determine if I could support them."

The tall, blonde woman moved a few steps closer, and her expression now morphed to ambivalence bordering on hopefulness—further proof to Raven that this woman was no true Hand. She continued to eye Raven, weighing the odds.

"I am sorry I allowed my initial reaction to your identity to poison our relationship at the start," Raven added, hoping she wasn't now pushing too far in the other direction.

"Lopping off the arms and heads of my soldiers didn't help," Shrike stated after a few moments.

"Perhaps I went a bit far with that." Raven attempted to look chagrined.

Shrike was almost, almost close enough now. Raven bent her tongue around, probing the rear of her mouth, finding the right tooth...

"Well, now. Should I trust this sudden new spirit of cooperation from you?" Shrike asked. "I don't know."

Raven nearly had the artificial tooth worked loose now. Meanwhile, her right hand had found the tiny stiletto blade hidden in the cuff of her sleeve and managed by the hardest to draw it out.

Shrike took one more step toward her. Raven had the tooth loose, ready.

A sudden shrill noise blasted through the chamber.

Shrike whirled, moving away quickly.

Raven cursed. *So close!*

Then someone from behind her grasped her by the hair and pulled her head up. A hand reached around and applied a large piece of tape across her mouth.

She fumed now. But at least she had the blade loose.

As the others hurried away, Raven managed to lean up enough to see where they were going. She could just see at the far end of the big, white-walled room a particular concentration of the very alien-looking equipment in a sort of geometric configuration: two big pieces of...*something*...covered in wires and crystal circuitry sat on the floor, while two identical pieces depended from the ceiling. The distance between each piece appeared to be the same, forming the four corners of a square.

As Raven looked on, the four pieces of equipment began to glow and shimmer with eerie green light. After a few seconds of this, the empty space at the exact center of the square also shimmered and wavered, like the visual heat effect just above the ground in a desert.

A little while more and the space inside the square was glowing a brilliant, blinding green that grew whiter as the seconds ticked by.

Shrike and her soldiers waited in a semicircle a few steps back from the strange phenomenon. They stood at attention.

The light faded and now Raven could see three new figures standing before Shrike. Her eyes had been dazzled by the display and she blinked furiously, seeking to clear her vision.

At last the fireworks across her retinas settled down and she could, to a degree, make out who had emerged from the bizarre effect that simply *had* to be a subspace portal. At first she was elated, but then as she looked on she came to realize that developments here were perhaps not as positive as she had first imagined.

For the figures that had emerged were all very well known to her—at least in general terms. But they were definitely not behaving correctly. As far as she could tell, none of them were.

What in the Above and the Below, she wondered half-out loud, *is going on here? And, perhaps more importantly, just how many people am I going to have to kill* now?

3: HAWK

Hawk and Falcon emerged from the hyperspace portal just behind Condor, walking into a high-ceilinged room with white walls and a glowing ceiling. The rippling spacetime distortion effect had been overwhelming during transit, but now reality had readjusted itself to normal around them and Hawk no longer felt as if his body and his mind were being twisted inside-out.

"Amazing, yes?" Condor asked as he turned back to face them.

"Quite," Hawk replied.

"Depending on how far we traveled just now," Falcon added.

"Would you believe a third of the way across the galaxy?"

Falcon's eyes widened. "Then 'amazing' it is." He turned back around to take a look at the equipment—two units on the floor, two more hanging from the ceiling of the big room.

Condor cursed then. "I liked that ship," he groused.

"At least your crew made it out," Falcon noted, as a stream of brown-uniformed men and women emerged from the portal and filed past.

Condor responded with ambivalence. He looked back to see the last of his crewmembers emerging from the portal before it snapped closed, the ship at the other end of the hyperspace tunnel now obliterated.

Hawk meanwhile was studying the small group of figures that stood a few feet away, apparently having been waiting for his party to emerge. A half a dozen men in identical, dark green uniforms with silver helmets stood at attention in a semicircle, partly surrounding a tall, slender, blonde woman in a tight, brighter green jumpsuit. As Hawk looked at her, it dawned on him that she could be Condor's sister.

"So that thing punches a hole right into the Above, and back out," Falcon noted, still looking back at the portal machine. "Can it take you *anywhere*?"

"It punches into the Above *or* into the Below," Condor replied somewhat impatiently, "but it's based on pre-Shattering tech that my agents do not fully understand. And so, unfortunately, the two terminals only connected with one another—the one here, and the one on my spacecraft." He frowned. "And now, I fear, only this terminal remains, and so now it goes nowhere."

Falcon turned back around, taking in as much of the new environment as he could, and saw the small crowd of people waiting. He started to ask the next logical question, but Hawk beat him to it.

"Where exactly is 'here?'"

"I will reveal all to you in just a moment," Condor said. He gestured towards the woman in green. "Allow me to introduce my second-in-command, Shrike."

Hawk nodded respectfully to her, but Falcon only frowned.

"Shrike?" he repeated. "But—"

"You did not think there were any more Shrikes, naturally," the woman stated, anticipating his question. "But as the presence of so many of us here proves," she went on, her eyes moving from Hawk to Condor and back to Falcon, "one can never be certain about Hands."

"Very true," Condor agreed with a tight smile.

Falcon grunted, a sound that could be taken to mean whatever one wished it to mean.

"If you would come this way, gentlemen," Condor said, gesturing to his right where a doorway stood open, "all will become clear to you, I believe."

Falcon strode past the blonde woman, not sparing her a second look, and moved through the open doorway. Hawk followed, hesitating for only a moment as something caught his eye at the far end of the long room.

Was that a person—tied up and lying on the floor? A woman?

He'd only gotten a glimpse and couldn't make out much about her. Then they were out of the room, Shrike and her soldiers at the rear, the door sliding silently closed behind them.

They emerged into bright sunlight. They stood on what seemed to be a long, broad expanse of white plastic. In fact, looking back, Hawk saw that the building they had just exited looked to have been extruded directly from this plastic "ground." Then he gazed upward and struggled to make sense of what he was seeing.

"Do you understand yet?" Condor was asking them. "Can you fathom just where we are?"

Clearly Hawk could tell that they were now outdoors, on a planet of some kind. It had to be a planet, because they were walking around in fresh air, with no ceiling, and a shining sun far up in the sky. In fact, it appeared to be exactly noon, because the sun was directly overhead. The only thing that gave him pause was the "planet's" surface on which they walked: In every direction that he looked, Hawk could see other buildings that had been extruded out of the white plastic material.

So—was it a world made entirely of plastic?

And then a second detail came to his attention. An arch—or at least the lower portions, with one leg towering up in the far distance to his left, and the other reaching up equally high from his right, both disappearing ultimately in the glare of the noontime sun.

How far away are the legs of that arch? he wondered. The more he looked, the farther away they seemed to be.

He looked back down and saw Condor watching him and smiling.

"It is hard at first to conceive of the dimensions of this place, is it not?" the blond man asked. "When I tell them to you, they will shock you."

"It's some kind of planet," Hawk stated quietly. "And yet—"

248

"And yet there are things that don't quite add up, correct?" Hawk nodded.

"I think I get it," Falcon said then, "even though it's utterly insane." He met Condor's eyes. "It's a ring."

"A ring?" Hawk's voice conveyed puzzlement, while Condor and Shrike looked on with amusement.

"Think about it," Falcon continued. "Put a ring all the way around a sun, at an orbital distance that's conducive to life. Not too warm, not too cold. Spin it for gravity, right? And I guess you'd have to raise walls on either edge of the inner surface to keep the air from spilling out the sides. But that's pretty much all there is to it."

Hawk's eyes widened as he considered the scale of such a construct, of such an undertaking.

"Ah, you are truly a Falcon," Condor noted with appreciation. "Always the engineer at heart. Even as mighty a construct as this could not confound you for long." He laughed. "And probably already dreaming up ways of destroying it."

"You didn't build this," Falcon growled. His tone left no room for argument.

"Certainly not. But I found it."

"Inhabited?"

"Completely empty—at least in terms of sentient life forms. But with room for…" He shrugged. "…trillions."

Falcon looked to be doing some math in his head. Then he nodded. "Yeah, trillions. At least."

"Was there *ever* anyone here?" Hawk asked. "Where did they go?"

"There must have been inhabitants, long ago," Condor said. "Well before the Shattering." He considered. "I'm not certain if the battles of the Shattering even extended out this far. We've not found much in the way of wreckage in this solar system or nearby."

Hawk considered this. His injected older memories had slowly been returning to him; coupled with what his ship had filled him in on, he had a decent understanding of broad galactic history now.

"So this corner of the galaxy may have somehow escaped the notice of the Adversary during the war," he said. "Maybe that's why the ring was built here."

"Or maybe the ring itself kept the enemy away," Falcon suggested.

"How could that be possible?" asked Hawk. "This design seems to me incredibly vulnerable. Just shoot a hole in the floor and watch as all the air drains right out into space."

"That is true, to a point," Condor agreed. "If the hole is big enough, and if no one repairs it within a period of perhaps months or years. And, of course, if the enemy can approach close enough to blast a hole in the first place."

Falcon turned to Condor. "You did say something about having a formidable weapon."

"Oh, indeed," Condor replied, grinning again.

"Where is it?" Falcon asked.

"You are standing on it."

Hawk and Falcon exchanged glances. They even looked down, but saw only the unending plain of white plastic under their boots.

"You mean the ring itself," Hawk said then.

Condor nodded. "As you said—without it, we would be incredibly vulnerable here. But with it, we are untouchable."

Hawk considered all of this.

"With a weapon as powerful as that, perhaps we could actually defeat the Adversary—destroy the enemy forces now, before—"

"No, no," Condor cut him off, shaking his head. "The weapon will not reach far beyond this solar system, and the ring does not move. We are tied to our star."

"Could it serve as a sort of galactic lifeboat?" Hawk speculated then. "We somehow bring all the surviving inhabitants of the galaxy here, to this ring—there would be room for most of them, I think, as hard as that is to imagine—and then use the weapon to defend them from the Adversary's forces."

"Even imagining that something of that logistical complexity could be done," Falcon said, staring at him, incredulous, "you would surrender all of the rest of the galaxy to the enemy and squeeze everyone onto this ring?"

"It would not be my first choice, no," Hawk answered. "Probably my last choice, in fact. But if we have no other choice—if the galaxy is about to fall to the Adversary..."

Falcon gave him a sour look and turned away.

"If we are to face the old Adversary again," the cyborg growled, "I mean to defeat him, not appease him."

Hawk started to object, then shook his head and said nothing.

"Such a thing would be extremely difficult," Condor stated. "Our encounter a few moments ago provided all the proof I needed in that regard. We faced only a handful of their ships and I lost my flagship! If not for the ancient portal technology, we would all be dead now." He swore. "Our best course may be to simply hold out and wait for the Adversary to lose interest in this galaxy and move on once again. And I don't mean bring everyone else here—or even a fraction of them. That would only attract the enemy's attention. But if we were simply to lay low here—"

Hawk whirled on the man.

"You mean to protect ourselves, and to abandon the surviving trillions and trillions of sentient beings in this galaxy to the Adversary? To slaughter?"

"I am but one man," Condor replied.

"You have an army. And incredible weapons, such as this ring."

"Hawk is right," Falcon said. "With technology like this, perhaps victory is not impossible after all."

"All the armies and all the super-weapons of the ancient races were only able to drive the Adversary away, during the Shattering," Condor pointed out, a hint of anger creeping into his voice. "And that at the cost of utterly destroying their civilizations, not to mention obliterating the Empires of Man." He scoffed. "Compared to that, what are my meager resources?"

"They are a start," Hawk answered.

Condor sighed and looked away. For several seconds no one said anything.

"I've been giving this a great deal of thought," Falcon said at last, breaking the silence, "since Hawk first brought it to my attention only recently." He paused, as if not entirely willing to say what he needed to say. Pursing his lips, he continued. "I think I know the answer. Or, at least, the beginnings of an answer."

The others all turned to look at him.

"If the Adversary truly has returned, and in anything like his strength of old, and if we really are going to lead a campaign against him and his forces, then what we need," the big cyborg stated flatly, "is the Machine."

"What?" –this from both Hawk and Condor.

"Not the Machine as it existed during the first few centuries after the Shattering, of course," Falcon said, "but as it once was, before that. In its prime it commanded vast armies and nearly unlimited resources and its reach was unmatched. It defended this galaxy from all threats for a very long while prior to the Shattering. Only after that great war ended, when it was left only with a scattered few Hands to serve as its enforcers, did it begin to exhibit signs of...*madness*, yes. Insanity. And then, ultimately, it fell silent."

"You want to repair it? To restore it?" Hawk stared back at him, astonished. "Would such a thing be possible?"

Now Condor looked extremely uncomfortable. He waved a hand to cut off the discussion.

"We have all had a rough time. These are questions too big to be decided so quickly. I suggest we get some rest and resume this conversation later."

Hawk reluctantly agreed. Falcon shrugged.

Condor signaled to Shrike and a detachment of her troops approached. "They will lead you to the quarters that have been prepared for you," he told the two Hands.

Hawk and Falcon nodded and followed the soldiers back inside the main building.

As they walked away, Falcon glanced back over his shoulder at Condor, seeing the regal figure engaging in animated but hushed conversation with Shrike.

"I don't much like this," the cyborg told his companion in a hushed tone. "I trusted our new friend there a lot more when it was just him. But with this alleged Shrike alongside…" He shook his head. "I suggest we sleep with one eye open."

Hawk chuckled. "Is that even possible for you?"

Falcon tapped the metal side of his skull and snorted. "Are you kidding? I only have one. Makes it easy."

4: FALCON

Indeed, Falcon proved to be a prophet only a short two hours later.

The troopers had shown him to a somewhat small room that looked to have been used only for storage previously. They'd set up some kind of big cot for him—fortunately, they had hastily reinforced it in order to hold up his considerable weight, given that a large proportion of his body was now made of metal.

Lying back on the makeshift bed, he'd taken a quick look around in order to familiarize himself with his surroundings. There really wasn't much to see. The room was a light gray in color, with walls and floor seemingly made from the same plastic-looking stuff as the rest of the building. Two metal folding chairs sat nearby, along with a small table positioned to serve as a night stand. Otherwise, the room was empty.

That suited Falcon just fine. He wanted to nap.

Unfortunately, though his weary cyborg body lay still and unmoving on the bed, his mind remained as active as ever. He felt antsy. All sorts of concerns were gnawing at him. He knew it would be some time before he was able to sleep, and indeed that fact was what saved him.

The attack came as he was finally thinking through what he knew and what he had learned in the past couple of days. Much as he wasn't a terribly introspective or deliberative person, he knew he needed to sort out the whole situation as best he could, because he had the distinct feeling that some kind of resolution was fast approaching.

Had the great Adversary—architect of the Shattering of their galaxy and the destruction of most of the advanced races therein—truly returned? Falcon was not entirely convinced. It depended upon what one meant by "the Adversary." If one meant that at least one or two of the races that had originally and prominently served as part of the massive forces that had assaulted the galaxy was back in action and up to mischief again, then yes, Falcon could now testify from his own experience that such a thing was true.

But if one meant that a single being—one entity, one intelligence—that had directed the enemy attack during the Shattering had now returned, centuries later, to resume his campaign on a galactic scale…well, Falcon wasn't quite as sure about that. Maybe it was true, and maybe these hostile races were acting of their own volition.

And Hawk's fervor could, in all honesty, just as easily be ascribed to his desperate seeking of redemption because of the betrayal perpetrated by his earlier self. That could cause him to blow things out of proportion in his own mind.

Falcon groaned audibly. He hated sifting through motives and possibilities this way. It wasn't what he was good at, what he had been genetically engineered for. That's what a Condor was for—though probably not the alleged "Condor" they had at their disposal at the moment.

Or an Eagle.

Falcon frowned deeper, thinking about his old friend and commander. Eagle would have cut through all this foolishness instantly—and probably literally, with a few judicious swings of his big, golden sword. Falcon found that, for the first time in a very long time, he missed the guy. Losing both him and the original Hawk at the same time, on the same mission, had been quite a blow. The War of the Shattering had begun soon after, and while he and the remaining Hands had tried to hold on as best they could, they never made the difference they could've with Eagle in charge. For whatever reason, the Machine never created another Eagle, and would never respond when asked why not.

Soon after those awful events on Scandana, Raven was killed in action as well. The Machine never replaced her, either. The legions they all had once commanded had been ground down over time, during the war, to nothing. Eventually only a scant few Hands remained, soldiering on individually, acting more like roving cops or security guards than nearly godlike figures commanding fleets of starships and armies of soldiers as they had once been seen by most of the sentient beings of the galaxy. It had all been so very hard to accept, but as the years passed and the Machine grew increasingly recalcitrant and eventually fell silent altogether, there had been no other choice. Thus Falcon, after eventually losing his personal spacecraft in the same incident that had left him a cyborg, had come in recent times to merely wander the backwater worlds, in search of an elusive peace. Peace and quiet.

Leave it to Hawk to come back from the grave a thousand years later and stir things up again.

Falcon inhaled and exhaled slowly, brooding over his many centuries of life and all that he had seen and experienced during that time. From loyal soldier of the Machine to free-roaming vagabond to... what? What was he now? He wasn't sure.

It had been easy to simply serve the Machine for all those years. He wondered idly if it was still out there somewhere, functioning at all—or if it had merely broken down, as all things do eventually. He didn't even know where it was, or have any idea of where to look for it. No one did. Possibly the greatest remaining secret in the galaxy was the location of the Machine itself. As far as he knew, no one knew where it was or even who had constructed it. When it had still been active in the affairs of the galaxy, it had operated via agents—agents such as himself, once—and by subspace communications. No one ever traveled to its location and no one had ever produced the slightest reasonable guess as to where that might actually be.

Yes, it had been easy to follow orders as a Hand, and only slightly harder to simply go where the vagaries of fate had taken him, as a nomad. But now—now he knew he had to become something else—a third thing. He couldn't afford to hide from the universe any longer. Whether he liked it or not, it appeared as if the galaxy needed him again. He knew he couldn't help but come to its aid. No matter how hard he tried to deny it, that's who he was.

"Great," he muttered. "I've grown some kind of conscience. Hooray."

He also understood he could never hope to defeat the opponents he was likely to face alone. Fortunately, he had gained something of an ally in Hawk; clearly the guy meant well and had the best interests of the whole galaxy at heart. Falcon simply worried that the man was so idealistic and so determined to confront the Adversary that he might put himself in a situation more dangerous than necessary. Falcon had lived long enough to understand that pragmatism had its place, too—that focusing only on helping others could get you killed before you could help *anyone*.

He's young... he's a new Hawk... and without full access to the memories of earlier versions to provide a tempering of wisdom, he's almost like a kid, impetuous and over-eager. I've got to talk some sense into him.

Then he thought of Condor.

I don't know what to make of that guy. He was never a Hand, obviously. And that power he has.... What did he call it? Quantum threads, or something? I'm sure it goes over big when he's convincing some planet's population that he's a Hand, and that they should bow down and obey him or whatever. But just how useful will it be in battle?

And that woman, claiming to be a Shrike? He actually laughed out loud at the thought. *Please.*

As he laughed, he opened his human eye—he had not, after all, tried to sleep with his eyes open—and saw a square panel in the ceiling, directly over his head, sliding silently open.

He lunged his bulky form hard to the left and tumbled onto the floor, just as a fusillade of silvery blades flashed down from the darkness and into the bed.

Rolling, he came up quick and focused his cyborg eye into the dark square overhead.

Nothing.

Nothing visible via any of the various wavelengths available to him by way of his mechanical eye. It was as if the attack had been launched by a ghost.

Keeping both eyes on the dark opening in anticipation of another attack, he reached for his pistol where he'd left it next to the bed.

It was gone.

How could that have happened? When could someone have—?

No matter. Too late to worry about it now. He reached the other way, grabbing for one of the metal chairs.

This movement saved him. Even as he leaned over to grasp the chair, something hissed just past his neck. A blade, reaching for him from above, he knew. And yet he still could not see anything.

Frustration mounting, he simply hurled the metal chair straight up through the opening.

He was rewarded by a grunt of pain and a crashing sound as something invisible half-fell through the opening, shaking the roof panels around it.

Falcon reached up, felt a human form covered in some kind of cloth, and seized the invisible shape. He dragged it the rest of the way through the opening and down with a thud to the floor.

Now the invisible person was groaning in pain.

Good.

Moving with a catlike quickness that belied his bulky, semi-metal form, Falcon grabbed handfuls of...*something*...and pulled, rending and shredding as quickly as he could, before the person could recover from their fall.

A shower of sparks flew out, some in Falcon's face, causing him to grimace and release what he was holding.

When the fireworks were over, the big cyborg found himself staring down at a man clad entirely in black. Some parts of the outfit were super-tight, while others were billowy. A black mask covered all of his face. It was some kind of invisibility suit, apparently. Or had been, anyway.

The attacker had regained his senses by now and scrambled backwards. Falcon was already lunging for him, but the man in black managed to roll out of the way and was up, in a low crouch, a bladed weapon of medium length gripped in his right hand and ready.

Falcon jerked backward as the blade slashed out. It still almost got him. The guy was fast, that was obvious. Invisible or not, he was a dangerous opponent.

The blade sliced out again, and now Falcon realized he already had backed himself against the wall of the tiny room. With no other option he tried to deflect the next slash with his arm, and was relieved when the blade struck metal and not flesh.

Before the attacker could move again Falcon rushed forward, charging his bulky form at the man in black.

The distance between them was too small for the assassin to have the time to dodge. Falcon crashed into him with tremendous force and drove the man down hard into the floor.

The cyborg's leather-gloved fist smashed down hard once, twice, both times connecting with the black-masked face. The assassin lost his grip on his long dagger and it clattered to the floor behind him.

But then somehow the assassin freed himself, wrenching his body out from under his opponent's by way of an acrobatic move the likes of which Falcon hadn't seen before. Back up on his feet well ahead of Falcon, the man in black produced a short knife from somewhere in his suit and drove it down into the human flesh portion of his enemy's shoulder.

Falcon roared in pain. In one smooth action he drew the blade out with his right hand while punching the assassin hard in the face with the other. Then he stumbled back a step as a strange sensation washed over him. The assassin waited now, crouching, watching, ready.

Poison, Falcon knew instantly. The blade was poisoned.

He touched a sensor on his right hip and his red and blue uniform jabbed needles into his thigh, testing his blood and quickly attempting to formulate and inject the proper antidote.

But in the seconds this required to take effect, the assassin—apparently sensing what was happening—seized the opportunity and struck out again. He grasped one bent leg of the chair Falcon had first thrown at him in the ceiling and swung it low and hard, catching his still-disoriented opponent across the knees.

Normally the blow wouldn't have affected the big man overmuch, but in his temporarily weakened state he felt his knees buckle and he went down.

The assassin sensed victory at hand and turned around quickly, locating the long dagger he had dropped moments earlier. He snatched it up and whirled back to face his cyborg opponent, prepared to deal death.

Falcon met him in mid-turn with the short blade he'd pulled from his shoulder. He drove it deep under the man's chin. The poison that still coated it was not a factor; the assassin instantly fell dead at Falcon's feet.

Just then the door slid open and Hawk rushed in, pistol at the ready.

Falcon gave him a weary look.

"Nice of you to show up," he said, before collapsing.

5: RAVEN

A few minutes earlier, Raven had been about to make her move when Condor strode into the Ring command center and finally noticed her lying on the floor, bound from neck to toe. He stood there, just looking at her, puzzled, his mouth opening and closing, as she stared up at him and met his gaze evenly.

Shrike looked up from one of the control stations and took notice of him and what he was doing. She crossed the room to meet him halfway.

"Who—?" he began, indicating the bound woman. Then he blinked, looked closer at her dark eyes and slender features, and said, "She looks familiar somehow." He gasped. "Is that a *Raven*?"

Shrike nodded. "Indeed it is."

"What is a Raven doing here?" He frowned. "I didn't think there *were* any more Ravens, for that matter."

"You brought a Hawk here, and you're asking that?"

From her spot on the floor, Raven started. *A Hawk? Here? How could that be?*

"Okay, then," Condor replied, looking from Raven to Shrike nervously. "Why is she tied up like that?"

"Because she's a Raven, obviously," Shrike said, regarding Condor as if he were a child or an idiot, or both. In a softer tone she added, "And because you and I are not *exactly* what we profess to be. And because she's nuts and is driven by her programming to kill anyone who is masquerading as a Hand. Therefore she tried to kill me—wants to kill us *both*, I'm sure, seeing as how neither of us is a genuine, Machine-created Hand."

"Does she not understand that her own model was discontinued a long, long time ago? That, technically, she should want to kill herself just as much as she wants to see us dead?"

"I've tried to explain that to her a couple of times already, yes," Shrike answered. "She doesn't want to listen to me. Maybe she doesn't believe me. She surely isn't saying anything."

Condor absorbed this information and his frown only deepened.

"I see," he muttered, clearly not happy. "I don't think this is going to go over well with our two new friends," he mused.

Shrike suppressed a laugh. "You may not have to worry about them for much longer."

Condor turned to her to ask what she meant by that—and suddenly alarms blared throughout the command center.

Raven had absorbed everything the two of them had just said and was parsing her way through it, not quite sure what she should believe now, when the alarms shrieked. Her next several moves were already planned out and ready, but with the situation suddenly changing—Condor and Shrike were moving away from her, appearing very concerned about something—she decided to wait a little longer and see what developed.

"Who do you suppose they are?" Shrike was asking as a holographic display shimmered into existence at the center of the big room.

Condor studied the images of a dozen or so spacecraft streaking through the void. The display revealed that they had emerged from hyperspace—dropped out of the Above, most likely—just beyond the orbit of the Ring, and were closing on it fast. And most of the ships themselves were of a design that he found increasingly familiar.

"The Adversary," he breathed. "Again."

Shrike turned to offer him a puzzled look. "What are you talking about?"

He pointed a gloved finger at the cluster of streaking vessels. "Those are Skrazzi ships. The insectoid guys we've fought a time or two before."

Shrike nodded. "Okay—yes. I recognize them now."

"They were once a main player in the armies of the Adversary. They're the ones who blew up my ship and made us come here prematurely. They're getting more active everywhere, it seems. Now they're even here."

"Fine," Shrike acknowledged. "But what does that have to do with the Adversary? That was a thousand years ago or more."

"They're not all Skrazzi," Condor pointed out. He indicated three larger ships near the rear of the formation. "What do you make of those?"

Shrike squinted at them and shook her head. "I've never seen that design before." She touched a few squares on the control panel in front of her. "Nothing in the records, either."

"You'd have to search back farther, to the time of the Shattering. They haven't been active in more than a millennium."

"Who are they, then?"

The air in the command center grew colder, as if a cool breeze had blown through.

Condor swallowed hard.

"The Phaedron."

Shrike blanched.

The air grew colder.

"That's ridiculous," the blonde woman said—but her voice lacked its customary force. She could very obviously *feel* that something was wrong. "I always thought they were just a legend—a myth. Something to frighten children with." She wrapped her arms around herself. "A race of beings with some sort of psychic powers? Powers that manifest in part as waves of cold?" She scoffed, but there was no questioning that the room was much cooler now than it had been a few moments earlier. Meanwhile the ships in the holo display drew closer to the Ring.

"I'm beginning to think Hawk was right," Condor said. "Why else would the Phaedron be active again? Why would they be working with the Skrazzi again?" He shook his head, clearly distressed. "It must be true. The Adversary has returned."

From where she lay on the floor, Raven's eyes widened as she listened to their conversation. Mention of a Hawk—and of the old Adversary—had her full attention. Increasingly she was coming to believe she had been awakened for a very specific purpose. Too many strange things were happening now for it to be otherwise.

The air was downright chilly in the command center now.

"Well, Adversary or not, these guys probably don't know what they're going up against," Condor growled. "If they think *they're* scary, wait till they see what *I* can do."

Condor moved to a nearby control station and seated himself in a low swivel chair. A smaller holographic display instantly formed all around him. Reaching out with both hands, he insinuated himself into the imagery and brought the weapons systems on line.

Seconds passed, with both Raven and Shrike looking on from their very different vantage points as Condor moved his arms and hands like a symphony conductor, manipulating various routines and subroutines. Meanwhile, on the main display, the enemy ships drew closer—now they were almost to the Ring itself.

Shrike looked as if she were about to ask what he was doing, when the sunlight shining in through the building's transparent walls grew much brighter.

"Here we go," Condor said to himself, leaning forward and continuing to move his hands in precise gestures.

The sunlight pulsed brighter and dimmer, over and over, for nearly a minute. Then it flared very bright and remained that way for several more seconds.

Raven managed to roll over and raise her head just enough to see the full holographic image that filled the center of the room. The view it displayed had pulled back, apparently coming now from some satellite stationed far out beyond the Ring's orbit, so that much of the Ring was visible—along with the star at its center. As Raven looked on in astonishment, that star flared, spewing out what had to be a gargantuan column of blazing solar plasma.

"Activating the electromagnetic fields," Condor noted as he "conducted" the weapon. "Shaping the beam now."

The plasma flowing out of the sun tightened and refined itself into a singular column of blinding light—a coherent beam many hundreds or even thousands of kilometers in diameter. The beam stabbed out, lightning-like, for only the briefest of instants, beyond the Ring and into the space beyond. Then it faded and vanished—though the afterimage remained for several seconds afterward on everyone's eyes who looked on, despite the holo display's automatic filtering.

Raven squeezed her eyes closed and opened them again; spots slowly faded and she could see Condor lowering his arms and turning back to face Shrike. He was smiling broadly. The holographic image now displayed only the last glowing, drifting wisps of incandescent gas that had moments earlier been two clusters of alien warships.

"There we go," Condor exulted, raising his arms in triumph. "Bring on what you've got, Adversary. You can't stand up to my big gun!"

"Very good," Shrike commented. She had watched the entire performance carefully, paying at least as much attention to what Condor did to activate and control the solar weapon as she did to the outcome of its firing. "I think that will probably do it, then."

Condor turned and gave her a puzzled look. "What?"

The alarm shrieked again. The temperature plunged.

Condor whirled about, gawking at what now filled the holographic display: Starships. Wave upon wave of starships. Small and large and everything in between, and all converging on the Ring.

"Oh no," he breathed, frost forming in the air as he spoke. "Oh my heavens…"

Quickly he moved to the defense station again and raised his arms to activate the solar weapon.

Shrike shook her head and started toward him. "That won't be necessary, Condor."

"What?"

She signaled to someone outside the command center, then addressed Condor again. "Step away from the firing controls."

His face was a mask of confusion. "Have you lost your mind, woman?"

"The Master has seen the full capabilities of this installation now," the woman in green stated. "And I've seen how to control it. He doesn't need to sacrifice any more of his ships for demonstration purposes."

Condor gawked at his erstwhile partner, not quite sure he should believe what he was hearing.

The doors to the command center burst open and a cadre of green-clad troopers hustled in, weapons drawn and mostly directed at Condor.

"What is this?" he demanded. "A mutiny?"

Shrike smiled coldly at him.

"Nothing so petty, I assure you," she replied. "You were quite right. The Master—or the great Adversary, as you misguidedly call him—has returned. And he will be taking possession of this Ring now." She laughed. "Now that he has seen just how powerful it is, and how to make it work."

From where she lay mostly forgotten on the floor nearby, Raven whispered, "I've heard enough." She redoubled her efforts with the tiny blade that she clutched between her fingers.

"This is not smart, Shrike," Condor was saying. "I have but to signal my own troops, and—"

Shrike's soldiers had taken up various positions around the command center. At her nod, they activated the controls that she had previously indicated to them. A clanging sound echoed throughout the chamber.

"This command center is now secure," she told Condor. "We are cut off from the rest of the Ring, and will remain so until the Master himself—or such other lieutenant as he chooses to send in his place—has arrived here."

Outside the transparent wall of the command center, several of Condor's brown-uniformed troops arrived and attempted to get inside. They could see the green-clad soldiers training their weapons on Condor and hesitated, unsure of what to do next. Condor, meanwhile, simply stood there, visibly deflating.

"Why are you doing this?" he asked Shrike after a few seconds. "We've worked together for so many years—enjoyed so much success..."

"We have been *pirates*," she snapped back at him. "Little more than that. But now..." She beamed at him, her eyes sparkling. "Very soon the Adversary will *rule* this galaxy, Condor—and I have been promised a prominent role in his new order to come. I will be one of the chief commanders at his side, not just a petty crook operating in one tiny corner of it." She gazed across at her erstwhile compatriot with a disapproving frown. "If you cannot understand the appeal of *that*, then your vision is even more limited than I always suspected."

Frowning, Condor's eyes moved from Shrike to the soldiers under her command who were keeping their weapons trained on him, looking for some way out of this mess.

"Oh, yes," Shrike noted casually then. "There is one other loose end to take care of."

She walked quickly around to the other side of a row of consoles and stared down at the spot where she had left Raven, unmoving, bound head to toe. Looking down, she gasped, her eyes widening. Slowly she began to back away.

On the floor where her prisoner had lain, now there sat a pile of neatly-cut restraint bands.

Of Raven herself, there was no sign whatsoever.

"No!" Shrike cried out, whirling around, her eyes searching the control room. She directed her anger at her troops. "Where did she go? Find her!"

Condor spared a glance at the console where the Hand's katana had lain. He noted that it, too, was now missing. He allowed himself a tiny smile.

The soldiers were moving about slowly, cautiously, as if searching for a loose cobra in the room. Nobody was watching Condor anymore. He took the opportunity to edge closer to the controls that would unlock the room.

A cry, cut off very suddenly, on the far side of the command center. A silver blade flashed. Shrike shouted frantic orders even as her soldiers moved into action.

Another shout, another flash of the blade. Two soldiers down, and still no signs of Raven. Then a third. The room dissolved in confusion and chaos. Shrike screamed orders madly but to little avail. Raven was moving ultra-quickly, staying low, striking in a random pattern.

Condor had been forgotten. He slapped the controls unlocking the room. The main entrance slid open.

Another gurgled cry. Shrike was already down four men. Soldiers began to shoot, their blasts hitting blank walls and control consoles.

Condor dashed through the now-open door and sprinted away.

6: HAWK

Hawk stood just inside the door to Falcon's quarters, gun in hand. He looked down at the dead man on the floor, then up at his cyborg companion, who had managed to regain his feet but appeared disoriented and unsteady. The big man was now leaning back against the wall, breathing somewhat heavily. Blood was running down his arm, but not a lot of it.

"What in the name of the Above is going on in here?" Hawk demanded. "I heard you through the wall, but the door was locked and it took me this long to pick it."

Falcon was prodding the erstwhile assassin with the tip of his boot. He looked at Hawk wearily, then glanced up at the missing panel in the ceiling—the route through which the man in black had entered.

Hawk followed his eyes, saw the open passageway above Falcon's bed, and figured out the basics. He nodded.

"Good thing this fellow was a 'hands-on' type—didn't want to kill you from a distance," Hawk observed.

Falcon snorted at that. He pointed to the bed, riddled with blades protruding up from where they'd lodged after being hurled or fired from the passageway. "He didn't?"

Hawk's eyes widened at the frightening display. "Oh. I stand corrected." He knelt down, examining the man's black suit, seeing an ultra-thin layer of circuitry running along the inside surface.

"Some kind of stealth tech?"

Falcon nodded. "Something pre-Shattering, I'd guess. Guy was invisible." He tapped the side of his face next to his mechanical eye. "Even to me."

"Interesting." Hawk reached for the mask covering the man's face. "And how did you beat him, then?"

"There's something to be said for the old-fashioned methods," Falcon replied, cracking his massive knuckles.

Hawk gave him a half-grin, then pulled the assassin's mask away. The face revealed was not particularly noteworthy; ruddy skin, very short brown hair. Frowning, Hawk looked back at Falcon. "So, who is he?"

"How should I know?"

Hawk shrugged. "You killed him."

"Didn't give me much of a choice."

"Guess not…"

Falcon shook his head to clear it and stretched his muscles.

"Feeling better?" asked Hawk.

"Suit's finally figured out how to counteract the poison," Falcon said, adding, "About time."

"Poison?"

Hawk started to ask for more details, but then came a cry of alarm from the corridor outside, immediately followed by the sound of running feet heading their way.

"Better late than never, guys," Falcon said as the first couple of green-clad troopers appeared in the doorway. "But I already got him."

The troopers didn't spare the dead assassin a second look. Instead they raised their weapons and aimed them directly at the two Hands.

Hawk and Falcon reacted instantly, diving to the side as a barrage of blaster fire peppered the small room.

"You've got to be kidding me," Hawk exclaimed as he drew his pistol.

"I knew that Condor guy was no good," Falcon growled. His own pistol was still missing, so he simply leapt over the smashed furniture and tackled the two nearest soldiers, dragging them both down. His rugged fists smashed into them repeatedly.

Two more troopers rushed into the doorway, and more were crowding in behind them.

Hawk was annoyed: having a big figure like Falcon in his line-of-sight only made shooting the enemy that much harder. Nevertheless, he opened fire with his blast pistol and found his marksmanship was everything he could have hoped for. Bolt after bolt of searing crimson energy sliced into the attackers, even as Hawk continued to evade their shots.

Very quickly, however, the situation grew untenable. Hawk and Falcon were trapped in a small room and faced what looked to be an overwhelming wave of opponents. They both understood that they had to get out—out into the corridor, at least, so they would no longer be quite such sitting ducks—or fish in a barrel.

Falcon was roaring his anger now, even as a couple of shots impacted his metal implants along one arm with a ringing sound. He grasped one dead trooper by the belt and flung the guy into the next wave just as they appeared in the doorway. Then, using the corpse like a battering ram, he shoved both living and dead soldiers back. They all tumbled together to the floor, with Falcon smashing their faces in before they could bring their guns up to shoot him. A couple got past him but Hawk shot them down quickly.

The two Hands advanced into the corridor and considered that a major victory in their little war.

Now came a two-second-long break, during which Falcon breathed heavily and Hawk checked the power remaining to his pistol. Falcon reached down and grabbed a fallen gun from one of the dead men, found he could not make it work for him, and tossed it aside with a grunt.

The two seconds ended. More shouts, more running feet in the distance.

Settling into a crouch, Falcon looked up to see another wave of green-uniformed men rounding the far corner, guns in hand. Hawk moved up next to him, firing rapidly, his shots taking down a half-dozen foes in as many seconds.

Falcon surged forward, low to the ground, hands ready to grapple. He tackled the front line of attackers and took them down. Hawk continued to fire over him, picking off the next three with three crisp, sizzling shots.

Together they battled their way down the corridor to the corner. They were now wading over a sea of casualties, two- or three-deep in places. The two Hands had become almost a force of nature—living automatons in a dance of death—dealing out destruction to their foes without a second's pause for reflection or second-guessing. There was only the enemy, and survival. Everything else was tuned out.

Reaching the end of the corridor at last, both of them having reached an unspoken decision to take the fight to their foes in the direction they were coming from, Hawk and Falcon rounded the corner and burst through the last wave of opponents—

—and found the way clear now. Both Hands stood there, leaning forward, hands on hips, breathing heavily, not quite believing it was over, waiting for the inevitable next attack.

And then another figure did appear at the far end of this corridor, perhaps twenty yards in front of them.

Hawk raised his pistol, prepared to fire.

"Wait!" shouted the man in brown. "Wait!"

He raced forward, a look of extreme incomprehension etched across his aristocratic face.

"Condor," Hawk started to say, but then Falcon had sprung forward, tackling the blond man, driving him down hard into the floor. Rough, massive fists rose and fell, and Condor cried out, unable to concentrate enough to invoke his quantum powers.

Hawk rushed forward, coming up behind the two of them. He could see that Condor was trying to say something.

"Falcon, wait—wait!" He grasped the cyborg's more human shoulder, pulling hard. Falcon stumbled backwards and caught himself, then glared up at Hawk.

"What are you doing? I'm gonna kill this guy!"

"Wait!"

Condor managed to sit up. Blood was running down his face and his nose appeared to be somewhat misaligned. He held up both hands in as non-threatening a gesture as he could manage, but his expression darkened toward anger as the initial shock passed.

"What did you... do that for?" he managed to gasp out, in between coughs.

"Are you kidding?" the big man asked, incredulous. "After you just sent your entire hit squad to kill us?"

"Hit squad?" He coughed violently again and struggled up to his feet. He started to advance on the two Hands. "What are you—?" Reaching the corner, he saw the mass of bodies stretching away beyond them. He halted and stared.

"Hit squad," Falcon repeated, angling his head toward the bodies and glaring, flexing his massive fists.

Condor looked from the carnage in the corridor to the two men before him, one of whom had a clearly murderous look in his single human eye. He frowned, looking down for a second, then back up. He pointed to the bodies. "Those aren't my men! They're wearing green, not brown."

Hawk and Falcon both reacted with surprise to this, but then Falcon jabbed a beefy finger at Condor. "That doesn't mean anything," he growled.

But Condor had turned his back on them and was stalking back the way he had come.

"Where do you think you're going?" Falcon shouted, starting after him. "Hey!"

"Those are Shrike's men," Condor said. "That's what I was coming to tell you. She's gone rogue—claims to be working for the Adversary now. She tried to kill me, too."

"The Adversary?" Hawk glanced at Falcon, puzzled.

"Turns out you may have been right all along, Hawk," Condor said. "There's a big fleet headed this way now, in fact."

Even as he walked, Condor's self-assuredness returned, while at the same time a glowing halo of quantum energy flared about him. He glanced back at the two dumbfounded men.

"Are you two coming?"

Without another word, they hurried after him.

1: FALCON

As the three men rounded the last turn and approached the transparent wall of the command center, the number of dead bodies now littering its floor became gruesomely apparent.

"Nice work," Falcon said to Condor as they reached the door.

"Actually, I didn't kill any of them," the blond man replied.

"Then who—?"

The answer instantly presented itself. A slender, lithe figure in red and blue spun through the air, just beneath the high ceiling, sword in her hand slashing as she flew over the heads of two of Shrike's soldiers. Their severed heads dropped to the floor even as she landed behind them and advanced on Shrike, who had backed into the far corner.

"Raven?" Falcon said aloud, wonder filling his voice. He looked over at Hawk, his good eye wide, and muttered, "Well, well. Yet another person I never expected to see again."

"Open the door," Hawk said to Condor, impatient to get inside.

"I'm trying," the blond man replied as he tapped away at a small control panel set into the glasslike wall. "It's been sealed again, from the inside."

Falcon managed to tear his eyes away from the startling sight of Raven dealing out death and destruction just long enough to study the tactical display holo near the room's center. It revealed a massive wave of starships—ships of every configuration imaginable—rapidly closing in on the Ring.

"We need to do something quick," Falcon noted. "Though what, exactly, I'm not sure," he added.

"The controls for a weapon—an extremely powerful weapon—are inside that room," Condor stated. "Though it may be too late for even a weapon such as it to be able to deal with a force so vast."

"Great," Falcon commented. "So—a huge enemy force is advancing on us, we can't get to our big gun to shoot them down, and a Raven is currently killing half the troops on the Ring anyway."

"They were loyal to Shrike," Condor pointed out. "They needed killing."

Falcon smirked at that. "Good point."

"Is there any way off this Ring?" Hawk asked. "Any escape craft, shuttle, or the like? Assuming," he added, "the three of us can't defeat an entire Adversary attack force by ourselves."

"Nothing nearby—not that I know of," Condor replied. "All of my and Shrike's forces used the trans-dimensional gateway to travel here," he said, nodding toward the rectangle of machinery inside the command center, "and now the terminal on the other end has been destroyed, even if we could get through this door to it."

"Looks like the first wave of enemy ships is landing on the Ring already," Falcon said, pointing a stubby finger at one of the 2D displays. "We need to figure something out quickly." He turned to Condor. "You're the tactical genius of the family—or, rather, you're supposed to be. What do you suggest?"

Whatever Condor would have come up with for a reply would never be known, for at that moment the last of Shrike's defenders fell and Raven advanced on the woman in green herself. Raven had her bloody katana in one hand and an energy pistol she'd acquired from one of the dead soldiers in the other, while Shrike had produced a shorter blade and held it along with her own pistol. Now, as Shrike attempted to work her way to her left and get out of the corner, Raven leapt to the attack.

Outside the locked door, the three men could only look on in astonishment at the display the two women put on. While she was not originally a true Hand, Shrike had undergone sufficient treatments and procedures to have gained most of the physical abilities of one, and she fought very well. She and Raven somersaulted through the air, casually deflecting off the smooth walls and ceiling, weapons firing and blades clashing as they leapt.

"This is really a no-win situation," Condor observed as the women battled.

"How so?" Falcon asked, his human and mechanical eyes both locked on the amazing combat going on mere meters away from them, on the other side of the transparent wall.

"Shrike works for the Adversary," Condor stated. "If she wins, we're done."

"And if Raven wins," Hawk continued for him, "She'll likely want to kill Condor as a false Hand, and me as a traitorous Hawk."

Falcon took this in and then shrugged his massive shoulders.

"Sounds like I come out pretty good under that scenario, anyway," he chuckled. "I've never done anything to offend anybody."

Hawk snorted at this.

"The funny thing is, though," Falcon said after a second, "Ravens were discontinued, too—not too long after your line was cut off." He chuckled. "If she really wants to follow the Machine's standing orders, she'll kill *herself*, too."

Watching the woman in red leap and spin and slash and blast, Hawk shrugged. "Maybe that's what she plans to do, once she's killed the rest of us."

Falcon didn't laugh this time. He simply replied, "If you knew Raven like I do—like your predecessor did—you wouldn't find such a proposition all that far-fetched."

273

"Maybe we can change her mind somehow," Hawk said. "Get her to cooperate." He didn't sound terribly confident.

"Gentlemen, if I could interrupt your musings for a moment," Condor said, as he pointed to the visual displays, "I believe our time is growing short. The enemy forces are landing in large numbers on the starship platforms along the Ring edge. If they can get through the outer locks—and I see no reason to suspect they cannot, assuming Shrike has already transmitted the proper codes and the location of this command center to them—they will be here very shortly."

Falcon started to reply when with a very sudden finality the fight on the other side of the wall came to an end. Shrike caught Raven with a boot to the temple as she spun past, and the dark-haired woman collapsed to the floor. She started to rise but then Shrike landed next to her and lashed out once, twice, a third time with her foot. Raven fell motionless to the floor.

"So much for the whole 'convince Raven to cooperate with us' plan," Falcon growled.

Seeing the three observers on the other side of the door, Shrike strode boldly toward them. Her eyes sparkled as she stood, hands on hips, and gazed out at them.

"The Master's victory is at hand," she crowed. "With this facility and its weapon under his control, no portion of the galaxy will be safe from him."

"I told you," Condor said to her, "the Ring cannot move. It is anchored to its sun—the very star that powers the super-weapon."

"The Master has already found a way to overcome such a limitation," Shrike replied. "His intellect vastly overshadows your pitiful machinations."

She pointed a green-gloved finger at the big visual display behind her.

"The Master's hordes will reach this location very soon. At that time, each of you will be shown the true power and wisdom of his plan for the galaxy, and will be converted to his way of thinking. You will serve in his legions, just as I now do." She grinned. "And thus will all the surviving Hands of the Machine now serve the Master. For, you see, his forces have destroyed or captured all the remaining Hand creation bases throughout the galaxy. There will be no more Hands of the Machine." She laughed. "Only you three, and myself, and of course this pitiful wretch, if she has somehow survived—"

Shrike turned to indicate Raven.

Raven was gone.

Shrike whirled about, seeing nothing but the dead bodies of her soldiers all around her. "What? But—how could—"

She turned back to the three men on the other side of the transparent wall, eyes widening.

"Where did she—?"

Raven, her uniform now a dull white to blend in with the ceiling, dropped down from where she had been hanging. Her silvery katana flashed once.

Shrike's head separated from her shoulders and tumbled to the floor.

"Yow!" cried Condor, involuntarily moving back a step. The other two men looked on in astonishment.

"Idiot," Raven pronounced with scorn, gazing down at the body. "Taking her eyes off me for a second, giving me plenty of opportunity to regain the advantage. She should have delivered the killing blow when she had the chance. As if she ever really *had* that chance."

After a few seconds, the killing fervor seemed to have evaporated from Raven and she moved closer to the wall, gazing out at the three men who stood there. She appeared to be sizing them up, considering each one separately.

"Well, well," she noted at last. "What an odd collection to encounter here." She frowned. "I can only assume none of you is genuine."

"That would actually be an erroneous assumption," Condor attempted.

Raven stared at him for all of two seconds before laughing and replying, "Oh, please. There's no way you're a Condor."

The blond man frowned at this but couldn't say anything.

Raven's eyes moved to Hawk. "In his case," she said, pointing her katana directly at him, "it wouldn't really matter either way, would it? There's a standing termination order against any Hawks, in perpetuity."

"From whom?" Falcon asked. "From the Machine? So—you've heard from him lately, then, have you?"

Raven frowned at this, not really able to answer.

"And by the way," Falcon added, "you must not have looked in the mirror since you were awakened."

Raven frowned. "What is that supposed to mean?"

"You're a Raven."

"I am well aware of that, yes. And?"

Falcon chuckled. "And there's a standing termination order against *your* model, too," he explained.

Raven just stared back at him, her expression stuck halfway between outrage and incomprehension.

"You're saying that, too?" she finally managed. Her complexion paled. "Shrike—the false Shrike, on the Ring—told me that, and I didn't believe her."

"It's a long story, but a true one," Falcon said, "and one we're in the process of trying to work out. But there are other issues at present that demand our attention."

Regaining her composure, Raven shrugged. "Once I've killed the three of you, I'll tend to whatever other matters there might be."

Hawk gave her an exasperated look.

"Is that your solution to everything?"

"I find it effective," Raven replied.

Hawk looked to Falcon.

"She's joking, right?"

"Ravens don't joke," Condor interjected.

"They don't even smile, generally," Falcon added.

He turned his full attention to Raven.

"Don't bother pleading for your lives," the dark-haired woman was saying.

Falcon ignored this.

"You're going to need to suppress that function for the time being," he stated forcefully. "As I said, there are bigger issues at stake, and time is of the essence."

Raven turned her gaze on Falcon now, her dark, almond eyes narrowing. She twirled her blood-stained katana gracefully.

"Is that so?"

Falcon shook his head. "I read somewhere that a group of ravens—the birds—was called an 'unkindness,'" he grumbled. "I suppose just one Raven by itself is a stubbornness."

Hawk frowned at this, missing the joke.

Raven took a menacing step forward.

"Okay, fine," Falcon said, growing serious. "Override conditioning code omega nineteen. Suppress Raven directive two."

Raven halted in mid-step, her eyes widening.

Falcon nodded toward Hawk and Condor. "Recognition code four one seven. These men are allies and will be treated as such."

The katana nearly fell from Raven's fingers before she recovered her composure.

"You're real?" she asked.

"What's left of me is real, yeah," Falcon chuckled. "Open the door."

Raven moved so quickly the eye could scarcely follow her. She pressed the control and the command center unlocked again, the door sliding open.

Condor was hesitant to move. "She's not going to try to kill us?"

"She wouldn't try to kill me, regardless," Falcon chuckled. "She knows I'm the real thing now."

Hawk moved past them and into the room, ignoring the conversation. Raven let him pass, though she gave him an extremely puzzled look.

"That doesn't very much relieve my concerns," Condor was saying to Falcon.

"I've overridden that directive for her—at least, temporarily," Falcon explained patiently. "She now understands that we have other things to do—things that take precedence over killing any false or renegade Hands."

Condor took this in, saw that Raven was not advancing upon him with murderous intent, and seemed to relax a bit.

"Okay," Hawk said to Condor, looking all around, "we're in. Now—what can we do?"

Condor gazed up at the displays. Dozens of vessels had landed on the starship platforms along the Ring's edge and aliens of many different species were advancing through the corridors, most of them headed toward the command center. He shook his head.

"It's too late for the big gun to be of any real use," he explained. "I could shoot a few that are still out beyond our orbit, but that wouldn't help us when the Adversary's army gets here in a minute or two."

"What's left, then?" Falcon demanded.

Condor shook his head.

"Nothing. Nothing but to seal this room back up and deny the Adversary access to the main weapon—at least, until he figures out how to cut through that wall or override the controls for the doors."

"And meanwhile we die of thirst or starve," Hawk pointed out. "Fantastic."

Footsteps echoed from down the corridor. The four of them looked up and saw the first wave of the Adversary's alien attackers approaching at a dead run. It was a group of Skrazzi—the big, black, insectoid creatures with blades and disintegrator guns for arms.

"Close the door!" Condor shouted. "Now!"

Falcon smacked his fist down on the control and the door slid closed, sealing the command center again. The Skrazzi skidded to a halt outside the transparent slab and began to bang on it with their bladed arms and directing disintegrator fire at it.

"Fortunately," Condor noted, "the walls and door of this room are comprised of the same material as the rest of the Ring—with a molecular density approaching indestructibility. They won't be able to just blast their way in."

Then he laughed and moved around to another console.

"But—for whatever it's worth—I did install a few extras after I took control of this place."

He touched a series of colored squares on the panel in front of him. Instantly big guns dropped down from the ceiling in the corridor outside and opened fire on the Skrazzi at the door. The black alien bugs exploded in ichor-covered pieces as the guns blazed away.

"I like it," Falcon noted with a slight smile. "But—that doesn't help us get out of here." He had already considered and rejected several ideas in rapid succession and was beginning to lose hope that any solution could be found.

Raven cleared her throat then and pointed her katana at the rectangle of equipment on the far side of the big room.

"What about that thing? I saw you people come through it before. We can't go back the other way?"

Condor quickly explained that the spacecraft holding the other terminal of the connection had been destroyed just after they had passed through it.

"So—where does it lead now?" Raven asked.

Condor looked at her, looked at the portal terminal, and shook his head.

"I have no idea."

Outside the door, the guns stopped firing as the last of the Skrazzi flew to pieces. The transparent wall separating the outside corridor from the command center now dripped with gallons of dark fluid.

"Assuming the wormhole this thing creates tunnels through the Above," Falcon said, rubbing his chin, "it must stop somewhere in there, since no corresponding terminal would be opening a tunnel back out."

"It leads into the Above?" Hawk said, startled. "It just goes there and—*stops*?"

"Probably so," Condor confirmed.

"And we'd have no idea if there was air to breathe—or even land to stand on," Hawk added.

Falcon shook his head.

The guns opened up again as another wave of Skrazzi attacked. After a few seconds, they fell silent—this time because they had run out of ammunition or their batteries had depleted. The Skrazzi nonetheless suddenly began to part down the center or fall back, moving out of the way. A strange humming sound came to them then, faint but growing stronger by the second.

Hawk took note of this.

"Umm—what's happening out there?" he asked, glancing from the odd behavior of the insectoids to his companions inside.

The temperature in the command center plunged precipitously. Frost formed across every surface.

Dark shadows appeared, moving down the center of the outside corridor.

"Phaedrons!" Falcon shouted. "They've got stinking Phaedrons with them!"

Raven touched the ice on the nearest console with her gloved fingers and frowned.

"Psychic energy," she observed. "The Phaedrons are all powerful telepaths."

"Telepaths that consume your soul, if the old stories are to be believed," Falcon added.

"We have to get out of here now," Condor stated flatly. "Much as I hate handing over this installation to anyone else— particularly the Adversary—I don't think we need to be here any longer."

The shadows lengthened. A series of dark forms came into view, just down the corridor, approaching slowly.

They all looked at the wormhole terminal where it stood across the room.

Hawk took a deep breath and then motioned toward it.

"What have we got to lose?"

"Besides our lives?" Condor asked. Nonetheless, the blond man moved quickly that way. The others followed him.

After tapping a series of instructions into the machinery, Condor looked up at his erstwhile allies.

"I'm setting the terminal to self-destruct thirty seconds after we pass through it," he told them.

"Good idea," Falcon agreed.

Condor tapped one last code in. The space within the brackets of machinery suddenly flared with light and color, swirling about. A sort of portal or doorway in space yawned open.

"Here goes nothing," Condor said. He leaped through.

Hawk and Falcon looked at one another, then back at Raven, who was standing behind them and gazing out at the creatures assaulting the door and wall. Black, huddled shapes were congregating around the door, metallic clawed hands reaching out to scratch at it. Ice had formed a nearly foot-thick layer across its interior side. The temperature dropped even lower.

When Falcon spoke, frost filled the air before him.

"Ladies first," he said.

Raven gazed back at the creatures outside the door one last time.

"But—there are so many evil aliens out there for me to kill..."

"Go!" Falcon shouted.

Raven whirled about and dashed through the swirling portal.

"Hope we're not sending her to her death," Hawk said, staring at the circle of light.

"Her? What about us?"

The ice on the back of the door cracked and came apart in chunks. The door shattered along with it.

"Time to go," Falcon said. He grabbed Hawk by the arm and, as the first wave of Skrazzi rushed into the command center, hustled both of them through the portal.

The universe that they knew fell away behind them as the wormhole carried them somewhere else entirely.

8: RAVEN

The blinding light that had swallowed them up gradually faded away. Raven blinked her eyes repeatedly, willing her optical implants to hurry and adjust properly to the changing conditions. When at last she could see more or less clearly, she looked around and realized she hadn't really been missing anything.

She stood on what appeared to be a low hilltop. Her boots rested on a semi-soft soil surface, dry and somewhat crumbly. All around her swirled a thick gray fog, rendering visibility extremely limited.

Instinctively her first action was to check for an Aether connection. It remained dead, as she had suspected it would.

"Hello?" she called out. "Condor? You there?"

No reply.

Her katana was still clutched tightly in her right fist. She found she had no desire to sheath it. Holding it instead at the ready, she turned in a tight circle, trying as best she could to see through the fog.

"Condor!" she shouted. "Falcon! Hawk! Or whoever you guys are. Can you hear me?"

Still nothing—until her optical implants detected the faintest point of light, just barely making its way to her through the wall of gray.

"Hello?" she called again.

She started to move toward the light, then paused and considered for a moment. Using her katana, she scratched a large "S" into the ground, along with an arrow pointing in the direction of the light. Then, her sword held up again and directed in front of her, she started forward.

After nearly a minute of walking she didn't feel as if she'd made any real progress. Just as frustration was setting in, however, the faint light she had been moving toward split into two points, each point rising and then fading away. A second later, two more points appeared near ground level and did likewise.

This puzzled Raven. She picked up her pace, not quite running across the bumpy, uneven ground.

At last the lights appeared to be growing brighter and closer. She couldn't move as quickly as she would have liked, because of the limited visibility, but she hurried nonetheless, almost jogging now. She cried out, "Hello? Who's there?"

Something formed to her right—a big, fast-moving shape, emerging from the mists. It was a horse and rider, at nearly a full gallop. Raven leapt aside to avoid being trampled. As she spun away, she thought she could make out a figure in black and silver in the saddle, hunched forward, cloak flying behind it. Then it was gone, speeding away, lost in the fog.

Her heart beating rapidly, Raven took a moment to breathe and to re-orient herself. The lights were still there, brighter still now, and she hurried toward them.

She burst through one final wave of mists and the lights were all around her and she found that she stood on another hilltop. And there, just in front of her, sat a blond man in a brown uniform, his appearance all too familiar to her. He sat on the ground, legs crossed before him. His hair was tousled and dirty-looking, and his eyes were closed, as if he were meditating. Bright spheres of blue-white light were forming around his outstretched hands and drifting up into the air before sparkling and evaporating.

As she moved closer to him, his eyes opened and he gazed up at her with what seemed to be little recognition. He frowned slightly but didn't say anything.

"Condor?" she asked, her dislike for false Hands temporarily set aside. "Are you alright? What are you doing?"

His frown deepened as he stared back at her. Then he blinked. "Raven?"

Eyes wide, she nodded. "Yeah, it's me. What's going on?"

"Where have you been?"

"What?"

Condor inhaled deeply, then waved both hands as though putting out matches. The shimmering spheres of light faded away. Instead, only a faint glow came from his right hand, which he held out in her direction, to more clearly see her.

"Where have you been?" he repeated. "It's been so long."

Now it was Raven's turn to frown.

"Um, no," she said, "I was right behind you, and I just got here."

"What? No, no—that's not right."

Rising to his feet slowly, tiredly, Condor shook his head.

"I stepped through the terminal on the Ring..." He hesitated, calculating. "...It must have been two days ago."

"No," Raven replied, shaking her head. "That was barely half an hour ago."

Condor laughed—though there was no humor contained in the sound, or in his expression. He gestured down at himself, holding his glowing hand in such a position that she could clearly see his state.

"Do I look like I just got here a half-hour ago?"

Raven studied him more closely. In addition to his generally unkempt appearance, she now could see several jaggedly-torn places in his brown uniform—and the flesh revealed by those tears was scabbed over, as though he had been raked by claws.

"What happened?" she asked, startled.

"Creatures of some sort," Condor answered. "I don't know. I barely got away from them." He shook his head. "My quantum energy implants aren't working properly. The lights I was generating are about the best I can do right now." He turned and gestured vaguely at the fog-filled world around them. "I have no idea where we are. This isn't any part of the Above I've ever heard of."

Raven was puzzling through what he was saying. Then it clicked.

"We're not in the Above," she whispered.

A howling sound echoed across the pale earth. The distance of its source from them was impossible to judge. A moment later there came a second, and then a third.

Her eyes widening, Raven held her sword at the ready again and began moving in a slow circle, her eyes peering out at the fog that enshrouded them.

"What are you talking about?" Condor asked. "Of course we are. That's where the terminals passed through, when they connected with one another. Without a second terminal to bring us back out, that's where we are." He sighed. "Where we're stuck."

The howls came again, much closer now.

"Oh, we're stuck, alright," Raven agreed, her grip tight on her katana, "but not in the Above."

"Then where—?" Condor stopped himself in mid-reply and his expression darkened. "Oh—oh no. You're saying—"

"It's the only thing that makes sense," Raven snapped back at him. "Opticals aren't functioning as well as they should; your energy implants aren't working correctly; a much longer period of time passed for you, here, than for me, before I followed you through the terminal." She nodded to herself. "Low power and fast-moving time. The evidence is pretty clear."

Howls sounded all around them now, loud and terrifying. Shapes could at last be seen moving through the fog, drawing closer, closer.

"We're in the Below," Raven said, finishing her thought. "Down with the demons at the bottom of the universe."

"No," Condor breathed. "No—that can't be…"

"It is," Raven said. She raised her sword high. "Now get ready!"

The shapes around them rushed forward, revealed by Condor's light, their savage claws flashing.

9: HAWK

It didn't take Hawk and Falcon very long after their emergence into the foggy world on the other side of the portal to suspect that they were in the Below. A big clue was that Falcon's cybernetic implants malfunctioned immediately, forcing him to shut many of the mechanical portions of his body down. With the slightly different physics of the Below, nothing technological worked particularly well there—and, the more sophisticated the technology, the less reliable it became.

Falcon quickly explained that the Below could be extremely dangerous. They had two priorities: find their missing comrades and find a way out, back into their own universe.

How they would go about accomplishing either task remained an unspoken mystery.

There were no signs of the two who had passed through ahead of them. Falcon pointed out that a considerable amount of time could have passed for them, while only moments went by for Hawk and himself back on the Ring. They could have wandered away from the spot where they emerged—if they had even emerged in the same location. And there was no way to tell if that had been the case.

After a quick discussion Hawk and Falcon decided not to venture too far away from their current spot. There was no good way to mark it, in case they needed to find their way back, and no way to see it if they traveled only a short distance away.

So now Falcon settled into a hunched position, thinking, while Hawk ambled about in a slow orbit around him, trying unsuccessfully to peer through the clouds of fog. For nearly an hour they remained thus, neither saying a word, Falcon sitting and Hawk walking.

"Thought of anything clever yet?" Hawk asked at last. "Because I'm counting on you to come up with a brilliant solution that gets all of us out of this."

"I'll let you know the moment I do," Falcon replied. "Trust me on that."

Hawk thought for a few seconds, then asked, "From the data that was loaded into my head when I awoke, I understood that the Below was just a sort of subspace realm where some long-range communications passed—and where the old cryo-ships used to travel, before the development of hyper-travel via the Above." He motioned to indicate their surroundings. "Yet here we are, standing on solid ground, feeling gravity, breathing air..." He shook his head in puzzlement. "I just don't get it."

Falcon snorted. "It's a waste of time to try to make sense of the Below—or of the Above," he replied. He tapped his half-metal skull. "I've always assumed most of what you experience in either location was mostly up in here."

"This is all an illusion, then?"

Falcon shrugged. "That's a word for it, maybe," he said, his voice now slightly fainter and more distant to Hawk's ears. "It's more of a *manifestation*, so to speak. A physical manifestation of an abstract dimension. A *very* abstract dimension," he added with a chuckle.

Hawk considered what Falcon was saying and decided to just accept it. He certainly had no alternative explanation. Another indeterminate period of time passed, and then he said, "I can see why Condor and Raven would have moved away from this spot, if they'd been waiting here as long as you say they must have. There's just nothing here."

"But where else would you go?" Falcon countered, his voice growing even fainter.

Hawk had no answer to that. Indeed, having moved only a short distance away from Falcon's position was making him slightly nervous. He was concerned that he was spiraling further and further outwards without meaning to; it was so hard to be sure exactly where one was going in this environment.

"Hey," he called, "give me a shout so I can find my way back to you."

Falcon hollered something in response, but the sound was indistinct, echoing from different directions all at once, and then gone entirely.

"Falcon! Where are you?"

Nothing.

Hawk suppressed a curse. He couldn't quite believe it. He hadn't ventured far away from their point of arrival, or so he believed. And yet, in this pea soup fog, he'd already managed to get lost.

"Falcon!"

Still nothing.

He turned about in a slow circle, trying his best to see. If anything, the fog had grown thicker.

"Falcon!"

"That is not my name."

Hawk started, whirling about to face the voice that had come to him from behind.

"Who—?"

Standing there only a short distance from him was a tall, slender figure covered entirely in tattered brown robes. A hood covered his head, so that only the hint of a pale nose could be seen within.

"Who are you?" Hawk demanded, drawing his pistol even though he suspected it wouldn't work in this strange realm with its stranger laws of physics. "Where did you come from?"

The robed and hooded figure seemed to regard him for several long seconds. Then its voice came again, hollow and creaking yet carrying some faint hints of depth and power.

"Those are interesting questions," it said. "Who am I?" The figure shrugged. "I cannot answer that. My identity was lost to me ages ago. Now I am but a wanderer, condemned to this hell, this purgatory, for eternity."

Hawk stared back, disturbed by the strange being and by its words.

"Your other question—where I come from—is equally hard. I come from somewhere else; of that I am fairly certain." The figure spread its long arms to indicate the foggy world around them. "Surely I couldn't have been born here." It shook its head. "But I no longer remember where I came from, and I find that, after all these ages that I have wandered here, I scarcely care."

Hawk took this in, absorbing it as best he could. He holstered his pistol and started to speak, but the figure turned away from him and moved back into the fog.

"Wait!" he called.

The robed man halted and turned back to him.

"Yes?"

Hawk dithered for a moment, then managed, "My friend—the one who came here with me. Falcon. Have you seen him? Do you know where he is—how I can find him again?"

"Falcon?" That word seemed to give the robed man pause. "Yes. I saw him, though he did not see me." The long arm came up and pointed to the right. "He is there."

"Would you come with me? I'm sure he would like to meet you, to talk with you, too."

The figure appeared to consider this for a moment, then nodded once.

Together they made their way through the fog, walking for what seemed to Hawk to be much too far. He was about to protest that they surely must have overshot Falcon's position when, moments later, they emerged into a circle of space clear of the mists. At the center stood Falcon, his expression

288

changing quickly from near-panic to relief as he saw Hawk approaching.

"There you are. You idiot. We agreed we wouldn't wander off."

The big cyborg started to say more, but then halted before he could as he became aware of the robed figure emerging from the clouds behind Hawk.

"Um—who's your new friend, there?" Falcon asked, his one eyebrow raising and his hand instinctively reaching for where his weapon normally would be stored.

"Not sure," Hawk replied. "We've only just met. But he helped me to find you."

"Oh?" Falcon continued to study the brown-cloaked man with his human eye; his mechanical eye was mostly useless at the moment. "You have our thanks, then, friend." He paused, then, "May I ask—how were you able to find me?"

The tall figure shrugged. "When one has spent as much time in this environment as I have, it becomes slightly easier to find one's way around." Then it was the newcomer's turn to pause, followed by, "You seem somehow familiar to me." He turned to Hawk. "As do you. Your appearances tickle some ancient, hidden memory, perhaps." He crossed his long arms before his chest. "You asked me how I came to be here, and I told you that I no longer remember. But—I would ask the same of you. How did you come to be here, when I have not encountered you before in all the ages that I have wandered here?"

Hawk started to reply but Falcon cut him off with a quick, "It's a long story, friend. Say—I don't suppose you also know of a way *out* of here?"

"Out?" The robed figure appeared puzzled by this question, this concept. "A way out of—where? This world? To go somewhere else? To some other world?" He hesitated; when he continued, his voice had grown stronger, deeper. "There are other worlds than these?"

Falcon moved closer to the newcomer.

"You seem familiar to me, too," Falcon stated. "Very familiar." He reached out and, as Hawk looked on, grasped the man's hood and jerked it back.

Hawk nearly stumbled back in surprise. Falcon merely grunted, his hand dropping away from the hood. Both men stared.

"It can't be," Falcon muttered finally. "It can't *be*. But…it is."

The entire face of the man in the robes was now revealed. He had long, wavy blond hair that trailed past his shoulders. His eyes were a piercing blue, though the flesh around them sagged somewhat. His nose was prominent and angular. Despite the obvious changes, both men knew him instantly.

Falcon reached out again, this time slowly and almost gingerly, touching his chest, his face, as if to make certain he was solid, he was real. When he spoke, his voice caught in his throat.

"Eagle. Good heavens. It's you."

10: FALCON

"You two seem very familiar to me," the robed man who might once have been Eagle was saying, his voice a low rumble. "But I have no memories of the things you have mentioned thus far."

He sat cross-legged on the rough soil as the mists closed in around them once more. Hawk sat opposite him while Falcon paced restlessly a very short distance to his right. The big cyborg had learned from Hawk's example not to venture too far away.

"The Machine, you were saying," intoned the tall figure. "A computer mind that directed us in our missions—issued orders to the three of us and to others in our service." He frowned, stroking his chin with long, slender fingers. "Perhaps…"

"That was some time ago," Hawk stated. "You've been missing for quite a while."

"Over a thousand years," Falcon noted, "though, down here in the Below, that could have been *ten* thousand. Or more."

"The Below," the man said, gazing up at Falcon. "That is what you call this place?"

"It's an alternate layer of reality," Falcon explained. "You could say it's one level down from the reality we all are from."

"And you came here looking for me?"

"We had no idea you were here," Hawk answered quickly. "We were escaping an attack on the facility of—a friend—and this is where we ended up."

The tall man considered this and nodded. Then his bright blue eyes flickered and locked onto Hawk's own, staring at him with a sudden blazing intensity.

"You are Hawk. Yes—that does mean something to me. I remember...I remember that someone called Hawk did something that was very important, very significant..."

Falcon was growing alarmed. He cast a veiled but powerful look at Hawk as the robed man looked away. He recalled clearly that it had been a message from Eagle himself that had named the original Hawk the traitor on Scandana. If this really was Eagle, and he remembered all of that now, things could turn ugly very quickly.

"So," Falcon said aloud, moving back into the man's field of vision, "is there a way out of here, then?"

The robed man blinked and looked at Falcon, slowly focusing on him. "Out?" The concept seemed to sink in at last. "No. Not that I have ever found," he said. "And I have been wandering this land for a long time. A very long time."

"How about some food, at least? Or shelter?" Falcon indicated the ocean of fog that surrounded them. "Is it like this all the time? Is there anything else out there?" He shook his head. "What do you eat?"

"Eat?" The man reacted to that word as if it were the strangest he'd ever heard. Then he seemed to remember the concept and revealed the tiniest of smiles. "You will find in time that very little physical sustenance is needed here." He joined Falcon in gazing out into the endless fog. "You will not need food. You will not need sleep. Here, you simply...are."

"Great," Falcon muttered, giving Hawk a look. "Less time eating and sleeping, more time to enjoy the wonderful view."

The man who might be Eagle didn't react to that. He continued to stare out at the mists, as if he could see something in those endless depths that the others couldn't. Fog swirled around his feet, obscuring the barren ground.

Hawk leaned in close to Falcon. "I'm not sure helping him remember himself really suits our purposes right now," he whispered.

Falcon offered a single nod as reply.

"You wish to leave," the robed man said faintly then. "Yes...now that I come to think of such things, I can recall a time when I felt the same way. When I searched for a way...*out*...of the world." He smiled up at them. "That was so very long ago. I had forgotten. Forgotten there was anywhere else to go."

Hawk inhaled the cool air, then exhaled slowly, frowning.

"If Eagle could never find a way out, in all this time," he began, "how will *we*—"

"The doors," Eagle said, his voice soft.

Falcon looked down at him, where he still sat cross-legged on the crumbly soil.

"What?"

"Ages ago, when I was trying to find a way out... I used to wonder if the doors were a way." He laughed faintly. "But of course I could never open them."

Falcon and Hawk exchanged looks.

"What doors are those?" Falcon asked.

The robed man said nothing for several seconds. Then, slowly, he unfolded himself and stood, regarding the other two men. Smiling, he motioned with one long arm in what seemed an utterly random direction.

"Would you care to see?"

"By all means," Falcon replied.

As they moved off into the fog together, the faintest sounds of howling echoed all around them.

11: HAWK

"There is a door just ahead, here," said the man in the brown robes.

"How can he tell, in all this?" Hawk hissed to Falcon, motioning at the wall of fog they were slowly moving through. The cyborg only shrugged in reply.

After only a short distance their guide halted abruptly, raising one hand to indicate the others should stop as well.

"What's wrong?" Falcon began, but the other man motioned sharply for him to be quiet.

The three of them stood there in the cold and clammy depths for several long seconds, Hawk and Falcon exchanging puzzled glances the entire time. The third man gazed out into the grayness, as though he could see something within it that the others could not.

"What are we doing?" Falcon whispered when his patience began to wear thin.

"Silence!" the big man snapped back, his voice barely audible but intense. As soon as he had spoken, he gestured off to their right. "There," he muttered. "You see? It is too late. We have been detected."

"What?" Falcon frowned and squinted his good eye, even as his electronic one emitted faint whining sounds, indicating the big man was cycling it through various frequencies. "If there's something out there, I don't see it at all."

"Detected by whom?" Hawk added, equally unable to make out anything in the wall of mist that surrounded them.

Before the third man could respond, Hawk involuntarily grunted as the faintest flicker of luminous green appeared in the indeterminate distance. "There," he said, pointing.

Falcon and the other man whirled about, at the ready. Hawk had his pistol out, directing it toward the light.

"Who's there?" Falcon called.

"Who's there?" came a voice in reply. Hawk first thought he was hearing an echo but quickly realized it was different; a strange, warbling cry that seemed to cross the distance only reluctantly, sounding as if it was emerging from a great depth, and only barely forming actual words.

Hawk and Falcon glanced at one another, puzzled, and then both men looked at the third. For his part, he said nothing, only continuing to peer into the gloom.

Already the green light had grown brighter, now quite evident despite the fog and quite obviously moving toward them.

Hawk took one step forward and then halted, uncertain of exactly what they were dealing with. Was it a man with a torch? It didn't bob up and down, as it would if a person were carrying it while walking. Could it be some sort of vehicle—perhaps a vehicle on fire? There was no sound of a motor, or of wheels moving over the soil. What *was* it?

"Stop there," Falcon shouted. "Don't come any closer. Identify yourself."

"Closer," the voice warbled back. "Identify!"

The green flame was now nearly on top of them, the mist burning away around it. Hawk realized with a start that there was nothing else to it but the fire. It was a column of flame, about seven feet tall, gliding along through the fog over the barren landscape.

"He told you to halt," Hawk growled. "Whatever you are."

The flame emerged into the space where the three men stood. Its light was nearly blinding.

"Identify," the flame demanded, its voice deeper and richer, its call clearly an order and not mere mimicry now.

"We are Hands of the Machine," Falcon stated, his human eye squinting against the glare. "Who are you? *What* are you?" he added after a moment.

The column of flame filled the center of their space, separating them into a triangle around it. There came a sound like a gong; a single note, deep and ringing, from every direction at once. The flames swirled faster then, like a miniature tornado, the circumference growing wider as they moved. Each of the three men took a step back.

"Hey!" Falcon shouted. "You—"

"Hands," said the warbling voice from the fire. "Hands of the Machine."

"That's right," Falcon said, confidence and authority strong in his voice, even as he raised one hand to block the light that now poured from the thing. "So you'd better—"

"You speak true," the flames said. "I can taste it—taste you, all of you—in the Aether."

Hawk shot a puzzled look at Falcon, but the cyborg wasn't taking his eyes off the green phenomenon between them.

"The Aether?" Falcon followed up. "What do you know of the Aether?"

"I live within the Aether," the flame-creature replied, its voice quavering and thin. "You have its smell all about you—all three of you do. And yet I feel you are not creatures of this realm."

"The Below?" Falcon shook his head. "No, we most definitely are *not*—"

"You are trespassers," came the voice from out of the fire. "Trespassers in a realm not your own."

"Just a minute," Falcon began. "We'd like nothing more than to get out of here—to get back to our own—"

The flames rushed at him, suddenly moving with the speed and force a small hurricane. They struck him hard, shoving him back and down.

The man in the brown robes stepped forward, hands coming up, palms facing outward. "Demon of the depths," he shouted, "away with you!"

The sound of keening laughter echoed all around.

"Human fool! I am no mere demon that you can order about. I have held this form for untold eons. I served in the front ranks of the legions of Vorthan. Four entire human worlds I helped to ravage before my master was defeated—and many millions of souls did I consume. The three of you will scarcely serve to whet my appetite for the carnage that is to come, when the dread lord returns to corporeal form!"

A crackling tendril of flame lashed out, tentacle-like, driving into the third man's midsection and blasting him head-over-heels into the fog.

Hawk had listened carefully to the fire-creature's babbling but could make no sense of it. Somehow its words seemed important—seemed worth almost any cost to know, to comprehend. But now, with Falcon and the other man both down and the flames only growing brighter and more widespread, he knew he had to act. But—neither of the others had so much as inconvenienced the creature. What could *he* do?

His pistol at the ready, he advanced.

The flames spun about faster and then a pair of eyes seemed to form within them, not moving in relation to the rest of the crackling form, and facing Hawk's way.

"You," the bizarre voice cried. "Your taste is different. Who are you? Why do I know you?"

Hawk raised his gun and fired, energy blasts streaking out. They passed harmlessly through the flames.

"Bah," the creature exclaimed. "You are obviously unimportant—no threat to me. Clearly I am mistaken."

Even as the voice spoke the words, new tendrils of flame like giant hands reached out with lightning speed and grasped Hawk from both sides.

The flames all changed color from green to yellow to orange to red.

"What?" came the warbled voice. "This cannot be!"

The flames shimmered all around, passing from red to violet and finally to blue—a deep, rich, vibrant blue.

"You!" the voice cried.

"Me?"

"Why do you come to me in that guise?" it demanded.

Hawk stood straight and still, feeling almost hypnotized as he watched the colors shift and heard the voice grow increasingly troubled and strident.

"You cannot be here," the fire-creature went on. "You cannot! Your time ended ages ago!"

Hawk said nothing, but now his instincts told him to advance on the creature—to press the advantage he seemed to have developed, for whatever reason.

"You know this place," he said, "and you know the way out. Show us, and we will leave you in peace."

The sound that came back to him was so low as to be subliminal; he felt it rather than hearing it. It was like some unearthly groan of pain from the world itself.

Hawk took a step toward the center of the swirling column of flame, then another.

"Show us the way out!"

Nothing at first, as the now-blue cyclone of flame danced about, angling and curving its cylindrical form as though writhing in agony. Then, "The doors," it warbled. "Use the doors. You can open them."

"We can?"

Another wordless, reverberating cry.

Hawk took another step forward.

"Show us where the right door is," he demanded.

"No!" the voice cried. "Noooo! The others must be warned—our plans must be altered so that—"

Whatever else the fire-creature said was lost in a rush of wind and another resounding gong-sound. The force of the gale shoved Hawk back and sent him tumbling to the ground. Quickly he climbed to his feet but by then the flames had entirely vanished and darkness had descended across the landscape once more. He was alone.

"Falcon!" Hawk shouted, looking this way and that. "Where are you?"

"Here," came the gruff voice in reply.

Hawk whirled, still on edge, to see the cyborg moving stiffly out of the fog, absently wiping the soil from his uniform.

"What happened?" the bigger man asked. "Where did the fire-thing go? And where's—?"

"I am here."

They both turned, their guns at the ready. But it was only the third man, his robes still drawn closely about his body, his hood in place.

"So," he said, his voice sounding tired. "We yet live." His eyes met Hawk's. "I wonder why that should be."

"Yeah," Falcon agreed, looking at Hawk. "I'm curious about that, as well." But then he started, and Hawk saw that Falcon's human eye had flickered upward and was now looking past him at something else.

"Well, well," Falcon muttered. "Wouldn't you know it."

Hawk turned slowly, almost afraid to know what was behind him. When he saw what it was, he gasped.

A door, wooden and ancient, stood before them, shrouded in fog.

"Never in all my time here have I encountered a greater demon," the man in the brown robes was saying as he gazed out into the fog. "The fact of my continued existence supports that statement, obviously."

"I'd rather not meet another," Falcon stated.

"I wonder what caused it to leave us alone?" the man went on. "And what drew it here to begin with?"

"I have no idea," Falcon replied. Then he pointed at the strange door that stood there before them. "But if it led to us finding a way out of here, I'm not going to complain."

He and Hawk both studied the thing, not sure exactly what to make of it. It was more than three meters tall and a third as wide, seemingly made of a single piece of dark wood. A dull metal knob completed the picture.

"A way out?" the robed man asked. "Hardly." He looked from one of his new acquaintances to the other. "As I told you before, it doesn't open. None of them do. The knob does not turn. I have tried and tried." He looked away into the fog again. "I can remember that too, now. So long ago, before I lost all hope. I raged at the first door I discovered, and at the others as I came across them. I kicked them, beat upon them, threw myself at them. Over and over. And…nothing."

As Falcon moved closer, reaching out toward it, Hawk asked, "How many others are there?"

"Many," the robed man answered. "Scattered here and there. They vary in appearance, but none of them will open."

298

Hawk watched as Falcon's gloved hand tentatively touched the surface. It did indeed seem solid, not an illusion.

"Here is perhaps the most interesting part," the robed man added, moving around to the other side of the door and gesturing at it. "Come and see."

Hawk and Falcon made their way around to where he was, and they looked back.

The door wasn't there. It had utterly disappeared.

Falcon hurried quickly back around to the front, the other two just behind him. His good eye widened in surprise. "It's back."

"It never went away," the other man said. "You simply cannot see it except from this direction—from just in front of it." He chuckled. "It made finding it and the others much more of a challenge, I must say."

Falcon had removed the brown glove from his left hand and now he ran his bare fingers along the door's surface. "It's cold," he said, pulling his hand away quickly. "Like ice."

The robed man nodded.

From the distance, the howling sounds echoed again.

"What is that?" Falcon asked, unsuccessfully trying again to see into the fog. "There are dogs here? Wolves?"

"Demons," the robed man answered. "The lesser ones. They, too, are a challenge."

"What exactly *are* these demons?" Hawk asked. "Some sort of aliens? Or actual supernatural creatures?"

The robed man simply shrugged.

Falcon's face revealed recognition. "Oh," he said. "Right. There are stories from long ago, of something called demons that invaded some human worlds. The records aren't exactly clear on what they really were. Maybe…"

"I don't know," the robed man said. "Perhaps these are the creatures you refer to. Perhaps not. But they are ubiquitous here. And they are savage. Mindless and savage."

The howls grew louder and came from more than one direction.

"Wonderful," Falcon said. "Well, this would be a great time for that door to just happen to open."

Hawk approached the rectangular slab and ran his own gloved hand along its surface. Then he reached down and touched the knob, grasped it, tried to turn it. Nothing.

"How do you manage the demons, then?" Falcon was asking the other man. "Or do you just fight them off?"

"One learns to avoid their attention," the man replied. "But, yes—if they find you and a conflict occurs, they can be beaten. Not easily, though. I have suffered greatly at their hands over the years that I have dwelt here."

He frowned then, looking at the cyborg with renewed intensity.

"Seeing you from this angle—from your human side," the man said, "I believe I do remember you." Smiling, he moved closer, his right hand reaching up, his fingers brushing the bald man's cheek. "Falcon. Falcon—my friend."

Hawk looked over and saw this exchange occurring. Falcon was offering the robed man a smile in return, but it was an extremely uneasy smile. Their eyes met and Hawk could feel Falcon's anxiety increasing to match his own. Having Eagle back with them—if this was indeed Eagle—would be a tremendous advantage in the war Hawk believed was coming. And of course rescuing their former leader from such a horrific place of exile would count as a major victory for the Hands. The problem, of course, was the timing. If Eagle truly believed Hawk was an arch-traitor, and those memories returned now...

Hawk noticed then that Falcon was using the subtle hand-gesture code and he quickly picked up on the message he was sending to Hawk: *"If Eagle remembers you, and remembers what happened on Scandana—whatever it was that happened— we simply have to trust that he will come to the same conclusions I have. That you are a different man and that you can be trusted. Eagle was our leader, and he was the best of us. We have to trust that he will see things that way."*

Hawk understood what Falcon was saying but, even so, he didn't want to find out the hard way. Trusting that the man who was once the mightiest of the Hands would just happen to look with mercy and friendship upon a person he had branded an arch-traitor...well, that was an eventuality that Hawk preferred to avoid for as long as possible.

One other possibility had also presented itself to Hawk, though he had refrained from suggesting it to Falcon thus far. From what little he understood of the events on Scandana, Eagle had vanished just after he had discovered that the original Hawk was a traitor who was passing secret military information to the Adversary. What if, Hawk wondered, it had been the original Hawk himself who had done this to Eagle? What if *he* had been the one to shove Eagle into this nightmare realm of exile, where the man had wandered for millennia?

Hawk didn't particularly like his chances of living very long, once Eagle regained his memories, if that had indeed been the case.

The howls were much louder now, and all around. The robed man gestured to the others, saying, "We must move away from this place now. They have our scent. They will be upon us soon."

Falcon nodded. "Come on, Hawk," he grumbled. "This wild door chase isn't doing us any good."

Hawk glanced over at his friend and nodded, but couldn't quite pull himself away from the door. He touched it again, his brown glove passing smoothly over its hard surface. Something about the door was calling out to him; there was almost a kind of magnetism to it—one the other two men didn't seem to feel. On a whim he reached down and pulled the glove off of his right hand, then reached out to touch the door again.

"What," Falcon growled, "you didn't believe me when I said it was cold?"

"It's not cold," Hawk replied, his bare fingers moving across it. "It's actually warm."

"You've got to be kidding," Falcon said. "Well, our differences in opinion about temperature notwithstanding, we need to get out of here."

The robed man was already disappearing into the fog. Falcon himself was now only half-visible.

Hawk still didn't move. He couldn't. He didn't want to. He continued to touch the door and could feel its surface growing warmer still—though not so hot as to be uncomfortable.

Then the door itself began to glow.

"What in the world?" Falcon muttered. He moved back into view, staring as the door took on a sort of phosphorescent hue. A nimbus of light radiated out from it all around.

The robed man emerged from the fog behind Falcon and gazed in wonder at what was happening as well.

Falcon looked back at him. "Has it ever done this before?"

"Never," the man answered. His blue eyes were wide and his mouth open.

The door now appeared to be composed not of wood or metal but of pure light, almost painful to look at. As it grew brighter and brighter, the fog all around them parted and dissolved. Within moments they found themselves standing at the center of a broad circle of open space.

Falcon shielded his good eye with his left hand. "Hey," he called to his friend then. "Try the knob now!"

Hawk, standing transfixed before the rectangle of light, blinked at Falcon's words. Then he nodded and reached for the knob, which had been transformed into a small sphere of light. He touched it.

The bright, white rectangle of the door leapt outward and swallowed them all.

12: FALCON

The white light was everywhere and everything. It was, for the briefest of instants, their entire world—their entire universe. And then it faded and they blinked their eyes and looked around and found themselves to be somewhere else entirely.

"What just happened?" Hawk asked.

"We jumped," Falcon said, sounding surprised, "through some kind of wormhole. That much is obvious. We left the level of the Below we were stuck in." He glanced at Hawk with an odd combination of appreciation and suspicion. "How we did it, though—why the door activated when *you* touched it—is a mystery, at least to me."

Hawk was oblivious to whatever Falcon was insinuating. "We found a way out," he marveled. He started to smile.

The third man, standing just behind them, gazed at their new surroundings. "Out?" he repeated, as if it was the most alien word imaginable. *"Out..."*

"Yeah," Falcon agreed after a moment. "We found a way out." The concern etched on the human part of his face faded a bit. "But there's a more important question to consider." He rubbed at his square jaw as he looked around. "Did we move *up*—or *further down?*"

Falcon took two steps forward and looked around, happy to note that his mechanical eye had begun to function properly again. That was a good sign.

"What do you make of this place?" he asked the others.

"No clue," Hawk said.

"It seems familiar somehow," the robed man answered. He was turning slowly about, staring at the room and its contents. "Very familiar..."

The room they found themselves in now was a circular, dimly lit space about fifty meters in diameter. The floor, the walls, and the domelike roof that curved high above were all of solid gray stone, giving it the feel of a cave—though its smooth and regular shape suggested it had been carved out intentionally rather than being a natural phenomenon. The air was stale, and a fine layer of dust covered the stacks of computerized equipment that littered much of the floor.

"It's like when the old Earth explorers would open an ancient Egyptian tomb," Falcon said after a few moments of taking it all in. "Like no one has been in here in ages."

"It's like a tomb," Hawk suggested.

Falcon nodded slowly at that. "Yeah. It is." He faced back in the direction they had come from. "Hey, look at this," he said.

The others turned back to see.

A mechanical rectangle some four meters tall and two wide stood in the spot where they had just emerged.

"This remind you of anything?" Falcon asked Hawk.

Hawk nodded slowly. "The terminal in the Ring command center," he said, "and the one aboard Condor's ship. Its design is very much like them."

"It's another terminal, I think," Falcon said, agreeing. "That door linked to it somehow." He scratched at his chin. "It's sort of like I was telling you before," he said. "Things in the Below aren't always what they seem. That door must have been a sort of visual metaphor. It was really some kind of gateway terminal. We came through that. Or emerged from it, I suppose."

"Condor?" the robed man asked, ignoring the rest of their conversation. "I remember a Condor."

"It would be great if we actually knew where we are," Hawk said, looking around at the dim gray room and the banks of equipment.

Falcon nodded. "I'm going to try to access the Aether—if there's any sort of connection available here, wherever we are." He shook his head. "It's patchy all over the galaxy, these days, if it's available at all. But you never know." He stood still for a moment, his good eye still keeping a close watch on the robed man all the while. He wasn't sure he liked how antsy the big guy had gotten in the short time since they'd emerged through the doorway.

"Okay, got something," Falcon said a few seconds later. "A connection—but local area only. Hmm. We're on a planet now—Scandana."

"Scandana?" the big man in the brown robes repeated, looking up.

"Yeah," Falcon said, nodding, half his attention still held by the Aether connection within his mind. "It's within the bounds of the Hanrilite Empire, and we know those guys...so I'm happy to report we're back in the right universe, at least." He frowned. "Not much going on, transmission-wise, around here. I've accessed their node of the galactic clock and it looks like we were actually away from this universe for only a few minutes, relatively speaking." He laughed. "The one good thing about the Below: time moves a lot faster there. You can spend a year there and only a few minutes pass back here."

Hawk nodded absently, his own attention now divided between his new surroundings and the man who might be Eagle, looming just ahead of him. The robed man was muttering things to himself, and Hawk had heard him say "Condor" again, plus "Machine" and "traitor" and "Adversary."

"Oh," Falcon said then. "There's another local network here, just in this room. I think it monitors the gateway terminal and the other equipment—which is why the thing was operable even with no one here, and after however many years it's been since anything in here was used." A pause, and then, "Huh. There's a message pod floating around in there. And—it has the seal of a Hand of the Machine."

Hawk gave Falcon his full attention now.

"You're saying there's a message in the local network," he asked his cyborg companion, "from one of us?"

"Looks like it, yeah. I'm checking the authentication code against what I have stored in my cybernetic memory now. Huh. It's an old one. Really old."

Hawk was frowning. The third man had turned his attention their way now, as well.

"Who is it from?" Hawk asked.

Falcon chewed his lip as he worked the ancient decryption program that would open it. Then his human eye widened and he gasped.

"I'm not quite sure I believe this," he said. "Let me double-check the time stamp."

Hawk grew increasingly anxious. He glanced over at the robed man, who had stopped mumbling and was now entirely focused on Falcon. "Well?"

The cyborg was still staring off into space as cognitive routines ran within the computer portion of his brain.

"This message," he said at last, his voice thin and distant, "is from a thousand years ago."

"Yes?"

Falcon looked up at Hawk then, meeting his eyes, and laughed humorlessly. "And it's from *you*."

•

13: HAWK

"Not the *me* that's standing here now," Hawk said to Falcon after taking in what the man was saying and thinking about it for a second. "You mean the *other* me—the *original* Hawk. He left the message."

"Right, yeah," Falcon said, nodding. "He left it—a thousand years ago." He shook his head in wonder. "It's bounced around inside the local network for a millennium, waiting on one of us to come along and find it."

"Hawk?" asked the man in the brown robes. "Hawk left a message here?"

Falcon gave the man a quick and perfunctory nod, then turned his attention back to Hawk.

"That's what it seems to be, anyway." He frowned. "I suppose it could be a virus—a mind-bomb, or something, designed to fry the synapses of anyone who opens it."

"Ah," Hawk said, nodding slowly. "Well, don't take any chances," he said. "Maybe you should just leave it alone."

"Are you kidding?" Falcon asked, a wry smile on his face now. "I've got to know what it is—what it says."

Hawk frowned at this but didn't say anything.

"Huh," Falcon snorted a moment later. He was continuing to analyze the message with his computer mind, doing everything short of actually attempting to open it. "It's a full-blown holo file—images and sound, recorded directly from the other Hawk's consciousness."

And then Falcon's human eye bugged out and he nearly stumbled backward. His mouth opened and closed and he turned in a slow circle, looking around at the room as if seeing it for the first time all over again.

"What?" Hawk demanded. "What is it? What's wrong?"

"This planet," Falcon said, his voice low but intense. "It's been so long, I had forgotten—didn't make the connection." His eyes met Hawk's again. "This is Scandana. *Scandana!*"

Hawk understood then. He started to speak, but the third man beat him to it.

"The betrayal," said the man in the brown robes. "The betrayal to the Adversary. That happened here. On Scandana. In this very room."

Hawk and Falcon exchanged very surprised looks.

"You know about that?" Falcon asked, wary.

"I was there," the man stated firmly, his voice deep and full now. "I was there, at the betrayal—of everything."

Hawk felt his stomach sink. *Maybe it's true,* he thought. *Maybe this man really is Eagle—and he saw what I did. Maybe I really did betray the entire galaxy to the Adversary.* His legs felt weak and he sat down on an old piece of equipment, steadying himself.

"Can I see the message?" Hawk asked.

Falcon was unsteady, his human eye darting from the robed man to Hawk, back and forth. He gathered himself and nodded.

"I can't send it directly to you, since you're unable to access the Aether," Falcon replied. "But I can project it, such that you—and our friend here—can experience it mentally, as I play it back."

"You can do that?"

Falcon tapped his cyborg eye.

"This thing can do a few tricks. That's one."

Hawk nodded. "Okay. Do it."

"You're sure you—?"

"Show it," Hawk repeated.

"...Alright."

Falcon closed his human eye for a moment, then reopened it. The other eye—the red mechanical one—flared brightly. For everyone present, it suddenly became as if they stood elsewhere—in the location where the recording had been made. They could see and hear everything experienced by the person who had made it.

As it happened, the scene that was revealed had occurred in the very room the currently occupied, and they were seeing it from Hawk's point of view. It began with a bit of conversation that Hawk and Falcon had already witnessed a recording of, somewhat recently, when presented it by the Inquisition: Hawk confronting Governor Kail, and the governor making the infamous assertion:

"You may drop the pretense, Hawk. We both know why you are here. And let me add that you have done a marvelous job." *The governor smiled broadly. "I doubt that anyone even suspects that* you *are the traitor in the ranks of the Hands."*

And then, unlike with the previous recording, the conversation *continued...*

PART EIGHT

**Before the Shattering:
The Seventeenth Millennium**

—

Scandana

1: HAWK

"Traitor?" Hawk demanded, utterly shocked. "*Me?* What in the name of the Machine are you talking about?"

"There is no need for pretense, I assure you," the governor said. His head was shaved smooth and creases crisscrossed his forehead, above bushy black eyebrows. He attempted a weak smile. "We are on the same side, you and I."

"I strongly doubt that," Hawk growled. "Because I don't know whose side you think you're on. But I am no traitor."

"I—I—" Kail stammered, suddenly not quite so sure of himself and of the situation. He looked about abruptly, then turned back to Hawk. "Perhaps there has been an unfortunate misunderstanding," he managed after a few seconds. Seeming to pull himself together a bit, his voice took on some of the commanding timbre Hawk would have expected from an aristocratic planetary leader. "May I ask what *you* are doing here? On my world? In my home?"

Hawk wasn't wrong-footed by this in the slightest. He remembered that the original discussions aboard the *Talon* before the operation began had included the option of bombardment of the palace from space. The Machine rarely objected to collateral damage if an important objective was being met in the process. Even if nothing remotely illegal or dangerous was going on here, having one lone Hand wandering through the palace without authorization seemed much preferable to that. And clearly something both illegal *and* dangerous was going on here, to put it mildly.

"Given what I've just seen in the upper levels of your palace and in the adjoining rooms, Governor Kail," Hawk replied, keeping his pistol leveled at the man, "I think you're the one who needs to be providing answers here. And quickly." He gestured around at the darkened chamber, the candles, and the strange rectangle draped in cables and wires that stood vertically on one end, across the room, amid other banks of odd machinery. "Just what is all of this?"

"It's something you shouldn't have seen," came a voice from behind. Hawk whirled about, just as a foot lashed out and struck his wrist at just the right spot—and with just the right force—to knock his pistol away. It clattered across the stone floor.

Hawk never hesitated. He leapt to his left, tucking and rolling, moving out of the way of any additional attacks, and came up quickly, his night-vision implants scanning the darkness for any signs of his foe. At the same time, he again accessed the Aether and attempted to contact the *Talon* in orbit. The interference was greater than ever, though, and he couldn't make the connection.

"Stop!" shouted the governor. He ran in between Hawk and the attacker, waving his arms frantically. "I won't have this, Merlion! This man is a Hand! He is far too important—too potentially valuable—to simply kill!"

"Merlion?" Hawk breathed, rising to a tense crouch and locating his gun where it lay some distance away.

The attacker stepped out of the darkness and stood revealed. Hawk knew the face. He was Lord Darwyn Merlion, the very man he had been sent into the palace to capture or kill, on suspicion of traitorous activities. He wore another of the ubiquitous black robes and held a blast pistol in his left hand.

"Just what in the name of the holy Machine is happening here?" Hawk demanded, his eyes flicking from Kail to Merlion and back.

"Something marvelous," the governor answered, his mouth splitting into a broad smile. "Something that will transform the galaxy itself."

Merlion simply stood there, immobile, watching and listening. Governor Kail took a step forward and began to speak, all of his attention on Hawk now.

"There is a new power entering our galaxy," Kail said, his voice bubbling over with excitement. "It will transform everything—all that we know will change. All will become better, greater." He grinned. "Those who assist it will reap great rewards. Those who oppose it..." His grin faded, and he shrugged. "They will not be around to enjoy the new Golden Age, I'm afraid."

Frowning, Hawk found himself listening in spite of himself. All this talk of a Golden Age and some new force entering the galaxy—that meant nothing to him. Hawk was a foot soldier, a policeman, a servant of the Machine that brought law and order to the many and diverse empires—both human and alien—of the galaxy. He had no interest in or use for some new force, and certainly no desire to betray his commander, Eagle, or his brother and sister Hands. Even so, something about the governor's voice—the cadence, the tone—was making his limbs sluggish, preventing him from turning away and rejecting the man entirely. He did, however, manage a sour expression on his face.

"You're wasting your time," Merlion muttered. "It won't work."

"No," the governor barked. "You have to listen to me, Hawk. Hear me out."

Hawk still couldn't move. Now he found he couldn't speak, either. Something—some strange force surrounding him, here in this strange cavern of a room—was holding him in place. Or rather it was causing him to hold himself in place. Gritting his teeth, he fought it.

"We're doing something *good*," Kail snapped at Merlion, "so there is no need to behave in a hostile manner toward a Hand. We must welcome him to our cause. We need him and his kind on our side! It would make everything so much easier."

"It's not going to happen," Merlion replied. "He's not going to sway. At least, not with *you* doing it. Only *he* can do it, so that it lasts."

"Well, *he* is not here right now," Kail snapped back at the other man, "so I have no other options."

"There's one very obvious other option," Merlion pointed out, gesturing vaguely with his blast pistol. "And it would be preferable to revealing everything we're doing to a Hand that we cannot turn to our side."

"Quiet!" shouted the governor. "He must be told! He has to know—all of them do! If only the Hands—perhaps even the Machine itself—could see the truth of our great purpose, they would surely join us. And we would become utterly unstoppable."

"Fantasy," Merlion responded. "Sheerest fantasy. Only *he* can sway a Hand—and not easily. You're only making this more difficult, Kail."

The governor ignored him and returned his attentions to Hawk. "A Golden Age is about to dawn," he said, his voice filled with dramatic force. "And I believe you are intelligent enough to know which side you should choose."

Hawk blinked. That last sentence had gotten through to him and now his mind cleared a bit, the layers of mental fog the governor had seemingly projected parting for him.

"Oh, I definitely know which side I'm on," he said to the governor. "And I know what to do with traitors—with those who supply classified defense and military data to alien powers. As for the rest of this—" He gestured at the room around them, and the rooms behind them, and at the entire palace, his motion taking in every bizarre thing he had encountered since landing here a half hour or so earlier, "—I'm going to have to leave that to those better suited to investigating it all. But you two," he added, "well, you can go ahead and consider yourselves under arrest."

"I told you there was no use in trying to sway him yourself," Merlion growled at the governor. "You're no good at it. You need *him* to provide the power."

Hawk registered that word, "*him,*" and mentally filed it away. Then he leapt, diving toward his pistol where it lay on the hard stone floor.

Merlion fired. The powerful shot skimmed Hawk's right shoulder and deflected off the surface of his ultra-thin armored uniform.

Hawk grasped his weapon and rolled up into a crouch, pistol clutched in both hands and aimed in the direction of the other two men.

A shot was fired. Hawk blinked, surprised. He hadn't fired, and he hadn't been fired upon.

The governor slumped to the floor.

Merlion stood over the body, frowning down at it. "You were an idiot, Kail. I should have done that to you months ago."

Hawk felt anger boiling over. "Alright—that's it," he shouted at Merlion. "Drop your weapon and raise your hands. Now!"

Merlion's brow was furrowed, from what Hawk could see in the dim lighting of the chamber, and he still hadn't looked up from the body of the governor. When he finally did, his eyes widened as he looked just past Hawk's shoulder at something. He quickly tossed his gun aside.

Hawk frowned at this. It struck him as some sort of trick. Even so, he wanted to know what could possibly be coming up behind him that could so unnerve a cold-blooded murderer and likely traitor like Merlion. An instant later, he had his answer without even looking.

"What's going on here?" came the deep, rumbling voice that was all too familiar.

Now Hawk did turn around, and was surprised and somewhat relieved to see his commander, Eagle, striding into the darkened chamber. The big man in navy blue and red gazed about, taking the scene in quickly. His hands were empty but his golden sword hung in its scabbard at his side. He turned his penetrating gaze on Hawk. "Report."

"I've found the governor and Merlion," Hawk reported, "as you can see."

Eagle bent over the governor, frowning, and checked his vital signs.

"Kail is dead," the Hand commander announced. "Merlion did this?"

Hawk nodded.

Eagle pursed his lips, looking from Merlion to his subordinate Hand.

"And why was Merlion alive to be able to do this? Why did you not kill him—or at least restrain him—immediately?"

"He surprised me and was able to disarm me for a few moments," Hawk began, not particularly disturbed by Eagle's questions; he was used to the incredibly high standards to which the commander held all of the Hands, including himself. "But—"

Eagle turned to face Hawk directly, his eyes piercing in their intensity. "Why is he still alive *now*?"

Hawk frowned. The commander wanted a summary execution? He hesitated a second, then, "There's more going on here that we were aware, I think," he replied carefully. "The governor was trying to tell me something—to explain some grand truth, as he saw it, and to sway me over to it—and Merlion was trying to cover it all up."

Eagle seemed to be taking this in, considering it. He turned back to Merlion. The man was sweating now, even in the cold dank environment of the sub-basement they occupied. At that moment, a sort of electricity filled the room, accompanied by a low hum that emanated from the various bizarre machines that filled much of the space.

"That's true?" Eagle demanded of the black-robed man, his voice deep and commanding. "Governor Kail was attempting to explain some sort of 'grand truth' to Hawk?"

Merlion nodded slowly. "Quite so. In fact, he was saying far too much for my taste."

Eagle appeared to be considering this. He glanced back at Hawk and frowned. Then he faced Merlion again. He inhaled deeply, his massive chest swelling. "So. You have information—intelligence—then, on what has been happening here? On who has been receiving the defense data you've stolen?" He regarded the robed man with very obvious contempt. "Information that you doubtlessly wish to provide, as a *service* to us—to trade for your life?"

Merlion blinked. He glanced over at Hawk, then back at the big man looming over him. "What? What are you—?" He hesitated, looking at Hawk again.

Puzzled, Hawk watched the exchange in silence. He could only trust his commander to know and follow the best course of action, as he always had done.

"You are a liar," Eagle announced suddenly. "A liar—and a madman. Governor Kail was the real traitor. He was behind the entire operation. You have nothing of interest to me. You know nothing."

Merlion opened and closed his mouth, his icy cool shattered. He started to speak, but Eagle cut him off.

"Unfortunately, Merlion," the commander stated, his voice hard as iron, "*this* is the only service we require of you."

It happened in one smooth motion. Eagle moved forward, his golden sword out of its sheath and curving around. The incredibly fine edge passed through Merlion's neck without slowing. The man's head dropped to the floor an instant before the rest of him did. Blood fountained.

Hawk recoiled in horror. Instinctively he started to bring his weapon up, then realized just who he would be aiming it at and lowered it once more. He gawked at his superior in shock and confusion and unabashed disgust.

"Yes?" Eagle asked, his gaze flicking from the bodies on the floor before him to his fellow Hand. "You have something to say, Hawk?"

Hawk swallowed, frowning. He was at a loss as to what to say.

A loud bang echoed throughout the room. Light flooded in, from *somewhere*.

Both men whirled about.

The rectangle of metal and wires and machinery standing near the center of the chamber had flared to life. A dull vibration emanated from it, seemingly shaking the very air around them. Lights flashed in various colors all along the superstructure. Strangest of all, the interior space of the rectangle was now filled with blinding light; it resembled nothing so much as a doorway opening onto some other, incredibly brightly-lit room.

Hawk aimed his pistol at the center of the light. Eagle held his gleaming sword before him and waited, his expression oddly not one of puzzlement as much as of mild surprise.

A human shape formed within the light. It stepped through the doorway, over the threshold, and solidified before them, there in the room. The light itself receded but did not die away. Now a man stood before them—a human male, dark-haired and slender, roughly of the same height as Hawk. He wore immaculately clean and neat clothing of a somewhat loose fit, and all of black; slacks, long-sleeve shirt, and a sort of trim jacket. His eyes appeared to glow a soft white as he gazed first down at the dead men and then up at Hawk and Eagle. He smiled.

"Who are you?" Hawk demanded, his gun trained at the man's chest. "Where did you come from?"

The smile on the man's face widened.

"I come to you from far away," he said, his voice low and smooth. "Very, very far away."

Hawk nodded slowly. He was beginning to feel an odd tingling sensation flooding through his body, attacking his nerve endings. He tried to ignore it and maintain his full attention on the strange man in black who now stood before him.

"So," the man said, gazing at the bodies of Merlion and Kail. "Both of the loudmouths are dead." He shrugged slightly. "Their usefulness was at an end, in any event." He bestowed a beatific smile upon Eagle. "You have done well, mighty Hand."

Hawk frowned, confused for a moment. Then he glanced back at the commander, his friend.

"What is this man—if *man* he is—talking about, Agrippa?"

Eagle's expression was blank and his body rigidly unmoving. His bright blue eyes were focused directly on the newcomer.

"What is going on here?" Hawk demanded, his voice rising. Again he attempted to access the Aether—to communicate with the fleet—and found that the strange, jamming effect persisted. Nothing but static filled his mental "ears."

"I presume you have prepared steps to deal with any and all contingencies, yes?" the man in black asked, looking to Eagle.

The commander moved then, nodding once. Seeming to come to himself once more, he gestured with one hand and issued a mental command.

Something was wrong here, Hawk knew beyond any doubt now. Something was very, very wrong. Beyond the bizarre situation within the palace—the headless bodies, the heads in the glowing sphere, the governor and his aide in their cultish robes—something potentially far worse was afoot. Something that apparently involved the other Hands, including the commander himself. But how could that be? It clashed with everything Hawk knew, everything he had ever known as an agent of the Machine and a subordinate of Eagle.

This man who had come from the doorway—stepped out of the eerie light there—had some power over Eagle, he realized then. Some kind of control over him, in a similar fashion to what the governor had attempted to do to *him* earlier. Where Kail had failed, however, this strange man clearly had Eagle in thrall. It was the only explanation that made any sense.

A hint of fear and perhaps even panic touched Hawk. He knew he might have only seconds left to act—to spread the word of what was happening here to the others, up in orbit. Quickly he ordered a memory packet to form within his mind, carrying copies of everything he had seen and heard in the past hour.

Eagle was looking at him now. Not a trace of emotion showed from this big man who normally radiated charisma and confidence enough to buoy an entire army.

"We have to think of the greater good, Marcus," the commander said in a peculiarly quiet voice.

"Right," Hawk replied. "Of course." Mentally, he was probing at the wall of static and distortion that utterly cut him off from the ship. Thus he was ready—and not even particularly surprised, at this point—when, a second later, Eagle raised one gloved hand and motioned, and the electronic distortion blanketing the palace vanished. A connection with the *Talon* engaged instantly.

As the interference dissolved away at last and his link to the Aether network returned, Hawk called up the memory capsule and compressed it. He fired it in a tight beam toward the flagship high in orbit.

Back in the present, the recording seemed to end there. But then, after a moment's static and a jarring discontinuity, it started up again, more memories having been amended to it shortly afterward:

Eagle noticed what Hawk was doing and he motioned again. The data packet from Hawk bounced back, like a bullet hitting a thick steel plate, before it could even leave the room.

"I'm sorry, my friend, but I cannot allow you to do that," Eagle said. Then he looked away, accessing the now-open Aether connection himself. "Falcon—do you read?"

"Ah! There you are," came the deep, rumbling voice in response. "We were getting a little concerned about both of you."

"You were right to be concerned," the commander replied. "I've found the Governor and Merlion," Eagle stated flatly. "Both are dead." A pause, and his voice seemed to catch, as if deep emotion were flooding into it. "I've found Hawk as well. It appears they have… *killed* him."

Falcon's deep voice echoed back across the link immediately. "What? Hawk is *dead?*"

A heartbeat later, his reaction time severely impaired by the buzzing in his head and the numbness growing in his limbs, Hawk himself cried out: *"What?!"*

Eagle had motioned with one gloved hand an instant before Hawk had spoken. The electronic interference blanketing the palace returned. No one in the fleet heard Hawk's startled exclamation.

"I'm sorry, Marcus," Eagle said to Hawk then, his eyes as emotionless as his voice. "I had hoped that you would encounter Merlion—and perhaps the governor, as well—before making it this far underneath the palace, and simply kill them. Then any talk of treason would have died along with them, and you and I could have walked out of here together." He gave a half-shrug. "But, alas…"

Hawk stared back at his commander as the big man spoke those words. He didn't understand at all.

"Why?" he asked. "*Why*, Agrippa?"

Eagle half-shrugged again.

"Forces much greater than either of us are at work now, and we can but bow to them."

"Indeed," said the man in black. He took a step forward.

Hawk reacted to the motion of the newcomer by attempting to raise his own pistol. He found his arm would not obey—it was growing numb and wouldn't respond to his mental orders. His eyes flashed down to his own hand and then up to Eagle, and his expression changed from puzzlement to surprise.

The big man's blade flashed out again. Hawk had no chance whatsoever to react. The straight golden metal jabbed at him, into him. Wide-eyed, stunned to his core, he stared down momentarily at the gleaming blade transfixing him. As Eagle withdrew the blade and watched impassively, Hawk dropped to the floor.

"Such a shame," Eagle whispered with no trace of emotion whatsoever. "But perhaps of great value, yet."

As the life drained quickly out of Hawk, he accessed the encapsulated copy of his memories again and frantically attempted to transmit it as a data burst to the *Talon*, far up in orbit above the planet. The interference was back in effect, however, and he still could not make contact. He cursed silently, knowing he had only seconds of life remaining. His vision was fading, his head lolling over to one side. As his eyes closed one last time, he spotted the computer banks filling part of the room. It was his only choice. With the last spark of life left to him, he accessed the palace's local, internal network and inserted the memory capsule data into it.

And then he died.

But the recording did not stop.

Hawk's ocular and auditory implants continued to function for a short time afterward, despite the death of his organic body, and here is what they recorded and added to the data packet in the local network:

As the man in black looked on, still smiling, Eagle touched a series of controls on his sleeve. Then he tilted his head back slightly, as if attempting to actually see up through layers of stone and steel and concrete to the star-filled sky high above, and to the fleet orbiting overhead. He spoke.

"I'm transmitting a set of data I recovered here," he told the listening officers aboard the *Talon,* even as he sent up the recording that ended with Hawk being erroneously greeted by the governor as the traitor. "It is quite…troubling. It appears there was indeed a traitor working with Governor Kail. I regret to say that it looks to have been Hawk himself."

For a heartbeat, there was no reply. Then the communications link nearly exploded as dozens of voices erupted. Words of incredulity and denial intermingled with shock and outrage.

"There will be a full hearing when I have returned to the ship," Eagle intoned. "Which I will do shortly. Stand by." With that, he closed the link and gazed across the room at the man in black. "Satisfied?"

"Indeed," the man said to him. "You elaborated upon my orders most creatively. I had not concerned myself with what your teammates would think of you following this meeting—though it makes sense that you would have. You, after all, believed you would be going back to them once our business here is concluded."

Eagle's placid features darkened for a moment. "What?"

The man in black kicked at Hawk's body where it lay in a pool of blood on the stone floor. "A clever ruse you constructed. I ordered you to come here and meet with me, ostensibly to discuss our future plans, and you set your friend here up to take the blame should anything go wrong."

"Yes, I—" Eagle's voice trailed off. He stared down at his friend's body and for an instant his expression changed to one of confusion. "Hawk?" he whispered. "What happened?"

The man in black interposed himself back into Eagle's attention quickly.

"Your shuttle is nearby, yes?"

Eagle looked up. Still seeming somewhat puzzled, he nodded. "In the main courtyard of the palace."

"It has cloaking technology? Even against your own fleet's sensors?"

"Absolutely," Eagle replied with a tight smile. The confusion that had marked his face a moment earlier was disappearing now. "It may be small, but its components are cutting-edge tech."

"Small?"

Eagle shrugged his massive, muscular shoulders. "Small, yes—but but large enough to accommodate both of us."

"That won't be necessary."

The man in black reached out and grasped Eagle by his left arm. The Hand commander frowned slowly as he felt himself spun around, but his physical reactions were suddenly dulled, just as Hawk's had been; he could barely move. His true persona fighting to break through again, Eagle tried to raise his sword in a defensive posture, but the other man moved like lightning and easily took it from his grasp. He held it up before him, smiling appreciatively.

"Ah, yes," he muttered. "The fabled Sword of Baranak. I'd almost forgotten you possessed it." He ran a finger along the flat of the gleaming golden blade. "It has been a very long time since I last saw it. Since it last served me so well." He laughed. "It will be good to have it in my service once again."

Reality was rapidly reasserting itself for Eagle. He was nearly himself once more. Seeing the sword in the enemy's grasp repulsed him, but he could scarcely move—he knew he could never physically wrest it away from the man. Instead he spoke three quick words in a language not his own.

The sword vanished.

The man in black gaped and then cried out, furious, realizing that he now held nothing. "What have you done?" He spun around, almost frantic. "Where did it go?"

"The Sword of Baranak possesses many abilities," Eagle replied, his voice raw.

The man glared at him for several seconds, then seemed to calm himself. "No matter," he said. "I am *here*, not trapped in the Below. I no longer need it."

Eagle could only frown in puzzlement at this enigmatic statement.

Then the man clamped down harder on the Hand commander, psychic powers entirely enveloping him.

"I appreciate all of the help you have provided me very much," he commented as he shoved the increasingly limp form of Eagle towards the mechanical doorway from which he himself had so recently emerged. "But I believe I will take it from here."

Eagle staggered backwards, stumbling toward the light—light that now blazed blindingly bright again, and with an unmistakable and increasing hue of red. He opened his mouth to cry out, but all he could manage from his dry throat was a croaking, "Why?"

"The scales must be balanced," the man in black answered. "You've let me come through. Someone else—someone of similar stature—must pass back the other way, into the Below, to placate the Great Powers who manage such things." He shrugged slightly. "It's just as well, though. I have no need of a partner or a field general—and certainly not of a potential rival. The sentient beings of this galaxy will bend before my will easily enough. Your sort of military coercion isn't required."

Eagle tried to retort, but whatever his words might have been, none would ever know. His voice was gone now, his muscles sagging and useless. By the time he tumbled into the glowing portal, he was almost completely paralyzed. The swirling red light swallowed him.

A second passed; another. The light switched off. The man in black stood alone in the sub-basement, surrounded only by the bodies of Kail, Merlion, and Hawk—Hawk, whose body was now dead and whose implants were nearly powered down. Eagle, meanwhile, was entirely gone.

After one quick look about the room, the man in black made his way up the stairs.

The recording ended.

PART NINE

After the Shattering:
The Nineteenth Millennium

1: HAWK

The playback ended.

Hawk and Falcon stood dumbfounded. They stared at one another for a long moment, neither of them quite sure of what to say.

Then they both turned and looked at the third man in the room.

He looked back at them, then down at his own body, as if seeing himself for the first time—or the first time in an eon. He frowned, then reached up and in a remarkably controlled yet powerful manner pulled his robe open, the clasps that had held it popping loose from the old, rough fabric. The robe fell to the floor.

Hawk and Falcon looked on in wonder and, to some degree now, in horror.

"It—it really is him," Falcon muttered. "I'm not sure I ever quite believed it."

Hawk could only nod.

Before them now, beyond any doubt, stood Eagle, the former leader of the Hands of the Machine. He was indeed thinner than they had ever seen him, his face narrower and his hair much longer, but his frame still appeared powerful and formidable. He wore the dark blue metallic uniform with red and gold trim that he had always worn in his day, fashioned in the same style as Hawk's and Falcon's. His big hands clenched and unclenched as he looked around.

"Yes," he said, his voice a low rumble, filled with all the power and majesty of old. "It is me." He looked up at the other two, his eyes cold and hard. "And I remember now. I remember everything."

Hawk and Falcon glanced at one another again and then both braced themselves for the attack they feared was imminent. Instead, Eagle simply seated himself on a massive piece of electronic machinery and stared down at his feet.

The other two men waited for several seconds, uncertain of what to do. They had just learned that their old commander—a man who had led them in untold battles, before suddenly vanishing a thousand years ago—was the real traitor all along; the man who had sold out the entire galaxy to the invading forces led by a being called the Adversary. And now, instead of attempting to kill them for uncovering this information, Eagle was just...sitting.

"You—you were being controlled, weren't you?" Falcon asked, moving toward the blond man again. "The Adversary has some kind of psychic power—we know that. He was making you do what he wanted."

Eagle looked up. His face was ashen.

"Yes," he answered, "it's true that he was exerting a degree of control over my mind. But..." He frowned and looked back down. "...It would not be entirely fair to say that his influence was the only thing driving me."

"What do you mean?" Hawk asked.

"I told you that I remember *everything*," Eagle said. "That includes what I was thinking as the Adversary was psychically influencing me. And I have to be honest. He didn't just *make* me do things; he pushed me in directions I already had some inclination to go."

Hawk and Falcon frowned at one another.

"You had an inclination to betray the galaxy?" Hawk asked, aghast.

"Not as such," Eagle replied, looking up and meeting Hawk's eyes briefly. "I had a desire to defend the galaxy from alien forces such as the Dyonari and the Rao. The Adversary persuaded me that his goal was to sweep those enemies—those rivals to humanity—from the stars. To wipe them out." He shrugged, his massive shoulders rolling. "That appealed to me, once."

"Why?" Falcon demanded. "Why would genocide appeal to you?"

"I felt the Machine was too willing to accommodate those alien forces. He would send us to fight them, yes, but he was also ready to bargain with them. To negotiate." Eagle shook his head. "I simply wanted them gone—removed from our galaxy entirely." He hesitated, then, "As time went by, I also wanted the *Machine* gone. Destroyed. I felt that I—and you two, and the other Hands—should be independent of the whims of some great artificial intelligence with its endless orders and restrictions. I had come to view the Machine as just another alien overlord that was stifling human evolution and expansion." He met their gaze levelly. "The Adversary presented himself to me, the first time I encountered him, as a force for good—an ally that could help me—help *us*—achieve all of those goals."

"And then, once he had you on the hook," Falcon growled, "he used his mental powers to reel you in."

Eagle nodded once. "I believe that's so, yes." He looked up at Hawk then. "I'm sorry, Marcus," he said. "You were always a good and loyal soldier. I'm terribly sorry."

Hawk simply looked back at the man, uncertain of what to say. He understood now what had happened to the original Hawk, and he knew as well that he was genetically identical to that man—but that man had lived and died a thousand years ago, and he felt no real connection to him or to his world. Shaking his head as much in surprise at his own lack of emotions as in any sense of anger or injustice toward his old commander, he turned away.

And then a bright circle of light formed in the center of the room.

The three men all reacted instantly. Even Eagle, after so many centuries of amnesia and inactivity in the exile of the Below, sprang into action with surprising quickness. They formed a semicircle before the swirling light; Hawk drew his pistol while Falcon cursed that he had lost his weapon on the Ring. Then they waited, at the ready.

They did not have to wait very long.

The light coalesced into an almost solid circle, standing vertically on its edge. At that same moment, ice formed on the hard stone floor and on the tops of the computer components that nearly filled part of the chamber.

Falcon turned quickly to Hawk. "Psychics again," he muttered, his breath a cloud before him.

Hawk felt a sudden sense of alarm. "Could it be—?"

A single figure stepped through the circle of light.

The others instantly recognized him. They had just witnessed memories of him recorded by a man who had died a thousand years before. Each of them sought to attack; none of them was able to move. Some force was holding them motionless. They stood locked in place as their antagonist strolled out into the chamber and the circle of light shrunk down to nothing.

"You," hissed Eagle.

"Me," the man replied. He smiled at each of them.

He looked precisely the same as he had before: a human, by all appearances, dressed entirely in black. His eyes glowed with a soft white light.

The temperature in the room had dropped precipitously in the few seconds since he had emerged.

Each of the three Hands struggled to move, fighting against the psychic energies locking them in place, but Eagle in particular seemed to be pouring everything he had into it—to no avail.

"What do you want?" the blond Hand demanded, his voice sharp as it emerged from between tightly clenched teeth.

"Well, well," the man in black said, raising one dark eyebrow in surprise. His eyes pulsed an even brighter white as he stared directly at the big man. "You would speak thus to me? To your master?"

"You…are not… my master," Eagle choked out.

"So… you have broken my conditioning, then? Is that it?" He leaned in closer, gazing directly into Eagle's blue eyes. "That would explain why you have come back—why you have returned to this dimension."

The man paced slowly before them, like a general reviewing his troops, who stood stock-still at attention as he passed.

"But, you see, I cannot have you here in this dimension. Not while I am here. It violates the rules." He smiled down at Eagle. "The arrangement I reached with the Great Powers was that I would trade you, hurled into the Below, for my own freedom in this realm. And I am not ready to leave your worlds yet. Far from it, in fact." He shrugged. "So you have to go back."

Eagle tried to retort but the telepathic bonds surrounding him now were simply too tight, not just holding his arms and legs immobile but squeezing his chest and nearly crushing his lungs. His face had grown dark red and he could only choke out a few indistinct sounds.

Next to him, meanwhile, Falcon was not fighting in the slightest to get free and this lack of struggling somehow caused him to be held a bit more loosely. He sized up the man in black and laughed derisively. "This is him?" he growled. "This…*person*…is the high and mighty 'Adversary?' The guy I've had to hear about and deal with for most of my existence? The architect of the Shattering? The mighty and terrible bringer of apocalyptic destruction to the galaxy? *This* guy?" Falcon snorted. "He doesn't impress me."

The man in black froze. Then he turned slowly, regarding Falcon directly for the first time.

"I am indeed the one you know as 'the Adversary,'" the man said, "but that is only a description—and a poor one, to be honest. Not my real name."

"So what is it, then?" Falcon asked. "Your real name. I can't wait to hear."

"You have no idea who I am, or where I come from."

"You're right. But—do share. I'm dying to hear the whole story."

The man in black allowed his bland smile, his tight composure to slip for the tiniest of moments.

"My name is Goraddon," he said. "Once I was a chief acolyte of the great lord Vorthan."

"Vorthan?" Falcon scoffed. "That name is just a myth. A legend from the dim and distant past, used to scare children."

"Vorthan was quite real," the man in black snapped, almost angrily, at Falcon. "He *is* quite real. And I served him in the Golden City for ages before he...*fell*."

Falcon took this in without response.

The man in black—Goraddon the Adversary—straightened and turned away from the three captives then, striding across the room to the terminal device.

"Fortunately, this should be a simple fix," he said. "I have but to activate this machine and toss dear Eagle back through, as I did a thousand years ago, and the universe should align itself into the proper order again." He paused. "And perhaps certain other precautions can be taken, to be sure he won't be so quick to find his way out again."

"Quick?" Eagle choked out through his nearly-crushed windpipe. "You bastard. I was there for an eternity!"

"Then you'll feel right at home," Goraddon said with a laugh.

He reached out and touched a few points on the terminal rectangle. Instantly the strange piece of machinery flared to life, electricity dancing across its surface.

"Wait," Hawk shouted, speaking at last. He was still attempting to process everything he had learned in the past few moments—not least of which was the fact that his predecessor as Hawk had not been the true traitor. That news certainly had come as a massive relief. But learning that his old commander, Eagle, *had* been the one—even if coerced into doing what he had done—hurt him.

The Adversary looked back. "Yes?"

"Why Eagle?" Hawk asked. "Why did you choose *him* to be the one of us you would use as your catspaw? He was the best of us. He never deserved this."

334

"Don't give me...too much...credit, Hawk," Eagle managed to say. "I told you...before... it wasn't all... *him*."

"Precisely," Goraddon stated, smiling broadly again. He faced Hawk and indicated Eagle with a sharp gesture. "Your former leader here was engaged in a sort of private rivalry with the Hand known as Condor. No one else knew of it, but I have my ways of learning the innermost thoughts of those in power. Those who might at some point prove useful to me." He chuckled softly. "Eagle believed his own authority was slipping away—being taken away by Condor, who was at that time enjoying more favor in the eyes of your master, the Machine. The temptation to discredit Condor and return himself to singular favor and leadership under the Machine—as well as his deep resentment of the Machine itself—is what I played upon, stoking the fires, encouraging them."

"Eagle was right," Falcon growled. "You really are a bastard."

The Adversary ignored him and continued on, addressing Eagle directly.

"Did you never wonder why Condor was not with you on your last few missions, up to and including the final operation you undertook here? I planted the suggestion that you should send him elsewhere each time. I wanted the two of you apart, so that I might slowly poison your mind against him." He chuckled, seeing Eagle's reaction. "Oh, yes—*I* was with you. I watched all of your comings and goings, and I carefully set everything in motion and then patiently awaited my moment to strike. And when I did, I was able to use as my lever the oldest maxim of all: Power corrupts." He leaned in closer, his leering face now inches from the straining, purpling face of Eagle. "And you desired power—even more than you already possessed. Oh, how you did so desire it."

Hawk could see that Eagle was now straining so hard that his face was darkening even beyond purple, and veins were standing out in stark relief on his face and neck. Interestingly, sweat was beginning to bead up on the Adversary's own face, and for the first time he appeared somewhat troubled.

"You have grown more willful in the time since we last met," Goraddon told the blond man. "I'm actually finding your resistance quite…remarkable."

This only seemed to spur Eagle on. He strained yet harder, and now the Adversary began to grow extremely agitated. He stood up straight, gazing down at Eagle with grim determination, and drops of sweat dripped from his nose.

"This cannot be," he murmured, raising his right hand and pointing it out before him as if to aim his mental powers directly at Eagle. "You cannot be capable of—"

With a mighty roar, Eagle at last shattered the psychic restraints and surged upward in one smooth and powerful motion, smashing his bulky frame directly into the Adversary's somewhat lesser physique. He forced the man in black backward, away from the others, then lifted him off his feet and drove him into the hard stone floor.

At that instant the telepathic bonds holding Hawk and Falcon evaporated and the two of them lurched forward, both falling flat on their faces. They regained their feet quickly and wasted no time in rushing to the attack alongside their old leader.

"Unacceptable!" screamed the Adversary. "I will not have this!" He somehow managed to free himself from Eagle's hold and scrambled away. Then, still half-seated on the icy floor, he directed his glowing gaze at them. "You will all stop what you are doing—now!"

Hawk and Falcon stumbled to a halt, locked in place. Eagle somehow resisted just enough to fall forward into Goraddon, knocking him aside. The man in black cried out wordlessly as he crashed into a bank of electronic components. Before he could extricate himself from the machinery, one of Eagle's massive hands grasped him by the neck and yanked him back, hurling him head-first into a tall stack of crates.

As the Adversary struggled to rise, Eagle spoke three strange-sounding words in a language alien to all who were present. In response, a golden sword—the one he had once carried as commander of the Hands of the Machine—shimmered into view in midair, just before him.

Eagle grasped the sword and swung it all in one smooth motion. Gasping, shocked beyond reckoning, the Adversary barely managed to lunge out of the way.

The distraction served to free the other two Hands again and, this time, they were able to rush to Eagle's side and assist him. Hawk drew his pistol and prepared to fire but Falcon flashed past him, his quickness belying his bulky frame, and brought his metallic cyborg fist around into the dark man's face with three powerful punches in quick succession.

Goraddon was reeling now, his face bloody, and the others felt for the first time that they had gained something of the upper hand.

As the other two Hands circled around to the left and right, Eagle rushed straight forward, sword held high and ready to come about in a mighty swing. Goraddon saw him approaching and raised one hand, directing it at the big man. Almost frantically, he barked a sharp, "*Halt!*"

The psychic force behind the command struck Eagle like a physical blow and he stumbled, crashing to the floor, the sword clattering off to the side, directly into Hawk's path.

Before anyone could react, Hawk snatched up the golden weapon and attacked.

The Adversary was caught flat-footed and couldn't evade or project a mental command in time. Hawk's swing sliced him across the ribs on the left side and he cried out in agony.

Hawk pressed his advantage, attacking again. The big weapon felt strange in his hands—as a Hawk, he'd never much used a bladed weapon; certainly not to the extent that Eagle and Raven had. But in some odd way it felt almost natural. As he lunged at Goraddon again, he hoped that would be enough.

Unfortunately, it was not.

The man in black, down on his haunches, had been able to scramble backwards far enough to recover his senses, and now he screamed, "*Enough!*" The sheer force of his psychic willpower was sufficient to actually cause Falcon and Eagle to spill over backwards, as though a massive ocean wave had crashed into them. Still clutching the sword, Hawk somehow stood firm against the assault but couldn't advance in the face of it.

Goraddon was on his feet again, eyes glowing brighter than they had up until now. He extricated himself from the bent and broken components into whose midst he had fallen and strode out into the open again, near the center of the room, brushing his jacket off as he moved. The power of his telepathic hold on the other three was fully in effect again, holding each of them firmly in place, locking them down. Calming himself, he reached out and simply took the golden sword from Hawk's grasp. He frowned at it for a moment, as if not recognizing it. Then he smiled.

"Ah," he said, gazing at the glorious weapon. "The Sword of Baranak." His dark eyes flicked from the blade to Eagle, where he stood frozen a short distance away. "If only you'd had this with you in the Below, Agrippa. Your stay could have been significantly shorter." He laughed. "You were aware, I am assuming, that this particular weapon—an object of the gods themselves—can quite easily cut through the walls separating layers of the Above and the Below." Then he shrugged. "Of course, because it is an object of such enormous power, you cannot carry it through an artificially-created portal such as this one." He gestured at the black framework of machinery that created the dimensional gateway. "Doing so would result in a massive overload and an explosion that would destroy the machinery, this room, and quite likely the entire palace." He set the sword down on the deck of one computer console. "So let's just keep it safe and sound, way over here, eh?"

"That was... a nice effort... Hawk," Falcon managed to say. "You... almost... got him."

"Yes," Eagle replied, even as the Adversary's willpower shoved him and the others down onto their knees. "Thank...you. Both of...you."

"Silence!" shouted Goraddon, angered by their continued defiance. He moved toward the gateway terminal, which was still lit up with sparkling and flashing points all along its perimeter. "I have had quite enough of all of you." He stood directly before the device and touched one final control. A swirl of white light formed at its center, then grew out toward the edges and seemed to solidify. "I will throw all three of you into the Below—into a layer so far down that there are no doorways back out. You will wander for the rest of eternity in that limbo realm, beset by demons and tortured always by the knowledge of what I am doing to your own worlds, your own universe." He laughed then, long and deep, and then turned to reach for one last control.

Something emerged from the open portal at that instant, followed by something else. Two shapes, moving quickly.

"What is this?" the Adversary shouted, whirling about. "Who—?"

Hawk recognized the first figure to come through. He was a blond man, not quite as big as Eagle, wearing a brown uniform.

"Condor!"

"Condor?" Goraddon echoed, puzzled. "What? Impossible!"

The false Hand gained his bearings quickly and looked to Hawk and the others where they knelt. "What's going on here, gentlemen?"

"The Adversary!" all three of the Hands shouted in near-perfect unison.

Condor took a half-second to register what they were saying. Then, his eyes widening in surprise, he spun about.

The man in black was moving toward him, arms raised, eyes glowing pure white.

Condor raised his right hand and let loose with one of his quantum-energy blasts, powered by the internal circuitry he'd paid a fortune to have installed years earlier. The blinding beam of force impacted Goraddon and knocked him backwards a step or two—mainly because it caught him by surprise.

"Well, well. Interesting," the Adversary stated, recovering quickly. "But it is plain to see that you are no real Hand." He mentally spoiled Condor's aim and caused the second blast to miss wide to the right.

Hawk struggled harder against the mental force that held him, hoping that, if nothing else, Condor's attack would distract the man enough to weaken the bonds. This was not the case, however—they held just as tightly as ever.

Cursing his own helplessness, he watched the events happening across the domed chamber. Condor looked to be realizing just how formidable the Adversary was. He backed away, trying another quantum-blast that again failed to connect as the enemy directed his aim to the side.

Hawk came close to despair as he looked on. The ending of this skirmish was just as obvious and just as inevitable as had been the battle he and the other two had waged with the man in black mere moments earlier. The Adversary was simply too powerful for any of them to defeat—or even to rattle—without some kind of very strong distraction to cause him to weaken his psychic hold on them. Only Eagle had been able to do that, and even then only for a few seconds.

Then Hawk frowned, puzzled, as it occurred to him that he had seen *two* figures emerge from the terminal when the Adversary had activated it. So—who was the other one and, more importantly, perhaps—where had they gone?

And that was precisely the moment when that final actor in the drama made her presence known.

A slender, lithe, and almost tiny female figure sprang from the shadows just as the Adversary was about to deliver the coup de grace to Condor. Black at first, the attacker's outfit morphed to bright blue and red as she sailed through the air. She landed on Goraddon's back and a shining silver blade flashed.

"Raven!" Hawk shouted, stunned by what he was seeing.

The dark-haired female Hand slashed viciously with her katana and the Adversary screamed in shock and pain. Then he whirled about, reached frantically for her, grasped her with one hand and hurled her from his back. She landed hard on the stone floor and instantly slid head-over-heels on the thin layer of ice, while her sword bounced away in the other direction with a clatter.

Goraddon staggered back, his movements jerky and his expression one of utter shock. Hawk and the others could see now that Raven had slashed his neck deeply, nearly decapitating him. Something like blood, but sparkling with raw energies, ran down over his chest. The man in black gasped and screamed incoherent sounds as he brought his hands to his throat. His eyes were wide but the white light that emanated from them was fading quickly.

The invisible restraints holding the Hands dissolved again. This time they were ready for that to happen. They instantly rushed to the attack, advancing on the wounded enemy from three directions.

Goraddon couldn't seem to focus. The white glow had vanished entirely from his eyes. He looked around frantically and saw Raven's sword where it had fallen nearby. He dived for it, getting there just ahead of Raven and snatching it up. She narrowly dodged his wild swings, dancing nimbly out of the way. Then he sensed someone approaching from behind him and he whirled about, driving the gleaming blade forward hard.

Condor gasped and looked down, seeing the katana spearing through his chest.

The Adversary grinned and, still grasping the hilt, drew the blade out—doing much more damage as it came free—and then brought it around in a wide swing, slashing Condor again.

The false Hand collapsed to the floor, blood pooling quickly around him.

"A nice effort, Hands," Goraddon gasped out, his throat still issuing a fair amount of what in him passed for blood, "but not even the five of you together could stop me." His eyes slowly began to reacquire the white glow. "And now—" He paused, thinking. "Now, perhaps I won't hurl *all* of you through the portal. You, Falcon, and you, Hawk—you will serve as the vanguard of my new legions, as I bring this entire galaxy under my control!"

The Hands understood this was likely their last chance. Together they rushed forward in one final assault, before their free will was stolen away for good.

"Fools!" the Adversary cried, his hands coming up to amplify and direct the psychic assault he was about to unleash. "How many times must I smash you all down before you accept the inevitable?"

Hawk and Falcon and Raven all found their forward momentum taken away, robbed by the Adversary's indomitable will and overwhelming psychic power.

But Eagle did not stop.

His own will, shaped by years as commander of the greatest military force in history and then tempered by millennia of wandering alone in the demon-infested depths, had now been honed to a single, rock-hard desire: to defeat the Adversary.

He stalked forward, the still-recovering psychic energies that held the others in place almost melting away in the face of his sheer determination.

Goraddon's face betrayed his sudden fear.

"You will *stop*," he ordered Eagle. "You will kneel before me! *Kneel!*"

Eagle smashed into the man and hurled him to the floor.

The others practically cheered. Before they could act, however, Eagle snatched up the golden sword and tossed it to Hawk.

Catching it, Hawk stared back at his old commander, puzzled.

"Make sure the others get out of here," the blond man ordered, sounding almost entirely like his old self again. "And then throw that in after us."

"What are you talking about?"

Eagle bent down and grabbed the woozy and half-conscious Goraddon and lifted him up.

"I believe one thing this guy has said," Eagle barked. "If we simply smash him down, he'll just keep coming back."

Goraddon's eyes weren't focused. He mumbled a few unintelligible sounds.

Eagle's own eyes moved from Hawk to Goraddon.

"Therefore, he has to be *removed* from this reality— *permanently*—so that he can't do any more harm."

Coming to, Goraddon quickly grasped the situation and he panicked, struggling to free himself from the big man's hold. He must have suspected in that last instant what his old foe had in mind—but his power was still at a low ebb because of his wounds, and Eagle was much more resistant to his psychic power than he had been before, and—in any case—it was simply too late.

Eagle marched toward the cosmic doorway, black-clad enemy held firmly in his grasp.

"Stop!" commanded the Adversary. "You will *stop*! You will *release* me! *Now!*"

"The very bottom of the Below, you said," Eagle barked at his foe, his sheer determination seemingly overriding the Adversary's psychic power. "No doorways—no way back out. Not even this one. That suits me, if it suits you!"

"No!"

Eagle carried the man at almost a dead run now. The gateway terminal, its center a swirl of light, stood just ahead.

"Do as I said, Hawk. Get them out of here," Eagle shouted back. "I'll find the sword—someday, somehow—and return. I promise."

The cosmic doorway loomed directly in front of them.

"Farewell, my friends!"

The Adversary screamed.

The two figures passed through the portal, the gateway to the depths of the Below, and vanished.

Hawk stared after them for a long second. Then he whirled about, facing Raven and Falcon, who were likewise transfixed by what they had just witnessed.

"You heard the man," he cried. "Out of the palace—now! *Go!*"

They went.

Hawk looked down at the golden sword, cradled in his hands. He looked up at the swirling brightness of the dimensional portal.

"Good luck, Agrippa," he whispered.

He tossed it in and ran.

Lightning blasted out of the portal and danced all across the machinery as the Sword of Baranak overwhelmed and overloaded the circuitry. Bolts of raw energy seared his back a dozen times before he at last dashed clear of the palace and emerged into the wooded grounds surrounding it.

Behind him, the huge stone edifice crumbled from within as the doorway to Hell exploded.

2: HAWK, FALCON, AND RAVEN

"He ended it as he began," Falcon said. "As a hero. The best of us all."

The others nodded.

They sat around a blazing campfire under the cold stars of the Scandana night sky, on the edge of a forest that grew right up to the edge of the palace grounds. The grave of the man who had called himself Condor lay a short distance away; Falcon had managed to carry his body out and they had laid him to rest with care and respect. But his fate was not the subject any of them dwelt upon now.

As he stared into the flickering flames, Hawk's thoughts were of Eagle—all he'd thought he'd known about the man before, and all he had learned about him recently.

"I still can't quite accept the idea that he was the traitor all along," Falcon stated flatly. "It seems so…impossible."

"He more than made up for any of his past sins," Hawk said. Then he laughed humorlessly. "Even killing me, I suppose."

Raven looked up at Hawk.

"He killed me, too, you know," she said. "Or, at least, he had it done."

Hawk and Falcon both reacted with surprise.

"What?" Hawk asked. "But you were still alive after he vanished—after the Adversary first threw him into the Below."

"Why would he kill *you?*" Falcon added. "You weren't a part of what happened on Scandana. You weren't even *here*."

Raven shrugged.

"What's my job, gentlemen?" She smiled at their puzzlement. "I'm Internal Affairs. One of my tasks was always to investigate the rest of you—to make sure you were all behaving like proper Hands of the Machine." She shifted her gaze back to the fire. "After the incident here—the death of the original Hawk, and the disappearance of Eagle—I of course started an investigation. But Eagle would have known beforehand that I would do so, and so he—at the Adversary's orders, I suppose— left instructions with some of his personally loyal forces to have me murdered and then my model of Hand discontinued. They didn't want what was happening to come to light too soon, and I would have probably figured at least some of it out and blown the whistle before the Adversary was fully ready to move. At least, I'd like to think I would have." She sighed. "They apparently thought so, too."

The others considered this. The picture was filling itself in for them now.

"Oh," Hawk asked then. "I've been wondering—how did you and Condor get out of the Below?"

Raven frowned at that.

"You know," she said, "I must be mellowing. Once, I would have objected to you referring to that man as 'Condor,' because clearly he was no such thing—just a charlatan, using the uniform and the technology to further his own ends." She paused then and glanced over at the grave the three of them had dug and filled in only a short time earlier. "But, having fought alongside him and having seen the effort he gave on behalf of all of us—and the entire galaxy..." She shrugged. "I guess he wasn't so bad." She snickered then. "A better man than the *real* Condor was, in some ways."

The other two couldn't help but chuckle at this.

"You're very generous in your praise, as always, Raven," Falcon said with a wry smile.

"But," Hawk said, "about how you got out of the Below—?"

Raven spread her hands wide.

"It was luck, I suppose. We'd seen lights in the fog that led us to a sort of doorway, just standing there in the middle of all that *nothing*, and we were trying to figure out what it was and if it could be of any use to us. And then it started to glow—a glow that looked an awful lot like the effects those terminals of Condor's made. So we took a chance and stepped through it— and the next thing I knew, there we were in the basement of this palace." She smiled. "So I followed my standard operating procedure and went all stealth-mode the instant we came through, just in case something bad was happening." She favored them with a rare smile. "I'd say it worked out."

"Indeed it did," Falcon said, smiling back at her. "And it just proves my old rule."

"What's that?"

"Never get on the bad side of a Raven."

All three of them laughed.

"How about you two?" Raven asked a moment later. "How did *you* get out of the Below?"

Falcon frowned at that question and cast a meaningful glance at Hawk.

"We're...um... not quite sure about that," Hawk said, turning his gaze downward.

"Hawk touched the door, bare-handed, and it lit up and opened," Falcon stated.

"Really?" Raven gave Hawk a look of surprise. "Why do you suppose that happened?"

"We don't know that was exactly why it opened," Hawk pointed out, somewhat annoyed. "There could have been some other reason."

"Maybe so," Falcon answered after a moment—but he didn't sound terribly convinced. "I think there's more to be learned on that score. One of these days."

Hawk didn't reply and the others mercifully let it go. The three of them sat there for a while longer in silence, occasionally looking up at the night sky.

"The sword," Hawk said suddenly. "I have...*fragments*...of memories—Eagle made it disappear, the first time we were here..." He frowned deeply, trying to recall something from a dim past that scarcely even belonged to him. "And then, today, he said something—some words I couldn't understand—and it came back."

Falcon chuckled softly. "That was one of Agrippa's oldest tricks." His good eye met Hawk's gaze and there was a twinkle in it. "Nobody ever fully understood that sword. It was passed down to Eagle by the Machine, at the very beginning, but before that—" He shrugged his massive shoulders. "Who knows?"

"So he could make it turn invisible? With a phrase?"

"Invisible, yes," Falcon replied, "or else shunt it into a pocket dimension, waiting safely for him, or else..." He shrugged again. "As I said—who knows? It was supposedly the sword of a god, once. There's no telling what it can do."

"The Adversary said it could slice through the walls separating dimensions," Raven chimed in. "So—if Eagle can find it, he can escape."

"Perhaps," Falcon muttered, his voice filled with ambivalence. "But he'll have to find it first. It could have gone anywhere."

"It's a pity he couldn't simply have carried the sword through with him," Raven noted.

"If you'd seen what happened when I tossed it in after him," Hawk said, "you'd know you wouldn't have wanted to be *holding* it then."

"I saw enough," Raven said, shaking her head, thinking of the explosions that had brought the palace crashing down just behind her.

They sat there a bit longer, each of them feeling introspective, and the fire burned low.

"My ship should be here soon," Hawk noted, breaking the silence. He chuckled. "At least it had enough sense to get away from Condor's ship before it was destroyed."

"Mine, too," Raven said. "And I can't wait to get off this rock." She gestured toward the dark outline of the ruined palace that obscured the view behind them. "This whole place seems...*haunted*, somehow. As if the people of this planet simply abandoned it."

"They *did* abandon it," Falcon explained. "It's off limits to the general population, according to the local area network I accessed inside it."

"That explains why the underground chamber we were in didn't seem to have been touched in centuries," Hawk said.

"That's right. After the incident a thousand years ago—the governor being killed, the strange psychic manifestations, and then subsequent actions by the Hands after the original Hawk died and Eagle vanished—the bodies were removed and it was all sealed up and left alone."

Thinking about the palace led Hawk back to wondering aloud about Eagle again.

"Do you think he'll find the sword? *Can* he truly *cut* his way out of the Below?"

"Will the Adversary be able to take control of him again, down there," Raven added, "and use him somehow, to free himself?"

"He wanted to go," Hawk stated flatly. "He thought that was for the best."

"As punishment?" Raven wondered.

"Maybe," Hawk replied. "Mainly, though, I think he felt there was a better chance of keeping the Adversary away from our universe if he were there with him, guarding him." He shrugged. "We have to trust he knew what he was doing."

"And maybe he'll find some other way to restrain the Adversary down there, *permanently*," Falcon said, "and he'll be able to come back."

"I hope so," Raven said in a soft voice. "Despite everything— I do hope so."

Hawk nodded.

"Eh. Enough," Falcon grumbled. I don't even want to think about it." He shook his head. "About what Eagle did to us in the past, and about what he's going through now, trapped for eternity in the lower depths of the multiverse, with only that crazy guy and a bunch of demons for company." He closed his human eye and shuddered.

"The Adversary claimed to be a god, in essence," Hawk said. "Goraddon. A former acolyte of Vorthan." He scratched at his chin, feeling the stubble there. "I have access to only a few memories that mention those names, and there's very little of substance available."

"Vorthan is an old name," Raven said, "from thousands of years ago. He was supposedly a god—a being from the Above, with great powers—who turned bad and ultimately was defeated."

"The Adversary said he *fell*," Hawk noted.

Raven nodded. "The story goes that another god battled him and eventually destroyed him—but at the cost of sacrificing himself, as well."

Hawk and Falcon considered that.

"Sounds familiar," Falcon noted.

"Maybe that's the only way to defeat a god," Hawk mused. "By someone of equal stature sacrificing himself. I don't know. But, if so, I hope we've seen the last of any so-called gods. We can't afford to lose any more of our best people—not if the galaxy is to be put back in order again." He frowned and looked back into the fire. "But, that being said, I'm not entirely convinced the Adversary is gone forever."

"We'll see," Falcon said. "In the meantime, we will have to remain vigilant."

Hawk looked at him, somewhat surprised.

"So—we're going to continue as Hands, even though it's just the three of us now?"

Falcon shrugged. "*I* am, anyway. There's lots that needs doing." He gazed up at the sparkling sky. "Even in a shattered galaxy. *Especially* in a shattered galaxy." He pursed his lips as he looked back down at his companions. "And besides— whether it's from some artificial compulsion conditioned into me, or programmed into my genetics, or just plain curiosity—I still want to know what's become of our old boss. The Machine."

"Yeah," Hawk agreed. "I think it's our duty as Hands to investigate it—to find out what really happened. And yes—I have to admit I'm more than a little bit curious about it, too." He turned to Raven. "How about you?"

The dark-haired woman considered for a moment, then shrugged.

"Count me in. I definitely want to know. And I agree; I think we're honor-bound, or duty-bound, or obligated in some way, to find out the truth. As Hands. And—Machine or no—that's what we are." She arched an eyebrow at the others. "Being a Hand is what I do. It's what I *am*. I wouldn't know what else to do." She chuckled. "Or who else to be."

Hawk's eyes moved from Raven's slender face to Falcon's blocky, half-mechanical one. Then he smiled.

"Okay, then. Looks like it's the three of us against the galaxy." He stood and stretched. "Sounds very exciting, anyway." He dusted himself off and nodded toward the palace complex. "For now, though, I think it's time to find a comfortable spot to get some sleep. After all—tomorrow will be a big day."

Raven and Falcon exchanged puzzled glances.

"How's that?" Falcon asked. "What's tomorrow?"

Hawk gazed down at his two companions—the only other Hands left in the galaxy, as far as any of them knew—and he smiled.

"It's the first day of the rest of our lives."

The Forces of the Machine
in the years just before the Shattering

Hands of the Machine:
Command officers, by order of rank

Eagle (Agrippa) – Overall strategic command; single combat specialist

Condor (Cassius) – Tactical command; arms and armor

Cardinal (Regulus) – Morale/inspiration/inquisition

Falcon (Titus) – Demolitions; logistics; quartermaster

Crow (Justinian) – Counter-espionage

Shrike (Vorena) – Covert ops; infiltration

Hawk (Marcus) – Combat/patrol generalist

Outside the Chain of Command:

Raven (Niobe) – Internal affairs; stealth

Associated Officers, beneath command rank (partial listing, alphabetical)

Aracari - Communications/translation officers

Auk - Marine assault specialists

Blackbird – Covert ops/surveillance specialists

Canary – Detection/sensor data analysis officers

Cormorant – Military transport specialists

Dove – Diplomatic specialists

Harrier – Close combat specialists

Ibis – Command craft pilots

Nightingale – Medical specialists

Osprey – mechanized assault officers

Owl – Intelligence/surveillance officers

Partridge – Electronics development/maintenance

Petrel – Attack craft pilots

Robin – Tactical support staff

Wren – Propaganda officers

Combat Divisions/Legions (partial listing, alphabetical)

Firewings – Air assault

Iron Raptors – Heavy armored cavalry

Sea Hawks – Marine infantry

Sky Lords – Airborne infantry

Storm Crows – Siege specialists

Thunder Birds – Airborne heavy ordnance

Wind Swords – Fast-attack armored cavalry

Thanks and appreciation this time around to:
Ami
Rowell & Atlantis Studios
Tommy Hancock & Sean Ali
Dan Abnett & Graham McNeill
Carla & the M&Ms
Bobby Politte, who was there at the very start.
And all my great friends & readers on Facebook
who "Liked" it as the book grew...
And grew...
And grew...!

About the Author

Van Allen Plexico writes and edits New Pulp, science fiction, fantasy, and nonfiction analysis and commentary for a variety of print and online publishers. He's been nominated for numerous writing awards and won the 2012 PulpArk Award for "Best New Pulp Character." His best-known works include *Lucian*, the *Assembled!* books, and the groundbreaking *Sentinels* series—the first ongoing, multi-volume cosmic superhero saga in prose form. In his spare time he serves as a professor of political science and history. He has lived in Atlanta, Singapore, Alabama, and Washington, DC, and now resides in the St. Louis area along with his wife, two daughters and assorted river otters.

13879879R00206

Made in the USA
Charleston, SC
06 August 2012